I0728953

PSYCHIC TEENAGE BLOODBATH PARTS I & II

DAVID SODERGREN

writing as
CARL JOHN LEE

This book is a work of fiction.
Any resemblance to names and people, living or dead, is purely coincidental.
No part of this publication may be reproduced or transmitted in any form without written permission from the author.
This book is not available to be used for training or use by artificial intelligence (A.I.) in any respect.

ISBN: 978-1-917910-05-7

Copyright © David Sodergren 2025
All rights reserved.

2025 INTRODUCTION

Hi friends, and welcome to the Drive-In!

You're holding two short novels I originally published under my 'extreme horror' pseudonym Carl John Lee; Psychic Teenage Bloodbath and Psychic Teenage Bloodbath II.

Back when I wrote Psychic Teenage Bloodbath, I couldn't decide whether to put it out under my own name or Carl's. I was really proud of this one, and thought it deserved a wider audience, but I eventually went with Carl. I was having too much fun writing as him, mostly because his books sold really poorly and it was very freeing to be able to write a story with the knowledge that absolutely nobody was going to ever read it.

Now, if you've somehow arrived here because you enjoyed The Haar and Summer of the Monsters, please proceed with caution. These stories are much wilder, with truly shameless amounts of outrageous bloody violence and gratuitous sex. However, they're both also ridiculously campy and silly and heartfelt, and intended to be taken in the spirit of a 1970s drive-in B-movie.

I considered re-editing them for this collection, as part one was completed in a fortnight, and part two in three weeks, and I know I could make them 'better' with a bit more polish and another draft. Ultimately, though, I decided to keep the stories as they were originally published rather than 'George Lucas' them. I love the raw, punk-rock spirit that flows through my Carl John Lee stories, and didn't want to risk sanding off the edges.

Instead, I'll just urge you to check out the content warnings at the back of the book if you're wary of what lies ahead.

Regardless, I hope you give both stories a chance. They're scrappy and nasty and gross, but there's also a lot of love in there, and though I may be alone in this, I still consider the sequel to be one of the best stories I've ever written. It's certainly the maddest!

If you're not aware, I created a backstory for Carl as a washed-up screenwriter of horror, exploitation, and pornography in the sixties and seventies, who was converting his unmade screenplays into novels. To this end, I've left in the original introduction by Judith Sonnet — who was very much in on the joke — and the afterwords to both books, as I treated them as little bonus short stories to add to the Carl mythos.

So once more, welcome to the Drive-In, folks. Find a parking spot, grab a hotdog and coke, and watch out for your date's roving hand.

Tonight, there's gonna be a bloodbath.

A Psychic Teenage Bloodbath.

And I think we can all agree that's the best kind, aye?

David Sodergren

2025

~

As always, I'd like to thank my wife, Heather, who is, quite literally, the best.

A pat on the head to Boris the pug for having a nice, squishy face.

A big thanks to Steve Stred for managing to keep Carl's secret for a surprising amount of time. I thought you'd break, dude.

A big cheers to you, reader. None of this is possible without you.

And lastly, thanks to Uncle Carl. Enjoy retirement, old timer. You've earned it.

PSYCHIC TEENAGE BLOODBATH

ORIGINAL INTRODUCTION

"You Ain't Ready for This"
A Foreword by Judith Sonnet

And I mean it. Even if you've read Carl John Lee before... you just ain't ready for the treats he has in store for you today. Psychic Teenage Bloodbath is everything that the title suggests, and then a whole helluva lot more. The book you have in your hands is filled to the brim with gore, intestinal drippings, feces, splattered flesh, sprayed guts, shattered heads... oh, and one of the sweetest love stories I think I've encountered in the annals of extreme horror.

So, an introduction. If you do not know who Carl John Lee is and this is your first time reading one of his books, then you are in for a whale of a time.

Lee — or 'Uncle Carl' — is a rather mythic figure in the field of indie horror. Not much is really known about him, other than the fact that he had a hand in the scene back in the seventies and eighties, where he did script work for many low budget exploitation films, a lot of which have never found the light of day.

I've talked to Lee a few times, and he seems humble, grateful, and curious. He writes for no one but himself, and yet he carves some truly entertaining yarns that should appeal to a bigger audience of horror-freaks. Upon discovering Lee, I wrote asking him which movies his name has been attached to. His response was cryptic:

"Too many. Not enough."

Now, in his later years, he's converting unmade scripts into books. Reading his work feels almost identical to a cinematic experience, because that's how these stories were intended to be told.

Why isn't his name more well known among film-fans and gore hounds? Well, the 'problem' a lot of directors seem to have had is that Carl John Lee never wrote with a budget in mind. His stories are huge, sprawling, bombastic, and go well beyond even the X-rated material of our favorite grindhouse flicks. So many of his scripts are — in Lee's own words — 'unfilmable'. I do hope this sentiment changes, and that ambitious, modern filmmakers catch hold of these books.

Cross your fingers, folks. It's never too late to adapt a really good book into a really gory film.

The other 'problem' is that Uncle Carl worked with a lot of scumbags and cheats, who took his scripts and did nothing with them. Some of the greatest horror movies imaginable are sitting in a dusty file-box in someone's grandpa's attic — if you have a grandpa, dear reader, maybe go check that out?

Reading a book by Lee is like uncovering a moldy VHS tape from the back of an abandoned storage bin and cleaning it up. It's putting that tape in your TV and watching a movie that hasn't even made it to IMDB or Letterboxd. It's a treasure hunt, minus the disappointment of digging in your backyard and not even claiming an arrowhead for your efforts.

You have to love horror movies to love Lee. The two just go hand-in-hand. You like cannibal exploitation flicks? You like shambling zombies? You like weird gel-lighting, horny narratives, and mean-spirited narrative shifts? Then you and Lee will be fine bedfellows.

But what should you expect from this book?

Well, everyone likes comps nowadays, so here you go:

Psychic teenage Bloodbath is a bold mix of revenge with supernatural splatter. It's Lucio Fulci directing Carrie, Scanners II, and The Sadness.

I don't want you to think that this book is merely gore for gore's sake, though. Even though this is very firmly a splatter novel, you will actually care about the characters and their plight. You will love to hate a lot of them, but your heart will go out for others. I don't want to spoil it for you, but as a queer woman that is constantly seeking good representation in the horror genre... Carl John Lee has done something incredible here. I feel seen, heard, exalted, and engaged by every sentence in this perverse, skin-ripping book.

Now, I've already yammered on too much. Turn on some ambient music from the '70's, butter your popcorn, sit back... and enjoy the bloodbath!

And remember, even if you think you're ready for what's ahead of you...

You ain't!

Judith Sonnet
Somewhere in Missouri
10/15/2022

For Leslie
I couldn't have done it without you.

(For the record, the Leslie in question is Hong Kong popstar and actor Leslie Cheung Kwok-Wing, because I was listening to his discography while I wrote the book)

1

———

It was with typical irony that on the night Charlie Bonner's life went to hell, she felt happier than she had in years. Perhaps the happiest she had *ever* been.

Charlie — only her mom still called her Charlotte, and only when she was mad — perched on the unmade bed, trying not to crease her dress. She watched Susan, smiling as the girl fussed over her own dress. She stood in front of the mirror, attempting to tug the perilously low neckline over her cleavage, with little success.

"Is it too much?" she said, watching Charlie in the mirror. "I feel like it's too much."

"Would you stop worrying? You look terrific."

Susan resumed pulling at the fabric. "Just a little higher. My nipples are practically on show."

Charlie smiled to herself. The dress covered plenty of Susan's chest, and her nipples were as likely to make an appearance at the Christmas dance as Robert Redford or Bigfoot. But Susan was self-conscious about her breasts, and it was up to Charlie to settle her nerves. After all, it was she who had convinced Susan to buy the dress in the first place.

"You're fine. Nothing's on show." She left the bed and went to Susan, placing a reassuring hand on the girl's waist. "You look far out."

Susan blushed, her cheeks turning as red as the crimson lipstick she wore, lipstick that Charlie had bought her especially for tonight. Susan glanced down at her feet, the way she always did when Charlie paid her a compliment.

"Are you sure you can't see anything? I think I should change."

"You can't wear sweats and a tee shirt to the summer dance, silly," said Charlie.

"I have other dresses," Susan protested.

"And those bulky gray dresses are *perfect* for when you travel back in time to Victorian England. But for now... keep this one on." She put her hand on Susan's chin and raised her head. "You look beautiful."

Charlie kissed her. Because of the lipstick, she tasted different tonight. Different, but still nice. Susan kissed her in return, their bodies pressing against each other, and Charlie could feel the girl's heartbeat pounding in her chest. She heard a noise — someone coming up the stairs — and quickly pulled away. God, Susan's mom's sense of timing was impeccable.

A knock at the door.

"Susan, honey... your dates have arrived. Are you two nearly ready?"

"Just a minute, mom," said Susan. "Keep them occupied. Get dad to talk to them about, I dunno... real estate, or something."

"Okay, dear." A pause. *"Does your dress fit? I told you, I told you every day, you shouldn't eat such a big—"*

"It fits fine," interrupted Charlie. She squeezed Susan's hand. "It fits her perfectly."

She waited for another snide comment, but for once Mrs. Ward's inexhaustible well of passive-aggressive insults seemed to have run dry.

"Okay. But be quick. I don't know what to say to teenage boys." Then, more quietly, *"Especially the weird ones."*

With that, she left. Charlie and Susan listened to her footsteps fading down the corridor. Susan looked at her reflection again.

"She's right. The dress doesn't fit. Maybe I should just stay home." She reached behind her back, fingers fumbling for the zipper. Charlie grabbed her wrist.

"Hey," she said. "Listen to me." She wrapped her arms around Susan, embracing her. "No offense, but... you know your mom's a dick, right?"

Susan giggled. "I know."

Charlie kissed her neck, letting her lower lip linger against the flushed skin. "So, who are you gonna believe? Your mom... or the girl who loves you?"

Susan closed her eyes and let Charlie kiss her. "You," she said, as Charlie's hands traced the contours of her hips, sliding over the unforgiving red satin. Susan had nothing to worry about. The dress looked stunning on her. It had taken Charlie six months to build Susan's confidence up enough to even *consider* going to the dance, never mind wearing a dress that highlighted her natural curves. But somehow she had succeeded, and the night had finally arrived.

The Clinton High Summer Ball.

Next year they would be seniors, and it would be prom time. Charlie harbored a secret fantasy of being able to go to prom with Susan as her date, though she knew that probably wouldn't be possible. Although it was 1978, American attitudes towards homosexuality were still mired in the Dark Ages. Still, it never hurt to dream.

Susan took one last glance in the mirror and tugged her dress up.

"Ah, screw it," she said, and turned to Charlie. "Shall we?"

Charlie offered her arm, and Susan took it. They walked as far as the door, then let go of each other. For the purposes of tonight, they were two perfectly ordinary, boringly straight girls. They certainly weren't planning to ditch their dates after the dance and go home together. No sir, that was not the plan at all.

Charlie grinned.

Not at *all*.

2
———

THEY ARRIVED AT THE SUMMER BALL AN HOUR LATE.

It was Susan's idea. She didn't want to arrive with everyone else and have them stare at her. That was cool with Charlie. She was here, and they were together. Oh sure, there were two boys with them too, a pair of science geeks called Kenny and Todd, but they were purely for decoration. They were nice boys, and Charlie and Susan had already agreed that they would give them a quick kiss at the end of the night as payment for services rendered.

Charlie chuckled, remembering the way Todd's hand had trembled as he tried to attach the corsage to Susan's dress.

"What's up?" asked Susan.

"Nothing," said Charlie, as the cab pulled away, leaving the four standing at the imposing entrance to the school hall. "Just buzzing." She looked at the boys. "You guys bring any alcohol?"

They shook their heads. Charlie had expected as much, and produced a small bottle of vodka from her handbag. "Well, luckily I did." She took a gulp, the liquid burning her throat, and passed the bottle around the group. Susan took a healthy swig, coughed a little, and handed the bottle back.

"Thanks," she said.

Charlie winked at her and linked arms with Kenny. "Come on. Let's go dance."

Susan considered asking Charlie for another sip of vodka. Her nerves were building, working their way through her bones, her veins. They made her legs weak, and her eyes blur. She looked down at her cleavage. God, what if Charlie was wrong? She had never shown this much skin before. Even when she went to the beach, she always wore a tee shirt over her conservative bathing suit.

There's still time to go home and change. You could hail a cab, and—

No.

She was staying, and that was that. Charlie was right about her. She was a good-looking girl with a great body, no matter what her mom said. Though, it was easy to *tell* herself that, and much harder to believe it. But that was the thing with Charlie. She *made* Susan believe in herself. It was one of the things she loved the most about Charlie. Well, that, and her peach of an ass.

Susan giggled. Charlie and Kenny were in front of her and Todd, and Susan watched Charlie's butt as she walked, her blue peplum dress accentuating the movement of her cheeks. *It's not intentional,* she would always protest. *It's just the way I walk.*

Then god bless the way you walk, thought Susan.

They climbed the stairs to the school, the entrance flanked by two white stone pillars, the Stars and Stripes hanging unmoving in the stillness of the evening. Mr. McDonald, the biology teacher, was on door duty. Susan worried he would check their bags and find Charlie's vodka, but he greeted them with a warm smile and ushered them into the hall.

As they entered, Susan tore her eyes from Charlie's ass and glanced around. The theme was Proud To Be An American, and the hall had been decorated with red, white, and blue strips of paper that reached from the ceiling to the walls. Susan thought a better theme would have been School Is Almost Over, Thank Christ, but she supposed this would have to do.

The first thing she noticed — aside from the music of the live band — was how many people there were. So many! It seemed like everyone was at the summer ball.

Everyone...

She tried not to think about that. The band was playing a Carpenters song, and she watched the couples dance awkwardly beneath a rotating mirrorball that cast broken shards of light across the hall. Some of the dancers she recognized, others she didn't. Susan, much like Charlie, liked to keep to herself. Individuality was frowned upon at Clinton High, and standing out from the crowd was inadvisable.

Susan felt eyes on her. Surreptitious glances, muffled voices. She felt exposed. Fighting back the urge to run, she followed Charlie's example, keeping her head high despite the nausea that threatened to overwhelm her.

You got this, she told herself, wondering if anyone recognized her. Normally her hair was up, her glasses on. She never wore makeup, and always hid her body under shapeless clothes.

"Nice dress," said a girl as she passed.

Susan's cheeks burned with shame, until she realized the girl wasn't being sarcastic. It was a genuine compliment. It felt nice. Weird, and unexpected, but... nice.

Todd asked if he could get her a drink, and she said yes. The vodka had settled nicely in her belly, and she wanted more. When Todd returned with a soda, she considered using Charlie's secret stash to top it up. Maybe tonight wouldn't be so bad after all? It was funny. She had been worrying about it for weeks. Months, actually. Any time she saw a poster advertising the ball, or overheard someone in class discussing it, her stomach would lurch. Only Charlie's dogged persistence had convinced her it wouldn't end in disaster. Speaking of which...

Susan glanced down. No, her nipples weren't on show. Her dress remained exactly where it should be. She patted her ass, checking to ensure her dress wasn't tucked in to her panties. It wasn't. Everything was fine. She was here, and Charlie was too, and that was all that mattered. She looked over at her girlfriend and raised her glass. Charlie smiled back, and Susan's heart filled with longing. She wanted to dance. More than anything, she wanted to dance with Charlie. It was such an intimate act. The closeness, the touching, two people moving as one. Her heart beat faster just thinking about it, though she knew they couldn't. The rumors had already spread around the school, the way they always do when two people of the same sex spent 'too much' time together. It was nothing to be ashamed about, Susan knew, but she only had one year left of high school, and wanted it to pass as smoothly as possible. And if that meant keeping their relationship under wraps for one more year, then so be it. It was a small price to pay for—

"What the fuck are you wearing?"

The voice came from nowhere, startling her. But despite

the loud music, and the general atmosphere of mingling voices and excited chatter, Susan recognized it. All at once, the carefully constructed facade of confidence she had built crumbled around her.

Maybe she's not talking to you. Maybe—

A hand on her shoulder, spinning her round. Susan's soda spilled over the rim of the glass as she came face-to-face with Greta Wendel.

Shit.

Greta's arms were folded across her chest. Beside her stood Michelle Strunk, Greta's best friend and partner in crime. They glared at her with disdain, Greta running her eyes up and down Susan's body. What was wrong? What had she done? Suddenly Susan understood.

She was wearing the same dress as Greta.

Double shit.

Susan looked around for Charlie, unable to locate her. Already, Todd was backing away from the brewing confrontation.

"I'm gonna get us another drink," he said, before vanishing so fast he practically left behind a puff of dust.

Greta seemed to be waiting for an answer. Had she asked a question? Susan couldn't remember. She looked helplessly at the bully. Greta's blonde hair had been immaculately coiffured into a Farrah Fawcett-style shag hairdo, her artfully applied makeup highlighting sharp cheekbones and full lips. She cocked her head. "Well?"

"Uh..." said Susan, trying to remember what Greta had asked.

"Uhhhhh," said Greta in a mocking tone. Michelle joined in, the two of them laughing at her.

Where was Charlie? She needed her. Tears sprang to her

eyes, and she hated herself for it. Why couldn't she stand up to her bully?

"I'm sorry," she said, apologizing in lieu of anything better to say. Sometimes she thought apologies were her default mode of expression.

Greta turned to Michelle. "Oh, you hear that? She's *sorry*."

"Sorry for what?" asked Michelle.

"Yeah," said Greta. "Sorry for what?"

Should she mention the dress situation? Or best not to?

"I don't know," said Susan.

Greta eyeballed her. "You don't know? So let me get this straight. You're *sorry*, but you don't know why?"

Susan nodded.

"God, you're pathetic," said Greta. She took a step closer, standing mere inches from her, and placed both hands on the neckline of Susan's dress.

My god.

Was she going to rip it? Susan thought she might black out from sheer panic. Not even Greta would go that far, surely. Not in front of *everyone*. Her classmates, her teachers...

Greta leaned in close. "You look like shit in my dress," she hissed. "So I don't want to see you again tonight. If I do..." she pretended to tug her hands apart, mimicking tearing Susan's dress down the front. "You dig?"

Susan nodded hurriedly.

Greta's eyes narrowed. "Then say it."

"I... I understand."

With a cruel smile, Greta released her. She turned without another word and strode away. It took Michelle a moment to realize her friend had left, then dutifully trotted after her.

Bile rose in Susan's throat. She was going to be sick, and wanted to run to the ladies' room, yet her legs didn't feel strong enough to support her weight. She stood there, trembling. Had anyone seen? People milled around, engaged in conversation, drinking and dancing. No one paid her any attention. She heard laughter. Was it directed at her? It usually was. It *always* was. She hiccuped, tasting vomit, and searched for the exit.

Then she saw Charlie pushing her way through the throng to reach her, and it took everything she had not to throw her arms around the girl and weep.

"Are you okay?" asked Charlie. "I came as quickly as..." She trailed off as she saw Susan's wet, red eyes.

"I have to go," said Susan. "I'm sorry."

"What did she say to you?"

"Forget it. I can't let her see me again. I'm wearing the same dress as her, and she... she threatened to... I'm sorry, I have to go. I can't stay here."

She elbowed past Charlie, heading for the exit. Charlie gripped her arm, halting her.

"Susan, wait. *Please.* She can't do anything tonight. Every teacher in school is here." She took Susan's hand. "You're safe. You hear me? You're safe."

She was stroking Susan's hand. It was a risk, and Susan appreciated the gesture, but there was no way she could remain at the dance. Not now, and certainly not while wearing Greta's dress.

You're not wearing her dress, her mind argued. *You're both wearing the same one. Or — and hear me out — maybe she's wearing* your *dress?*

It was all true, but in Susan's experience, bullies didn't concern themselves with semantics. Still, she could feel her heart slowing to a more acceptable rate. With Charlie by her side, the danger felt less palpable.

"Don't let that bitch spoil tonight," said Charlie. "This is meant to be special."

Susan offered an apologetic shrug. "We'll never fit in. You and me... we'll never belong."

"Yeah, maybe you're right," said Charlie. She smiled. "But so what? That doesn't mean we can't stay and have fun." She held Susan's hand lightly. "Do you trust me?"

Susan glanced around distractedly, searching for Greta. "What do you mean?"

"Do you *trust* me?"

Susan looked her in the eyes. "Of course I do. You *know* I do. That's why I'm here, isn't it?"

Charlie didn't answer. Her grin broadened, lighting up her soft features. "Then come with me. I've got something to show you."

3

THEY TRAVERSED THE DANCE FLOOR, GLIDING BETWEEN FACES that barely registered their presence, two softly spoken ghosts haunting the Clinton High Summer Ball, invisible to all but the keenest eyes.

Charlie led the way, stopping frequently to make sure Susan was close behind. The girl was shaken by her encounter with Greta, and Charlie understood it perfectly. With a cowardice typical of bullies, Greta only bothered them when they were apart. So, she figured, as long as she and Susan stuck together for the rest of the night, they would be okay. But to do that, they would need to ditch their dates and find a quiet place.

Charlie knew exactly where they had to go.

She brought Susan to a door in the corner of the gym hall. With a quick glance to ensure no one was watching, she pushed it open and pulled Susan through.

"Where are we?"

"Somewhere we can be alone," said Charlie. It was dark inside the room, so she hit a switch. Several lights came on, revealing a flimsy staircase that led up high. "Follow me."

With her heart beating fast, she took Susan's hand, and together they ascended the stairs, the music and chatter of the dance muffled by thick walls. At the top of the stairs was a sturdy metal door with a sheet of paper taped to it.

ENTRY FOR OFFERISED PERSONAL ONLY, read the handwritten scrawl. Charlie had seen the sign before when she had scouted potential hiding locations, but she gave Susan enough time to read it and chuckle at the spelling mistakes before pushing the door open.

"Oh, wow," said Susan, her eyes widening.

Charlie grinned, putting her arm around Susan and leading her out onto the roof of the school. The music bled from the dance hall into the evening air, the sweet sounds of summer surrounding them.

"You like it?" asked Charlie. "There's no one else here. Just the two of us."

"Just the two of us," breathed Susan.

"They never lock the door. I scoped it out weeks ago, in case... well, it doesn't matter. Here, come and see this."

Aside from a vast air conditioning unit in the far corner, a large pyramidal skylight in the middle of the roof was the only notable feature. Colors throbbed through the glass, the music growing louder as they approached.

"Keep low," said Charlie, crouching and inching towards the window as best as her tight dress would allow. "From here, you can see everyone." They pressed their faces to the glass, their breath steaming it up. Below them, the dance continued in their absence. Teenagers spun in hypnotic circles, the girls' dresses billowing around them like umbrellas, the boys resplendent in colorful suits.

"Look, over by the drinks table!" said Susan. "Is Mr. Quinn..."

Charlie looked. Mr. Quinn, their English teacher, stood

beside Miss O'Neill, the economics teacher, his hand resting on her ass. Someone wandered over to the table, and Quinn gave Miss O'Neill a subtle pinch, then dropped his hand, using it to ladle some punch from the bowl into the kid's glass.

"Did he just..."

"He did!"

They laughed, moving away from the window, and stood, hand-in-hand, overlooking the town. The sun was setting, reddening the sky, the trees casting long, wizened shadows that reached for the car park with grotesque black fingers.

"God, Clinton looks so pretty from up here," said Susan.

"So do you," said Charlie.

Susan gave her a wry glance. "You're so lame, you know that?"

"I know," smiled Charlie. "We can't all be as cool as you."

The band was playing a Jackson Five song, the singer attempting a falsetto wail that resembled a strangled boy. Charlie squeezed Susan's waist. "Are you glad you came?"

Susan waited a moment before answering. "I am now. If you'd asked me five minutes ago..."

"Don't worry about Greta. She can't find us up here."

"I know. It's just that when she speaks to me, I feel like I'm five years old. I'm going to be eighteen soon. This time next year we'll be finished school. We'll be adults."

"And you'll never have to see her again."

"That's not true," said Susan. "She might take my order in McDonald's."

Charlie laughed and pulled her close. The sun dipped below the faraway mountains, the sky flaring a brilliant crimson. "It's not often I say this about school," she said, "but I don't want this moment to end."

Susan nodded. "Same."

They turned towards each other. As The Jackson Five song ended, the band launched into a new tune. Both girls knew it. *If You Leave Me Now* by Chicago. It was the song that had been playing on the radio when they first kissed in Susan's bedroom. Old memories bubbled to the surface, enveloping Charlie like a warm bath. She was positive Susan felt the same.

"May I have this dance?" she asked, feeling absurdly nervous.

Susan put one hand on Charlie's waist, and Charlie rested hers on Susan's shoulder.

"I'd be honored," said Susan.

And there, on the roof of the school beneath the dying light of the sun, they danced with practiced grace. Neither stumbled, nor giggled. Nothing could break the spell. Susan rested her cheek against Charlie's and closed her eyes. They twirled slowly, shuffling in time with one another, blissfully unaware that down on the dance floor, Michelle Strunk was standing slack-jawed, staring up through the skylight at them.

"I love you," said Susan. "I love you so much."

"I love you too."

"I was thinking," said Susan. "Maybe tonight... we could go all the way."

The last six words came out as a hushed whisper.

"I'd like that," said Charlie, and they kissed again, Susan's hands gripping her ass like she was hanging on for dear life. "You wanna go now?" she said, aware of the almost comic sense of urgency in her voice.

Susan laughed, and tried to hide it. "Cool it, tiger. We just got here. I've never danced with you outside of our rooms before. It makes me feel funny. In a good way."

It was Charlie's turn to be embarrassed. "Yeah, no, I didn't mean *now* now... I meant *soon* now, y'know? Whenever. There's no rush."

Their song finished, replaced by *My Lover,* the latest ballad from the heavy rock group The Slaughtered Lambs. Charlie wasn't a fan.

"How about I get us another drink?" she asked.

"What about your vodka?"

"It tastes better when it's mixed with something," smiled Charlie, tracing her fingers down Susan's cheek. "I won't be a minute. Don't go anywhere."

"Damn, and I was planning on jumping off the roof."

"You're cute when you're sarcastic, you know that?" said Charlie, as she slipped free of Susan's grasp and headed for the door. "And quit staring at my ass, you creep."

"Never," said Susan. "See you later, Charlie-gator."

Charlie grinned and opened the door to the stairs.

In the months that followed, she would often reflect on her decision to leave Susan alone on the roof. What if she had stayed? What if they *had* just left and gone home together? How differently would things have turned out?

And — most importantly — would everyone still be alive?

4

———

Susan kept her distance from the skylight, instead leaning on the stone barrier that circled the roof. The sun slipped out of sight, the sky moonless. House lamps switched on across the town, the occasional passing car briefly illuminating the shadowy roads like distant explorers.

She was happy. Happier than she could ever remember being. All she could think about was Charlie's embrace, and her tender kisses. In that one perfect moment, Greta Wendel was the furthest thing from her mind. So when the door to the roof groaned open, Susan spun around with a goofy smile plastered to her face.

"That was quick," she said, taking a step forwards. No one replied.

Shit.

What if a teacher had spotted them coming up here? Or worse, maybe Mr. Quinn had brought Miss O'Neill up for—

"Well, well, well," said a voice in the darkness, interrupting her thoughts.

Susan's stomach dropped.

"Oh no," she whispered involuntarily, as Greta emerged through the doorway, her arms folded. She wasn't alone. When was she ever? Michelle was with her. Then two more bodies, two boys. Susan knew one of them was Freddy McAlmond, Greta's boyfriend. He was a sports jock, football or baseball or wrestling or some dumb shit like that. He had to duck his head to clear the door, his six-foot-plus frame towering over all of them. The other boy, Susan assumed, was Michelle's date.

"What are you doing here?" she asked, surprised to hear the words leave her mouth.

"Oh, I just came to make out with my *girlfriend,*" sneered Greta. "How about you?"

Susan swallowed hard. God, they must have seen them. Did the whole school know? Why hadn't she and Charlie been more careful?

"Please," she said. "I don't want any trouble."

Greta shook her head. "You turn up to the summer dance... with your *girlfriend*... wearing *my* dress... and you say you don't want any trouble? Girl, you are fucking *begging* for trouble."

Susan's eyes flicked to the door. Where was Charlie? Where the fuck was she? "I'm sorry, I didn't know. I wouldn't have worn it if I'd known, I swear."

"Don't speak to me," said Greta, her voice dripping venom. "Don't you *ever* speak to me, you fucking disease. Your kind disgusts me." She took a step closer and raised her hand. Susan flinched away, stumbling over her heels.

"Eww, don't touch her!" shouted Michelle. "Her lesbianism might be contagious."

Greta's boyfriend looked aghast. "Can that happen?"

"What if I catch it?" asked the other boy. "Will I become a lesbian?"

They were so fucking stupid, and it pissed Susan off, though the anger was not enough to replace the dread that had settled in her stomach. Her lips were dry, and she licked them subconsciously.

"Don't lick your lips," said Greta. "What, you got a crush on me, is that it? You want to kiss me?"

Susan shook her head. Events were spiraling out of control, and she was powerless to stop them.

Greta made a show of looking offended. "Why not? Don't you think I'm pretty?"

It was a trick. Susan tried to think. What would be the correct response here? Was there one?

"No," she said, then quickly added, "Yeah." She felt hot, too hot. "I don't know."

"You don't know? Then why are you wearing *my* dress? You must like me. That's why you're dressing like me."

Susan's mind was a blank. Her lip quivered.

"Oh shit, she's going to cry!" laughed Michelle, nudging Greta with her elbow. Then the tears came, running down Susan's cheeks, smearing the makeup that Charlie had helped apply only an hour before.

Charlie.

Where *was* she? Susan chanced a glance through the skylight, her eyes scanning the dance floor, stopping on the drinks table. There was Mr. Quinn, and a queue of kids... and there was Charlie, three from the front.

Look up, look up... please look up.

But she didn't.

Greta advanced, Michelle and the boys following, sticking close to her.

There was nowhere to run.

Charlie reached the front of the queue. God, there was only a choice of punch or soda. That was it. How did it take people so long to decide?

"Two sodas, please," she said, waiting patiently as Mr. Quinn filled two plastic tumblers and handed them to her.

"Enjoying yourself?"

She nodded and smiled, afraid to talk again in case he smelled the vodka on her breath. She needn't have bothered, as he immediately turned his attention back to Miss O'Neill. Charlie noticed the wedding ring on his finger.

Bad boy, she thought, then headed for the door. Two kids were making out beside it, but Charlie figured she wouldn't have any problem sneaking past. She took a final glance back at the flirting teachers, then almost screamed as she bumped into someone, the drinks spilling down the front of her dress.

"Oh my, I am sorry," said a man.

She looked up, staring into the face of her math teacher, Mr. Carradine.

Fuck, she cursed internally. She hated Carradine. Creepy Carradine, that's what she and Susan had dubbed him. As if keen to live up to his nickname, Carradine produced an embroidered handkerchief from his tweed jacket and dabbed at her chest with it.

"Here, let me get that," he said in his plummy English accent. "Can't have a pretty young girl like you with a stain on her che—" he stopped, correcting himself — "her *dress.*"

"Thanks," she said, squirming away from probing fingers that lingered too long. "I have to—"

"Charlotte Bonner," he said, his brow creasing into a frown. "I never expected to see you here. You are a quiet one, aren't you? You rarely speak in my class. Are you afraid of me?"

"No, I just... look, I'm sorry, I really—"

"You don't need to be afraid. I'm always there if you need to talk. After class, or... after school. I'm rather approachable."

"I'll remember that." She glanced up at the skylight. No one there. That made sense. Susan was probably keeping out of sight. When she looked back at Carradine, he was inspecting her breasts.

"It was nice talking to you," she said, and made to leave.

Carradine gripped her arm. "Wait," he said. "Have you ever considered private tutoring?"

Charlie sighed. She looked at the skylight again.

I won't be long, she thought. *Just gotta get rid of this creep.*

Susan wouldn't mind.

Charlie was sure of it.

∼

"You want me to *what?*"

Susan's breath came in short, ragged gasps. She felt her knees might buckle at any moment.

"You heard me," said Greta. "Take the dress off. Then you can go."

"I can't. I can't do that. I just can't."

Greta took a step closer, her face inches from Susan's. "You can, and you will. Or things are going to get much worse. I won't have you wearing my dress. You cheapen it. You get to wear dungarees, while we wear pretty dresses. That's how things work."

"We don't make the rules," added Michelle.

Greta dropped all pretenses. "Strip," she snarled. *"Now."*

Michelle was laughing. So, too, were the boys.

"Come on, take it off," said Michelle's date.

Michelle glared at him. "Don't sound *too* excited."

"What? She's got nice tits. I want to see them."

"Mine not good enough for you?"

As they argued, Susan stepped back, horrified. Surely Greta was joking? She couldn't actually expect her to... she couldn't... she couldn't expect her to strip to her underwear. Her heart hammered frenziedly in her chest.

"Please..."

"I'm waiting," said Greta. "Show us what your little lesbo friend gets to play with every night. Come on, let's see what you've got going on under there."

Greta lunged forwards, her fingers closing over Susan's neckline. She yanked down, *hard,* but Susan moved with the motion, falling to her knees to remain in her dress.

My god, they were really going to do it.

They were going to strip her.

Hands groped for her, scratching at her clothes. She swatted them away, trying to get to her feet, but every time she did, someone shoved her. She fell, Greta and Michelle attacking her, the boys standing back and enjoying the spectacle of public humiliation. Fabric tore, though she wasn't sure where.

"Charlie!" she screamed. "Charlie! Help!"

"No one can hear you, bitch," said Greta.

Susan struggled to her feet. The dress sagged, and she held it up. She was too busy looking at Greta to notice Michelle behind her. Susan was aware of two hands on the back of her dress, pulling the fabric into tight balls... and then came an almighty tearing sound.

～

"Okay, Mr. Carradine, I'll keep that in mind for next year," said Charlie.

Why wouldn't he stop talking? And could he not look her in the eyes for more than five seconds without glancing down at her chest?

She thought she heard something. A scream, high-pitched and terrified. It cut through the music. She looked around. A couple of other revelers tilted their heads up, as if they too had heard it.

"Susan?"

"Excuse me?" asked Carradine, but Charlie wasn't listening. She pushed past him, heading for the door.

Someone else screamed, this time from inside the hall. She glanced up at the skylight and paused. What *was* that? She squinted, the lights glaring off the disco ball and impeding her vision. Then the skylight shattered, raining sparkling glass over the dance floor, and *there*, sailing through the air in what seemed like slow motion, was a pale white body, the limbs loose and doll-like.

Susan.

The body hit the drinks table, smashing it, upending the punch bowl and sending it flying. The sound of bones breaking could be heard over the music, as Susan came to a stop with a sudden, dreadful finality. Her head smacked hard off the wooden floor, shards of glass still drizzling down around her, catching the light like fireflies.

Charlie dropped her drinks and ran. She fell to her knees as she reached her friend.

"Don't touch her!" someone shouted. "Her neck could be broken."

And despite the adrenaline, despite the emotion and the horror that flooded through her, Charlie knew the voice was right. She kneeled by Susan and wept.

Blood poured from the lifeless body, pooling around the pair of them. No one else dared come close. The sight was too ghastly. Susan's eyes were wide open and staring, but with no trace of life behind them. They may as well have been made of glass. More blood spurted from myriad wounds, tiny pieces of fractured skylight embedded in her skin.

And where the fuck was her dress? She lay there, bleeding and dying in the middle of the hall, in her bra and panties.

"Don't look!" Charlie screamed at the crowd that had gathered around her. "Stop looking at her!" She got to her feet, slipping in the blood, and retrieved the gingham cloth from the broken table. She laid it across Susan to preserve her modesty, blood seeping through the thin linen in a maddening Rorschach Test pattern.

"Someone call a paramedic!" she roared at the crowd, most of whom stood stock still, their jaws agape. She caught movement out of the corner of her eye. The stair door opening, and several figures making a hasty exit.

Charlie made a mental note of each one.

Greta Wendel. Michelle Strunk. Freddy McAlmond. Peter Herbert.

They had done this. She knew it. She would find proof, and go to the cops, and...

Someone grabbed her hand.

Charlie screamed.

It was Susan.

She looked at Charlie and tried to lift her head.

Charlie leaned in close. "It's okay, you're going to be okay, everything is going to be—"

Susan coughed a mouthful of thick blood over Charlie's

face, and by the time Charlie wiped it off, her girlfriend's eyes had closed.

"Oh, fuck you," whispered Charlie. She lay down next to Susan, blood soaking into her dress, tiny pieces of glass jabbing into her.

"Fuck you all," she said.

5

———————

ELEVEN MONTHS LATER

Charlie stared down at her gym shoe-clad feet. "Come on," she said in a small voice. "Just let me in."

Michelle put her palm against Charlie's forehead and lightly pushed her. "What, so you can spy on us while we're changing? You think we'd let you watch us in the shower? Fuck off, you creep. You can wait outside until we're done, like you always do."

Charlie opened her mouth to argue, and Michelle slapped her across the face. The blow wasn't hard, but it was enough to shame her into silence.

She trudged around the outdoor locker room, finding her usual concrete step to perch on. She had sat here so often over the past year, she was surprised it didn't have an indentation of her ass cheeks. As she listened to the girls' laughter drift through the frosted glass window, she heard the showers spurt into life.

A group of boys ambled by, walking towards their own locker room. "Hey lesbo! Bet you wish you were in there with them, huh?" one of them shouted.

She ignored him, sitting with her head down as they passed, peals of laughter echoing across the sports field.

"One month," she said to herself. One month, and then she could say sayonara to high school and all its wretched occupants. Ever since the dance, life had somehow gotten worse. It wasn't just that she didn't have Susan by her side anymore. That would have been bad enough. It was that Greta had stepped up her bullying to apocalyptic levels. Not a day passed by without some cruel remark, an incident of random violence, or a new humiliation. It had been tolerable when Susan was still around, but facing it alone was unbearable. That they had kept it up for almost the entire senior year was testament to Greta's guilt, or so Charlie believed.

Greta had been responsible for Susan's 'accident', as it had been written up on the official report. Traces of alcohol had been found in Susan's system, so the brainiacs in the police department had surmised that she had gotten drunk, torn her own dress off, and fallen through the skylight.

"Bullshit," said Charlie. It was obvious that Greta was responsible. Greta and Michelle and Freddy and Peter. The four of them had never faced any consequences for their actions, and that thought, more than anything, was what kept Charlie going. On those long nights, where she would sit staring at an unopened bottle of pills, or when she would stand in the shower and gaze at the sharp edge of the razor blade, holding it to her skin, daring herself to cut her wrists... on those nights, the idea that one day those bastards would answer for their crimes was what kept her from ending her life.

The locker room door opened.

"You can go in now, clit-licker," said one of the girls as they filed out and headed home, laughing and play-fighting.

The girl — who Charlie barely knew — held her fingers up in a V and flicked her tongue between them.

"Very original," muttered Charlie, picking herself up and scuffing her gym shoes along the gravel. The locker room was empty when she entered. With no one else there, it had an eerie quality. Locker rooms should either be bustling with activity or completely abandoned, Charlie thought. Whenever she had to change by herself after class, it felt like she was in a horror film.

She kicked off her shoes and disrobed, laying her gym shorts and tee next to her bag, then placed her underwear on top. Grabbing a towel, she padded barefoot into the shower block. The joke was on those idiots; she preferred showering alone. Regardless of what *they* thought, she didn't want to see her classmates naked. They may have attractive faces and beautiful young bodies, but to Charlie, their ugly personalities made them repulsive.

She stepped into the jet of lukewarm water.

"One month," she said again, repeating it like a mantra. The water ran down her legs and swirled around the drain as she scrubbed at her body. Once, she thought she heard the door open. "Is someone there?" she called out, but there was no response, so she carried on, washing the soap off and reaching for her towel.

She couldn't find it.

"Shit," she said, unable to remember whether she had actually brought it or left it by her bag. She stepped out of the stall and looked. No towel. With water dripping from her hair and fingers, she walked towards the changing area with a mounting sense of unease. Her fears were justified as she entered the locker room and found her belongings missing.

The room was bare.

Usually, they only tied the shoelaces of her sneakers together and hung them from the beam, or threw her clothes into the shower with her. But this was the first time they had stolen them. Suddenly, that one month felt like an eternity.

"How am I supposed to get home?" she whispered to no one, her voice cracking. She got down on her hands and knees and checked under the benches. They must have left her *something* to wear. But there was nothing. No clothes, no shoes, no towel. She lived twenty minutes from the school. There was no way she could make it back without someone seeing her.

The water on her body was getting cold. She leaned forwards and ran her hands through her hair, wringing it out as best she could, then walked towards the door leaving a trail of damp footprints. In her head, she planned her route home. If she took the long way, there were bushes to hide behind most of the way. But the short route passed through a residential area, and there might be clothes hanging out to dry that she could steal.

Borrow, she corrected herself. She would return them tomorrow.

"Fuck you," she whispered, too cold and afraid to cry. She took a deep breath.

No time like the present, huh?

Steeling herself for the most stressful walk of her life, Charlie pushed open the door and looked out.

She screamed.

Someone was standing there.

Charlie covered her naked body and slammed the door, pressing herself up against it. What now? What more could they do to her? She didn't think it was possible to humiliate her any more than—

"*I've got your clothes,*" came a quiet voice.

"Leave me alone," sobbed Charlie. Then, quietly, "I don't deserve this."

"*I'm not one of them,*" said the voice. It was a girl. She waited a moment, then added, "*I honestly have your clothes.*"

Fuck it, thought Charlie. If they wanted that badly to torment her, they would force their way in. She stepped away from the door and squatted, covering herself. *Let them do their worst.*

The door creaked open, and a small bundle slid through the crack before it closed again.

Her clothes and bag! She ran for the garments, picking them up and dressing before any further calamity befell her. The fabric smelled funny, and stuck to her wet skin, but she didn't care. Everything was present and correct, except her panties. It was a small price to pay.

When she opened the door and stepped out into the sunshine, a short girl with shoulder length auburn hair was waiting for her. She looked shyly at Charlie, her hands stuffed in the pockets of her denim jacket.

"Hi," she said.

"Hey," said Charlie. "Where did you—"

"I saw them laughing and stuffing something in the trashcan at the end of the block. When I looked, it was a pile of clothes. Figured they belonged to someone in here."

"That explains why they stink, at least," said Charlie. She wiped away her remaining tears and offered the girl a smile. "Thank you. I didn't know what I was going to do."

"S'alright," said the girl. "My name's Lynette."

"Charlie."

"I know," she replied, then bit her lip, adding, "I'm in some of your classes."

"Oh. I'm sorry, I..."

"It's okay. I keep a low profile most of the time."

Charlie's smile widened. "I hear you. I do the same." She glanced down at her clothes and peeled a used bandaid from her sleeve. "It's working out pretty well for me, as you can see."

"I hate those girls," said Lynette.

"They pick on you, too?"

"No, they don't know I exist. But I know their type. In my old school, I... anyway, that doesn't matter. Are you okay?"

"I am now," said Charlie. "Thanks to you." The girl blushed. "Hey, can you show me where you found my stuff? I'm missing... uh, something."

"Sure. Follow me."

They walked together down the street, and Lynette identified the trash can. Charlie lifted the lid and peered in. The smell was overpowering, and she half-heartedly rooted around, searching for her missing undergarments. Unable to locate them, she gave up.

"Nothing?" asked Lynette.

"Nah. It's fine." She smiled at the girl. "Thanks again. I mean it. You didn't have to do that for me."

"It's okay," said Lynette. "I wanted to." She kicked a stone, refusing to make eye contact. "Hey, you wanna hang out this afternoon? My parents just got a VCR. We could—"

"I can't. Sorry."

Lynette looked crestfallen. "Oh, okay. I understand."

"No, I mean, I can't *today*. There's something I have to do. But how about tomorrow?"

For perhaps the first time, Lynette looked her in the eyes. The connection was fleeting, and she quickly turned away. "Yeah, sure. Groovy. Maybe I'll see you in class first?"

She sounded so keen. Not only did it make Charlie smile, but it also broke her heart a little. Imagine being so desperate for a friend that someone would want to hang out with *her*.

"Lunch time," said Charlie. "Let's sit together." She checked her watch. "Listen, I really gotta go. I'll see you tomorrow, okay?"

"Okay," said Lynette, lifting her eyes from the concrete long enough to meet Charlie's gaze. "See you later."

Lynette turned and walked away, her school bag dangling off her shoulder. Charlie was thankful, as tears were already forming in her eyes.

See you later.

It was funny how the weirdest things reminded her of Susan. She couldn't hear rain pattering off the window without thinking about her. Certain food (pepperoni pizza), certain songs *(If You Leave Me Now)*, and even that dumb and totally innocuous phrase, 'see you later,' always took Susan back to the good times.

See you later, Charlie-gator.

The good times. Ha! What a joke. Things were also pretty bad back then. But they had found each other, and between them created a small oasis of calm.

See you later, Charlie-gator.

Charlie wiped away her tears.

It was time to visit Susan.

6

———

Clinton Memorial Hospital was a relatively new addition to the town. Charlie carried the distinction of being the second child born in it, all eighteen years ago. The first, with crushing inevitability, had been Greta Wendel, beating her by thirty minutes.

A sinister, brutalist monolith, the five-storey building towered over the rest of the town, causing no end of complaints from residents whose houses sat in the hospital's shadow for much of the day, and who were woken at all hours by the furious blare of sirens.

"Good morning, Charlie," said an orderly as she entered through the glass doors.

"It's afternoon, Frank," she replied cheerily.

"Oh shit," he said, and hurried off down a corridor.

Charlie smiled. It felt odd to smile in a hospital, but this place made her happy. Her visits here were the only times she felt whole.

She passed the reception desk and waited for the elevator.

"A girl your age should take the stairs," said a man next to her.

She looked up at him. "Oh hi, Dr. Kevok. I've just been at gym class."

Kevok mopped sweat from his brow, his eyes focused on the numbers above the elevator, the dial moving from three to two to one. "A reasonable excuse, I suppose."

"How is she?"

"Same as always." The elevator pinged, and the doors slid open. Charlie and Kevok parted to allow two nurses to exit, then stepped inside. "No change, I'm afraid. And I wouldn't get my hopes up, Charlotte."

Charlie shrugged. "You never know."

"No," said Kevok. "I suppose you're right about that." He patted her on the shoulder. "I wish I had half your optimism, young lady. You're a good friend to her, you, uh..."

She waited for him to finish the sentence. Instead, he just stood there, beads of sweat running down his forehead. Charlie thought it was strange; the inside of the hospital was always cold. Maybe the doctor had come straight out of surgery?

The elevator doors opened, and Charlie exited. She turned to Dr. Kevok. "Is this not your floor?"

No answer.

"Are you alright?"

He was frozen to the spot, his arms dangling uselessly by his side. His head pivoted to look at her. There was something in his eyes that unnerved her.

"Doctor?"

The doors closed. Charlie waited, watching the dial move from five all the way back to one.

"That was weird," she said, then forgot all about it.

~

...so close so close so close so close so close so close so close so close...

~

Level five was the quietest floor in the hospital. Most of the patients here were not expected to make it out. Few people wandered the corridors. Today, a couple of visitors sat crying on a bench, comforting each other while a doctor glanced at a clipboard and spoke to them gravely.

Charlie walked by without a second glance. It was rude to stare. She made her way to the end of the corridor and entered the last room on the left.

Susan lay in bed, her white sheets crisp and undisturbed. Her eyes were, as usual, wide open.

"Hi," said Charlie, dragging a chair to the side of the bed and settling herself in. She laid her bag on the side table and unzipped it. "How are you feeling today?"

She took a brush from her bag and ran it through Susan's hair, careful not to lean on the tubes that entered her mouth and right nostril.

"I've had a shitty day," Charlie continued. "I mean, every day without you is a shitty day, but this one was special. They took my *clothes.*"

She finished with Susan's hair and placed the brush back in the bag.

"I found them in the trash, in case you're wondering what that smell is."

She wondered why she hadn't mentioned Lynette.

Don't want to make Susan jealous?

That was silly. There was no reason to be jealous.

"There's only one month left of high school. Can you

believe that? It'd be totally awesome if you could wake up before the end." She stroked Susan's face. "I don't have a date for the prom, and I was *kinda* hoping you'd ask me."

She noticed the photo frame on the window was empty. Last time Charlie had visited, she had left a photo of the pair of them. Susan's mom must have thrown it out. She always did. No problem. Charlie produced the same photo from her bag and placed it back in the frame. Susan's mom could throw out as many as she wanted. Charlie had a whole stack of that photo that she had printed in the dark room at school. She could keep this game going forever.

"There was talk of canceling the prom out of respect for you. They even had a meeting about it, with all the parents invited. But they agreed to have it anyway. They said that if you'd died, they would have canceled it. My parents voted not to hold it. I was proud of them."

She laid the frame on the windowsill and looked at the black-and-white image. They were so happy back then. They were both smiling, their arms around each other, the wind blowing Susan's hair across Charlie's face.

"I wish this photo was in color. It looks like this was taken a hundred years ago."

She took her seat again, and held Susan's hand.

"Want me to read to you? Well, bad luck. I'm going to, whether you like it or not."

She took a paperback from her bag — Peter Benchley's *Jaws* — and turned to the page with the bookmark.

The door opened, and a nurse entered. "Visiting hours are over."

Charlie closed the book and looked at her. "But I just got here."

"Out. *Now*. You know the rules."

Charlie did. But it wasn't every day that a gang of bullies

stole her clothes and made her late. She considered telling the nurse, but didn't believe she would get much sympathy. The woman looked old enough to have invented modern medicine.

"Okay," sighed Charlie. She packed up her things, then kissed Susan on the head. "I'll see you soon, okay?"

She slung her bag over her shoulder, the nurse's beady eyes following her as she walked. She reached the door and opened it, disappointed that her visit had been cut short.

"See you later, Charlie-gator," said the nurse.

The door slipped out of Charlie's hand. She turned to Susan, who lay still. The nurse faced the wall. A tremor ran through Charlie's body, almost imperceptible at first, then growing stronger.

"What did you say?" she asked.

But the nurse simply stared ahead. A trickle of drool rolled down her chin and hung there, before falling onto her uniform. It was flecked with blood.

"I asked you a question," said Charlie, her voice quivering. "What did you just say to me?"

The nurse's head slowly turned. The movement was jerky, like a mechanical toy that needed oiled. Her eyes rolled back into her skull, exposing blank white orbs. She took a lumbering step towards her.

The woman was freaking Charlie out. She reached for the door handle with clammy hands.

The nurse managed another faltering step.

"Okay, forget it, I'm going," said Charlie, keenly aware of the sudden panic in her voice. She grasped the handle and pulled, stepping out into the cool corridor and pulling the door shut behind her. It clicked into place, and everything felt normal again. What the hell *was* that?

See you later, Charlie-gator.

The nurse... she had said...

"You imagined it," whispered Charlie. "That's all." She walked to the elevator and pressed the button. "You're fucking losing it."

She looked down the corridor. The grieving couple were gone, as was the doctor. It was as quiet as a morgue.

Poor choice of words.

The soft creak of hinges broke the unforgiving silence. Somewhere down the corridor, a door was opening. Charlie didn't want to look. She didn't want to, and yet she did.

The old nurse stepped into the corridor.

Charlie couldn't understand why she was so afraid. There was a nurse... so what? She was in a hospital, for god's sake.

But something about the unnatural way the woman moved frightened her. One leg buckled, and she almost lost her balance, righting herself at the last minute, her arms swinging loosely by her sides.

"Are you okay?" Charlie called. She jabbed the elevator button again. "Do you need any help?"

The nurse never spoke. She advanced slowly, the white hospital lights reflecting off her eyeballs, making them glow.

Use the stairs, Charlie's brain urged her.

No. She wouldn't give in to fear. This nurse was a harmless old lady. Everything was fine. There was nothing to be afraid of.

The light above her flickered.

"You, uh, want me to call someone?" asked Charlie.

The nurse was getting closer.

Her heart beat fast. Too fast. Where was the damn elevator? Fuck it, she should have taken the stairs. She jabbed the button again. There was a ping, and the doors opened. Charlie entered, pressing the lowest button on the panel and waiting for the doors to shut. They took forever. The maddening footsteps of the nurse rang in her ears. She hit the button again, and again, until finally the doors started to close.

A hand, old and gray and wrinkled, appeared. It gripped the elevator door, preventing it from closing. Charlie screamed. She couldn't help it. The doors gasped open, revealing the old nurse, her eyes still blank, her jaw sagging loosely, blood and spittle running over her chin. Her head flopped forwards.

"See you later, Charlie-gator," she wheezed, and then all at once, the strange expression fell from her face. "What... where am I?" she said, as the doors closed and the elevator began its descent.

Charlie gripped the rail. She caught a glimpse of herself in the mirrored wall, her pure white face a ghastly vision of horror. Should she go back up and check on the nurse? She knew she should. It was the right thing to do.

"Well, fuck that," she said, and rode the elevator all the way to the bottom.

There, she ran from the hospital and didn't look back.

7

...see you later Charlie-Gator see you later see you later...

THE VISION FADED, AND ONCE MORE SUSAN RETURNED TO THE
yellow walls of the hospital room.

...I did it I did it that old whore that bitch I did it I fucking did it...

She stared at the only flicker of visual interest in the
room. The calendar. The image was of boats in a harbor,
their white masts forming an obscure pattern against the
clear blue sky. She hated that motherfucking goddam cunt
of a calendar. Next time she had control, she was going to
tear it down. How cruel of her parents to insist it hung there!
What were they, sick in the head? All fucked up? Those
monsters. She had lain here for almost a full year, staring at
that fucking calendar, watching each miserable day crawl
by, a grim reminder of her inability _to fucking do anything._

_...those cunts those bastards I'll kill them I'll fucking kill them I'll
work on my strength and practice and practice and practice_

because what else can I do and I'll kill them I'll rip them apart I'll kill them...

Lying alone in her hospital bed, unable to move, unable to even *blink,* and yet fully awake and conscious, had driven Susan quite mad. She couldn't sleep, hadn't for eleven months, electricity firing through her brain, electricity that she had learned to harness. It was difficult at first. It took her four months just to make Dr. Kevok clear his throat. But she was getting better. She had been so close with Kevok in the elevator.

...so close so close so close...

And then success at last! It took a lot out of her. More than she expected. Her synapses no longer sparked. Instead, they throbbed dully, the pain wracking her body. She would have screamed if she could. She would have started screaming eleven months ago, and never stopped.

But she would have her revenge. She would have the revenge she deserved. For her. For Charlie.

...see you later see you later see you later Charlie-gator...

She would have her revenge, and no one could stop her. Not even God. What was the worst that could happen? She would go to hell? The idea held no concern for Susan. Hell was this bed. Hell was being kept prisoner in her own useless body.

If there was a hell — and Susan was convinced there was — then she was already there.

8

———

THE NEXT DAY IN SCHOOL, CHARLIE SAT WATCHING THE CLOCK. The lunch bell would ring any second now, and the morning had elapsed without incident. Sure, some girls had giggled as she passed, and asked if she enjoyed her walk home, but she chose not to dignify the question with a response.

In fact, the episode in the locker room had been the furthest thing from Charlie's mind. Instead, she fixated on the bizarre happenings in the hospital. It had been so surreal that she questioned her own memories.

See you later, Charlie-gator.

It was a coincidence. It had to be. The alternative was... what, exactly? Nothing made sense. What she did know was that she should have gone back and checked on the nurse. The poor woman could have had an aneurysm or something. Well, she might see her today after school. She didn't normally visit Susan on a Friday, because that's when Susan's parents went, but after yesterday, she felt she owed her girlfriend a proper catch up.

She glared at the clock. Why hadn't the bell rung yet?

She wondered if Lynette would be there. She had said they would meet for lunch. Would she keep her word? Charlie thought she would.

In front of the blackboard, Mr. Carradine droned on. Some people claimed the English accent was sexy, or signified intelligence, but Carradine's voice bored Charlie to tears. It didn't help that she couldn't look at him without thinking of that night at the summer ball. If he hadn't stopped her — if he had let her go — would she have reached Susan in time to save her? The question had tortured her thoughts ever since, and she knew she would never receive a definitive answer.

Mercifully, the bell rang, and Susan joined her classmates in immediately shoving her notebook and pen into her bag.

"Class dismissed," sighed Carradine, as the students jostled past him. Charlie zipped up her bag and realized she was looking forward to seeing Lynette. It would be nice to have lunch with someone again.

She pushed away from her desk and walked to the door, trying not to make eye contact with Creepy Carradine. She was almost beyond him when she felt lecherous fingers grip her arm.

"Miss Bonner," he said, "I regret I must ask you to remain behind."

"But it's lunchtime."

He smiled thinly. "Some things are more important than lunch, young lady. Your inappropriate behavior, for example."

"My what?"

Carradine waited until the last of the pupils left the classroom. "You know fine well what I'm talking about," he said as he closed the door.

"Honestly, I really don't."

He made a grand show of looking disappointed in her as he slunk towards his desk and opened a drawer. "Are these, or are they not, your property?"

Charlie's breath caught in her throat. A pair of red panties dangled from his hand. *Her* panties, the ones the girls had taken from her.

"Give them back," she said, and tried to snatch them from his grip. He pulled them out of reach.

"So you don't deny it."

"Deny what? They're mine, give them back!" She lunged for the panties, and Carradine raised them above his head like a sad flag.

"I've heard of pupils giving apples to their teachers to curry favor, but this is ridiculous. And your little love letter, might I add, was riddled with grammatical errors, the likes of which suggest a career in literature should not be high on your list of priorities."

Love letter? What the hell was he talking about?

"I didn't... look, would you just give them back, *please?*" He must have heard the exasperation in her voice, for he started to laugh.

"In time. I think we need to have a discussion first. Then, and only then, will I furnish you with your undergarments."

Charlie rubbed at her temples. "This is so embarrass- ing," she muttered. Creepy Carradine, holding her under- wear in his gross fingers. He held them in both hands, stretching the waistband, the small black hearts that dotted the fabric distorting out of shape.

"I know you've always, shall we say, carried a torch for me," he said.

"Huh?"

"Please, Miss Bonner, don't make an even bigger fool of

yourself by denying it. I've seen the way you look at me. The way you bat your eyelids suggestively, and how, sometimes, when you know I'm watching, you spread your legs just wide enough for me to see..." — he cleared his throat — "...everything."

"I've... I've never done any of that."

"Oh, piffle. You leave your underwear on my desk, and then refute any prior wrongdoings? What do you take me for? A buffoon? A nincompoop? Is that it?"

His face was growing redder with each word. Charlie glanced at the door. She didn't like where this was heading. Should she make a run for it?

"Don't even think about it," said Carradine. He rubbed the thin cotton between his thumb and forefinger, then balled her underwear up and pocketed them.

"I could report you for this, you know. Trying to buy better grades with..." — he savored the words — "...*sexual favors*. It would not look good on your college applications, I can tell you that much."

"What do you want?" snapped Charlie. She was running out of patience. "You can keep the panties for all I care." She sniffed back tears. "What do you want from me?"

Carradine patted his pocket. "Oh, I *will* keep them. To teach you a lesson."

"Fine. Can I go now?"

She started for the door, and once more he stopped her.

"We're not done here." He walked behind her, placing his hands on her shoulders. "In my country, we have a little something called *corporal punishment*. This state banned it a few years ago, which I believe has contributed to the rotting of young people's minds. Don't you agree?"

Charlie couldn't control her breathing. Her body started to shake as Carradine marched her over to his desk.

"I'll tell the principal," said Charlie, playing her final gambit. "I'll tell, and you'll be fired."

He bent her at the waist, forcing her down over the desk. "And who do you think they'll believe? A respected mathematics teacher from England, or a juvenile delinquent who leaves her used underwear and perfumed notes lying around on his desk?"

"I didn't leave them anywhere, and I didn't write any fucking notes!"

Carradine's fingers tightened over her shoulder blades. She could hear his heavy breathing, his dry lips smacking against each other. "Such language," he panted. Though unable to see his face, Charlie knew he was smiling. "You've just earned yourself an extra ten strokes."

He lifted a wooden ruler, cracking it off the desk with a sharp report. Charlie flinched. She felt sick. She tried to wriggle free, but his hand pressed on the back of her neck, forcing her down. He used the ruler to raise her skirt.

"I hope you know, I take no pleasure in this," he lied.

Charlie braced herself, her hands tightening into balls.

"No pleasure... *at all.*"

She closed her eyes.

Whack.

Charlie winced, waiting for the stinging pain to flare over her butt. It never came.

Whack.

Again, nothing. Was the sick fuck toying with her?

"What in God's name..." she heard him mumble, then looked back over her shoulder. Carradine held the wooden ruler as two pink, rectangular marks formed on his cheek. He gazed at his hand as if it wasn't his, then struck himself in the face with the ruler.

Staggering backwards, he smacked himself again, this

time in the throat. He choked, emitting a reedy grunt, and stared at Charlie.

"What are you doing?" he asked in a strangulated whisper.

He brought the ruler down between his legs with savage ferocity, then dropped, whining, to his knees.

Charlie backed away. What *was* this? A fetish? Some sort of twisted game?

"Uh, I'm gonna go," she said. "You can keep my under-wear." She started towards the door, waiting for him to stop her. Instead, he increased the violence of his self-flagella-tion. His pink face was turning purple, and blood dripped from a couple of wounds. He rummaged in his pocket and threw her panties across the room. They landed at Charlie's feet.

"Take them, please! Just make her stop! Tell her to stop!"

Charlie nodded slowly, like she was humoring a child. "Yeah, okay, I'll do that. I'll tell her." She picked up her underwear, took one last look at Carradine, and slipped out into the corridor.

Whack! Whack! Whack whack whack!

"Fucking weird-ass English sex freaks," she whispered to herself, then jogged down the corridor towards the lunch hall, leaving Mr. Carradine to... whatever it was that got him off. She shook her head. Susan would *never* believe it when she told her.

~

...do it do it hit yourself you creep you sleaze you fucking cunt why are you hitting yourself huh why are you hitting yourself...

~

The voice rattled around in Edward Carradine's head as he stared at his hand in astonishment. The thick wood cracked against his cheekbone.

"I did it," he spluttered. "I gave her them back!"

He leaned on the desk with his free hand, then brought the ruler sharply down across his knuckles.

"Stop it! I gave the blasted things *back!*"

The ruler hit him just above his eye, splitting the flesh open. His vision turned red as blood flowed into his eyeball.

"Shut up! I never touched her! I was—"

It cracked against his teeth, the blow powerful enough to knock the front two at an angle, the roots bursting from his gums. His mouth filled with coppery tasting fluid.

"I was just trying to scare her! I wouldn't—"

Across his cheek again. The ruler fell from his hand, clattering to the floor, and then his hands — good God, both of them! — reached for the waistband of his suit trousers. They tugged them down, hauling them over his ass and taking his underpants with them.

"What? No! No, stop!"

He wanted to cry for help... but what if someone came in and saw him like this?

...look at that it's so small I've never seen one before is that all it is that's pathetic oh my god it's so small it's pathetic you scum you shit you...

With his trousers bunched up around his knees, he waddled over towards the desk on legs he couldn't control.

"Get out of my body!"

He collapsed over the desk the way Charlotte had been only moments before, then crawled over it, digging his nails into the wood and hurling himself forwards. He crashed into his chair, knocking it over, and those damn infernal hands fumbled with a drawer, sliding it open. His eyes widened in horror.

The stationery drawer.

"No... please dear God, dear sweet Lord Jesus Christ, I beg you..."

He got to his feet and stood by the desk, bending his knees so that his penis and testicles rested on top, right next to the pile of trigonometry tests he was due to grade. Sweeping his arm over the desk, he sent the papers flying. They glided through the air like oversized snowflakes, as his own traitorous hand plunged into the stationery drawer and emerged clutching something.

A mathematical compass.

"God... God..."

It hovered above his flaccid member in a hand that had once belonged to him. Powerless to stop it, he prayed that the loss of control below the neck would mean he was unable to feel pain.

He was wrong.

The pointed tip of the compass slammed down into his cock, easily piercing through the soft meat. Blood fountained over his white shirt, drenching him. He pushed down on the compass, grinding it into the desk, pounding it with his fist until it dug firmly into the wood. He looked down at his mangled cock, blood leaking through his urethra, and vomited over himself. Agony wracked his body, sparking from his crotch to his extremities, every nerve ending alive and on fire with unholy intensity.

∽

...he's crying he's crying oh my god Charlie look he's crying...

∽

"Shut up!" he roared, as he groped inside the drawer and produced a twelve inch steel rule.

"Good God, no!"

It trembled in his hand. He had to stop her. He knew what she had planned.

Carradine concentrated hard. He focused all his attention on his hand, on his fingers, willing them to open, fighting against every urge within his body.

The fingers began to uncurl. The steel rule slipped through them a couple of inches.

"Come on, come on," he said, straining with every fiber of his being. The measuring implement slid further through his grasp... and then his fist closed tight.

He angled the ruler so that the sharp edge faced down, and rested it on the shaft of his cock.

"No! Help! Someone help me! Please!"

He no longer cared if someone found him like this. He would explain, and they would understand it wasn't him doing this, it was—

He started to saw. It only took a second for the steel rule to burst the skin. Blood bubbled and frothed as he dragged it back and forth, back and forth, hacking through the tissue of his penis. Each motion sent waves of sickness coursing through his body. His knees were weak, though he couldn't faint even if he wanted to. The metal scratched along his scrotum, slicing it open, bursting one testicle. It oozed fluid, mingling with the spurting blood and the chunks of vomit that covered the desk.

Still he sawed, his penis attached by thin strains of ragged foreskin, and only when those last cords were severed, and the steel rule scraped uselessly across the empty desk, did Susan allow Edward Carradine to stagger backwards, blood gushing from his torn crotch, and fall, sobbing, to the floor.

9

———

Charlie found Lynette sitting alone at a table in the corner of the lunch hall. The girl looked up at her with something resembling nervous excitement.

"I wasn't sure if you were coming," she said.

Charlie took a seat next to her, still trying to process what had happened in Carradine's class. "Yeah, I got, uh, held up." She wondered if the weirdo was finished beating himself up yet.

Lynette nodded. "Are those..."

Charlie followed Lynette's gaze to her hand, where she clutched the crumpled panties she had picked up from Carradine's floor. "Oh, yeah." She blushed, and stuffed them in her bag. "That's what I was looking for yesterday. I found them." She laughed at the absurdity of it, and a puzzled Lynette laughed with her. The girl had a sweet smile when she laughed, and she tossed her hair back the way Greta and the cheerleaders did when they were flirting with the jocks.

"Where were they?" asked Lynette.

Charlie unpacked her lunch. A ham and cheese sandwich, a carton of orange juice, and a candy bar. "Mr. Carradine had them," she said, then took a bite of her sandwich.

Lynette peered at her curiously. "Creepy Carradine?"

"You call him that too?" Charlie was still chewing, so she covered her mouth as she spoke. "I thought that was just us."

"You mean you and Susan?"

Charlie swallowed her food. She heard the name out loud so rarely, that when she did, it always sent a dagger through her heart. "Yeah," she said quietly. "Susan."

"I wasn't at the dance, but I... I heard what happened. How is she?"

"She's okay. Alive, but unresponsive. The doctors say she might be like that forever. They don't hold out much hope."

"I'm sorry."

"You've no reason to be. It wasn't you who put her there." She finished her sandwich and washed it down with some juice. "Anyway, I don't wanna talk about that. Tell me, what do you do for fun? Apart from digging clothes out of trash cans, I mean."

Lynette cracked a smile. "Oh, not much. I read a lot. Go to the movies."

"Oh yeah?" said Charlie, glad of the subject change. "What's your favorite?"

"I saw this horror a few weeks ago called *The Hills Have Eyes*. It was pretty hip."

"They played *that* at The Regal? I thought they only showed Disney movies. Isn't it run by some religious wackjob?"

"It is. But I have a car, so I go to the drive-in. There's one the next town over. The—"

"Starlight," finished Charlie with a smile. "I went there

once. They show all the scary movies, right? All the really gross ones?"

"They do." Lynette leaned in close and giggled. "The kind your parents don't want you to see." She pulled back, her cheeks coloring. "You like those sort of films?"

"I love them. I went to The Starlight on a date and saw one about these two female vampires who lived in a castle and drank people's blood."

"Were they lovers? The vampires?"

Charlie nodded. She hadn't intended to bring up the lesbian angle. "Yeah, I think they were. It was a couple of years ago, I can't remember."

"I think I saw that one. I thought it was cool... and kinda sexy." Lynette whispered the last word like if she said it loud, she would be struck by lightning. She looked down at her clasped hands, clearly embarrassed.

"Maybe we could go together sometime?" said Charlie. "I'll pay for the gas."

"Really? I'd like that. You busy Saturday?"

Charlie laughed. "Oh, Lynette, I'm *never* busy."

"Me neither!" said the girl, and she flicked her hair again in that endearing way. The sight warmed Charlie's heart, and before she could stop herself, she said, "You're cute when you laugh." She realized what she had said. "I'm sorry, I didn't mean that. Like, okay, I did, but I shouldn't have said it. I'm sorry. Should I go? I think I should go."

She was already packing up her lunch when Lynette put her hand on Charlie's wrist.

"Don't go," she said. "It's nice to talk to someone. It's nice to have a friend."

Charlie gazed into the girl's eyes. They were so sincere, and they matched her auburn hair perfectly. She felt she could stare into them for hours.

"Sorry. Sometimes I overreact."

"It's okay," said Lynette. "So do I." She seemed to realize she was still holding Charlie's wrist, and let go.

"So how about tomorrow?" asked Charlie. "Wanna catch a movie?"

"Sure thing. Saturdays are always a horror double bill. There's a diner there too, so we can get supper, if you like."

"Oh shit, is this the designated lesbo table now?"

The deadpan voice startled both of them. Michelle stood with her palms on the table, a sneer on her face.

"You know she's a lesbian, right?" she said to Lynette. "You should probably sit somewhere else. People talk. Well, except her girlfriend," she said, gesturing at Charlie. "She's a vegetable."

"She's not—"

"Not what?" snapped Michelle. "Not your girlfriend, or not a vegetable?"

Charlie clamped her mouth shut. She wouldn't rise to the bait.

Michelle turned back to Lynette. "So, what's your story? You a queer too? You guys are like weeds. You cut one down, another springs up in its place."

A loud crackle echoed across the PA. Michelle briefly looked up, then continued. "What are you, mute?" She put her elbows on the table, looking directly at Lynette. "I'm talking to you, bitch."

"I'm just trying to eat my lunch," she said.

The PA crackled again. Then a curious thing happened. Distant horns drifted through the speakers. It was enough to silence the lunch hall. The assembled kids looked up in surprise and confusion. A song was playing. But not just any song... it was *If You Leave Me Now* by Chicago.

Charlie stared at the PA system. "What the hell...?"

A loud gurgle cut through the music. It came from Michelle's stomach. She glanced down at it, then straightened up, shifting uncomfortably.

Charlie listened to the music. She hadn't heard this song since... since her and Susan's last dance. Despite the memories it held, she had actively avoided the song, promising herself that the next time she heard it, Susan would be in her arms again, and they would be dancing. And now—

Michelle farted. It was a tremendous sound, a great ripping blast of juddering flatulence. Her mouth opened, her body going rigid. The smell was foul. Charlie and Lynette kicked their chairs back, retreating to a safe distance. They made brief eye contact, then turned to the frozen statue of Michelle. The bully fidgeted in her pleated floral skirt, and the music abruptly stopped as she farted again. It echoed across the hall, and there was utter, devastating silence for several seconds, before one of the football jocks burst out laughing.

"Holy shit, Michelle had the tacos!" he shouted.

The bully tottered forwards, then froze, her body clenching. Without turning her head, she addressed Charlie. "What... did you do to me?"

Another burst of wind. Charlie could have sworn she saw the girl's skirt billow. More laughter, everyone in the hall now staring, backing away from the terrible odor that surrounded Michelle like an impenetrable force field.

Then the unthinkable happened.

Michelle raised her head to the heavens and screamed as a torrent of murky brown shit flooded down her legs. Chaos erupted. People nearby fled, far enough to avoid the splatter of feces on their shoes, but not so far that they wouldn't get to witness the event. Michelle took a step forwards, and more shit blasted out of her. Her panties, filled with her own waste, dropped to her ankles. She kept going, walking like a malfunctioning robot, leaving a trail of excrement in her wake.

She turned and pointed at Charlie. "You did this!" she cried, as her bowels emptied over the slick floor. Michelle stood there in a pool of her own shit. She gagged, doubling over, clutching her stomach.

"What the fuck?" someone shouted. The laughter had begun to die away, though traces remained. The stench was too much for some, who ran from the hall and vomited in the corridor. Michelle fell to her knees in the lumpy puddle.

"Ewwww," a girl cried, but no one was prepared for what happened next.

Michelle arched her back and farted again. Blood exploded from her anus, evacuating at such force that it hit several boys standing on a table to get a better view, knocking one of them off his feet.

Charlie pressed up against the wall. She turned to Lynette. "Let's get the fuck out of here!"

They slid along the wall as Michelle writhed in agony. The girl staggered to her feet, arms outstretched. Something pink and slippery dangled from between her buttocks. It looked like her intestines. They kept coming, sliding out of her asshole and coiling on the ground between her feet. Laughter turned to screaming and wailing and crying and vomiting... so much vomiting. The lunch hall stank like the inside of a portable toilet.

The last of Michelle's long intestine slopped out in a steaming pile. She stood straight and raised her hands in the air, her belly visibly vibrating, her ass cheeks rumbling. She bent over, fingers clawing through the muck, and unwittingly pointed her filthy bare ass at a large portion of the student body. They scrambled to get away, falling over one another in panic, one girl trampled underfoot as the stampede began.

"Oh shit," said Lynette.

"Oh shit, indeed," said Charlie, grabbing Lynette's hand and running for the exit. They didn't look back, not even as Michelle's desperate cries hit a cacophonous fever pitch. They reached the doors ahead of the remaining student body, making it through just in time. Two seconds later, Michelle Strunk's ass exploded.

Charlie slammed the door as gallons of blood rained down against it, then thumps of fleshy chunks splattered down on the few students who hadn't fled the scene. It sounded like a thunderstorm had broken out.

Charlie and Lynette stumbled down the hallway, holding their noses and gagging, never slowing in their desperate quest to reach fresh air.

A stern-faced janitor passed them, carrying a wet mop that dripped water as he walked. "What's that smell?" he growled. "One of you goddam kids shit themselves?"

Charlie, her face green with nausea, looked at him. "Man," she said, "you're gonna need a bigger mop."

10

———

They walked until their feet hurt.

Lynette was the first to break. She located a park bench and sat, saying nothing. For what could be said?

Charlie joined her. They watched the trees blowing in the wind for a while, before their gaze fell upon a frantic woman chasing after her dog, his lead trailing behind him.

"What the fuck just happened?" asked Lynette. "Did she... is she..."

"Oh, she's *dead*," said Charlie definitively.

"But how? What could do that..." It all seemed to catch up with Lynette at once. She abandoned the bench, ran from Charlie, and threw up in the bushes. Eventually, she trudged back, wiping her mouth and looking sheepish.

"Feel better?" asked Charlie.

"Not really. How 'bout you?"

Charlie shook her head. "She *exploded*. I heard her guts hit the wall. How does that happen?" The loose dog scampered past them again, its owner racing after him. Charlie could swear the dog was smiling.

"You remember that song that played over the PA?"

Lynette had zoned out. "Huh?"

"That song. The one by Chicago." She half-heartedly hummed the opening notes.

"Oh yeah. I forgot about that." She gave Charlie an askew glance. "It was hardly the most memorable thing that happened."

"I know. But that song... it played at the summer ball last year. I danced to it with Susan, up on the roof. It was the last thing we ever did together. Five minutes later, she fell through the window." Lynette remained silent. "I say *fell*, but she was pushed. I know she was. Greta was up there, along with her boyfriend Freddy, and that Peter asshole no one likes. And you know who else was? *Michelle.*"

The dog was running circles around his owner, the poor woman frantically trying to grasp the errant lead.

"Pretty weird coincidence, huh?" said Charlie. "That song comes on, then Michelle dies like that."

"Guess so. Crazy."

"That's not all, Lynette. Something happened after Mr. Carradine's math class. It's why I was late for lunch." She explained the events as best she could. The panties, the attempted punishment, and the way she had left him beating himself across the face with a ruler.

"Tell her to stop. That's what he said to me. *Tell her to stop."*

Lynette looked puzzled. "Tell *who* to stop?"

Charlie had an idea, but if Lynette wasn't thinking the same thing, she wasn't willing to say it out loud. It was too insane. "I don't know. But what I *do* know is that I would have reached Susan in time if he hadn't stopped me at the dance. In a way, it's his fault as much as anyone's."

Charlie felt Lynette's hand rest on hers.

"Charlie, you've been through a lot today. You want me to take you home?"

"No, I'm fine. It's just... I dunno, maybe you're right. I'm not sure how to process it. The Carradine thing is whatever, y'know? He's a creep. But Michelle..." She laughed drily. "I mean, maybe no one deserves to die like that. But the fact she's dead? I know I'm supposed to care, but I don't think I do. In fact, I *know* I don't. If anything, I'm glad. Does that make me a bad person? She made my life a living hell. Her and Greta. I think the pair of them put Susan in a coma from which she might never wake up." She smiled. "Fuck her. I'm glad she's dead. There, I said it." Her voice cracked. "You hear me? I'm *glad* she's dead. I'm..."

She broke down in tears. Lynette pulled her close, resting her head against her shoulder. She stroked her hand through Charlie's hair.

"I know how you feel," she whispered. "The reason I moved here last year was because I was getting bullied. They found out I was... different. The girls there would beat me up after class, two, sometimes three days a week. One time, they dislocated my jaw. Another time they hit me so hard on my ear that I lost my hearing in it. That's why I talk funny."

"You talk funny? I hadn't noticed," said Charlie honestly.

"I talk out the side of my mouth, because that's the side I can hear out of. My hearing never came back in that ear." She laughed humorlessly. "After a while, I was costing my parents too much in medical bills, so they moved us across the country."

"Jesus. That's terrible. I'm so sorry."

Lynette shrugged. "It's okay. It's better here. No one knows me, so they leave me alone. Though back home," she added, "no one ever exploded."

"Did you have someone to talk to in your old school? A friend, or..."

"No. That's how they found out. There was this girl. I thought she was, y'know, like me, and I asked her out. I considered her a friend, but she told everyone. That was when it started. After that day, I never knew a second's peace."

"And you had no one to talk to? That must have been awful."

"It's okay. I found a way to manage on my own."

"Tell me," said Charlie sadly. "I'd love to know."

"You'll think it's dumb."

"I won't," said Charlie. Lynette was still stroking her hair. It felt nice. "I promise."

Lynette took a breath, like she was about to reveal a great secret. "Meditation," she said. When Charlie didn't laugh, she continued. "I learned to meditate. I used to do it at night to clear my head. I couldn't sleep, just lying in bed with all the day's pain and humiliations rattling around in there. Meditating helped. It got to the point I could do it any time. If someone was teasing me, or being horrible, I could shut them out."

"Teach me."

Lynette looked unsure. "I'm not much of a teacher. It took me a long time to get good at it."

"Then give me the basics. I could use a little help sleeping."

"Okay." said Lynette. Then, more confidently, *"Okay. Let's try it."* She shuffled around on the bench to face Charlie. "We'll start with keeping your eyes closed. Eyes open is much harder. You ready?"

"Super ready," grinned Charlie.

"Okay. Well, close your eyes, silly!" Lynette playfully slapped her arm.

"I knew I'd be terrible at this," giggled Charlie. "Right,

I'm relaxed." She forced the smile from her face. "Let's do this." She closed her eyes, and her thoughts immediately turned to the sight of Michelle standing shrieking in the lunch hall, floods of—

"Picture yourself in a corridor," said Lynette. Charlie was glad of the interruption. She hoped this meditation business would work. Without it, she knew she would be seeing Michelle's face in her nightmares.

"Why a corridor?" she asked.

"Just do what I say. Can you see it?" Lynette's voice was soft and kind, her words like velvet. Charlie relaxed. As requested, she imagined a corridor. It resembled the upstairs hallway in her childhood home in Pasadena. Funny. They had moved out of there when she was five.

"I can see it."

"Good," said Lynette. "There are doors. So many doors, more than you can count. Can you see them?"

Charlie could. The corridor, which at first had seemed to fade into darkness, was now illuminated by ornate brass lamps along the walls, one between each door. It stretched on as far as she could see.

"Charlie? Can you see the doors?"

"Yes," she said, smiling. "Hundreds of them."

"More," said Lynette. "Oh, I almost forgot. Breathe deeply. It's all about breathing. Breathe in... and breathe out. Keep the rhythm."

"There's a lot of admin to this."

"Keep quiet, or you'll ruin it. Now breathe."

Charlie did.

"You still see the corridor?" asked Lynette, her voice strangely distant.

"Yes. I can't see the end of it."

"And you never will. Those doors represent infinite

possibilities for you. Behind each one lies a happy place. A happy memory. Walk down the corridor and choose a door. Any door. They're *all* happy places."

"I haven't thought of a happy place yet."

"You don't have to. It'll reveal itself to you. It's easier when I'm not telling you what to do. Are you still in the corridor?"

"Yeah." In her mind, Charlie stood before a door. They all looked the same, but this one smelled different, a nostalgic odor of sea and sand. "I've chosen one."

"Open it."

Charlie put her hand on the wood, surprised by its comforting hardness. It didn't feel like her imagination, or a dream. It felt real. The door opened, and she walked through.

"Jesus," she said, stepping onto the sand and squinting into the sun. The wind ruffled her hair, blowing it across her eyes.

"Where are you?" Lynette's voice was so faint, it sounded like she was speaking down the phone from the other side of the world.

"I'm at the beach," said Charlie, unsure whether Lynette could still hear her. Was she speaking out loud back in the real world? Or just in here, in her mind? "I can smell the sea air."

"Good. That sounds calming. What are you smiling at?"

"I feel the sand between my toes."

"It's nice, isn't it?"

"Yeah." Charlie remembered the beach. Her family had visited relatives in Martha's Vineyard when she was a kid, and she had spent much of her time out here, on the private beach, while the adults talked and drank and did whatever adults did. "It's not changed," she said. "It's exactly as I remember it. I'd sit and build sandcastles and watch the tide roll in, then out again. The sea was so blue... it still is. It's so peaceful."

Lynette said something, but she was so quiet Charlie couldn't make it out.

"It's working," said Charlie. She broke into a run, leaving her shoes behind, heading for the water. The waves lapped lazily at her feet, the water refreshing beneath the glare of the sun. More than anything, she wanted to get in the ocean, maybe wade up to her waist.

Why not? It doesn't matter if your clothes get wet. This isn't real, remember?

But it *felt* real... frighteningly real.

"Lynette, you still there?"

"I'm here."

Lynette's voice soothed her, and she turned around to check the door was still there.

It wasn't.

Okay, she thought. *No problem. It's my head. I can leave whenever I want.*

The door had to be somewhere. She looked around, at the beach and the trees and the adorable white wooden house they were staying in, a beacon against the blue sky. Following her footsteps, Charlie wandered back up the beach. The indentations her feet had left in the sand came to an abrupt end. She held her arm out in front of her, searching for a door that wasn't there.

"Lynette? How do you get out?"

The fear hadn't quite set in yet. She felt too safe, in her own mind, in a happy place, with her new friend watching over her. She sighed and looked down the beach. The gulls cawed in the air, circling something on the sand, something limp and putrid and—

Charlie turned away. She didn't want to know what it was. It was nothing good. She could smell it — god, it fucking stank — so she walked the other direction, leaving the gulls to fight over their grisly prize. She stopped in her tracks. There was someone far ahead of her, on the beach.

A lone figure.

Shielding her eyes from the sun, Charlie squinted at the person. They took a step closer.

"Hello," Charlie called out. She raised a hand and waved. They didn't wave back. She realized Lynette hadn't answered her question. How *did* she get out of here?

"Lynette?"

No answer.

The dark figure took another step closer, and suddenly Charlie was very, very afraid.

On the park bench, Charlie's body jerked. Lynette glanced around, seeing nobody, and took Charlie's hand. You could never be too careful in public spaces.

"Are you okay?" she asked. Charlie had been silent for too long. Lynette knew she shouldn't have done this; not without proper practice. She realized Charlie was saying something.

"There's someone here," she said, the whispered words catching in her throat. *"I don't know who."*

"Walk away from them." Lynette kept her voice calm and moderate. She had experienced this before during her meditations, uninvited guests appearing in her happy places. It was always a risk. Dammit, she shouldn't have rushed into this! "If you see anything odd, just walk away. And remember, nothing can hurt you there."

She knew that wasn't true, though.

"Okay," whispered Charlie. *"I'm turning away."* Her brow wrinkled into a frown. *"They're still in front of me. Wherever I look, they're standing there."*

"It's okay. Don't worry. Find the door and go back into the corridor."

"I can't find it. I can't find the door."

"Then open your eyes. Remember, you're here with me in the park. I'm holding your hand right now."

A long silence.

"I can't open them. What the fuck, I can't open my eyes."

This was bad. Shit! Lynette placed two fingers above Charlie's eye and lifted the lid.

"What are you doing? Are you touching my face? Who's doing that?"

"It's me. I'm trying to open your eyes." She stared into the sightless, milky pupil. "I... I don't know what's wrong."

"They're coming closer. They're coming towards me. Why can't I see their face?"

"Stay cool. Just walk away."

"I tried that! They're always there." Her voice exploded in anger. *"Who are you? What do you want?"*

"Charlie, relax. It's all in your head. You're in control, don't forget that."

"Then why can't I open my eyes? Who's there? Fuck, why won't they say anything?"

"It's okay. Just—"

"It's not okay!" screamed Charlie, the words echoing through the quiet park. *"They're getting closer!"*

"It's alright, just—"

Charlie's voice dropped back to a whisper. *"Wait... I can see their face. It's blurry, but... oh my god..."*

"Listen to me, Charlie," said Lynette. Panic gripped her with a frosted fist. *"Run."*

Charlie's body stiffened, her shoulders twitching. *"I see the door,"* she panted.

"Go to it! Run through and don't look back. You hear me? Whatever you do, don't look back."

"I'm almost there. I hear them. They're behind me. They're close."

"Keep going. Are you there yet?"

Charlie drooped, almost sliding off the bench. Lynette held her.

"I'm there," she said. *"I'm at the door."*

"Come on!"

"It's okay, I'm opening it. I think they're gone. I..."

Charlie's eyes shot open.

"Jesus fuck!"

All Charlie could see was green. As her vision swam into focus, she realized she was on her hands and knees, staring at the grass. She grabbed two handfuls of earth and squeezed the fine grains of dirt between her fingers. Her eyes were wet, her breathing labored.

Lynette was by her side, her hand gently massaging between her shoulder blades. "Are you okay?"

Charlie took a moment to gather herself. Her limbs trembled, and she wasn't sure she could stand. "Yeah," she croaked.

"What did you see? What happened?"

"I'm sorry," said Charlie, struggling to her feet and brushing the mud from her knees. "We shouldn't have tried. It was a bad idea. I knew it wouldn't work."

"Charlie, what did you *see?*"

But she couldn't bring herself to talk about it. "It doesn't matter." She began to walk. "I'm sorry," she muttered, as she forced her feet to move. "I have to go."

Then she ran, leaving Lynette kneeling on the grass. She wanted to turn back, to apologize again, to wave goodbye, something, anything to show Lynette it was nothing to do with her.

But she was afraid.

She was afraid that she might look once more at the maddening visage that had haunted her dream, or hallucination, or whatever the fuck it was.

That face.

That pale, sinister face, consumed by rage, and drained of all humanity.

Susan's face.

The face of her corpse, leering and misshapen.

And most of all, Charlie was afraid that this time, she wouldn't be able to wake up.

11

———

WITHOUT EVEN THINKING ABOUT IT, CHARLIE FOUND HERSELF standing at the entrance to Clinton Memorial Hospital. She supposed, in a way, it was her *real* happy place. The only time she truly felt safe and secure was when she was with Susan.

And yet a sick sensation slithered in her stomach like she had a belly full of venomous serpents. She had already seen Susan today.

In her fucking *mind*.

Susan — or something old and dead and resembling her — had stalked her across the sand dunes, arms outstretched. It wasn't the Susan she knew and loved. It was something different; a doppelgänger, a twisted reflection.

She looked up at the imposing monolith of the hospital.

Just go in.

She entered, offering a perfunctory smile to the receptionist, and headed for the elevator. She went to press the button, then glanced around before her finger made contact, yesterday's events still fresh in her mind despite the madness and horror she had witnessed only that afternoon.

Satisfied there were no zombified nurses stalking towards her, she took the elevator to the fifth level.

"Hey," she said as she walked into Susan's room. Her friend — girlfriend, she reminded herself — lay as lifeless as she had for the last year. Charlie studied her face, though for what, she couldn't say. She dragged the chair over to the bed, the metal legs screeching across the floor, and sat.

"So, I don't even know where to start," she said. "Michelle's dead. That's the biggest deal, I guess. She died in the lunch hall in front of us. Susan, she — and I can't even believe I'm saying this — *she shit out her guts*. Like, all her internal organs. And somehow, that's not the craziest part, because after that... her ass kinda exploded." She laughed to herself. It sounded ridiculous out loud. She caught an odd flash of white, and glanced down. Her skirt was up around her waist, her panties on show. She snorted and pulled her skirt down, covering herself. "Sorry, I totally flashed you. Anyway, wanna know something even weirder? Just before it happened, a song came over the PA. *If You Leave Me Now*. You remember that, don't you? Yeah, of course you do. Lynette didn't understand, she wasn't at the dance. Oh, yeah, that's *another* thing. I made a new friend. At least, I think we're friends. She's called Lynette. You'd like her. She's..."

Charlie looked down again. Her skirt was once more bunched up at her waist. This time she tucked it between her thighs.

"I, uh... what was I saying?" But she had forgotten. She looked around to make sure no one was in the room with her. There wasn't. She was alone. She glanced at the ceiling. The air conditioning hummed softly, and she could feel the cool air drifting through the room. Enough to lift her skirt? No way. Not a chance.

She checked her skirt was still firmly clamped between her legs, then looked at Susan for a long time.

"Was... was that you?"

Silence, except the beep of the heart monitor and the almost imperceptible rustle of fabric. Charlie felt friction on her skin, and looked down to see her skirt curling up. She placed her hand on it, holding it down.

"Stop it," she said in a quiet voice. She felt ridiculous. "Shit, I'm losing my mind." She rubbed her eyes and stood. "I'd better go. Your folks will be here soon, and you know how much your mom hates me." She paused, checking the photo of her and Susan was still in the frame. It was. Leaning one hand on the bed, she kissed Susan's forehead.

"See you soo—" Then she froze, her stomach dropping.

Someone had their hand on the inside of her thigh.

There was no mistaking it. A human hand, cold and dismal, applied pressure to her flesh. It crept upwards. Charlie wanted to turn around, to see who was doing it, to see who was assaulting her like this.

But she didn't. Because deep down, she knew that there was no one there, and to acknowledge that would be the potential end of her sanity.

The hand slid further up her thigh. It was cold, so cold, five icicles tracing the contours of her thighs.

"Susan," she breathed, her voice trembling. "Stop. Please."

The invisible fingers caressed her. They brushed her cotton underwear with a lover's touch. Tears filled Charlie's eyes.

"Susan. I asked you to stop."

The digits found the leg holes of her panties and wormed their way under the fabric, investigating the soft fat of her buttocks. Had she gone insane? Had the pressure gotten to her? She looked down at Susan, into her open eyes, and when the icy finger probed at her vagina, she screamed and threw herself from the bed, stumbling over the chair and nearly falling.

Charlie stared at the motionless girl, her heart thudding erratically. She wanted to throw up. "That *was* you, wasn't it? Answer me! Was that you? Did you kill Michelle? Huh? Was that *you* that beat Mr. Carradine? Can you hear me? If you can, then fucking answer me!" She shook Susan's shoulders. "Answer me, you—"

"Leave my daughter alone, you slut!"

Charlie had just enough time to think, *oh shit,* before Susan's mother yanked her head back by the hair. She lost her balance and crashed to the floor.

"Mrs. Ward, I'm—"

Susan's mom kicked her in the ribs with smart black shoes that tapered to a wicked point. Charlie raised her hands defensively, and Mrs. Ward smacked them away.

"Bitch! Slut!" the woman ranted, punctuating each word with a hard slap to Charlie's face.

"Hilda, please!" Susan's dad was attempting to physically restrain his wife, but to little avail.

"Get off me, you useless man!" She pushed him back and whacked Charlie across the head, a thick wedding ring connecting with her skull. Charlie scrambled onto all fours, crawling away as Mrs. Ward repeatedly kicked her. Then the woman stopped, long enough to step back and admire her handiwork. "So the great corrupter returns!" she ranted. "The harlot dares to show her face!"

"Mrs. Ward, please, I'm—"

A vicious open hand slap knocked the words from Charlie's mouth. She crawled forwards, and Susan's mom planted a kick between her legs. Charlie yelled in pain, curling herself into a protective ball. Mr. Ward had seemingly given up trying to stop his wife. Instead, he fumbled in his pocket for a cigarette and lit it, shaking his head.

"You're not welcome here, jezebel!" shrieked Mrs. Ward.

"Please, I only—"

"Ah, listen to the gilded tongue that turned my sweet, innocent daughter towards Satan! A whore's tongue, that's what you have. A filthy, degenerate..."

Mrs. Ward trailed off, and Charlie braced herself for more abuse. When none followed, she chanced a glance up at the woman.

Mrs. Ward was staring at Susan. It took Charlie a moment for the insistent, high-pitched beeping sound to register.

Susan's heart monitor.

Without looking at him, Mrs. Ward said to her husband, "Mort, get the doctor."

Susan's dad jogged from the room, leaving Charlie alone with Susan and her mom. Thankfully, the older woman was more concerned with her only daughter, and seemed to have forgotten about her. What was up with Susan? Her heart monitor had maintained the same steady beat ever since she had been moved from the main ward, yet now it had increased considerably.

Charlie picked herself up and backed towards the exit. She wanted to stay and see what was happening, but this was also her chance to escape.

Footsteps pounded down the corridor. The doctor must be on his way. Susan's mom turned towards the sound, looking at Charlie, looking through her. She lifted her hands, the fingers curling into hooks, her eyes glazing over.

"What's happening?" asked the bewildered woman.

Charlie gasped.

Not again, please not again...

The doctor barged into the room, almost knocking Charlie over. "Mrs. Ward?" he said, pacing towards her, already out of breath from running. He was too late.

Susan's mom pressed her fingers into her cheeks with feral strength. She scratched at the flesh, stretching it to breaking point, burrowing her nails until they tore through, her fingers sinking into her own cheeks up to her knuckles. Her mouth opened in a silent scream, and for one stomach churning moment, Charlie saw the woman's fingertips waggling inside her mouth, her nails clacking together.

"Mrs. Ward..." said the doctor, stepping back in horror and surprise. The woman looked at him with tears in her eyes... and then tore her cheeks apart, her fingers dragging eight ragged splits in her face, her teeth and pink gums visible through the grisly slashes. The doctor grabbed her wrists, attempting to wrestle her hands out of her mouth. Mrs. Ward kept screaming, the holes lengthening, dark blood spilling from her mouth and running in a thick river down her chin. She shoved the doctor, sending him careening backwards into her husband, the two men collapsing like felled trees. There they lay, shock setting in, as Mrs. Ward dug her nails into her forehead and sliced open the skin below her hairline. It came away in a meaty flap, sagging over her eyes. Mrs. Ward gripped the loose flap and pulled.

Charlie closed her eyes, but it was the *sound* of Mrs. Ward's face peeling away, and the wet splat it made when the discarded epidermis hit the floor, that turned her stomach.

"Hilda!" roared her husband, but it was far too late. As Charlie raced from the room and stepped into the waiting elevator, she could hear Susan's father's cries reverberating off the cold, bare walls. She could still hear them even when she stumbled, dazed and weeping, from the hospital and into the warm and deadly embrace of the lazy summer evening.

12

———————

...so horny so horny so horny you felt so good Charlie you felt so good where did you go I'm sorry about my mom now come back here and let me touch you god it felt so good it felt so good I want it I want you I want you so bad I want to fuck you I want you to fuck me I...

Nurse Donna Matthews watched as Lloyd, one of the hospital's longest serving porters, squirted sanitizer on the floor. His mop rested in a bucket, the water as red as a sunset, the fluorescent lights glinting of the calm surface.

"Hell of a day," she said, stifling a yawn.

Lloyd squatted and sprayed the disinfectant under the bed. "Rough one?"

"Like you wouldn't believe. You hear about the girl from the high school?"

"I saw them take her out of the ambulance in bags. What the hell happened?"

"We don't know. Apparently, the poor girl exploded in the lunch hall."

"Shit," grinned Lloyd, "is the food really that bad?"

"Terry — I mean, Dr. Freudstein — thinks she must have eaten a cherry bomb or something."

Lloyd grimaced as he leaned on the bed and stood, his old bones cracking as he did so. "A cherry bomb wouldn't do that. Now, a stick of dynamite on the other hand..."

Donna half-smirked and checked her watch. Her shift had officially finished forty-five minutes ago, and if she didn't leave soon, she would be late for her date with Xander. Her friend Jenny was supposed to take over, but she was running late, leaving Donna to change the sheets of Coma Girl. Donna didn't know the girl's name, and didn't care to. Not for malicious reasons; the more she knew about the patients, the more it upset her when they died. And very few people made it out of Level Five still breathing.

Lloyd tucked the sanitizer into his belt and gripped the handle of the mop. "Well, I'll see you later, Donna. Hope it gets better for you."

"You mean you hope no one else rips their own face off tonight?"

"Something like that," chuckled Lloyd. Gallows humor was an integral part of working at the hospital. Without it, most medical staff would be hopelessly lost in a pit of despair. Lloyd opened the door, then turned back to her.

"Hey. They brought in someone else from the school, right? A teacher?"

"They did. He was all messed up."

"Is it true... about... oh, you know!"

Donna peered at him over her glasses. "Yeah. It's true."

Lloyd shook his head in a mixture of disbelief and admiration. "How the hell does a man accidentally cut off his own co—" He grinned. "I mean, his own penis?"

"You'll have to ask him that, Lloyd. I just work here. Now, are you done? I've gotta change the sheets in here, or Kevok will have my ass."

~

...her ass yes her ass Charlie's ass oh I felt it again I touched it it was so soft so round...

~

"Yeah, I'm done." Lloyd's wrinkled brow creased. "Goddam bloodbath in here tonight, and it's not even a full moon."

Donna glanced out the window. "Don't get all superstitious on me, Lloyd. I need you to keep me sane."

"I'd rather keep you up all night," he mumbled as he left the room, the wheeled bucket trundling down the corridor. Lloyd was nearing retirement age, and had an unfortunate habit of saying exactly what he was thinking. Donna wasn't sure if he knew or not, but it always made her laugh.

"In your dreams, Lloyd," she whispered, and walked to the girl's bedside. Splatters of blood decorated one side of the top sheet, the droplets forming an intricate pattern. It was bad, but not bad enough to be taken to the incinerator. They could be cleaned in the great industrial washing machine down in the basement, and then reused. The incinerator was reserved for the really gross stuff, and luckily, most of the woman's blood — and the fleshy mask of her face — had ended up on the floor. They would have transferred Coma Girl to another bed, but it was a busy night in Clinton, and none were available.

"Dang budget cuts," Donna grumbled, as she stripped the sheets and bundled them up, stuffing the soiled bedding into a black bag. She looked at the girl, and her heart broke a little. Barring a miracle, everyone knew she would never wake up. And Donna had worked at the hospital long enough to know that miracles were thin on the ground these days. She thought about the poor young girl who dutifully came round most days to read and talk to Coma Girl.

"You've got a good friend," she said. "Some folks have no one."

She smiled to herself, then realized her hand was up the girl's gown and groping her vagina. Shocked, Donna pulled her hand away and stepped back from the bed. She looked around to make sure no one had seen. She was alone.

"I'm sorry," she said to the girl. "I don't know what happened."

She stared at her hand. She could smell the girl's sex on her fingers. What the fuck? It was a mistake. She must have rested her hand on the girl's leg without thinking, then accidentally slid it up and into...

No, that was absurd. She couldn't understand. It made no sense. Where was Jenny? That lazy idiot should be doing this, not her. She had to get home, shower, do her hair, her nails, and pick out an appropriate outfit for her date.

Appropriately slutty, she thought, grinning, and then she lost control of her mind.

~

...that's it that's right take it off take it off take it all off...

~

Donna watched what was happening through her own eyes. She wished she could shut them off like a TV set, or close them, but she was nothing more than a prisoner in her own body, a witness to a crime, helpless and unable to prevent it.

Her fingers went to work, dextrously unfastening the buttons down the front of her uniform.

"I'm not doing this," she said in a short, breathless gasp. Halfway down, her hands seemed to grow impatient, grabbing both sides of the garment and ripping it open. One button popped clean off, rattling across the floor. She shrugged the uniform over her shoulders, letting it fall to her waist.

"I'm not doing this!" she repeated, louder this time. Her heart pounded, relentless horror seeping through her pumping veins, as she shimmied the outfit over her hips, her thumbs hooking into the waistband of her colorful patterned panties and taking them down too. As they landed at her feet, she clambered gracelessly onto the bed in just her white socks.

"No! Stop!"

But she couldn't. Someone was controlling her, a sick puppet master with a lust for degradation. Tears streamed down Donna's face as she pivoted one-eighty and backed onto the girl, planting her bare ass above the patient's head. Leaning over, she pulled the hem of the girl's gown up past her breasts, then pressed her crotch into the girl's face, smothering her.

"Please don't!" she urged her invisible abuser, lowering her head to the girl's pubic area. "Please... mmmmph!"

~

*...that's it that's it lick me lick me lick me Charlie kiss me there oh
Charlie oh Charlie I've missed your touch...*

Grinding her pussy against the near-dead girl's face, Donna
went to work on her. She buried her face between the girl's
legs, her tongue probing. She rested on her elbows and
gripped two handfuls of cold, lifeless ass while moving her
hips in slow circles, her tears soaking the girl's thighs. It was
like screwing a corpse. The idea repulsed her, disgusted her,
but no one had told her body. Her legs stiffened with
obscene satisfaction, revolting warmth spreading through
her, as if even her sense of pleasure had been taken captive
and forced to do someone else's bidding.

She took the girl's hand, pressing it to her own breast,
squeezing it, watching in mounting horror as the door to the
room inched open.

Stay out, she wanted to scream, but her jaw was pressed
against Coma Girl's pubic bone.

"Sorry, Donna," said Lloyd as he entered. "I forgot my
antiseptic..."

The words died on his lips.

He stood motionless, staring in confusion as the naked
Donna rose up on her knees over Coma Girl. The girl was
also nude, her gown bunched up around her neck.

"Get out!" Donna screamed. "Don't look! It's not me!
Someone else is doing this!"

She leaped from the bed with a feral roar, landing clumsily but maintaining her balance. Lloyd's face registered
nothing but shock as she came for him, grabbing his shirt
collar and throwing him across the room. She slammed the
door shut as Lloyd hit the window, his head breaking

through. His legs went slack, slumping out from under him, and he managed to turn to her as he slid down the wall. The glass had scratched his face, and as he opened his mouth, several cuts revealed themselves, expelling bright red blood down his wrinkled features.

"Why?" he spluttered. His words were slurred, and she noticed his false teeth were missing.

"It's not me! It's not me!" she said, weeping as she did so. Lloyd cowered before her, raising his feeble hands. Against every wish in her mind, against everything Donna believed in, she snapped off a large shard of broken glass from the window.

"Don't kill me," said Lloyd.

Donna wished she were dead. She had known Lloyd for the ten years she had worked here. He was a sweet man, a kind man, who sometimes drove her home from work, and spoke reverentially about his beloved grandchildren, and about how one day soon he would retire and buy a small cabin in the country where he would teach the youngsters about the beauty of nature and—

She brought the glass screaming down into Lloyd's face, gashing it open, unleashing a crimson river down his stubbled cheek. He tried to take the shard from her and she sliced open his palm, brushing him aside and plunging the razor sharp glass into his chest. It struck bone, jamming between his ribs, and Donna pulled the glass sideways, snapping it in two. With the remaining piece still clenched tightly in her hand, so hard that it cut into her own fingers, she slashed his face again. The glass split his upper lip and neatly sliced off the tip of his bulbous nose.

"What the fuck is going on in here?"

Donna — or the person controlling her — turned to see Dr. Freudstein staring wide-mouthed in the doorway. A clipboard fell from his hand. He took a step closer, then retreated as Donna rose.

"What... what the hell have you done?" he said, glancing from the girl lying on the bed with her legs spread to the mutilated body of the porter. Donna looked down at the glass in her hand. Lloyd's blood ran down her arms, her breasts. It pooled on the floor.

"It wasn't me, you have to believe me..."

She turned from the doctor and faced the window. Somehow, she knew what was to come next.

"No! No, no, no!"

Gripping the frame, she raised one leg and placed it on the broken glass. It pierced her foot, but she didn't let that stop her. Donna clambered onto the ledge, more shards tearing long scratches down her back, exposing raw, gleaming musculature. She peered over her shoulder. The doctor raced forwards.

"Don't do it!" he shouted.

Donna felt her lips curl into a smile. She leaned over, gazing down at the street below her. The people were so small.

Then she released the frame, letting herself fall.

The car pulled up outside the hospital.

Jenny Fenton grabbed her backpack from the footrest and lifted it onto her lap, unzipping it to double check her crumpled uniform was in there.

"I'll see you tomorrow, right?" said Luca in the driver's seat.

"Yeah," said Jenny, rifling through her clothes. Everything was present and correct. She pulled the door handle, letting in the cool air, and Luca placed his hand on her wrist.

"Hey, don't I get a kiss?"

Jenny moved closer, giving her lover a quick peck on the cheek.

"That it?" asked Luca.

"Haven't you had enough?" grinned Jenny. "Listen, I'm already an hour late thanks to you and your dick. Donna will be bugging the fuck out."

Luca pulled her close and pressed his lips to hers. Jenny let him kiss her, then opened the car door fully.

"I gotta go. Call me, okay?"

Backpack in hand, she exited the vehicle and waved at Luca as he drove off, then scampered towards the building, her heels clicking along the sidewalk. Light sparkled off the ground ahead of her, and she slowed. Something littered the sidewalk. It looked like shattered glass, with a pink and white object in the middle.

When she crouched to investigate, Jenny realized it was a broken set of dentures. Most of the teeth were scattered around, but a few remained set into the waxy gums.

Disappointed it was nothing more exciting, Jenny rose. She checked her watch. She was so fucking late.

"Shit," she said, shaking her head. "Donna is gonna *kill* me."

"Don't do it!"

The loud voice roared into the night, traveling for miles around. Jenny tried to place it. It sounded like Dr. Freudstein. She looked up, searching for the source, and locked eyes with the naked woman plummeting towards her.

There was just enough time for Jenny to recognize Donna's screaming, terrified expression, before their heads collided. Donna's cranium barreled into Jenny's face like a lead weight, obliterating it in a crimson explosion, her body continuing on, plowing through Jenny, snapping her spine before thudding to the concrete, and when the first medics arrived on the scene, alerted by a horrified witness, they weren't immediately sure whether they were looking at one body or two.

13

THE RAIN STARTED TO FALL AS CHARLIE NAVIGATED THE QUIET streets on her way to Lynette's house. She had rung her friend from a phone booth and gotten her address, crying breathlessly down the line, unable to answer Lynette's panicked questions.

She felt better now, though. The rain always helped clear her mind, even as it soaked through her thin sweater. Already the day had begun to feel like a dream. She patted her skirt down, irrationally afraid that it was up around her waist again. But *was* she being irrational? It had happened in the hospital. More than once.

When you were with Susan.

"Stop it," she muttered to herself. What did she think — that Susan was somehow responsible? That she had used ESP to peek at her panties? It was ridiculous. If Susan could really harness the power of telekinesis, wouldn't she use her powers for something more useful?

Like revenge?

A chill ran down Charlie's spine. Yes, revenge. Why not?

Carradine and Michelle fit the bill nicely. But her own mother? Surely Susan wouldn't go that far. Unless—

"Fucking *stop* it," she said, louder this time. There was no sense in thinking about it. No sense at all. She was tired, and in shock. In the last six hours, she had watched a man brutally beat himself, then a girl shit out her intestines, and a woman tear her own face off. It was enough to make anyone question their sanity.

She reached Lynette's street, striding alongside the white picket fences and counting the numbers on the doors. Ten, twelve... and there it was, number fourteen. A mustard-colored Oldsmobile was parked in the driveway, the trunk open. A harassed-looking man in a blue shirt and thick mustache wrestled with a suitcase, trying to force it inside. He gave up, leaving it jutting out, and rested against the vehicle, wiping sweat and rain from his furrowed brow.

"Hello," said Charlie, fighting against her natural anxiety when talking to strangers. "Does Lynette live here?"

The man's face brightened. "She sure does. Go right inside, she's upstairs." He almost looked surprised, as if Lynette didn't get many visitors calling around. Charlie headed for the door, entering in time to catch Lynette bounding down the stairs.

"I saw you from the window," she said breathlessly. "Are you okay? On the phone, you sounded—"

"I'm alright," said Charlie, though when Lynette embraced her, she hugged her back tightly. "I'm sorry about before. At the park, running away. I had to—"

"Wait. Let's go somewhere else to talk. It's too crazy in here."

As if on cue, a dark-haired older woman emerged in the hallway. "Hank, you've not packed your toothbrush!" She noticed the girls, eyed them suspiciously. "Lily... who's your friend?"

Lynette rolled her eyes and turned to Charlie. "That's my mom. She always calls me Lily."

"It's such a pretty name," said Lynette's mom. "That's what I would have called you, if your father hadn't insisted on Lynette. Now, are you going to introduce us, or am I gonna have to tell your friend some embarrassing stories about you?"

Lynette's cheeks reddened. "Mom, this is Charlie. Charlie, this is Mom."

"Pleased to meet you," said Charlie.

"My folks are going away for the weekend," said Lynette, "so the house is in chaos. You still up for that drive-in movie tonight?"

"Is it a scary one?" asked Lynette's mom.

"I don't think I invited you," said Lynette, then looked expectantly at Charlie.

The idea appealed to her. She doubted they would get much privacy in here. "Sounds good."

"What about your supper?" asked Lynette's mom.

"We'll get food with the movie."

"Well, we'll be gone by the time you get back."

"Jeez, you promise?"

Lynette's mom smiled at her. "Very funny. Is your friend going to be staying over?"

"No," said Lynette, at the exact moment Charlie said, "Yes."

They looked at each other.

"Maybe," said Lynette.

"We've not decided yet."

Lynette's mom nodded distractedly, rummaging through a toiletries bag. "Hank, I found your toothbrush."

"Crisis averted," he called back from the driveway.

"We gotta go," said Lynette, ushering Charlie out the door. "Don't wanna miss the start of the movie."

"Don't I get a goodbye kiss?"

"Mom," said Lynette, reluctantly trotting back to give her mom a quick kiss.

"Have fun, girls. It was nice to meet you, Charlie. I hope we'll see you again soon."

But Lynette had already dragged Charlie outside and past her father, who was now standing on the suitcase and attempting to squash it flat.

"Sorry about them," said Lynette once they were out of earshot. "They're going away together for the first time since I was born. They've packed everything except the cat."

"It's okay," said Charlie. "I thought they were cute."

"You don't have to live with them."

They reached a beat-up fifties Ford Thunderbird, and Lynette opened the passenger door, holding it for Charlie.

"Why thank you," she said, blushing. She got in and closed the door. Something about being around Lynette made everything feel okay again. The driver door opened and Lynette got in, her tight jeans and red and blue striped tee clinging to her curves. Charlie noted she wasn't wearing a bra. When she raised her eyes, Lynette was looking at her. Dammit, she had totally caught her staring at her tits.

Lynette pretended she hadn't. "We don't have to go to the movies if you don't want. I just made that up to get us out of—"

Charlie kissed her. She couldn't help herself. She took Lynette's face in her hands, kissing her passionately. After a startled moment, Lynette responded in kind. Charlie ran her hands through the girl's hair. It was soft and damp.

Lynette pulled away from the kiss, keeping her forehead

touching Charlie's. "Sorry, I just got outta the shower. Hair's still wet. I was in my pajamas when you called, so I had to rush. I... I wanted to look my best for you." She smiled sheepishly. "That's the fastest I've ever got ready."

Charlie felt the girl's warm, minty breath on her face. She smiled back and stroked Lynette's cheek.

"I would have kissed you anyway," she said, and then she did.

14

———

As Lynette drove them to the drive-in, Charlie told her about her visit to the hospital.

"Holy shit," Lynette said when she finished. "Is her mom okay?"

"I doubt it. I hope so, I guess." She half-smiled, then tried to hide it. "She never liked me much."

They arrived at The Starlight Drive-In, bought their tickets, and parked near the back. On the big screen, an animated hotdog strutted through the streets in some sort of advertisement for the concession stand. They held hands and watched in silence, while Charlie thought of how best to word what she was about to say.

"There's something else," she said falteringly. "When I was there... with Susan..." Goddam it, how to explain?

"You can tell me," said Lynette.

"It's gonna sound crazy. You'll think I'm nuts." She sighed. "You remember I told you about the song playing when Michelle died?"

"The one you and Susan danced to?"

"Yeah. That's not the only weird coincidence. When Mr.

Carradine was hitting himself, he shouted something at me. *Tell her to stop. Make her stop.* I didn't understand it at the time." She paused, looking at Lynette, waiting for her to laugh. She didn't. Charlie swallowed and continued. "Three people are dead or injured, all in one day. And all of them had, y'know, pissed off Susan."

Lynette was silent. She watched the hot dog cavort on the screen as an animated ketchup bottle chased after him. "What are you saying?" she asked slowly. "Do you think Susan is somehow... responsible?"

"In the hospital, before Susan's mom attacked me. Someone *touched* me. Every time I looked down, my skirt was up around my waist. I felt someone stroke my legs, my thighs, my... listen, it wasn't my imagination, I swear. I could feel her hands on me. All *over* me."

"She's been in a coma for a year," said Lynette. "How could she touch you? Or do any of that other stuff?"

"I don't know. When I say it out loud, it sounds dumb." She chuckled softly.

"You've been through a lot. You just need a rest. If you like, we can try meditating again?"

"After last time? No fucking way."

She fell silent, and knew exactly what Lynette's follow-up question would be.

"What did you see? In the park, I mean?"

"Her," said Charlie. "I saw *her.*"

"Susan?"

Charlie nodded. "She was coming for me. She was angry, or confused, or—"

Lynette cleared her throat. "So is she, uh, still your girlfriend?"

"I don't know. No, I don't think so. I suppose I would have moved on earlier, but she was all I had. There was nothing to move on *to*. Then you came along, and... shit, what am I trying to say?" She laughed. It felt good. "I like you, Lynette. I like you a lot. I know we've just met, but... you make me feel happy again. I haven't felt that in a long time."

"So, is this a date?"

"Yeah," Charlie decided. "It is. Our first date. Even though we've already kissed, this is our first date."

Lynette giggled. "I mean, *I've* already seen you naked..."

"What?" Then Charlie remembered their first meeting, Lynette returning her stolen clothes as she tried to cover herself. "Damn, that's not fair! You've seen me, but I've not seen you."

"There's an easy way to fix that," said Lynette. Her voice dropped to a whisper, and Charlie imagined the adrenaline pumping furiously through her veins. "I mean, my folks are away all weekend."

Charlie didn't know what to say. She was too excited and nervous and turned-on and afraid, so she responded by kissing Lynette. Their kisses were urgent, their touches charged with desire. The gear shift pressed into Charlie's belly, so she swung her leg over Lynette and sat atop her, looking down into the girl's hungry eyes. They kissed again, and when Charlie felt Lynette's hand under her sweater, a heat rose inside that made her tremble. Lynette cupped her breast through her bra, their kisses growing more passionate. Charlie moved down to Lynette's neck, jutting her ass out to create more room.

Beeeeeeeeeeeeep!

"Oh!" said Charlie, realizing that her butt was pressed up against the car horn. She burst out laughing, the spell momentarily broken, and fell back into the passenger seat. "Sorry, that was my fat ass," she giggled. "It always gets in the way."

"Oh, your beautiful ass!" said Lynette, grinning. Her cheeks were flushed the color of her lips. "You know, I was once late for class because of your ass."

"Okay, what? You're gonna have to explain that!"

Lynette's face turned beet red with embarrassment. "Shit, I can't believe I'm telling you this. Like, this *one* time, you were walking through the corridor in tight pants, and I was behind you, just, like, totally staring at your ass, and I walked past my classroom and missed the start of class."

"Because of my ass?"

"I knew I shouldn't have told you."

"Well, you did, and now I'm *never* gonna let you forget it."

"Shut up, the movie's gonna start soon."

"You think you can concentrate with my big, juicy ass next to you? Want me to sit in the back so you don't miss the movie?"

Lynette shook her head, laughing, and Charlie decided to let her off the hook... for now. "Listen, I'm gonna get some fries. You want anything?"

"Fries sound good," said Lynette. She flipped down the glove compartment. "I'll get you some money."

"No need, my treat," said Charlie. "Back in a minute." She opened the door and stepped out. The coming attractions were playing on the big screen, a preview for a gnarly looking film called *I Spit On Your Grave*. Charlie went to close the door, then had an idea. "Hey, Lynette?"

"Yeah?"

Charlie turned her back on her, bent over, and flipped her skirt up. She looked back over her shoulder. "Just in case you miss my ass while I'm gone."

Then she lowered her skirt, slammed the door, and walked, giggling, in the direction of the on-site diner. God, she felt fucking great! There was a swagger in her step, and a pleasant tingle in her belly and thighs.

It was warm inside the diner, the hot air mingling with the intoxicating scent of fried food. Most of the patrons were teenagers, and their excited chatter drowned out the jukebox. Charlie reached the counter, mentally going over her order in her head. What had Lynette asked for? Her mind whirred. Fries, that was all. Nothing but fries. She decided to get her a Coke too. Everybody liked Coke.

"What'll it be?" asked the bored-looking server behind the counter. She chewed gum, twirling a pen between her fingers.

"Two fries and two Cokes to go," said Charlie, with all the confidence of someone who was falling in love. Nervous energy flowed through her. Already she was worried about whether flashing her panty-clad butt had been too much. Would Lynette think she was easy? Too forwards? Or would she be reclining in the car and thinking about how Charlie's ass would feel in her hands? Charlie smiled. She knew she was blushing, but figured no one was watching her.

The waitress didn't bother writing the order down. Without turning her head, she bellowed, "Two fries, Petey."

"Gotcha," came the shouted reply. Charlie knew the voice.

"Shit," she breathed.

The waitress looked at her. "You say something?"

"No. Nothing." She turned from the counter. That voice... Petey... it had to be Peter Herbert. She glanced sneakily over for confirmation, and there he was. Michelle's ex-boyfriend, and one of the last people to have seen Susan before she smashed through a skylight and slammed into a table sixty feet below.

Charlie's blood boiled. She hadn't seen Peter since the

dance. He had left school that summer after a huge fight with his girlfriend. Apparently Michelle had cheated on him with most of the basketball team, and — if the rumors were to be believed — most of the football team too.

She peered at him over the counter as he scooped out a portion of fries. He looked different. Older, and a lot greasier. She supposed working with fast food did that to you. Did he know about Michelle? He must. It had to be all over town by now. Perhaps he simply didn't care, or even secretly relished the manner of her demise the way that, deep down, Charlie did.

Two kids lounged near her, awaiting their order. She watched their reflections in the window. The movie had started — *Night of the Living Dead,* an old black-and-white one — and the boys' spectral images played out over the screen.

"They found him with his dick in his mouth," one of them was saying. "His own *dick.*"

"Bullshit," said the other dismissively.

"It's true. My dad fuckin' found him, man. He said he had his pants around his ankles and his dick in his mouth. His balls too. Fucking Carradine, man. Totally gross."

"What did you say?" Before Charlie knew it, the words were out of her mouth. She wished she could grab them and shove them back in, but it was too late for regrets.

The first boy turned to her. He had piercing blue eyes and severe acne that he hid behind long hair that flopped over his face. He looked her up and down, then decided she was okay to talk to. "You go to Clinton High?"

Charlie nodded.

"Then you know old man Carradine, right? They found him *dead* today. And get this... he'd cut his own *dick* off."

"No..."

"Yup," smirked the boy, clearly relishing telling the story. "My dad's a cop. They think it happened right around the time that girl in the lunch hall... hey, where are you going? I've not got to the best part yet!"

But Charlie was already backing away. She bumped into the door, and a couple of patrons laughed at her as she shoved it open and left.

The waitress's bored voice echoed after her. *"What about your order?"*

Outside, the air hit Charlie hard. Dead? Carradine was *dead?*

"They're coming to get you, Barbara."

The voice from the movie emanated from miniature speakers mounted on the dashboard of every car. Where was Lynette? She couldn't remember where they had parked.

Carradine's dead.

It must have happened just after she left the classroom. What if she had stayed? Would he still be alive?

Susan would have killed him anyway.

She spotted Lynette's Thunderbird and stumbled towards it, sickness rising in her stomach. The film played on, the disembodied voice all around her.

"They're coming for you, Barbara."

Throwing open the door, Charlie collapsed into the seat alongside Lynette.

"Good, I'm starving," said the girl, turning to take the food from her. She stared at Charlie's empty hands in disappointment. "Oh. You change your mind?"

Charlie turned to her. She must have looked awful, because Lynette's expression changed to one of deep concern.

"Are you okay? What happened? Did someone—"

"Carradine's dead."

It took a moment to register on Lynette's face. "Creepy Carradine? How do you know?"

"Someone in the diner told me."

"Who?"

"Some kid. His dad's a cop."

Lynette raised her eyebrows. "Shit."

"Do you believe me now?" The question was loaded. Charlie watched Lynette squirm as she tried to think of a suitable reply.

"You mean..."

"I already told you. If it wasn't for him, I might've reached her in time."

Lynette rubbed her eyes. "It's just... things like that don't happen. This isn't a movie, Charlie," she said, gesturing through the windshield at the screen. "This is real life, and things like ESP and astral projection and shit don't—"

"Where the fuck am I?"

The voice cut her off. Lynette stopped talking and turned towards the speaker. "Did that come from—"

"What the fuck? Where am I?"

Charlie's fists clenched, her stomach tying itself in knots. The voice crackled from the tinny speaker, but it was unmistakably that of Peter Herbert.

She didn't want to look. More than anything, she wanted this day to be over, and for all the death and madness to be forgotten like a hazy dream. But she *did* look, and as her eyes fell on the screen, she could say nothing, do nothing, except for point at it with a shaking hand.

Lynette followed her gaze. "Wait, is that... no, it can't be..."

"It is," said Charlie.

Peter was onscreen. He was in the movie, a strange shimmering black-and-white projection standing in the middle of an outdoor cemetery alongside the two main actors. They regarded him curiously.

"*Who's that, Johnny?*" whispered the woman.

Her companion pushed his glasses up the bridge of his nose. "*I...*" A grin broke out on his face. "*He's come to get you, Barbara! Look, here comes another one of them!*"

The screen cut to a shot of a man shambling through the graveyard. Charlie had seen the film once before on late night TV after her parents had gone to bed, so she knew the man was a zombie. Any minute now, he would lunge for the heroine and attack her. But last time she watched the film, her old classmate Peter hadn't been there.

The movie cut back to a shot of the couple. Peter stood by them, spinning on the spot. "*Where did I go? What happened? Jesus fucking Christ, what the fuck is going on?*"

Suddenly the camera was behind the zombie as he staggered past gravestones, coming for them. The male actor ran from the screen with a cry of, "*I'm getting out of here!*"

"*Johnny!*" cried the woman.

Peter glanced around. "*Shit, you can stay lady, I'm getting out of here too.*" He chased after the man, nearing the edge of the screen, and then smacked off the side as if running into an invisible wall. He stumbled backwards, rubbing his nose as dark blood ran down his face. "*What? Help! Someone help me!*"

Charlie's stomach churned.

"What the hell is going on?" breathed Lynette. "This isn't what happens. This isn't what happens!"

"It's her!" screamed Charlie. "She's doing this! She's going to kill him!"

"No, that can't happen, that—"

"We have to stop her!"

But did she really want to? Hadn't Peter contributed to Susan's accident? Charlie grappled internally with her indecision. He might have done, he might not. She couldn't be sure. If Susan was going after him, then she supposed he must have been partially responsible. But did he deserve to die? Did he deserve to be massacred on the drive-in screen in front of hundreds of people? Was that justice?

Tears rolled down Charlie's face. She had always thought she was a good person. Or at least, she tried to be. To rise above the bullies, and the people who mocked and ridiculed her and made her life a living hell. She couldn't stand by and let someone die, no matter what they had done to her friend.

"Where are you going?" asked a panic-stricken Lynette, as Charlie opened the car door.

"I have to stop her," snarled Charlie, and then she bounded from the vehicle, racing towards the diner. Would Peter still be in there? Or had his entire physical form been transported into the movie? She couldn't be sure. There was no precedent for this shit.

"I coulda sworn I'd seen this film before," muttered someone as she passed, their eyes transfixed on the screen. They shrugged and took a bite of their burger. "Guess not."

Charlie skidded around him, heading for the glass door.

"Get the fuck off me!" Peter was shouting, as the zombified man overpowered him, his fingernails scratching at Peter's arm. They dug four deep channels in his skin, more blood gushing from the open wounds and showering the zombie's face. People in their cars cheered. A truck was parked nearby, four jocks on the trailer hooting and thrusting their fists in the air in appreciation of the onscreen carnage, their beers foaming and spraying wildly over themselves.

Charlie slammed into the door with her shoulder, stumbling as she did so.

"That chick needs to learn how doors work," someone in a nearby booth muttered.

She ignored the voice, racing for the counter, listening to the shrill screams from the kitchen. With a burst of adrenaline, Charlie vaulted the counter, throwing her legs over and landing awkwardly. Ahead, she saw the waitress, and beyond her, Peter. Blood poured in rivers down his face. The waitress heard her approaching footsteps, and turned.

"I can't wake him up!" she sobbed.

Peter was frozen rigid. In his hand, he held a plate with a cheeseburger, fries, and slaw on it. The plate was red with his blood. It soaked into the burger like watery ketchup, turning it soggy, the bun limp. His neck shuddered as dozens of small, toothlike marks pressed into his flesh, further and further until the skin burst. Gore erupted from his neck, and a huge chunk of bloody muscle dropped and splatted onto the checkered floor.

"Oh God!" yelled the waitress. She turned away, then collapsed onto the floor in a faint. More people had come to join them, drawn by the noise. One vomited, while another demanded someone call an ambulance.

Peter's shirt tore open, revealing his finely sculpted chest and stomach. Charlie backed away. There was no way to stop this. Susan was in control, somewhere out there, beyond this realm.

Car horns honked loudly outside. Peter's jeans worked their way down his hips, his jockey shorts following. His penis moved, extending in all directions as if someone was tugging on it. More bite marks appeared on the shaft of his cock. Crimson fluid dribbled out of them, before the tip of his penis wrenched itself free and smacked wetly between his feet.

His stomach was next. The skin rippled, then tore open with an excruciating sound. Steaming viscera slopped out of the gaping cavity.

"Charlie!"

She turned at the sound of Lynette's voice, thankful to tear her eyes from the macabre scene. Lynette shoved her way through the gathered spectators behind the counter. "Charlie, come here! You have to hear this!"

She stepped away from Peter, taking one last look at his remains.

My God, she thought. She could have sworn he was looking at her. Not just in her general direction, but right *at* her, at her *specifically*. His gaze followed her, and she knew she was right. A tear rolled down Peter's cheek, mixing with the blood, as his lower ribs splintered from his torso, jutting out like branches from a tree, before snapping clean off and clattering to the ground.

"Oh god, oh god, oh god," said Charlie. Lynette dragged her outside, where she gulped in vast lungfuls of air. The pervasive stench of fried food was all she got, and she dropped to her knees, her gorge rising in her throat.

"Charlie, listen!" screamed Lynette, pointing at the screen. "Listen to what he's saying!"

She tried, raising her head as vomit spilled out of her mouth and down her sweater.

Peter was still on the screen, his torso a hollow shell, greedy hands raking around in his guts, slobbering mouths chomping on fat, slippery intestines. His face was unrecognizable, a mask of black blood, his eyes barely visible. Once again they seemed to stare at Charlie, from across space and time itself, as if he could somehow look out of the screen and identify her.

"*I'm sorry!*" he cried, his voice a wet gurgle. "*Please, Charlie... tell her I'm sorry! Do you hear me? I'm sorry! I'm sorry! I'm sorry!*"

Charlie looked at Lynette. The girl was staring at her, pale and distraught, her whole body trembling. As Peter's gurgles faded to nothing, the jocks on the truck started honking their horn at the gleeful devastation.

"*You see that?*" hollered one of them. He cracked open another beer and belched loudly. "*Now* that *is the good shit!*"

15

───────

THEY DROVE IN SILENCE.

The rain came down hard, the Thunderbird's wipers struggling to keep up. Charlie looked at her hands. They were covered in blood. It had dried to her skin, and now cracked as she clenched and unclenched her fists. The front of her sweater and skirt were coated in a mixture of blood and vomit. She wound down the window and leaned her head out, letting the raindrops pound against her face.

They had left before the cops arrived, sneaking out amidst the chaos. The film was still playing as they drove away, though word was spreading through the audience that someone had died.

Lynette slowed the car as they came to the lights on the edge of town. The engine idled, purring contentedly. Charlie noticed Lynette's knuckles were white as she gripped the wheel, the tension causing her forearms to vibrate soundlessly. Charlie touched her, and she flinched. They looked at each other, neither sure what to say. It was Lynette who broke the silence.

"Want me to take you home?"

Charlie shook her head.

The lights turned green.

"Want to come back to mine?"

Charlie nodded.

Despite the minty gum she chewed on, her throat was dry, so she opened her mouth and let the rain in. The droplets wet her tongue, and she closed her eyes as the car moved again, her hair trailing behind her in the wind.

Lynette pulled into her driveway. The mustard Oldsmobile was gone.

They exited, and hurried through the rain towards the house. Once inside, Charlie smelled herself. She stank. Her clothes were beyond repair; there was no washing powder in the world that could clean her soiled garments, and hell, she wouldn't want to wear them again anyway.

The house was still. Without a word, Lynette took her hand and led her up the stairs. At the top, she opened the door to the bathroom. Charlie kicked off her shoes before stepping on the plush, blue carpet, as Lynette pulled back the plastic curtain and switched the shower on.

"I'll get you some clothes," she said.

Charlie gripped her arm urgently. "Don't go."

Lynette nodded. She had splatters of Peter's blood in her hair and on her face. Charlie removed her sweater and reached for the buttons on her blouse. She managed the first with a bit of effort, but the second proved too much. She broke down crying. Lynette stepped forward, her fingers working the buttons loose, one at a time until the stained shirt hung open. She pulled it over Charlie's shoulders and tossed it in the basin.

"Turn around," she said in a choked voice. Charlie did, letting Lynette unfasten her bra as she tugged the zipper down on her skirt. It fell to her feet, and she stepped out of it, standing with her back to Lynette. With a deep breath, she pulled her panties down and climbed over the side of the tub. The high pressure jet of water hit her chest, and she turned, catching a glimpse of her blood-caked face in the mirror, two white lines from her eyes to her chin carved by her tears.

Someone touched her shoulders. She almost screamed.

"It's okay," Lynette whispered in her ear. Charlie turned to face her, their eyes meeting. Lynette was in her underwear, a bar of fresh soap in her hand. "Let me," she said. Charlie took a step back, letting the water cascade over her head and shoulders, closing her eyes as Lynette ran soapy hands over her face. Charlie imagined the scarlet water pouring over her body and swirling down the drain. She felt Lynette's hands in her hair, rubbing shampoo in, and the soap sliding over her cheeks and neck. Her hands unconsciously reached for the girl, finding her waist and lingering there. Lynette froze for a second, her body tensing... and then she went back to cleaning Charlie's face.

Charlie opened her eyes and looked at Lynette. The girl's white bra was wet, the thin material transparent. Lynette wiped the soap down Charlie's sternum. Charlie stopped her, taking the girl's hand and gently prizing the soap from it.

"Let me do you now," Charlie said. They traded places. Charlie lathered up her hands and cleaned the blood from Lynette's face, her features so delicate that Charlie was afraid she might crush her.

She reached around to Lynette's back and found the clip of her bra. "Do you mind?"

Lynette's lips parted and she let out a low, almost inaudible moan. Charlie unhooked the bra and removed it. Lynette watched her, their faces inches from one another, their breasts pressing together.

"I don't want to be alone tonight," said Charlie.

"I don't want to ever be alone again," said Lynette.

Charlie leaned in, her hand on the girl's neck. "You won't be."

She smiled as Lynette's hands slid down her soapy back and rested on her ass.

"You promise?" said Lynette.

"I'll never leave you," said Charlie. She kissed Lynette, tasting her, their tongues finding each other, hands exploring uncharted territory. Charlie pulled away, looked deeply into Lynette's eyes, and wiped a strand of wet hair from her pretty face.

"Never," she said.

They left the shower and hurriedly dried off with a towel.

Lynette led the way to her bedroom. There, they tumbled onto the sheets, lying side by side, kissing and caressing each other. All the death and horror of the last twenty-four hours seemed to evaporate as their flesh touched, their lips meeting, their hot breath in each other's faces. Lynette panted softly whenever Charlie kissed her neck, their bodies still damp, soaking the bedding. Charlie lay back as Lynette kissed her breasts, her tongue flicking her nipple, taking it between her teeth and pulling on it. This was further than she and Susan had ever gone, much—

No, she couldn't think of Susan right now. She wouldn't.

Suddenly nervous that she would accidentally say her ex-girl-friend's name, she pushed up, forcing Lynette roughly onto her back and swinging her leg over the girl, sitting on her hips. She glanced down at Lynette's white panties, at the dark triangle visible through the sodden cotton. She leaned forwards, nuzzling between Lynette's breasts, shuffling back-wards down the bed as she went lower, leaving a trail of kisses down her stomach. When she reached Lynette's bellybutton, she wiggled her tongue inside. Lynette burst out laughing.

"Sorry," she giggled. "I'm ticklish."

Pleased to find Lynette wasn't laughing at her, Charlie continued her descent until her tongue reached the waist-band of Lynette's underwear. Turning to the side, she kissed Lynette's inner thigh. Then, heart racing frantically, she did the same to Lynette's crotch. It was warm, and she felt bris-tles of hair through the thin fabric. She hooked her fingers into the waistband and pulled.

"Hey," said Lynette. From between her spread legs, Charlie looked up at her. "I've..." She sounded nervous. "I've never done this before."

"Me neither," said Charlie. "You want me to stop?"

"I never said that," Lynette smiled, her face flushed. She raised her ass off the bed, allowing Charlie enough room to slide her underwear down. It wasn't smooth, the wet fabric sticking awkwardly to her, but once they were at Lynette's knees, they came off easily, and she tossed them aside.

"Come here," said Lynette, beckoning her forwards. She motioned for Charlie to lie face-down beside her, then got on top, massaging her shoulders and neck. Lynette's wet hair trailed down Charlie's back, and her body tingled, every nerve ending alive in a way she had never experi-enced. Gentle fingers caressed every inch of her, as she mimicked Charlie's movements from before, running kisses down her spine. Then she kissed Charlie's ass, licking between the cleft of her buttocks, teasing her with playful bites.

It was surprisingly forward of Lynette, who moments before had seemed so shy and cautious. But her tongue felt so good that Charlie didn't question it for long, not even when Lynette took Charlie's arms and crossed them behind her back. Lynette slipped fabric — it felt like a tee shirt — under Charlie's arms and used it to wrap them up.

"Hey, don't do that," Charlie said kindly. "I want to touch you."

Lynette didn't listen. She began to tie the shirt into a knot.

"Come on, it's my first time too, y'know. We've got all the time in the world to get kinky. Let's just—"

Lynette pulled the knot.

Hard.

"Ow!" yelped Charlie. "That's too tight. Come on, stop. Let me go."

Her heart pounded, but it was different from before. The excitement was gone, replaced by something else. Fear. She tried to break free, but her arms were tied tight.

"Lynette, please, I don't like this."

Why didn't she answer? Charlie looked over her shoulder, but Lynette put her hand on the back of her head and pressed it into the pillow, smothering her. She kicked, and Lynette shifted her weight, pivoting atop her, grabbing her legs. Charlie forced her head away from the pillow.

"Stop! Stop, or I'll scream! I'll fucking—"

The stilted voice that interrupted her stole the breath from Charlie's lungs. It sounded like Lynette, but something was off, as if she was reading the words phonetically. As if someone was speaking *through* her.

"*No... one will... hear... you.*"

Charlie froze. She knew that voice.

The tone, the inflections.

She knew it all too well.

16

———

Lynette watched it happen.

Vignettes that throbbed from blue to purple to crimson obscured the edges of her vision, growing larger with each passing second. She tried to move, to stop herself, but she was merely a spectator, a passenger in her own corporeal form.

Helplessly, she stared as her own hands bound Charlie's wrists. The image shook as Charlie frantically kicked. It was like watching a movie during an earthquake. Whoever was controlling her located a stocking from the bedside cabinet and used it to bind Charlie's ankles.

No! Lynette wanted to scream. *It's not me! I'm not doing this!*

But she couldn't. She supposed Charlie already knew. She had been right all along. Goddamnit! Why hadn't she listened to her? Why hadn't she believed her? They could have done something, they could have stopped this, but now Charlie lay face down on the bed, naked and tied up like a Thanksgiving turkey as Susan — for it had to be her — used

Lynette's hands to press Charlie's face into the pillow, smothering her.

As the vignettes pulsated, Lynette became aware of a presence inside herself, in her own head. She pictured herself standing in a darkened theater, the ghoulish assault on her friend playing out in Panavision on the big screen. She concentrated harder, visualizing herself in a front-row seat. Someone was behind her. She craned her neck, attempting to tear her eyes from the screen, upon which Charlie now lay on her back, squirming like a worm on a hook as Lynette's fingers spider-walked up her bare leg.

"Please," said Charlie, her voice muffled, as if the speaker in the theater had blown. *"Don't do this."*

Lynette managed to turn away, gazing over her shoulder at the empty rows of seats. A dark shape sat just out of her line of sight. She turned the other way, wishing she could close her eyes so as not to witness her hands on Charlie's breasts, the nails digging into the soft mounds, almost hard enough to break the skin. Charlie wailed in horror, but the sound was growing softer, the image receding.

Lynette knew she had to hurry, but panic had stricken her. She could no longer turn her head, instead forced to watch as her hand occupied the screen, taking hold of a half-finished glass of milk and smashing it off the bed frame. The white liquid spilled onto the pillow, the circle of jagged points sparkling in the moonlight that poured through the bedroom window.

My god, thought Lynette.

The sight galvanized her. She knew what she had to do. Despite the chaos playing out before her eyes, her breathing slowed.

It's like back in your old school. When the kids were shouting at you, calling you names, beating you. What did you do? When they spit in your face, when they followed you home, when they threw stones at your window. How did you manage to get to sleep at night?

She relaxed, and the theater started to shift. The lights gradually flickered on, one at a time, revealing crisp white walls.

And when they cornered you down that alleyway, and the boy with the switchblade cut the straps on your dress, his friends sweating in anticipation, the girls laughing and cheering them on... how did you get through that?

Doors. Hundreds of doors spiraling down an endless, brightly lit corridor.

Find it. Find your happy place. Susan's in one of them. Get her out.

Lynette pinched the webbing of her thumb and forefinger, finding the pressure point, zoning out. The comforting blanket of meditation was within reach. She just needed to slip under it.

Her feet were soundless as she walked calmly from the theater and headed down the white corridor. Somewhere in the dank recesses of her mind, she heard Charlie whimpering and crying.

I'm coming. Hold on.

She pushed open the first door, stepping unafraid into her grandmother's hallway, listening to the comforting tinkle of wind chimes on the porch. The TV was on, playing softly from the front room.

Lynette reached up to the door bhandle — it was as high as her head — and tugged it down, entering the room. Her grandmother sat in her rocker, a puzzle book in one hand, a pen in the other.

"Hello, dear," she said. "Would you like some candy?"

Lynette looked around the room. No sign of Susan.

"No thanks, Grandma," she said. Through the window, storm clouds amassed, darkening the sky. She glanced at the TV set. Charlie's face filled the screen, screaming in terror.

"The things they put on TV these days," her grandmother said with a smile and a shake of the head.

Keep control, keep control.

Lynette backed out, closing the door as she heard her grandmother call out, "Come back anytime, my little lamb."

Where was Susan? The fear returned, the corridor lights a few doors down fizzling out, the bulbs popping. She gripped her pressure point harder, terrified to release it, and headed for the next door.

Lynette couldn't suppress a smile as she entered into The Louvre. Her family had vacationed in Paris back in seventy-five, the highlight of which had been a visit to the famous art gallery. Even now, standing before *Gabrielle d'Estrées et une de ses soeurs,* she felt a welcome serenity flow through her. All around, art lovers stood transfixed, murmuring and nodding in appreciation.

Yet as she gazed at the painting, the image swirled, the paint dripping from the canvas and melting down the wall.

"Look at that," one of the gallery patrons commented. *"I don't recall seeing this one before."*

"Is that a breast?" replied their companion, running their fingers through their thick beard and nodding sagely.

It *was* a breast. Lynette knew it well. After all, it was hers.

The painting had vanished completely, and a moving image of her bare breast was now framed on the walls of The Louvre.

"Oh shit," she said.

A hand that had once belonged to her raised the broken milk glass and held it to her nipple, the razor-sharp edges digging in. Lynette stumbled back, looking for the door.

It wasn't there. She glanced around in panic, her eyes falling on a lone girl sitting on a circular bench. She wore nothing but a hospital gown, her matted hair masking her grim face.

Susan.

Lynette had seen her photo on the front of some anti-bullying pamphlet that the school had distributed. Every time she saw one, it had been grossly defaced; knives drawn sticking out of her face, cocks probing her mouth, the usual bullshit. But still she recognized her.

Blood gushed from both of Susan's nostrils, splattering on her lap, the excess running down her legs. She didn't seem to notice Lynette as she sat staring at a blank wall.

"Get out of my head," said Lynette.

Susan didn't react.

Suddenly every painting in the gallery displayed the same image, that of Lynette's point-of-view as she held a broken glass to her own breast. Charlie lay beneath her, blood dripping from a small wound on her cheek, tears running from her eyes.

Then Susan spoke.

"Never... see her... again."

Her voice boomed through the gallery, echoing off the walls. The occupants fell to their knees, clamping their hands over their ears and grimacing in agony. Only Lynette remained standing.

"Susan!" screamed Charlie. *"Why are you doing this?"*

"Never again..." said Susan, and then she started to grind the glass against Lynette's breast, twisting it with infinite slowness. *"...or else..."*

Lynette lunged for a fire extinguisher on the gallery wall. Unbearable pain wracked her body, emanating from her chest. She ignored it, wrenching the extinguisher free and racing towards Susan, raising it above her head and bringing it down on the girl's skull.

Clang!

Susan had no time to react. Her body crumpled, her spine snapping as the force of the extinguisher bent her at the waist. She dropped from the bench, landing face first on the floor.

Lynette loomed over her, clutching the metal safety device in both hands. Susan was still moving.

"Get out of my mind," snarled Lynette. She brought the extinguisher down on the back of Susan's skull. The metal base struck the floor, obliterating Susan's head. Chunks of brain matter sprayed over Lynette's feet, shards of bone skittering across the wooden floor. "Get" — she slammed it down again — "out" — and again — "of my fucking head!"

From the neck up, Susan was a sticky, pulped mess... and yet still her fingers twitched, scratching at the floor. Lynette kicked her onto her back and hoisted the extinguisher up one last time.

Susan's face resembled nothing more than a flap of wretched skin with teeth puncturing the soggy membrane. Her eyes were gone, her nose crushed beyond recognition. As the lips moved like dead leaves fluttering in a fall breeze, Lynette's stomach churned. They were trying to form a word.

"*You...*" said Susan.

Lynette brought the extinguisher down hard.

The gallery lights flashed, dazzling in their luminescence, and then Susan was gone and Lynette opened her eyes to find herself in her bedroom, a broken glass in her hand pressed against her own skin.

"*No!*" she roared, hurling the container towards the wall. "Get out of my head! Get out of my fucking head!"

She flung herself to the side, stumbling off the bed and away from the bound Charlie, tripping over her laundry bag and thudding to the floor. There, she retreated to the corner of the room and hugged her knees tightly, shivering and crying.

"Get out of my head," she muttered. Her whole body trembled. She ran her hands over her legs, over the floor, the wall. She had control again, control of her own body. Susan was gone. But for how long? Could she come back? The idea horrified her. She had forced Susan out once, but next time… no, there wouldn't be a next time. There couldn't be. She would rather die than lose control like that again. To be trapped inside her mind, watching powerlessly as her own body betrayed her, abusing the girl she loved, puppeteered by a psychopath, a killer, a—

"Lynette? Is… is that you?"

It took her a second to place the voice. Charlie. Oh god, *Charlie!*

Lynette got to her feet, hurrying towards the bed. As she reached it, Charlie flinched. The sight broke Lynette's heart.

"It's me. It's me, Charlie, I swear to god, it's me. She was in there, she was in my head, but she's gone now. I wouldn't do that to you, you have to believe me. I swear, I wouldn't… I couldn't…"

Tears rolled down Charlie's face. "I believe you. Please untie me."

Lynette removed the knotted stocking from Charlie's ankles, then rolled her onto her front and released her wrists.

Charlie stretched, trying to get her circulation flowing again.

Lynette reached to touch her, then withdrew her hand. "It wasn't me, Charlie. It wasn't me, you have to believe me. I wouldn't do that. If you asked me to stop, I would. I love you. I swear, you have to believe—"

"I believe you," said Charlie. Then, quieter, "I believe you."

She touched her cheek, inspecting the blood that came away, then looked at Lynette.

"It was Susan," she said, and this time, Lynette didn't argue.

17

———

The cuts on Lynette's breast weren't deep.

Charlie cleaned the wounds with soap and hot water, then used band-aids to attach some gauze she found in the bathroom cabinet. After, Lynette gave her some pajamas, and they lay together in bed, wide awake and holding each other as if desperately clinging to their sanity.

"What was it like?" whispered Charlie. "When... y'know..."

Lynette did know. What she did *not* know was how to put it into words. She thought for a moment. "Did you see that movie *Halloween,* where the guy in the mask kills the babysitters?"

"No. I saw a preview on TV, though."

"Well, there's this scene at the start where you see through a kid's eyes. You see what he sees, his hands as he picks up the knife, the way he stabs his sister to death. It was like that. I saw you lying there. I watched myself tie you up, but I couldn't do anything about it. I couldn't stop myself. Inside, I was screaming. I was begging for it to stop."

Charlie hugged her tighter. "And did you see her? Was she there?"

"Yeah. Yeah, she was."

"So what happened? How did you stop her?"

Despite the warmth of Charlie's body, Lynette shivered. "I meditated. It was hard, because I was so scared, but I managed to regain control. I found her in one of my happy places."

"What did you say to make her stop?"

"Nothing. I hit her over the head with a fire extinguisher."

That made Charlie laugh. It was hollow, and tinged with sadness, but it was a pleasant sound, and Lynette found herself smiling.

"I'm sorry I didn't believe you," she said.

Charlie pulled her into an embrace. "It's okay," she said. "I wouldn't have believed me either."

Lynette didn't want to ruin the moment, but she had to ask. "What are we going to do?"

"We have to stop her."

"How?"

"You've beaten her before... could you do it again?"

Lynette looked her in the eyes. "I don't know. I took her by surprise. I doubt she expected me to find her."

"But we have to try. And soon. What if she comes back? She was going to cut your—"

"Don't say it." Lynette touched the gauzy pad beneath her pajama top. "I know what she was going to do."

"What if she gets in *my* head?" said Charlie. "What if she makes me hurt you? I can't fight her like you did. I'm not strong enough."

"Maybe I stopped her forever? I hit her pretty hard."

"And what if you didn't? You want to live the rest of your life never knowing if she can come back?"

"Then what are you saying?" asked Lynette, exasperation creeping into her voice. "What do *you* think we should do?"

Charlie swallowed. "We have to kill her." Lynette started to protest, and she cut her off. "We have to kill her, before she kills you."

Lynette settled her head against the pillow. It was wet from her tears. She knew what Charlie was saying was true. She was living on borrowed time. Susan would come for her next. There was no doubt about it. But what could they do? March into hospital and switch off her life-support machine?

Actually...

"It might be dangerous," she said softly. Charlie just looked at her. "If we get caught, we'll go to jail. And Susan will try to stop us."

"I know. But we can't wait and find out what she's gonna do next. By then, it'll be too late. I can't lose you." She stroked Lynette's face. "Do you remember what you said after you untied me?"

"Uh, yeah, I told you it wasn't me, and that I wouldn't do that to you."

"You said something else. You said you loved me. Did you mean that?"

It came back to Lynette the way embarrassing moments always did. Well, fuck it. It was true. "Yeah, I meant it."

"Good," said Charlie. "Because I love you too. And if I have to die or go to jail to save your life, then I don't care. I'll do it. I'll do it for *you*."

She kissed her, once, on the cheek.

Lynette let her hand rest on Charlie's waist. "We should

go now. I might have knocked her out for a while, but we need to go before she gets her power back."

"And before I lose my nerve," said Charlie.

"Yeah. That too."

They kissed again, one more time, and got out of bed. Lynette gave Charlie some clothes to wear. As they dressed in silence, she checked the wound on her breast. The gauze was stained red. But it could have been worse.

Much worse.

"She's so angry," said Lynette. "When she was in my head, I could *feel* her anger. That's what drove her. Just this all-consuming rage. She wants to hurt people. She wants to hurt *me*." Her voice dropped to a whisper. "And I think, if it came down to it, she'd hurt you too."

"We'll stop her," said Charlie. "Whatever it takes, we'll do it."

Lynette took her hand and squeezed it urgently. "I can't let her in my head again, Charlie. Never. She's insane. She'll tear down everything I've built in there. She'll destroy my mind."

"I won't let her," Charlie said definitively. She crouched and tied her shoelaces. "I know her. I can reason with her."

Lynette doubted that would work, but kept quiet. She tried not to think of what they were planning to do, but what else *could* she think about? They were about to wander into a hospital to murder a girl.

Murder.

It was self-defense — if they didn't succeed in their mission, Susan would kill them — but no jury in America would ever believe them.

"You ready?" asked Charlie.

Lynette nodded, though more than anything, she

wanted to say goodbye to her parents. Should she write them a note? Sure, and what the hell would it say?

Hi mom and dad, my new girlfriend's ex is in a coma, and she's using ESP to kill people, so we've gone to stop her. Be home for dinner. Love, Lynette.

She looked over at Charlie and saw the worry etched onto her features. That was good. They *should* be afraid.

"Let's go," said Charlie. There was no more time to kill, no more excuses. They were dressed and ready for battle. All that stood in the way was the traffic, and at this time of night, that wouldn't be a problem. They would hit the hospital in fifteen minutes, tops.

In fifteen minutes, you might be dead.

"Fuck it," said Lynette. "Don't wanna live forever anyway."

Charlie smiled at her, and together they left the bedroom and headed down the stairs to the front door in silence.

Lynette pulled back the chain and unlocked the door with her key. She felt an immense sadness to be leaving her home, and took one last look up the stairs. Part of her — a larger part than she would care to admit — wanted to run back up there and hide under the covers like she used to do during thunderstorms. Hell, maybe if they did what Susan had asked, and never saw each other again, the crazy bitch would leave them alone? She could get revenge on the people that had wronged her, and that would be that.

But she kept thinking about that rage she had felt pulsing from Susan. That sheer, unbridled fury festering within her. She wouldn't stop. She would carry on killing, over and over, her power growing until—

"Lynette?"

She tried to smile. "Sorry. Just thinking."

"Best not to," said Charlie.

"Yeah."

Without another word, Lynette turned the handle and opened the door. It was dark outside, but not so dark that she didn't see the two figures cloaked in shadow on her doorstep. Acting quickly, she tried to slam the door shut, but it was too late. The first figure lunged forwards, forcing her back into the hallway, the other pouncing on Charlie, and then the door slammed shut and the long night of unimaginable terror truly began.

18

ONE MOMENT LYNETTE WAS THERE, AND THE NEXT SHE
vanished, like a trapdoor had opened beneath her. Charlie
had no time to react. Rough hands slammed her against the
wall, her head striking plaster, before bundling her
forwards. She rebounded off the opposite wall, then
someone had her by the hair, dragging her behind them.

"Lynette?" Charlie managed to say, before a gloved hand
attached itself to her mouth, silencing her. The intruder
manhandled her to the nearest door and shoved her
through. Her ankle caught the edge of a coffee table and she
ended up on the floor, the thick carpet breaking her fall.

Lynette wasn't so lucky. She appeared in the doorway as
her assailant hurled her towards the table. She slammed
into it and fell, taking two empty mugs and a glass fruit bowl
with her. The bowl shattered, loose apples rolling onto the
carpet.

The light came on, and both girls looked at their
attackers.

"Jesus," said Charlie.

"You'll fucking wish it was," said Greta Wendel. Beside

her, Freddy McAlmond stood with his arms folded across his letterman jacket, his jock's body an immovable fortress of pure muscle. Charlie glanced at Lynette. The girl was doubled over. The impact from striking the table had knocked the wind from her, and the cut on her breast must have reopened, for bright red blood seeped through her cream sweater.

"What do you want?" asked Charlie, as Greta glared down at her. But there was something different about the bully tonight. Her usual confidence was notable by its absence. She looked afraid, her eyes darting around the room as if searching for some hidden clue.

"Where is she?" said Greta.

Confused, Charlie couldn't think of a reply. Greta stormed towards her and kneeled, then slapped her across the face. The crack was as loud as a gunshot.

"Leave her alone," wheezed Lynette. She came for Greta, but Freddy was too fast. He took Lynette by the collar and yanked her towards him, backhanding her.

"Answer her," he roared, staring at Charlie. "Where's that little bitch girlfriend of yours?"

The realization dawned on Charlie. No wonder Greta was afraid. "You've seen her, haven't you?"

Greta stared at her. "You know where she is. You can make her stop. She's killing my friends."

"And you know you're next," said Charlie, allowing a smile to creep across her face.

"Not if I can help it," said Freddy. "Ain't no bitch gonna kill me." He produced a knife from the waistband of his jeans, the four-inch blade glinting dangerously.

"You think that's gonna stop her?"

Freddy's bravado momentarily faltered. "Sure it will. I'll... I'll cut her throat, and then I'll cut *yours*."

Charlie chuckled at him. Funny how he and Greta weren't so scary anymore. Sure, they had barged into Lynette's house, overpowered them, and threatened them with a knife... but that was the least of her worries. Bullies paled into insignificance alongside the paranormal threat of her deranged psychic ex-girlfriend.

Greta looked at her feet, at the table, anywhere but at Charlie. "Tell her we're sorry," she mumbled.

"What?"

"I said, *tell her we're sorry*. I didn't mean for her to go through the window. I was just—"

"Just what?" snapped Charlie, scarcely able to believe she was finally getting an admission of guilt from Greta. "What were you doing up there? What happened?"

Greta squirmed with embarrassment. "She was wearing my dress. I told her to take it off. She wouldn't, and, y'know, one thing led to another..."

"She's going to kill you," said Charlie.

"You won't know when, and you won't know how," interjected Lynette. "Maybe she'll make you shit yourself in front of the school like she did Michelle? How'd you like that for your legacy?"

Greta glanced fleetingly at Lynette. "I don't even know who the fuck you are."

"We're wasting time," said Freddy. He stalked towards Charlie, stepping on the table to reach her. She tried to crawl back, but one burly hand wrapped around her neck, the knife in front of her face. He scratched it down her nose. "Tell her to stop... *haunting* us, or I'll kill you, right here, right now."

"She wants us dead, too," said Charlie. "She's out of control."

"It's true!" shouted Lynette. "We're on our way to kill her!"

"Bullshit," said Freddy. "Time to die, bitch."

Greta placed a hand on his shoulder. "Wait. Let her talk." She looked at Charlie. "I'm listening."

As fast as she could, Charlie filled Greta in on the events of the last twenty-four hours. Greta listened without interruption. Once Charlie was finished, she turned to Lynette and said, "So you can stop her?"

"I don't know. I think so."

"You've done it before," said Charlie.

"No. I pushed her out of my head. But we don't know if that actually *did* anything. We need to kill her in real life, I think. Unplug her from the machine or something."

"Or cut her throat," said Freddy.

"Sure, whatever works," said Charlie. "But we need to get to the hospital. For all we know, she's already dead."

"She's not," said Lynette. "Even after I killed her — in my head, I mean — she spoke to me." She shook her head sadly. "She'll be back."

"So we're all fucked," said Greta. "Unless we stop her tonight."

"Then what are we waiting for?" said Freddy. "I'll drive."

19

THE STREETS WERE DESERTED AS THEY SPED THROUGH THE night.

The absurdity of sitting in a car alongside her greatest tormentor was not lost on Charlie. Greta had conspired to wreck her life. She had belittled her, mocked her, ruined her high school years, and almost *murdered* her girlfriend. Now, the bully sat in the passenger seat of Freddy's convertible, nibbling her fingernails. Charlie watched her in the wing mirror. An old saying rattled around in her head.

The enemy of my enemy is my friend.

Well, she wouldn't go that far. If Greta ended up as collateral damage on this doomed venture, would she shed a tear? Doubtful. But there was safety in numbers, and if Greta and Freddy could occupy Susan's attention long enough for her and Lynette to put a stop to her reign of psychic terror, then they would have served their ghoulish purpose.

"What's the plan?" asked Freddy, breaking the silence. "We just gonna walk right on in?"

"What time is it?" asked Charlie.

Freddy checked his watch. "Almost eleven."

"Then visiting hours will be over."

"Think you can talk your way in?" asked Lynette.

"Maybe. Depends who's on reception. They sometimes make exceptions for me."

"We could just wait til tomorrow," said Greta. She sounded nervous.

Freddy smacked her arm. "What, and give her time to kill us? You want to wake up with your guts falling out of your ass?"

Greta didn't reply.

Charlie took Lynette's hand. They looked at each other with worried faces. Ahead, lightning forked across the sky against a miserable blanket of obsidian storm clouds. Had Susan caused that? Charlie rubbed at her eyes. Of course not. She could control people, not the weather. She wasn't *that* powerful. *Yet.* She wondered how long Susan's mind had been active. Just recently? Or had she been aware this whole time, lying awake in hospital and unable to signal to anyone or let them know? If that was the case, it must have been hell.

Freddy slowed for a red light, pulling up alongside a sign that read Clinton Memorial Hospital, with an arrow pointing to the right. They were almost there.

The end of the line.

The lights turned green, and he navigated the bend, turning onto Laymon Avenue. Ahead, the hospital loomed into view, lit up like a Christmas tree. Charlie's heart hammered in her chest. What the hell were they doing? Did they think they could just stride into a public building and murder someone without anyone noticing?

You've no choice.

But there was always a choice.

Sure. Kill Susan, or let her kill Lynette. That's your choice. Live with it.

Freddy braked sharply, jolting his passengers.

"The cops," he said grimly, spinning the wheel to take a sharp turn down a side street. Charlie gazed out the window at the assembled officers. An area outside the hospital had been cordoned off with brightly colored tape, while serious-looking men in white suits stood around smoking. She glanced up at the broken window on the fifth floor.

Susan's room.

Charlie's stomach lurched. Could it be? Could they possibly be so lucky? At that moment, she hated herself. Lucky? Lucky that Susan might have thrown herself out of a window? She had loved Susan, and been loved in return. Her happiest memories were of the time they had spent together, which is probably why the meditation experiment had failed. How could Charlie have somewhere to hide in her mind when the only true happiness she had ever known was in Susan's warm embrace?

Freddy parked the car and killed the engine. Wordlessly, the four left the secure confines of the vehicle and walked to the avenue. There, they stood on the sidewalk, gazing up at the hospital. More lightning split the night, striking the imposing building and exploding in a shower of sparks. Thunder rumbled ominously overhead.

"She's awake," said Lynette.

"Yeah," said Charlie, as heavy raindrops pelted her face. "And she's pissed."

〜

It wasn't the storm that alerted Lynette to Susan's state of being.

It was the vision.

As she left the car, her mind flashed to the inside of a hospital room. In her periphery, she saw the machines with their glowing buttons and the drip supplying her with fluids. A deep, foul resentment swirled through Lynette's brain, as if she and Susan were somehow linked. It lasted only a second, but it was enough to know Susan was alive and waiting for them.

Lynette pictured herself in her safe white corridor. The image fluttered in and out of focus. She couldn't enter her meditative state yet, but she had to be ready.

Her and Charlie's life may depend on it.

From somewhere above, a scream drifted from an open window, sending a shiver down Lynette's spine.

It's okay, she told herself. *It's a hospital. Nothing to do with Susan.*

She didn't believe it, though. Susan was waiting for them. And she would kill them all. Nerves skittered through Lynette's body. She looked at Charlie and made a decision.

"It's too dangerous for you," she said. "You should wait outside."

"What?"

"If she gets in your head, it's all over. What if she uses you to attack me? I can't hurt you. I can't—"

"This isn't your fight," said Charlie. "It's *ours*. You think I'd let you go in alone?"

"But in the park. You tried to meditate, to control your mind... and she won."

"You remember what else happened in the park? I said I'd never leave you. And I'm not a liar. We either go in together, or we don't go at all."

"Oh, you're fucking going in," said Freddy. He pulled the knife from his waistband and concealed it in the sleeve of his letterman. "We all are."

Lynette looked into Charlie's eyes. Though they brimmed with tears, the girl's jaw was set, her mind made up. Lynette kissed her.

"Disgusting," said Greta, though when Lynette pulled back, she saw Freddy watching them with interest.

"Hurry the fuck up," he said, hawking up some phlegm and spitting it onto the sidewalk. Then he took off towards the main doors of the hospital.

"Wait!" Greta shouted, struggling to catch up.

High above, something smacked into a window. Lynette looked up, spotting cracks along the glass in a pane on the second level. A man's face appeared at it. The window broke, and the man — who wore hospital scrubs — hurtled out of it, flying through the air. He slammed into the roof of a parked car, the windows exploding outwards, then rolled over the top and thumped lifelessly to the concrete.

"Jesus Christ!"

The four paused. Lynette and Charlie shared a glance.

It was beginning.

Lynette took a tentative step towards the dead man, and Charlie grabbed her hand.

"There's no time," she said gravely. Instead, they ran for the hospital. Two medics appeared through the sliding doors. From all around came the sounds of screams. Men, women, children... so much screaming. Another body hit the ground near the entrance, this one a woman wearing a hospital gown. Her head smacked into the concrete and burst like a watermelon. The medics hesitated, unsure who to attend to first. Lynette knew it didn't matter. Both were dead. And if they didn't hurry and find Susan, a hell of a lot more people would soon be joining them.

In her head, Lynette heard a distant sound. She pictured the white corridor. One of the doors shook, the padlock rattling. Someone on the other side of the door was pounding their fist against it.

They were trying to get inside her head.

"You okay?" asked Charlie, snapping Lynette back to reality.

"Yeah," she lied. "I'm fine."

They reached the entrance, the doors gasping open to allow entry to the reception area. The desk was set in the middle, with dozens of uncomfortable metal chairs on either side acting as the main waiting room. Some of the prospective patients had left their seats and stood at the window, watching the bodies fall to the street with uncomprehending faces. Others remained seated, scribbling their details on white forms or simply staring at the walls, looking bored or unwell or a combination of the two. A woman cradled a crying baby, ignoring the man in front of her, who kept turning around and shooting her irritable glances.

Charlie headed straight for the desk. Behind it sat a harried-looking nurse talking breathlessly into a phone. Charlie tried to get her attention, and the woman waved a dismissive hand.

"Fill in a form and sit down."

"Corrine, it's me," said Charlie. "I need to—"

"Fill in a form and *sit down*."

Charlie turned to Lynette. There was a dull thump from outside as another body slammed onto the ground. Two nurses hurried past, almost knocking Lynette off her feet.

"What's going on out there?" one of them shouted.

"We've got another jumper!"

As more people noticed the carnage in the street, the waiting room chairs began to empty.

"Stay back," someone shouted, but the natural inclination to gawp at a dead body was too strong for most. They crowded the doors, a few brave souls stepping outside, watching eagerly. It sickened Lynette. Charlie was arguing with the receptionist, who didn't seem to be listening, while Freddy glanced around nervously, the tip of his knife jutting out from his sleeve.

"We should just go up there," he whispered to Greta, loud enough for Lynette to hear. For once, she agreed with him. She looked at the waiting room, at Susan's potential victims. One man caught her eye. He was sitting in front of the woman with the crying baby, his head in his hands. Blood streamed from his nostrils. As Lynette watched, it started to leak from his ears, then his eyes. He trembled, his fingers scratching down his face. He got unsteadily to his feet, his cheeks inflating, his cranium bulging.

"Oh shit," said Lynette. She knew what was coming next.

The man's head exploded. Blood drenched those around him, the stump of his neck issuing thick gouts of crimson fluid. The woman behind him clutched her baby to her chest, screaming as the gore flooded over her. The baby cried harder.

"Shut that thing up," said a nearby patient, seemingly oblivious to the dead man whose blood covered him. He limped towards the woman on wooden crutches. She turned to him, her pale face splattered with blood and small chunks of brain that resembled uncooked mincemeat.

"Did... did you see..." she stammered.

The man raised one crutch and brought it down on the

baby. The small bundle dropped to the floor, and before its mother could stop the man, he started to pound the infant with his crutch. She jumped for him, knocking him off his feet, but it was too late.

The baby had stopped crying, its white shawl stained dark red.

"Call the cops!" someone bellowed, as violence erupted between the patients. Lynette backed away, bumping into the reception desk. Charlie had given up trying to talk her way in, and now stood staring at the woman behind the desk, who was holding the phone and clubbing herself across the face with it. Her eyes were wide, as if she couldn't believe what she was doing.

Lynette knew why. Good god, was Susan doing all of this at once? The thought terrified her, and she tugged at Charlie's arm.

"Come on!"

As they ran from the desk towards the corridor, the receptionist shoved the phone receiver into her mouth, using both hands to force it down her throat. Her eyes followed them as they ran, glowing with recognition.

She knows we're here.

The receptionist hopped over the counter, the telephone halfway out her mouth, and chased after them. The phone reached the end of its cord, jerking her back. She fell, then yanked the receiver out of her mouth, taking several teeth with it. They dropped into her lap like small bloody shells. Behind her, the occupants of the waiting room scrambled over fallen bodies, crushing them underfoot, attacking each other with the ferocity of feral dogs.

She can't be this powerful, thought Lynette. *I can't beat her.*

As Charlie hammered the elevator button, the receptionist advanced, her fingers curling into vicious fists, eyes locked on Lynette. She was coming to kill her.

"*Warned... you...*" she drawled through her smashed teeth, her face swelling from the self-inflicted abuse. Lynette searched for a weapon.

She didn't need one.

Freddy appeared between them, his knife bared. He thrust it into the receptionist's stomach, opening her up. Lynette looked away. She knew the woman was innocent, and hoped she wasn't cognizant of her actions.

"Don't kill her," she said, but already she could hear blood splattering onto the floor like a leaky faucet.

"Too late," said Freddy, his voice tinged with a strange glee. She watched him, gazing in awe and horror at his grinning, triumphant face. The woman's blood soaked his jacket as he dragged the knife upwards, opening her belly. He shoved her backwards, and she fell, her head striking the floor.

Freddy looked at Greta and grinned maniacally. "You see that, babe? I fucking got her. I got the bitch *good*. I gutted her like—"

Then, without warning, he plunged the knife into his own eye.

"Jesus fuck!" he screamed, as the orb burst, white fluid dribbling meekly down his cheek.

"Freddy!" said Greta.

He pulled the blade out, then jabbed it into his remaining eye, twisting it around, the sound of the metal scraping against bone turning Lynette's stomach even more than the nightmarish visual.

The speaker system crackled into life. "*Emergency, emergency, would everyone please leave the building in—*"

It cut off, replaced by the familiar opening notes of *If You Leave Me Now*.

Freddy dropped to his knees, stabbing himself repeatedly in the face, his once-handsome visage now pockmarked with dozens of bleeding cuts and lacerations. Greta went to him, recoiling as he lashed out at her with the knife.

Charlie punched the button for the elevator.

"Stop him!" shouted Greta. She shook Lynette by the shoulders, tears streaming down her face. "Make him stop hurting himself!"

The music filled the air, haunting in its incongruity. The waiting area had calmed down, and when Lynette looked beyond Greta, she understood why.

Everyone was dead. Everyone except one man, who she thought she recognized as the owner of Murphy's Hardware Store. She *thought* it was him, but when she had met him once while applying for a part-time job, he hadn't been covered in blood, and he hadn't been stark naked.

"God, no!" he cried, as he stepped out of his pants and crawled over the mound of dead bodies, hungrily shoving his throbbing erection into the first hole he came to. "I don't want this! Someone stop me!"

"Where's that elevator?" breathed Lynette. Greta had let go of her. The bully leaned against the wall, stealing glances at Freddy, who lay on the floor, utterly lifeless apart from one arm that continued to stab himself, over and over, his face and torso resembling tenderized beef, a deep puddle of blood spreading around him. It reached Greta's feet, soaking the soles of her sneakers.

"You did this," she said, staring at Charlie with hatred in her eyes. "It's all your fault."

The elevator pinged, and Lynette and Charlie turned to face the doors. They opened, revealing two male orderlies and a patient on a gurney. The patient, a young man, was naked, his crotch a mangled atrocity, his penis half-sticking out of the mouth of the first orderly as he chewed savagely. The other orderly's scrubs and underpants were at his ankles, and he masturbated violently as his counterpart crunched down on the severed cock. "Help me!" he screamed as he ejaculated, blood-flecked semen spurting from the tip of his dick.

"Uh, we'll get the next one," said Charlie, backing away. She didn't see Greta coming for her. Lynette did, but she was too slow to react, her shock at the grisly tableaux rooting her feet to the spot.

"You did this!" shrieked Greta, as she lashed out with a wicked right hook. It caught Charlie on the jaw, rocking her backwards. She stumbled, falling into the elevator and cracking her head against the gurney.

The doors started to close.

"No!" screamed Lynette, drawing on hidden reserves of strength. She ran for the doors, reaching out to stop them closing, but Greta shoulder-barged her out of the way. Lynette skidded on the blood, falling, landing hard on her side. She made brief, heartbreaking eye contact with the dazed Charlie, and then the doors closed fully.

On her hands and knees, Lynette scrambled towards the elevator, jabbing the button with her finger so hard she thought something would break. But she was too late.

Charlie was gone.

"No... no..." she mumbled, watching as Greta scurried back towards her prone boyfriend, who was still stabbing himself. Greta steeled herself, then reached for Freddy's hand, snatching the blade from his grip. His arm continued to move up and down, but with the knife gone, it looked to Lynette like he was making a jerk-off motion.

His final insult.

Lynette watched the counter above the elevator start climbing. She would have to wait until it came back down. Charlie could still be alive in there. Forcing herself to her feet, she leaned one hand against the wall, filling her lungs, trying to mentally prepare herself for whatever was waiting behind those elevator doors when they reached level one again and opened.

Then she felt the knife against her throat, and a hot breath on her ear.

"Just you and me now," said Greta.

"We gotta wait for Charlie. She—"

"Fuck that cunt! We go now, or I'll slit your fucking throat!"

"I can't leave—"

Blood spurted across the wall as Greta jabbed the blade partially into Lynette's neck. "Upstairs, now!" she demanded.

"I don't know where Susan is! Only Charlie does!"

"Well, you'd better fucking find her. She killed my boyfriend, and I'll be goddamned if she kills me before I get to go to prom!"

Lynette felt the knife slip further inside her, and she knew that if she didn't acquiesce, Greta would kill her. "Okay! Okay! I'll take you!"

Greta shoved her down the corridor. "Lead the way, bitch," she said.

Lynette looked back at her, at the knife in Greta's hand, smeared with her own blood. She touched the wound on her neck, felt the blood pulsing from it. The man in the reception area had moved on to another body, his hairy ass thrusting his cock into some poor corpse's rectum.

"Tell my wife I'm sorry!" he shouted, as Lynette reached

the door to the stairs, pausing for a second before barging it open, wondering what new horror awaited her on the remaining four floors of the forsaken hospital. As Greta pushed her onwards, the knife occasionally piercing her skin, only one thought kept Lynette going.

Charlie.

She might still be alive. And if she wasn't? Then Lynette swore that once Susan was dead... Greta would be next.

20

THE REMAINS OF THE CHEWED PENIS SLOPPED OUT OF THE orderly's mouth and dribbled down his chin. "Forgive me," he said, tears in his eyes.

Charlie crawled into the corner of the elevator, putting as much distance between her and the men as possible. The orderly who had been masturbating turned his attention to her, venomous fluid dripping from his sagging cock. He, too, was crying, and his whispered voice kept repeating The Lord's Prayer over and over.

"Our Father, who art in heaven," he said, as he raised his hand to his mouth and smeared his filthy seed over his lips and face. "Hallowed be thy name..."

Charlie kicked the leg of the gurney. It smacked into the half-naked orderly's hips, knocking him off balance. She felt the other man's hands clawing at her, so she slid down onto her back, aiming the soles of her shoes at him and kicking. He struggled to hold her as she connected with his flailing hands. One of his fingers snapped backwards, but he didn't seem to notice.

More hands, the other orderly groping at her face with

rubber-gloved fingers that invaded her mouth. They tasted of his own ejaculate. It was foul, but Charlie did what she had to do — she clenched her jaws shut, digging her teeth into the hard flesh of his thumb. Blood filled her mouth as her teeth clamped shut on bone. The orderly recoiled, leaving thick strips of flesh in Charlie's mouth. She spat them out and crawled beneath the gurney, coming out on at the opposite corner. The bell pinged again, the doors sliding open. Charlie glanced at the readout above the entrance. Level three.

The children's ward.

She bit down on her fist to stop from screaming.

The level three corridor was sheer chaos. A doctor ran shrieking, bumping from wall to wall. His eyes were gone, burst and smeared across his cheeks and forehead, while a giggling toddler clung onto his optic nerves with tiny fists, their feet swaying. The floor was awash with blood, bodies everywhere. One woman was still alive. She lay on her back, covered in mewling infants like writhing maggots. They scraped at her flesh, ripping open her blouse and scratching at her breasts, tearing her nipples off and lapping up the spurting blood. Dr. Kevok strolled past the elevator, casually pushing a woman in a wheelchair and whistling along with *If You Leave Me Now*. The woman was on fire, her skin crispy and charred, and steam rose from Kevok's hands as he pushed the flaming wheelchair. He paused at the elevator and looked in, spying Charlie in the corner. Tears rolled down his cheeks.

"Please, make her stop," he sobbed, then resumed his walk.

Charlie curled into a ball. She couldn't get out here. She would be torn limb from limb. My god, what hell had Susan unleashed?

The doors started to slide shut again, and the two orderlies turned back to Charlie. She aimed both feet at the gurney and kicked it with all her might. The trolley knocked into one of the men, catching him unaware. He staggered, and Charlie leaped to her feet and shoved him through the quickly narrowing gap. He landed in the corridor as the doors shut, and the elevator jerked into life again.

One down, one to go, she thought madly.

Charlie faced the remaining orderly. It was the man who had been eating the patient's penis. She held the gurney, angling it so that it remained between them. If she could keep him at bay for a few seconds, they would arrive at level five and she could get out. It wasn't long. She just had to—

The elevator juddered to an abrupt halt. The lights went out, plunging the cramped interior into darkness. Seconds later, tiny red strip lights came on, offering scant illumination.

"Oh, fuck," said Charlie.

The power was out.

She was trapped.

Lynette climbed the stairs.

If she stopped for even a second to catch her breath, Greta pressed the tip of the knife into the small of her back.

The stairwell itself was curiously silent, which, she reasoned, was A Very Good Thing. If they could make it up the various flights without encountering any more of Susan's victims, they stood a reasonable chance of stopping her and finding Charlie.

She hoped.

Would she be strong enough? Did she have the self

control to keep Susan out of her head? She pictured her corridor again, each door an entryway into a happy memory, and then Greta jabbed her and she resumed climbing.

"Move," said Greta.

"I'm trying. Not everyone's a fucking cheerleader."

"No shit, fatass."

Lynette ignored the jibe. They had passed level two, and now approached the third floor. A door opened far above them, the sounds of a life-or-death struggle echoing down the stairwell, and though Lynette was tiring, the sound spurred her on. At any moment, one of those doors could open and—

A body rocketed past her, falling between the stairs. It clanged off the rail, bones snapping, and rebounded onto the lower set of stairs, rolling to the bottom and coming to a stop in a tangle of shattered limbs. High above, someone choked, then vomited. Fabric tore... or was it flesh? She wondered if there was an alternative stairwell in case this one became impassable. There had to be. It was a big place. But finding it would mean wandering the corridors, and Lynette didn't know how bad it was out there. By the sounds of it, things were out of control.

They reached the third level, and she walked towards the doors.

"Where are you going?" asked Greta.

Lynette listened. The chilling voices of the dying and the damned screeched on the other side of the doors. She dared not open them. A child's mocking laugh rang out, a vision assaulting her eyes of a man lying dying, his throat torn open, wild-eyed children using their small hands to scoop up his blood and lap at it with swollen gray tongues.

She backed away slowly.

Halfway there. Only two more flights to ascend. She could do this.

Another vision, this time taking place in an operating theater, a nurse screaming in horror as hands slashed and cut her face with a scalpel.

Lynette gripped the rail and started up the stairs, her body tense and coiled.

"Wait," she said. Footsteps on the landing above. No, not footsteps. It sounded like hands slapping against the stairs, followed by something scraping across them.

"What *is* that?" said Greta.

There was no time to consider the question. A white hand smacked onto the landing between levels three and four. Then another. The fingers hooked onto the stair, dragging themselves along. A woman's face appeared, the neck snapped at an obscene angle. She started down the stairs, and Lynette realized the woman had no legs, her broken spinal column cracking emptily against each step. The bloodshot eyes fixed themselves on Lynette, the lips curling, trying to form a word.

"*You again,*" it said, dragging itself forwards, tumbling down the stairs, arms pinwheeling. It landed at Lynette's feet, the hands grasping feebly for her legs.

The pounding in Lynette's head increased in intensity. Susan had found her. She kicked the half-dead abomination across the floor and closed her eyes, visualizing the white corridor. Every door trembled as invisible fists hammered against them. Lynette took off down the corridor, checking each door, ensuring the padlocks were secured.

She fought back another maddening vision, a man bent over a hospital bed, his pants pulled down, a bone saw hacking through his buttock, the flesh folding over, the skin tearing.

Then another, a woman's hands squeezing a baby's throat, the infant's head turning blue, then purple, as it gasped for air.

Then—

"Stop!" screamed Lynette. *"Stop!"*

All at once the knocking stopped, and a deep, throaty voice echoed past her.

"I see you."

One final vision followed.

In it, a teenage hand with chipped red nail polish clutched a knife, the blade rusted and stained with blood. It rose, revealing the potential victim, and Lynette saw herself, her eyes closed, oblivious to Greta and the knife.

She tore herself from her meditation, and suddenly she was back in the hospital, turning to face her assailant.

Greta thrust her arm forwards, the blade penetrating Lynette's belly.

"You... will... die..." said Greta, though Lynette knew it wasn't her. Blood poured from Lynette's side, and as she staggered back, she stared helplessly into Susan's blank, emotionless eyes, and knew she was going to die today.

21

___

"GET THE FUCK AWAY FROM ME," SAID CHARLIE.

She looked around for an escape. There was a hatch above her, outlined by the emergency lights, but no way to reach it without standing on the gurney. She glanced at the alarm button, but what good would that do? The whole damn hospital was fucked.

With only the gurney — and a castrated corpse — between them, the orderly lunged forwards, clambering over it. Charlie punched him in the face, her knuckles cracking against his jaw. He fell at her feet as she dodged to the side. His fingernails raked down her arm, drawing blood, and she put her hands on the gurney and climbed over, landing safely on the other side. But how long could she keep this up? The orderly rose, saliva dangling from his lips. He looked like a clown that had been caught in the rain, bloody crimson makeup dribbling down his leering face.

"Your tits," he said. "I'm going to eat your tits!"

Charlie was unprepared for the sentence. Her stomach lurched. The orderly stared at her chest, his fists reflexively opening and closing. Then he came for her again, scrambling over the gurney, arms spread wide to catch her. Charlie had no options. She leaped towards him, slamming her shoulder into his chest and catching him off-balance. He crashed backwards, his head thumping against the metal wall. He moaned, and then... nothing.

Charlie stood in the elevator, panting. Was he dead? Unconscious? Breathing through her mouth to avoid the rancid odor of dead flesh, she peered over the side of the gurney, into the darkness where the emergency lights didn't reach.

The orderly's body was gone.

"What the fu—"

Then hands clutched her ankles, reaching from beneath the gurney. She had no time to react, her legs pulled out from under her. She fell heavily onto her ass, the impact jolting her bones, and then he was pulling her, dragging her close and crawling atop her. Frenzied hands tore at her shirt, attempting to tear it to shreds. His face appeared from the darkness, teeth champing together as he neared her chest.

"Gonna eat you, gonna eat you all up, gonna eat your tits, your fucking tits," he murmured, the deranged ramblings of a lunatic in a psych ward.

Charlie worked her legs up between them, keeping him at bay with her knees. The orderly clawed at her face and neck, his fingers cloaked in surgical gloves.

"Just try it!" she roared. "Just fucking try it!"

She tried to shuffle back, and something touched her head. A limp hand dangled over the edge of the gurney, the arm belonging to the poor man whose genitals the orderly had been eating when the elevator arrived.

Pushing with her hands, she managed to move back a few inches. Her shirt tore open, the manic fingers dancing against her chest and hooking into her bra as the orderly's teeth snapped together with a revolting enamel *clack*. He forced his head against her knees, trying to prize them open. Desperate for any sort of distraction, Charlie yanked the dead man's arm. The corpse rolled over the edge and landed on top of the orderly.

Rivers of blood flooded over the elevator floor. The dead man's stomach had already been torn open, and now the orderly's head was stuck in the makeshift cavity. Confused by this latest development, he lifted the body off, depositing it to the side. His head was now soaked with red blood, and a long string of intestine hung around his neck like a scarf.

Without missing a beat, the salivating orderly forced himself on top of Charlie, his hands finding her bra.

A long string of intestines...

He tore her bra apart.

...hanging around his neck...

He pinched one breast in his hand, leaning over towards it, mouth open, teeth bared.

...like a fucking scarf!

Charlie grabbed the intestine in both hands, pulling in opposite directions. The soggy innards tightened around the orderly's neck. The repulsive organ was slippery in her hands, so she twisted it around her wrists, and as the man's teeth scraped against her nipple, she pulled him away from her. A look of panic fell over his face. He reached for the internal organ, but his rubber gloves prevented him from getting a firm grip, his fingers sliding off the smooth, wet surface. He backed away on his knees, and Charlie got to her feet, never releasing the fleshy cord.

"Ack!" he choked, as Charlie positioned herself behind him, placing her foot against his spine and pulling harder. The guts stretched, threatening to break... but they didn't.

As the orderly's arms slumped to his sides, Charlie released him. He fell forwards, his face smacking onto the blood drenched floor. In the near-darkness, she looked closely at him. Was he moving? Were his fingers twitching? Was—

She raised her foot above his head.

"Get your hands off my fucking tits," she whispered, and brought her foot down. The skull cracked, but didn't break. It did on the second try, bursting beneath Charlie's sneaker like a ripe tomato. She lifted her foot, crimson gore dripping from the sole of her shoe. Adrenaline flooded her veins, and she knew she had to get out of here before it wore off. Stepping over the bodies, she climbed onto the gurney and reached for the hatch. She unclasped the release and lifted the hatch, then hauled herself up, scrambling onto the roof of the elevator. There, she rolled onto her back, waited a second, and got to her feet. The shaft was cold and dark. She looked around at the thick steel wires that stretched above her into the unforgiving blackness, wondering if she could climb them.

Of course she couldn't. That was ridiculous. But maybe she wouldn't have to. The doors to level four were within reach. She walked to them, tried to slip her fingers between them. They wouldn't budge.

"Come on!" she cried, pounding her fists against the chilly metal. From the other side, she heard muffled moans and footsteps. Soon, others were banging their fists against the doors, and she backed away. What if...

The door jolted open. Just a fraction of an inch at first, but then it happened again.

Charlie wiped tears and snot from her face. "Oh, you *gotta* be fucking kidding me," she said, as another hand appeared and the doors to the fourth level started to open.

22

The blade slipped out of Lynette's belly.

She shoved Greta as hard as she could, and pressed her hand to her stomach, horrified by the sensation of her own warm blood evacuating her body. Greta stumbled backwards and stood there, unmoving. Blood dripped steadily from the tip of her knife. Lynette's heart hammered unceasingly in her chest. After a moment's respite, Greta shrieked, coming at her again, the knife raised.

Lynette dodged to the side, the metal blade striking the wall with a piercing crack. Greta turned to her.

"Kill me," she said, tears running down her cheeks.

"Fight her," said Lynette. "She's in your head!"

But Greta was beyond saving. She pivoted, swinging the knife wildly, forcing Lynette back towards the stairs. Greta's movements were jerky, each swing more of a violent spasm, exhibiting none of the usual grace and poise inherent to the head cheerleader. The blade whistled past Lynette's face, and she pushed Greta again. The girl skittered backwards, her feet sliding on the bloody floor. She almost overbalanced, and Lynette knew this was her only chance. She charged forwards, gripping Greta in a bearhug and barreling into the double doors. They burst open, and the two girls landed in the corridor of level three. Immediately, tormented wails filled the air. The stench of death clung to the walls like foul moss. Lynette looked to her left and saw an orderly staggering towards her, his arm dangling from his shoulder by thin strips of veins and tendons, the fingers low enough to scrape along the floor. In his other hand, he carried a man's severed head like a grisly jack-o'-lantern.

Lynette turned to her right. From that direction, a doctor jogged towards her, pushing a woman in a wheelchair. Both of them were on fire, and both were laughing.

Lynette grunted as Greta managed to angle the knife and cut her forearm. She had never been involved in a fight before. Sure, she had been beaten up, but she hadn't ever fought *back*. She had always just taken it, accepting that life was there to trample her at every opportunity, and that she had no hope of winning. But now there was more at stake. Not just her life, but Charlie's too. And who knew how many more?

She slammed her elbow into Greta's face. The girl's nose burst juicily, but she didn't stop, trying to wrestle the knife into a stabbing position. Lynette pinned her hand down, lying atop her. The flaming wheelchair approached. The rubber tires had melted, the metal rims trundling along the floor. Lynette felt the heat on her skin. She pinned Greta's other hand down and headbutted her. Greta's eyes closed as she emitted a thin shriek of pain, and Lynette took her chance. She reached for the knife and stole it from Greta's hand, plunging it into the girl's shoulder.

The heat from the approaching wheelchair bristled against Lynette's skin, and she threw herself backwards. As she hit the double doors and landed in the stairwell, she had enough time to see Greta pull the knife free and rise to her feet. The doors swung shut, the momentum carrying them so that they opened again on the sight of the fiery wheelchair slamming into Greta. She fell onto the flaming woman, who wrapped her arms around Greta with a wicked cackle... and then the doors closed for good.

Greta screamed in agony for a few moments as her body caught fire... and then Greta screamed no more.

There was no time to celebrate. Lynette touched a finger to her stomach wound. Her fingers traced the outline of a narrow cut, bile rising in her throat. She was losing blood. She had to hurry.

With a low moan, she forced herself up and towards the stairs, placing her hand on the rail. Susan was still two levels above her. Provided that Lynette encountered no one else on the stairs, she would reach her soon. She had to prepare.

Closing her eyes, she took a deep breath and pictured the crisp, white corridor.

A welcome serenity flooded over her. It was good to be back, to escape the insanity and the violence, though she couldn't fully relax. She had to keep part of her mind in the present, ready for one of Susan's vessels to attack her again. As her physical body climbed the hospital stairs, she opened the nearest door in her mind and walked through, feeling the soft whisper of long grass against her ankles.

She was back in her grandmother's yard, where she had spent so much of her youth. A swing hung from a tree branch, and she sat on it, kicking off from the ground and letting gravity do its thing, enjoying the rush of air against her face. She knew if she swung high enough, she could see her grandma through the window, and so she kept kicking, tucking and untucking her legs to increase her height. Sure enough, she spotted her grandmother, sitting in her chair and lit by the faint blue glow of the television.

Lynette's heart skipped a beat.

Someone was standing behind her grandmother. A dark shape. A phantom.

The backyard crackled like television static, and for a second Lynette was back on the hospital stairs, blood leaking down her legs, before she forced her mind to return to her grandmother's yard, kicking her feet out to stop the swing. She jumped from it and ran for the back door.

"Grandma!" she shouted, barging the back door open and bursting into the kitchen, pausing only to grab a knife from—

But they were all gone. The wooden knife block sat empty on the counter beside the cookie jar, five thin slits where the knives usually rested.

"Oh god, oh god no," muttered Lynette. She left the kitchen and headed for the main room. The noise of the TV seeped through the doors. It was *The Rockford Files*. It always was, in the happy place. Nothing ever changed here. Nothing. It couldn't, because Lynette controlled it. No one else could access her thoughts, her memories. No one else could—

She opened the door.

"No," she cried, when presented with the image of her beloved grandmother in her chair, the missing knives jutting out of her like a human pin cushion. One in each thigh, one in each breast, and the third — and worst — was the butcher knife protruding from her crotch like a gleaming, bloody phallus.

It must have been recent, as great gouts of blood jetted from each wound, and the woman's fingers still twitched in her death throes, tapping out a dire funereal rhythm on the arm of the rocking chair.

Susan. Susan had done this. And if she had done it here, then...

The thought rocked Lynette. She ran from the room and exited into the white corridor, glancing down it. The doors were all open. All of them. Lynette stood before the next one, afraid to enter, afraid not to. She stepped into The Louvre, standing before her favorite painting, *Gabrielle d'Estrées et une de ses soeurs.* It had been slashed in two, the sides hanging like canvas drapes.

Everyone was dead. They lay in pieces. Men, women, and children had been dismembered, disemboweled, their limbs spread around the floor, their bodies torn asunder. Lynette noticed movement, and spun to face a woman. She stood before Lynette, naked, her arms crudely severed in a sick parody of the *Venus de Milo.*

"Where did she go?" asked Lynette.

The woman trembled, trying to remain still. "I'm not allowed to move," she whispered through pursed lips. "If I do, she'll come back for me."

Lynette took a step closer.

"Go!" said the woman. "Get out! Get out of here! It's okay... I'm art now. I'm art! I'm fucking art!" She started to laugh, the sound turning to throaty screams. Lynette noticed the woman wasn't simply standing there. She had been impaled on a pole that was wrapped in barbed wire, a makeshift stand that vanished between her legs and up her—

No, it was too awful. Too indescribably awful.

"I'm a work of fucking art!" screamed the woman, and Lynette ran from The Louvre, emerging in the white corridor, facing a never-ending array of open doors. She peered

through the next one, at the rollercoaster of screaming limbless children at Disney World, and slammed it shut.

Susan had destroyed her happy place.

Desecrated it.

Lynette allowed herself to drift back to reality.

And there, in the hospital, a set of double doors loomed before her. She looked over her shoulder. There were no more stairs. She had reached the fifth level. All that separated her from Susan were these doors. But now she had nowhere to hide. Her mind was wide open. It was Susan's for the taking.

She pushed the doors and stepped into the intensive care ward. Snow crunched beneath her feet, a howling gale blasting along the hospital corridor. Snowflakes fell from the ceiling, landing on her face and dissolving. It was impossible, and yet Lynette was unsurprised. Nothing was impossible, not anymore, and this frozen hell was simply another display of Susan's immense power.

Suddenly, Lynette struck herself across the face. The slap resounded throughout the corridor. She looked at her hand, saw it clench into a fist, and then she punched herself. She tried to avoid the blow, but had no control of her head and neck. The fist connected with her brow, and she almost fell.

∼

...why are you hitting yourself huh why are you hitting yourself cunt...

∼

"Get out," cried Lynette, closing her eyes and drifting back into her head. Her vision dimmed, and she found herself back in the theater where she had first encountered Susan. Tearing her eyes from the screen, she turned and scanned the rows, searching for Susan. There she was, in the back row.

The room stuttered, crossfading into the hospital, where Lynette watched as her fist pummeled her own stomach. It was agonizing, but not enough to stop her. She focused her mind, blocking out the pain and returning to the theater of her mind. The red velvet drapes were closing on the screen with infinite slowness.

Time was almost up.

Lynette staggered towards the back row, gripping onto each seat as she passed. The dark shape of Susan calmly stood and walked along the row.

"Come back," snarled Lynette, her mind clouded with fury and a sense of impending vengeance. Susan ignored her. She walked towards a strange green light. There, she waited, then opened a door beneath the light and walked through. Lynette approached, wincing in pain as, back in the hospital, she beat herself harder. She arrived at the door and looked up at the backlit sign.

EMERGENCY EXIT, it read.

Fuck it, thought Lynette.

She didn't know where it led, but if it meant stopping Susan, she would follow the bitch all the way to hell.

Charlie watched in horror as the metal doors to the elevator shaft jerked further open. Where could she go? She was stuck here. She was *trapped*. There was nowhere to run to, nowhere to escape.

She looked down at the open hatch between her feet. Well, she supposed it was safer down there than up here. She lowered herself back into the elevator, her feet finding the gurney, and pulled the hatch closed. She had forgotten how bad the smell in the elevator was, the putrid stench of blood and offal clinging to the walls.

Listening closely, she heard the doors above her groan open. What was—

The elevator jolted as something landed on the roof. Charlie bit back a cry of terror. Footsteps throbbed above her.

What was up there? What in god's name was *up there?*

It stalked back and forth, nails scratching against the steel.

Then the footsteps stopped. Charlie heard nothing but her own labored breathing, and the blood rushing through her head. She sagged down onto the floor, looking up at the hatch.

It was moving. It rose, revealing the darkness of the elevator shaft, before being tossed aside with a metallic reverberation.

Whatever was up there... was coming in.

23

———————

The emergency exit opened at Lynette's touch.

The door seemed to dissolve into nothing, and she fell through, bumping her knees as she landed on a gravel path surrounded by freshly mown grass. It was a path she knew intimately, due to her habit of walking with her head down and focusing on her feet so as not to make eye contact with anyone. But why was it here in her happy place? It didn't belong, and never would.

She had no good memories here. None at all.

Lynette stood, brushing the loose gravel from her knees, and looked up at the bronze sign by the path.

CLINTON HIGH SCHOOL.

Why was she here? Why the hell was she outside her school?

Two jocks walked by, one of them elbowing her sharply as he passed. They laughed as they strolled away, and Lynette felt the familiar burn of shame on her cheeks. There were teenagers all around, doing whatever teenagers do — talking, flirting, skateboarding. Some of them lurked in the shadows of the elm trees, smoking sly cigarettes, extinguishing them when a teacher strode past.

The noise was deafening, people shouting and laughing, music blaring from the radio of some beat-up old jalopy. Someone else bumped into her, a girl this time.

"Outta my way, deadbeat," she said.

"Sorry," said Lynette, shuffling from the path and onto the grass. The sun hung low in the sky, hot against her skin.

"Why am I here?" she said to herself, then turned back to the doorway. It floated there like a mirage, and she peered through into the theater. A scream blared out over the speaker system. Lynette recognized it as her own. On the big screen, she saw her hands drawing a scalpel across her arm. The flesh parted like the expectant lips of a lover, blood oozing to the surface and running down to the crook of her elbow.

Then suddenly Susan was there, in the doorway, staring at her through cold, dead eyes.

"You're mine, now," she said, smiling, and slammed the door shut with dreadful finality. It shimmered as if in a heat haze, then vanished.

"No!" gasped Lynette, reaching her hands out in front of her, searching for the door. A couple of schoolkids laughed at her.

"What's she *doing?*" asked one girl.

"She's a fucking weirdo," replied the other.

Lynette dropped to her knees, groping around the grass. "No, no, no," she said. "It has to be here. It has to be here."

But the doorway was gone. She looked around for help, for another exit, for *anything*. All she found were more people pointing and laughing at her, mocking her.

She was alone. Much like her entire life, Lynette was surrounded by hundreds of people, and yet she was utterly, hopelessly alone. She sat there, weeping, on the grass, as students filed past her, some ridiculing her, others paying scant attention to the pathetic sobs that wracked her body.

That was it, then. The end. Like an idiot, she had followed Susan in here without considering the consequences, and fallen into her trap. There was no way out, no access to her happy places, no escape route. She tried to imagine the white corridor, tried to wake up in the hospital, but her mind was an utter, total blank. She could visualize nothing. Her imagination had been scrubbed clean.

She lay down on the grass and curled into a ball.

"I'm sorry, Charlie," she whispered, the jeers of her schoolmates ringing in her ears. "I'm so, so sorry."

Fear prevented Charlie from moving.

It constricted her throat, wrapping its freezing arms around her as she watched two thin hands, horribly burned, appear above her, gripping onto the edges of the hatch. Charred skin hung in flakes, crisp white bone visible between black muscle. Slowly, a head lowered through the gap, loose strands of hair dangling from the roasted scalp.

Charlie managed to drag her weary body over to the gurney. She pulled herself under, hugging her knees to her chest, and waited.

The hideous creature lowered itself into the elevator. It weighed nothing, for it was just a skeleton with a light coating of crispy, burned flesh. The gurney moved as the creature stood on it. Charlie held her breath, her body vibrating with crazed terror. Maybe it wouldn't find her?

The creature hopped down from the gurney onto two bony feet. Chunks of gristle fell from its torso, hitting the floor, reminding Charlie of the time her dad had dropped a tray of barbecued chicken all over the kitchen tiles. The feet turned in her direction, a grotesque hand taking the loose sheet of the gurney and lifting it up.

The adrenaline was wearing off, and Charlie knew her body had given up the fight for survival.

The creature peered under the gurney. Its eyes, which resembled two bright rubies set into a scorched black skull, sparkled as they settled on her. What remained of the lips curled into a smile, the skin around them crumbling to ash and raining down like black snowflakes.

"Found... yooooouuuuuu," it said, in a voice choked with the grim fires of hell. It was a voice Charlie remembered. She hadn't heard it in so long that it seemed to come from a different lifetime.

It was the voice of Susan.

The bell rang, signaling the beginning of class.

Lynette wandered, dazed, towards the school. What else was there to do? This was her home now. Susan had imprisoned her within her own mind, in a place where no good memories would ever dare intrude.

Fucking *school*. She had spent her whole life looking forward to getting out of here. Her parents had once told her that school days were the best days of your life. That was the day she had realized her parents were fools. School was tribal warfare, and only the strong survived, each day a catalog of misfortunes to be deftly navigated lest the overwhelming humiliations weigh you down into an early grave.

She hesitated by the doors, and thought — not for the first time in her life — about killing herself. It wouldn't work, though. Not in here, not in her mind. She knew this, because she had tried it before, after the incident with the boys in the alley.

It had taken her weeks to even locate a happy place after that day. All the doors in the white corridor had led only to that damned alleyway, her torn clothes lying discarded next to the trash can and a small pool of her blood. Even when she had managed to access a pleasant memory, it had been tainted by the laughter of the boys, their grunts and snorts as they—

She could hear them now. Jesus Christ, *she could hear them now*.

Lynette glanced back at the school lawn and saw them sauntering up the path. The boys. The ones from back *then*, from the alleyway. The leader, a lantern-jawed bastard with a crew cut and the devil's eyes, smiled at her. Sunlight glared off the switchblade in his hand, the one he had used to—

Lynette ran into the school, her heart racing. They couldn't find her, oh god, they couldn't, not again. Never again. Her feet pounded down the corridors, the lockers blurring by, tears stinging her eyes. She felt sick.

"They're not real, they're not real," she panted, speeding round a corner and pressing herself up against a wall. Sweat dripped down her forehead, down the back of her neck, her body trembling, her vision narrowing.

"You're going to be late for class, young lady."

She looked up into the stern face of a teacher. He flicked his wrist, the switchblade snapping out with efficient deadliness.

"You'd better hurry," he smiled emptily.

She ran, further down the corridors, spiraling into madness. Which class was she due in? She chose one at random, opening the door and entering the classroom. Except it wasn't a classroom. It was a bedroom.

Her own bedroom.

"Oh my god," she cried, running into the room and throwing herself down on the bed, almost bouncing off it. Burying her face in the pillow, she smelled the achingly nostalgic scent of her childhood. Had she really done it? Had she found a sanctuary within her own private hell?

The door closed, and she rolled onto her back, staring up at the ceiling. A candle was lit, and posters of Rock Hudson and Elvis Presley decorated the walls. It was exactly as she remembered it. Well, of course it was! It was her memory. But what about Charlie? What good was being here if she never saw Charlie again?

She left the comfort of the bed and walked to the window, gazing out into the night. The moonlight illuminated the yard in a serene lunar glow, and she pressed her forehead against the glass.

"Charlie," she whispered.

Something clicked to her right. A door handle. She looked towards the walk-in closet and felt a curious churning sensation in her stomach.

Oh god.

All at once a memory, long suppressed, came back to her. Years ago, she had buried it, buried the trauma so deep that it could never be found, and then forced herself to forget about it. And it had worked.

Until now.

"No," she whimpered, as the door creaked slowly open.

The closet was dark, a curious void. But as her eyes adjusted, she saw a shadowy figure leaning against the frame. He was tall, impossibly tall, with simian arms that reached down to his knees.

"Hey, Lynny," croaked the tobacco-fueled voice of her Uncle Harv. "How you doin'?" He was naked, his penis engorged, a half-empty whisky bottle clutched in his hand. "Been thinkin' 'bout you again, pretty baby."

Lynette screamed and ran for the door, her uncle giving chase. He caught her shoulder, tearing her nightdress down her back, and she threw the door open and ran into the school hallway, slamming it behind her. Through the door, she heard him call out.

"It's alright, Lynny. I've been waiting a long time. I can wait some more."

Screaming, she clawed at her face and retreated, staring at the door, afraid to take her eyes off it.

"We've always been here," he shouted through the door. *"All of us."* He paused, then added, *"Welcome home, bitch. Welcome to hell."*

24

———

Charlie closed her eyes.

The creature moved closer. It smelled of spoiled meat and misery.

She flinched away as something touched her cheek. A finger. It traced her dry lips.

"Miiiiiiine," said Susan. *"Aaaaaalllll miiiiiiine."*

The stench grew stronger as the face came towards her, close enough that she felt its rasping breath on her skin.

"Please," said Charlie. "Stop."

The charred skull nuzzled up to her. Its flaking skin was hot to the touch. It found her mouth, and Charlie shuddered as the skull kissed her. The lips crumbled to nothing, until cracked teeth scraped at her chin and mouth.

"Kisssss meeeee," said Susan.

"I can't," sobbed Charlie. "You're not her. You're not the Susan I knew."

Susan grabbed her hair and yanked her head back. Charlie smelled burning follicles as the hellish fingers singed her locks.

"Kisssss meeeee."

Charlie swallowed, loud enough to reverberate around the elevator. Forcing herself to do it, she kissed the rigid bone of Susan's cheek.

"More... passsssiiiiooonnnn."

Susan's dry tongue flicked across her lips. It was like being poked with a log from the fire. Charlie dry-heaved. She opened her eyes and looked into the blazing fires of Susan's eyes. Powdery hands caressed her breasts.

"Touch... meeeeee."

Charlie placed her hands on Susan's waist, the cracked muscle abrasive to the touch. She ran them up to the two small mounds of burned meat on Susan's chest, skin flaking off as she did so.

Susan forced Charlie onto her back. To her left lay the corpse from the gurney. To her right, the flattened face of the orderly. And on top of her, a withered, gnarled nightmare that Susan — or what had once been Susan — now occupied. It slid its withered digits into the waistband of Charlie's pants and tugged them down.

"Don't..." she whispered, as the hideous skeletal monster ripped her underwear from her body and calmly spread her legs, the ghastly tongue scratching across the discolored teeth. Wizened hands reached for her ass, raking sharp talons down the plump flesh, and as Susan's head descended, and the rotten nub of the tongue prodded at her labia, Charlie vomited.

She clamped her eyes shut and tried to think of something, *anything* else. What she pictured was a long white corridor with doors on either side as far as she could see. Lynette's sweet voice crept into her head.

Those doors are infinite possibilities for you.

That's what she had said that day in the park.

Behind each one lies a happy place, a happy memory. Even a happy dream or wish.

But she had *tried* that. Susan was in there already. She was—

Charlie screamed as Susan's tongue entered her. The corridor faded, and she was back in the elevator, the metal floor freezing against her spine, Susan's head chafing her thighs.

Walk down the corridor and choose a door. Any door, it doesn't matter. They're all happy places.

She closed her eyes and tried again. The corridor yawned before her like a chasm of dreams. She ignored her physical body, centering all thoughts and feelings on the corridor. Which door? It didn't matter. She had to try *something*. Lynette told her that meditation worked, and Charlie believed her. She believed her, because she loved her, and that was that.

She reached for the nearest door.

She placed her hand on it.

She pushed it open.

The school bell was still ringing. It wouldn't stop.

"Shut up!" screamed Lynette. She pulled at her own hair, tearing out two handfuls in trembling fists. "Shut up!"

She was going mad. There was no doubt about it. Uncle Harv — that vile, sadistic pervert — was right. This was hell. Her very own hell. Behind each door doubtlessly lurked some twisted evocation from her rotten existence, memories she had locked away or forced out of her head. She hadn't thought of her sick uncle in ten years, maybe more, but now his nocturnal visits came back to her with nauseating clarity. Susan had weaponized Lynette's one defense mechanism.

Her memories.

She looked from classroom door to classroom door. Should she try another one? She couldn't stay here, not when the boys from the alley roamed the corridors, switch-blades and cocks in hand.

No, there had to be a way out. She would keep searching. She would search forever if she had to.

Footsteps behind her. Lynette's body tensed. Were they here? Had the boys found her? She spun on the spot, ready to flee should the need arise, blood pumping through her veins so fast she feared she might explode.

It was a girl.

She walked quickly, her head down, books tucked in to her body. She wore a light blue sweater and tan slacks, her canvas shoes squeaking on the floor as she walked. As she approached Lynette, she kept her head down, letting her hair fall in front of her face.

"Charlie," whispered Lynette.

The girl didn't look at her. She quickened her pace, though between the strands of hair, Lynette could see the girl's cheeks flushing with nerves.

"Charlie, it's me," said Lynette.

"Leave me alone," said Charlie, perilously close to breaking out into a sprint. She passed by, and Lynette turned to watch her go.

And then it all came back to her.

Charlie. That outfit. Those tan pants. That was what Charlie had been wearing the day...

Lynette followed. Yup, she was right. Charlie's pants clung tightly to her ass. The fabric hugged every curve, fitting her like a second skin, her big ass bouncing with every hurried step. Lynette licked her lips. She couldn't help it. Everything was falling into place. The day she had told Charlie about, when she was late for class because she was following her and staring at her butt... this was it. She burst into tears of joy. She had done it. She had found one happy memory in Clinton High School, and that memory was Charlie's fat, beautiful, perfect ass. She watched each cheek rise and fall as Charlie walked, mesmerized by the movement. The pants were so tight, Lynette saw the lines of her panties, and, just like she had that day, she fantasized about what color of underwear Charlie was wearing. Pink... no, black. Maybe red.

She smiled. The smile blossomed into a grin. She shook her head and wiped away a tear.

"God bless your ass, Charlie," she said. "God bless your—"

Wait a minute. Wait one goddam, motherfucking hot minute.

With one eye firmly locked on Charlie's posterior, she partially abandoned the fantasy and—

—opened her other eye. "Holy shit," she said, as she gazed up at the ceiling of Clinton Memorial Hospital.

She had done it. She was free!

She was fucking free!

Lynette got to her feet, keeping her mind's eye on Charlie's ass, and her physical eyes on the hospital corridor. There was no time to waste.

Susan Ward had to die.

Charlie stepped out onto the roof of Clinton High School. She knew the door would lead her here. Had she ever felt happier than that night on the roof? That fleeting moment of joy, before her entire world had crumbled around her?

Susan was, naturally, there already. She stood, her palms resting on the edge of the building, staring out over the town. When she heard Charlie's footsteps, she turned and smiled. She looked so beautiful in her dress, the neckline plunging dangerously low.

"Hey," said Susan. "Why are you crying?"

Charlie hadn't realized she was. "I don't know. Guess I'm just happy, that's all. You look incredible."

It felt so real, like it was actually happening. She supposed, in a way, it was.

Susan did a little spin, teetering on her heels, and stumbled forwards into Charlie's arms. They embraced, and shared a tender kiss.

"God, I can't stand in heels for more than five minutes," laughed Susan. "I don't know how people do it."

Charlie ran her hands through Susan's hair, searching for flaws in the memory, for imperfections to pull her from the fantasy. She found none.

"Hey," said Susan, "don't mess up my hair!"

"Sorry," smiled Charlie. She stared at Susan. How could she reconcile the sweet, shy girl before her with the deranged psychopath who was killing indiscriminately back in the hospital? Back in real life?

"What's up?" said Susan. "You're looking at me funny."

Charlie's throat was all choked up. "I've... I've not seen you in so long."

"We *literally* just arrived at the dance together."

"I know. But it feels... longer."

Susan's hands found Charlie's waist. "Are you okay?"

Charlie nodded. "Yeah. Fine."

"Then why don't you kiss me like you mean it?"

Charlie did. Their lips touched, delicate at first, then with more passion.

...more... passsssiiiiooonnnn...

Charlie pulled back, momentarily leaving Susan kissing thin air, and for one moment, she was back in the busted elevator, the charred skeleton between her legs, its teeth grazing her most sensitive areas and sending waves of tortuous agony coursing through her.

No!

She couldn't lose control right now. She drifted back to the school roof, where Susan looked at her with hurt in her eyes.

"Why'd you pull away?" she said, and Charlie took the girl in her arms, kissing her with such fervor that even Susan seemed surprised. But only for a second. She leaned into the kiss, their bodies rubbing against each other, Susan's hands finding Charlie's ass, squeezing it through the satin.

"God, I love your butt," said Susan.

"I know," said Charlie.

You're not the only one.

She thought of Lynette, and wondered if she would ever see her again.

Then, as the girls held each other and gazed out towards the setting sun, a song started playing. Charlie turned to Susan, a shiver of anticipation dancing down her spine.

"That's our song," she whispered, as *If You Leave Me Now* filtered through the glass skylight.

"It sure is," said Susan. The sparkling reflections of the mirrorball played across her face, making her seem unreal, like an angel.

"May I have this dance?" asked Charlie, and Susan nodded.

"I'd like that," she said, and took Charlie's hand for the very last time.

25

————

EVERY FIBER OF LYNETTE'S BODY ACHED. SHE LOOKED DOWN at her bloodstained limbs. Susan had really done a number on her. She touched her face. It felt puffy and swollen. Dried blood was caked around her mouth and nose, and shallow cuts zigzagged her arms, but the damage could have been much worse. Susan could have killed her. So why hadn't she?

The snow that had coated the floor on level five was melting, turning to a slushy paste. The wind, too, that had wailed mournfully through the building, had stopped. Silence reigned. There were no tortured screams, no cries of horror. Somehow, the quiet was worse.

The scalpel Susan had used to inflict the damage on her body lay abandoned. Lynette picked it up. She tried to walk, almost collapsing when she did. Blood poured down her legs, her arms. There was a wide puddle of it on the floor, and she had to assume it was all hers. Leaning against the wall, she shuffled down the corridor, leaving a smeared red trail on the paintwork.

In her head, she pictured Charlie walking ahead of her, her ass cheeks barely contained by the thin fabric of her pants.

"Just in case," she said, and smiled, knowing that in a few moments, it would all be over.

Charlie and Susan clasped hands. Whenever they danced, Charlie always adopted the traditionally masculine position, and this time would be no different. She rested her hand on Susan's shoulder, letting Susan take her by waist, and as the song started, they began to turn, waltzing atop the roof, while below them, the summer ball continued, the revelers unaware of their presence, the way it should have been that balmy night all those months ago.

"Susan... you know I love you. And I always will."

"I know," said Susan innocently.

"You were my first love, and despite everything, I think I'll *always* love you."

They glided across the roof, Charlie guiding them, moving closer to the big glass skylight.

"Careful," said Susan, looking over her shoulder. "People might see us."

"Let them," said Charlie. "Let everyone see. I'm not ashamed. Are you?"

"Of course not."

They reached the skylight, dancing in front of it. Charlie dropped her hands to her sides.

"Kiss me," she said, and Susan did. As they kissed, Charlie looked down into the skylight behind Susan. Everyone stood still, staring up at the pair of them, some pointing, others with shocked or appalled expressions on their young faces. Mr. Quinn ran from the punch table, trying to force his way through the gawping onlookers to reach the stairs.

"I can't believe you came back to me," Susan said quietly. She sounded different. "She's still alive. That girl you like. I didn't kill her. I kept her alive for you."

Charlie pulled back. Susan didn't just sound different. She *looked* different. Her face was harder, crueler.

"Susan... is that you? The *real* you?"

Susan ignored the question. "I can use her body," she continued. "I've been practicing. I've had a lot of time to practice, just lying there, unable to sleep. But it's okay now. I'm back. And I can be anyone I want to be. Anyone *you* want me to be. I think, with a bit more practice, that I can stay inside forever. Maybe I can teach you how to do it? Wouldn't that be neat? You and me, staying young forever, going from body to body. We'd never have to grow old. *Never*. And if you want me to use *her* body for a while, then that's okay. It's quite a nice body. Though I think you could do better."

She spoke like everything was normal. Like she hadn't killed people. Dozens of people, perhaps hundreds.

"So what do you say? You'll have to be quick. She's bleeding out. I cut her up real bad, but I didn't kill her. She'll heal. I can go right now and become her, if you want." She kissed Charlie on the cheek, then the lips. "Then we can finish what we started... in her bedroom. It'll be nice. Oh, hey, what about if I was Lynda Carter? You might have to get her to come to Clinton, but I can do it. Imagine the faces of everyone in school if you turned up to prom with Wonder Woman!" She laughed at that. It wasn't a pretty laugh. "So whaddya say? You better hurry and decide."

"Susan, you can't—"

"You'd better hurry," she said, still smiling, "or else I'll rip that cunt to fucking shreds, and decide for you."

~

Lynette found Susan's room. It was easy to identify, as it was the only room in the hospital that still had power. The machines beeped steadily as Susan lay in bed, calm and lifeless, her covers tucked in around her as if everything was normal.

It was the first time Lynette had seen her in real life.

She looked so fragile. All the violence, all the death and horror, and somehow this frail young girl with the tube coming out her nose was the epicenter of it all.

Lynette stood a moment, thinking. What was the quickest way to kill her? The scalpel felt painfully insignificant in her hand. So small... but if she slit the girl's throat, surely that would be enough? Or maybe she should throw her body out the window? No, that might give Susan enough time to escape. Too big a risk.

Fucking decide already!

"Scalpel," she said. "The fucking scalpel."

The blade trembled in her hand. Her lips were dry, her throat parched. She felt weak from loss of blood.

Get it over with.

Resting one hand on the firm mattress, she moved the scalpel to Susan's throat, the tip of the blade pressing into the white flesh.

"Die, bitch," she said, and dragged the scalpel across Susan's jugular.

~

Blood erupted over Charlie's face.

One second she had been looking at Susan, trying to reason with her... and the next, Susan's throat had torn apart as if invisible, spectral hands had cleaved it wide open. Susan's hands shot up to her throat, blood gushing over her grasping fingers, spurting from her neck and spilling down her cleavage. She staggered backwards, eyes wide and staring and full of fury.

This is it, thought Charlie.

She lunged towards Susan and shoved her.

The bleeding girl fell backwards, landing against the skylight, blood fountaining from her arteries. The glass groaned, long, spiderweb cracks forming, splintering in different directions and heading for the edges.

Susan didn't dare move. The glass crackled like a frozen pond on the first day of spring.

"I did it all for *you,*" she said to Charlie, blood gurgling from between her lips. "I *love* you."

Charlie wept. What she had said earlier had been the truth. She would always love Susan, no matter what. She didn't want her to die... and certainly not like this. She could have forgiven her the killings of Greta and the others. Quite easily. But the bloodbath in the hospital... and the threats against Lynette...

She wiped the blood from her face.

"I love you too," she said.

Susan smiled, and something in her expression chilled Charlie to her marrow.

"See you later, Charlie-gator," said Susan, as the glass gave way and she plunged into the gym hall.

She was still smiling all the way down, until the last second, when the realization she was going to die finally seemed to set in. She let out one final blood-choked scream, before her head hit the gym floor and exploded like a close-range shotgun blast.

26

———

"It's been three months since the Clinton Memorial Hospital disaster that cost the lives of over two hundred civilians, and government officials have now concluded their investigation. A toxic gas leak from a faulty pipe in the basement is said to have been responsible for the mass outbreak of hysteria and violence that erupted one evening in the quiet town of Clinton. Officials, who initially blamed marijuana in the water supply, have announced that the area has now been deemed safe, and construction of a new hospital will began as planned this winter. We spoke to Mayor Greg—"

Charlie turned the TV off and lay back down in bed, pulling the covers up to her chin. "Toxic gas," she muttered. "My ass, it was."

Lynette stirred next to her. "What's that about your ass?" she asked, giving Charlie a playful swat on her rump. Charlie rolled over and faced her.

"Morning," she said, and kissed her girlfriend.

"Morning," said Lynette. She stretched, grimacing in pain as she did so.

"Feel any better today?"

"A little, maybe. I tried to sleep on my back, but I must've rolled over in the night. My nose hurts."

She spoke like she had a cold, her broken nose still giving her grief, though the doctors had done a fine job of setting it back into position. Her body was healing the way it should, though she would have the scars for the rest of her life. Some were more noticeable than others — her arms, especially, were covered in thin white lines that would never fully heal — but most could be hidden with judicious placement of clothing. Charlie didn't mind. She thought Lynette was still the most beautiful girl she'd ever seen, and since she had gotten out of hospital a month ago, the two had been inseparable, spending most days and nights together.

Charlie bit her lip and lowered her voice, even though her parents were both out. "So you don't feel up for..." she shrugged, "...a little fun?"

Lynette smiled shyly. "I don't think so. Believe me, I'm horny as sin... but give me a week, okay?"

"Okay," said Charlie. "But you know... if you're not well, you don't *have* to do anything."

Her palm rested against Lynette's thigh. The girl's long tee had ridden up during the night, and Charlie's hand slid up until it brushed Lynette's panties. Her fingertips slipped beneath the satin. Lynette moaned softly.

"You're bad," she smiled, as Charlie ducked under the covers and removed her girlfriend's underwear.

Afterwards, they lay in bed, holding each other.

To Charlie, the last few months felt like a nightmare from which she had recently awoken. The cops had spoken to her, of course, trying to piece together what had happened that night, like why had they found her in a broken elevator with three corpses, and why she was one of only two people who had been unaffected. She had played dumb, and told them she remembered nothing. A shrink had sat in on one of the sessions, and deduced that shock had wiped the events from her memory. After that, the cops were less interested in her.

She did remember, though. She remembered everything, even if she wished she could forget. They hadn't spoken about that night yet, her and Lynette, neither wanting to relive it. She supposed, in time, they would discuss it. When they were older, and probably very, very drunk.

"What are you thinking?" asked Lynette, purring contentedly after their lovemaking.

"I'm thinking I need a shower. Want to join me?"

"You go. I don't think my legs are ready to stand yet." She closed her eyes. "God, where did you learn to *do* that? That thing with your tongue?"

Charlie smiled and kissed her, then reluctantly slid out of bed. Naked, she walked to the bedroom door and took her silk robe from the hook. "Okay. Gonna take that shower. After that, I'll make us breakfast. Pancakes alright?"

"Mmmmmm," said Lynette, rolling onto her side and taking the thin duvet with her, revealing her bare ass, her thighs clamped together. "You were so... *good.*"

Pleased, if slightly embarrassed, Charlie shook her head and grinned. She licked her lips, tasting Lynette on them. "Glad to hear it. So, you want pancakes?"

"I heard you," groaned Lynette. "Pancakes would be good."

"Groovy." Charlie slipped into the silk robe. "Okay, I'm gonna hit the shower. I won't be long."

"Mmmmmm," said Lynette. *"See you later, Charlie-gator."*

Charlie froze. The blood seemed to drain from her face, her feet rooted to the spot. "What did you say?"

Silence followed. Too long a silence.

"I said, enjoy your shower. I'll be here when you get back."

Charlie gripped the door. "Yeah. Okay," she managed to say.

See you later, Charlie-gator.

It was a coincidence, that was all. It didn't mean anything.

See you later, Charlie-gator.

A coincidence.

Nothing more.

A coincidence. Like all the other coincidences since Lynette had gotten out of hospital.

Charlie left the room, wandering down the hallway to the bathroom. Inside, she closed the door. Then, she locked it.

See you later, Charlie-gator.

It meant nothing.

Nothing.

What did she think, that Susan had somehow... no, no way.

No fucking *way.*

It couldn't happen.

She had watched Susan die. She had watched her fall, all the way down, her face calm... until the last second.

Then her expression had changed.

"Bullshit," said Charlie. "That girl in there is Lynette. I know it is."

But she didn't know that. And as she stepped out of her robe and into the shower, Charlie started to cry, because she realized...

She might *never* know for sure.

CARL'S AFTERWORD

I used to be friends with this fella back in the seventies who would shit himself at parties. I'm not kidding, it happened on at least three occasions when I was present. But rather than blame the booze or the Herculean amounts of cocaine he would snort, he was adamant that an ex-girlfriend was exacting psychic revenge on him.

He claimed that she could take over his mind and force him to do things. He really seemed to believe it too. I was present during his unforgettable appearance in court over a DUI charge, when he first made the outlandish claim. Needless to say, the judge was unimpressed.

To most of us, it sounded like a feeble excuse for his erratic behavior. But remember, this was the 1970s, and the occult and supernatural were all the rage. I don't know what it was — we seemed to have more open minds back then, or maybe we were just naive and high as fuck. I mean, I've certainly had experiences I can't explain. So yeah, it's fair to say that while we treated Shitty Pants Joe — an unfortunate, but well-earned nickname — with a fair degree of skepticism, we never fully discounted the idea of full-blown psychic warfare.

Then one day I met the ex-girlfriend.

Me and Joe had taken some quaaludes and were drinking at a bar in Queens. It was always fun to spend time with Joe, because you were never quite sure if he was gonna shit himself or not, which added an element of high suspense to even the most mundane encounters.

Anyway, he was telling me something, I don't remember what, and halfway through, his eyes opened wide, and he just stopped. He stared at me, and I swear I've never seen a man look so frightened.

"She's coming," he said.

A few seconds later this chick walked in alone. She was dressed head-to-toe in black, with a net veil that made it look like she'd come straight from a funeral. She walked over, took a seat at the bar, and stared at us. At least, I think she was staring. Her head was pointed towards us, though the veil made it hard to see her eyes.

Shitty Pants Joe, meanwhile, was trembling. I had to take the glass outta his hand and place it safely on the table.

"She's watching me," he said. "She's trying to get inside my head."

Then the crazy motherfucker started singing. Now, let me paint a picture for you. We're in a dive bar in Queens, full of bikers, pimps, hookers, junkies — basically, the New York Greatest Hits. And in the middle of all this, Joe starts singing *My Favorite Things* from the goddam *Sound of Music*. He starts quiet, almost a whisper, but by the time he gets to the second verse, he's on his feet and belting it out.

Everyone stops what they're doing and looks at him. I see some bikers in the corner. They look pissed. Next thing I know, they're at our table. Fists started flying, someone took out a knife, and we hightailed it out of there, bruised and confused. Those motherfuckers chased us for several blocks until we lost them. I asked Joe what the hell he was playing at, and he told me that when he felt this psychic chick trying to get inside his head, he would think of his favorite things to keep her out. He told me that singing the song helped.

Joe was, of course, as crazy as a shithouse rat. He died years later in an automobile accident. His funeral was sparsely attended, but I was there to pay my respects. During the ceremony, I saw a woman dressed head-to-toe in black, her face covered by a dark veil. Same woman? Who knows. But I'll tell you something — I didn't ask. Heck, I didn't go near her. You never know, man. You never know.

Anyway, that's where I got the idea for Psychic Teenage Bloodbath. No one was interested in making the movie without major revisions, as the budget would be too high for the sort of producers I dealt with (crooks and perverts, mostly), so I'm glad the story is finally seeing the light of day now, and I hope you enjoyed reading it. I've always said that I think we need more stories where our main character is saved by the memory of a really great ass.

Anyway, until next time,

Your friend,

Uncle Carl

PSYCHIC TEENAGE
BLOODBATH II

For all the dogs

PART I

AFTER

1

———

"See you later, Charlie-gator."

Though ten years had passed since she last heard those dreaded words, they still rang in Charlie Bonner's ears like the eerie toll of a church bell at midnight. She glanced around at the assembled partygoers, searching for *her*.

Lynette.

There she was on the other side of the room, clutching a gin and tonic and watching intently. She brought the glass to her lips and looked away as if she hadn't been caught staring.

Ten years wasted.

For a full decade, Charlie had been held captive by this sad, twisted mockery of Lynette. She *knew* it was Susan inside, and that somehow, her insane psychic ex-girlfriend had swapped bodies a fraction of a second before dying. At first, it had been impossible to tell. She looked like Lynette, sounded like her, smelled like her... even *tasted* like her. But the cracks had begun to show. Just a little initially, like a chipped vase turned to face the wall to hide the imperfections from visitors. But Susan, for all her strenuous efforts, couldn't hold it together. How could she? The girl was a maniac, a psychotic killer with the blood of hundreds of people on her hands from the devastating hospital massacre of nineteen-seventy-eight.

Charlie shivered. The nightmare of that night still haunted her, and would forevermore.

Keen to avoid Susan's prying eyes, even if only for a minute, she shuffled away in search of the bathroom. Sometimes, in bed, she tortured herself by wondering about the extent of Susan's powers. Back then, she had brought an entire town to its knees. And now? If Susan wished to, could she destroy whole countries? The world?

"Looking for the bathroom?"

The words startled her. She turned to a petite, pretty woman with a peroxide perm. The woman smiled at her. "I'm afraid this is the line."

"Shit."

"Yeah, I think that's what he's doing. Some guy's been in there for about ten minutes, so I figure he's either shitting or jerking off."

The woman banged her fist off the door.

"Hey, weird guy? Hurry up in there. I've had six vodkas, and I don't wanna pee myself before the bells."

Charlie grinned, momentarily forgetting about Susan. "I guess that wouldn't be a great start to the new year."

"Yeah, that's *not* how I want to enter the nineties." She offered her hand. "Say, I'm Marlene."

Charlie took her hand and gave her name. "Pleased to meet you. You friends with Nick?"

She figured the woman would be. Nick was friends with *everyone*. It was his party they were at, along with half the city, it seemed. Charlie had worked with Nick for a couple of years in the mid-eighties, back when Susan had allowed her to get a job. Those days were ancient history, of course. Now, Susan only let her out by herself to buy groceries and clothes with her meagre allowance. Other than that, she was confined to the apartment they shared in lower Manhattan, bought outright with Susan's inexhaustible supply of money. Once a year, however, Charlie was permitted to attend Nick's new year party. It was a way of keeping up appearances, so that the few acquaintances she had made during her brief career wouldn't grow suspicious of her absence.

She looked over her shoulder. No sign of Susan. She sighed deeply, savoring the freedom.

"Yeah, I know Nick," the woman was saying. "Dated him once. Nice guy. But then, who hasn't... hey, you okay?"

"Huh?" Charlie blinked and felt a solitary tear trickle down her cheek. "Oh, yeah, sorry. Something in my eye."

The woman nodded. "Yeah, okay." She pounded on the bathroom door again, shouted, "Hey, bozo! Shit or get off the pot!" and then smiled at Charlie. "Listen, if you wanna talk..."

"No," said Charlie, cutting her off. "I'm just happy to be here."

The woman furrowed her brow. "You don't get out much, do you?"

Charlie dropped her gaze.

If only you knew, she thought, struggling to conjure a reply. She conversed so rarely these days, it was like she had forgotten how. Sensing the awkwardness, the woman turned away.

"I'm sorry," said Charlie, reverting to her default apologetic behavior. "You're right, I don't get out much."

The woman brightened. "Work, huh?"

"Yeah. Work."

"What do you do?"

Oh god, enough with the questions!

"I... I sell... stuff."

"Stuff, huh? What kinda stuff?"

Charlie turned to the mingling bodies for inspiration, her eyes settling on a dude in a baseball cap. "Hats," she said, hoping that would satisfy the inquisitive woman. "I sell hats."

"Oh yeah? What's your best—"

The woman abruptly stopped speaking, as if the words had dried up on her tongue. A look of surprise and confusion dawned on her pretty face.

"You alright?"

"No," Marlene whimpered, her hand dropping to between her legs. "I think I..."

Charlie looked down at the dark patch on the crotch of the woman's corduroy pants. It spread across her thighs.

"Oh my god," said the woman, panic creeping into her voice. "It... it just *happened*. I... what am I gonna do?"

But Charlie wasn't listening. She looked away from the woman, scanning the sea of oblivious faces, and finding—

Susan.

The maniac stared at her through Lynette's blue eyes, her lips pursed. The gin and tonic glass had cracked in her hand and lay in pieces by her feet. One shard of glass remained in her palm, oozing thick blood.

No, mouthed Charlie with a shake of her head. But it wasn't a command, or even a suggestion. She was begging. It was the only language Susan understood.

She thinks I'm flirting, thought Charlie, and with that came the realization that the Marlene's life was in serious danger. She had to get away, had to show Susan it was an innocent conversation between two people waiting in line for the bathroom. Nothing illicit.

Nothing worth killing over.

Hating herself for doing so, she abandoned the woman, but Marlene wouldn't let her leave. She grabbed Charlie's arm, her fingernails digging into the flesh.

"Please," said Marlene. She was crying now, her pants drenched in urine. "You can't leave me like this. People will see... they'll *laugh* at me."

"Let me go," snapped Charlie, trying to shake her arm free. But Marlene refused to release her.

"You can't go!" she said, desperation in her voice, unaware that if Charlie *didn't* leave her, Susan's apocalyptic jealousy would bubble fully to the surface. And if it did? Well, Charlie knew what would happen.

It wouldn't be the first time.

"I'm sorry," said Charlie, fighting back her own tears. "I can't stay." She walked away, breaking free of Marlene's grasp, and when the woman tried to prevent her leaving, Charlie shoved her.

The woman staggered backwards, slipping in a puddle of her own piss and crashing to the floor. As she had feared, everyone at the party turned and looked at her. "No!" cried Marlene, and Charlie started to cry as she walked steadily towards Susan, trying not to draw attention to herself. It wouldn't have mattered. All eyes were on the drunk woman who had pissed herself and then fallen over. Some laughed, others grimaced in second-hand embarrassment.

But at least she was alive.

"Enjoying yourself?" Susan asked in a grotesque imitation of Lynette's sweet voice. God, that was the worst part of the whole sick charade; Charlie had grown to detest Lynette. Her face, her voice, her body... all of it.

"Susan, don't," said Charlie. "We were just talking."

"I'm not Susan, you dumb fucking *cunt*," she snarled through gritted teeth. "Susan's dead. How many times do I have to fucking tell you?"

Charlie swallowed. "I... I know. And I'm sorry. But please... let that woman go. Don't... don't *hurt* her."

Susan looked at the palm of her hand, where the large piece of glass was still embedded in her skin. She plucked it free, a jet of blood spurting from the open wound, and discarded the broken piece.

"Would you prefer I hurt *you?*" asked Susan, without looking at her.

"Yes. Yes, I *would*. Please, stop—"

Susan inspected her palm, watching as the blood slowed to a trickle. "I was planning on hurting you later, anyway." She turned, locking eyes with Charlie, her demeanour changing, hardening. "Is *this* how you show gratitude? I let you out to your party, and you say thank you by eyeball-fucking some bleach-blonde slut?"

"No, no, I wasn't, I promise. We were just waiting—"

"What was your plan, huh? To finger-bang her in the bathroom?"

Sweat formed on Charlie's neck. "I swear, nothing happened. I *swear*. I wouldn't do that to you. I love you," she lied. "You *know* I love you."

"You wanna see if her cunt is bleached too, is that it? *Yeah?* Because we can find out, Charlie. We can find out very fucking easily indeed, you fucking ungrateful, sniveling piece of fucking *shit*."

"Don't, Su— I mean, don't, Lynette. Let's go home, me

and you. We can bring in the New Year together, and I can wear that little—"

Without raising a hand, Susan slapped her. The invisible blow rocked Charlie's head to the side, stealing the words from her mouth, almost knocking her off her feet.

"Hush, sweet Charlotte," said Susan. "*You* wanted this, not me." She looked at Charlie with sheer contempt, eyes blazing in maddening fury. "*You* wanted to come to the party. *You* wanted to have a drink. And *you* wanted to cheat on me." Her expression softened into something resembling sadness. "After all I've done for you." She shook her head. "I'm disappointed. And you know what happens when I'm disappointed, don't you?"

The woman by the bathroom had gotten unsteadily to her feet, and now stood in a puppet-like manner hauntingly familiar to Charlie.

Susan was in control.

Marlene tugged her pants down.

"Please," urged Charlie, the slap still singing her cheek. "Don't do it."

"But don't you want to see her pretty pink cunt?" asked Susan.

The shamed woman was tearing her clothes off. A dark-haired lady covered Marlene's nakedness with a coat, but she pushed her away, stumbling as she tried to peel off her sodden panties.

"Nope," said Susan simply. "Not a natural blonde."

"I'll do *anything*," said Charlie. "Anything you want. Just stop, and come home with me."

Stark naked, Marlene wandered through the crowd, her face expressionless. But it was the eyes that were the give-away. They always were. Charlie saw the horror and panic deep within them.

"Do you think she can fly?" Susan asked casually.

"No," sobbed Charlie. She dropped to her knees, hugging Susan's ankles, kissing her feet the way Susan liked it when she was on a power trip. "Please... I'm begging you. I'm *begging* you."

"Too late," said Susan. "You really need to consider your actions. Don't you see? This is why I can't let you out by yourself. Because I can't *trust* you."

Charlie looked up in time to see the naked girl walk past her through the hooting and cheering crowd, her cute, dimpled ass jiggling with each step. She was heading for the glass door to the balcony.

"No, no, you *can* trust me," urged Charlie. "You can, I swear. I'll be good. I'll be *so* good, you'll see. You'll never have to worry again, I promise."

Marlene stepped through the doorway.

"Someone get that bitch a blanket," a man laughed.

"She's gonna freeze her bare ass off out there!" shouted another.

Charlie couldn't watch. She knew what Susan was capable of. If she wanted the woman dead, then she would kill her. For her, it was as easy as blinking.

"You know, Charlie. I wish I could believe you," said Susan.

"You can! You can!" She was shouting now, unafraid to be heard, though the whooping crowd drowned her out. A flash from a Polaroid lit up the room, and then the girl was outside.

"Hey, maybe we should stop her?" someone asked.

The balcony door slammed shut, creating an impassible barricade between Marlene and the rest of the guests.

Susan looked down at Charlie. "No more parties?"

"No more parties," sobbed Charlie.

"And you'll stay home with me, keep me company?"

What the hell have I been doing the last decade, Charlie wanted to shout, biting her tongue instead. "I'll stay home with you. I'll do whatever you want."

"Forever?"

The girl had climbed onto the barrier, fifteen storeys above the street, as the partygoers hammered on the glass door, trying and failing to open it. She wobbled precariously in the breeze and held one foot out over the vast drop.

"Forever," said Charlie, gazing at Susan with unconcealed hatred.

Susan stroked a hand through her hair. "Good girl," she cooed, caressing Charlie's head. *"Good... girl."*

The hallway was empty as Susan retrieved their winter coats. Marlene was safely inside now. Charlie watched a couple of younger girls wrap a towel around her and usher the shaking woman into a quiet room.

"I couldn't help myself," she was saying to them. *"I wasn't in control."*

The girls nodded sympathetically and closed the door behind them, probably assuming Marlene was on drugs. Billy Joel blasted over the stereo sound system as the party resumed.

"Come on, Charlie," said Susan kindly. "Let's go home."

She took Charlie's hand Tend led her to the elevator.

That was it, then. No more annual parties. She wondered if Susan would even let her leave the house for shopping. Her crazed jealousy knew no bounds, and it was only getting worse. But at least this time, the woman was safe.

She was *alive.*

They didn't speak during the elevator ride. There was nothing to say. Charlie had to accept her fate; she was Susan's plaything now. It was official; her life was over. One time, she had tried to kill herself, but Susan had stopped her. The punishment had been so severe, so twisted and agonizing, that she had hadn't tried again, though she dreamed and fantasized about it, praying for an end to the unremitting misery of her useless existence as the sex-toy of a deranged killer who wore the face of the woman she had loved, once, many years ago.

But even that felt like a dream now, and with each passing day, the memory of those brief, happy moments with Lynette faded further into obscurity. Or maybe they had always been a dream?

"I'm glad we came to an agreement," said Susan, as they reached the car. "I think you'll be happier staying home. The outside world, Charlie... it's a bad place. A terrible place. Your soul is too innocent, too pure. You belong with me."

Charlie opened the passenger door and got in. "You're right," she said, horrified to find herself questioning whether it was true or not.

"I know, silly. I'm *always* right." Susan smiled and squeezed Charlie's knee through her dress. "Haven't you learned that by now?"

Charlie fought not to flinch from Susan's touch.

Get home, lie still while she fucks you, and go to sleep. Perhaps tomorrow will be better?

Susan started the car. Flakes of snow fell onto the windshield, turning to liquid on contact and dribbling down the glass.

"Did you have a good time?" asked Susan, letting the engine idle.

Charlie looked at her. What the hell did she want? "Yeah," she said, her voice hoarse from shouting.

"You don't *sound* like you did."

Come on, you can do it. Put on the old act.

"I did, Lynette. I really did. I had a lovely time with you. Thank you," — she choked back a sob — "for taking me out tonight."

"And you learned a valuable lesson, didn't you?"

Charlie nodded. "Yes, I did."

Susan smiled. It was such an uncharacteristically warm, genuine smile, that it reminded Charlie of the real Lynette.

"Good," said Susan. "Now, it's almost New Year. Let's start off on the right foot, shall we?" She leaned forwards, and Charlie did the same, and they shared a kiss that made Charlie feel sick to her stomach, as, high above them, fireworks erupted in the sky, signaling the beginning of a new decade of misery and torment. "Look," said Susan, pointing through the windshield at the colorful explosions. "Aren't they—"

Smack.

Marlene's nude body crashed to the concrete in front of the car. She landed feet-first, her ankles and knees snapping violently, bones splintering and tearing through flesh like a blade through soft dough. The lower half of her body was obliterated on impact, while the upper half slumped to the ground as blood gushed from the myriad wounds, forming a widening puddle around her.

Susan turned to Charlie and grinned.

"Whoops!" she said, and started to laugh.

PSYCHIC TEENAGE BLOODBATH II

2

———

THEY DROVE IN NEAR-SILENCE, THE PEACE SHATTERED ONLY BY Susan's occasional hiccuping giggles, while Charlie experienced one of her frequent panic attacks. Her throat was tight, chest constricted, and black vignettes closed in around her vision. She raised her dress, enough to scratch repeatedly at her exposed thighs, leaving them raw, the skin broken. Words and thoughts didn't come easily to her. She kept seeing the woman, *still alive,* rolling back and forth in her own blood, wailing like an animal caught in a trap. They had left her there, left her to *die.* And why? Because she had dared to speak to Charlie in the line to the bathroom?

It was obscene. Susan had murdered her.

Susan, the girl who — once upon a time, in a different life — she had loved with all her heart, and who had loved her back. She had *waited* for Susan to wake from her coma, waited for a full year of heartbreak and loneliness. And when Lynette had appeared, she hadn't planned on falling for the girl. It just... happened. But was moving on so *wrong?* Was it so evil, so cruel? Did she deserve to be physically and psychologically tortured for the rest of her life for daring to *love?*

"You're quiet." Susan's words were fingers around Charlie's pale throat. "And stop scratching your leg, you know I hate that. You have such attractive legs."

"Sorry," muttered Charlie, lowering her dress to cover the marks.

"I didn't say put your dress down. I want to see you. Pull it back up."

Charlie did.

"Higher," said Susan. "Are you wearing those panties I bought you?"

Charlie raised the dress to her waist, revealing the see-through panties Susan had instructed her to wear.

Susan peered at her crotch. "I like them." She removed one hand from the steering wheel and ran her fingers over the smooth, translucent material. More than anything, Charlie wanted to recoil from Susan's touch. But she knew from cold, hard experience that to resist Susan was to anger her, and right now, Susan was calm. Reasonable. Perhaps now was a good time to talk to her?

"L-Lynette?"

"Yes, lover?"

"You didn't... y'know, you didn't have to do it."

"What, buy you the panties?" Susan smiled. "It's my pleasure. You know I like you looking sexy for me, baby."

That was certainly true. Susan only allowed Charlie to wear expensive — and extremely uncomfortable — lingerie, in case the whim took her and she wanted a fuck. The penalty for disobeying — for wearing a pair of stretchy cotton granny panties — was extreme, often the death of a random pedestrian.

"No, I don't mean that. I meant the woman."

"What woman?"

Charlie swallowed loudly. "The woman you killed."

Susan momentarily stopped stroking Charlie's crotch, then resumed. "I didn't—"

"I know you did. We both know it. And *Susan*... it has to stop."

Silence reigned, the atmosphere in the vehicle as frosty as the snowy streets outside.

"My *name* is Lynette."

"Susan, please. You can't keep killing. I was just talking to her. We weren't doing any—"

"*How fucking dare you!*" roared Susan. Her nails dug into Charlie's crotch, shredding the thin material of the panties. "I do everything for you! I've given you a home! I've fed you, I've clothed you, I've fucked you! And this is the thanks I get? *This* is the thanks?" Susan stared at her, one hand gripping the wheel, the other scratching between Charlie's legs.

"Keep your eyes on the road," whispered Charlie, suddenly afraid.

"Don't tell me what to do! You don't get to tell me what to do! I crawled out of hell for you, you nasty little whore! I crawled out of hell, and forced my way back from the fucking *dead,* just for you... and this is how you repay me? I lay there, staring at that ceiling and listening to you, unable to move. Do you know what that *does* to a person? *Do you know how that fucking feels?*"

The car sped up, Susan's foot a brick on the pedal.

"No, I don't," said Charlie. Tremors wracked her body. "Come on, slow down."

They raced through the streets, running a red light, a passing vehicle honking at them. Susan didn't notice.

"I did all that for you!" she continued, screaming in fury.

"All that... and not once did you stop to say *thank you*. Not once!"

A pressure built in Charlie's head, more intense than her usual stress-induced migraines, as if a medieval torture device was clamped over her skull and being slowly tightened.

"Susan... you're hurting me."

"You're lucky I love you. Because if I didn't, you'd be dead by now. You'd be dead. Dead, dead, dead, dead, *dead.*"

Liquid poured from Charlie's nose. Blood.

They rocketed through another set of lights, a couple of New Year revellers leaping out of the way. One of them, an older man, wasn't fast enough. The car struck him. Charlie heard him thump onto the roof, and then he was gone, far behind them, his broken body rattling across the road as the car picked up speed, the dial nudging sixty.

Tears fell from Charlie's eyes as she squeezed them shut to combat the awful pain in her head. She knew she should stop antagonizing Susan, but a thought crept insidiously into the back of her mind.

Was Susan finally going to kill her?

God, it would be a relief. She had no life left to lose, not anymore. Charlie welcomed death with open arms. She would embrace it, she would kiss it. Hell, she would fuck death's brains out if it meant she was free from this prison. When she was younger, and bullied relentlessly for her sexual orientation, she had thought of suicide as an easy way out, a coward's option. Now, she felt differently.

She knew death was her only escape.

"You know, Susan," she groaned, blood flooding down her chin. "You're a real bitch."

Susan's voice dropped to a cruel whisper. "What did you say?"

Charlie tasted blood, and licked it from her lips. "I said, *I hate you*. I've hated you for so long, I've forgotten what it felt like to love you. Hell, I've forgotten how it felt to even *like* you."

"Don't you fucking speak to me like that," snarled Susan.

"I hate you! I hate you so much!"

Unbuckling her seat belt, Charlie leaned towards Susan and punched her. It wasn't a hard punch — her strength drained from her as her head continued to throb — but it felt good. So, so good. She did it again, and then Susan turned to her with bloodshot, manic eyes. Charlie flew back against the passenger door, the back of her skull smashing the window. She felt the cool night air against her face, ruffling her hair, the tops of the buildings racing by in a frenzied blur, and then Susan's hands were around her throat, throttling the life from her.

As Charlie's vision blurred, she managed to look to her right. They were approaching a T junction, an apartment block dead ahead. Time slowed as they neared.

This is it, thought Charlie. If there was any justice in the world, they would both die.

Susan loosened her grip.

"What are you smiling at?" she asked. "Is something—"

The car hit the brick wall at close to one hundred miles per hour.

The impact was devastating, the front crumpling against the wall, both women shooting forwards. Susan hurtled through the windshield, while over the roar of metal grinding against stone, Charlie heard her ribs snapping. She felt no pain, not even when the sharp edge of the window frame cleaved into her neck and warm blood erupted across her lap.

~

Seconds passed like days.

As Charlie's life ebbed away, she glanced with one eye — the other hung down her cheek, knocked loose by the force of the blow — at Susan.

She was still alive.

Susan's breaths came in thick rasps, her lungs punctured. The crash had sent her through the windshield, and she lay sprawled across it, her face ragged and bloody from the glass that pierced it in multiple places, her party dress torn and shredded. The top of her head was flat, like Frankenstein's monster, from where she had collided with the wall.

Yet still she breathed.

Die, thought Charlie. *You have to die.*

Then the fine cords of stretched skin and veins that attached Charlie's head to her neck snapped. Somehow, she was painfully aware of her own severed head tumbling from the car window and bouncing on the frozen ground, before her eyes closed for the last time and all was quiet once more.

PART II

AFTERLIFE

3
___

When Charlie awoke, she was alone in the car.

Afraid to move, she lay a while, waiting for the pain to tear through her body. But the pain never came, and so she pushed herself away from the dashboard and settled into the passenger seat.

She felt fine. Absolutely one hundred percent A-OK. She touched her head, surprised to find it still attached to her neck. Oh, she *remembered* the trauma, and the memory of the searing-hot agony lingered like a tumor... but not the actual, physical pain itself. Reaching for the rearview mirror, she angled it towards herself.

"Oh god," she said.

A girl stared back at her in the reflection. A girl she hadn't seen in a good ten years. It was herself, aged eighteen, fresh faced save for a hint of acne on her forehead. Her hair was its original color, the way it had been before Susan made her dye it when the first streaks of gray had appeared.

"This isn't real," she whispered. "I'm dreaming."

If she was, it sure as hell didn't feel like a dream. She

stared at the mirror and pressed at the tight skin on her face. God, she looked good. The bags under her eyes had gone. Without checking to see if anyone was watching, she tugged her dress down and inspected her breasts. No scars, no bruises. Not like there usually were.

She cried. Sitting by herself, with a soft wind moaning through the city streets, Charlie Bonner cried for a long, long time.

She was dead. It was the only explanation. There was simply no way she could have survived the accident — her fucking *head* had come off — and certainly not emerge from it as a teenager. The idea didn't frighten her, the way it would some people, because she, unlike most of the population, was aware there was more to this world. She had glimpsed the other side before, during her meditation with Lynette in the park. Another dimension, a dream state... whatever it was, Lynette had harassed the power to control it, something she had tried — and failed — to teach Charlie to do.

So yeah, Charlie wasn't surprised there was an afterlife. She was just amazed it looked so... dreary.

The car door wouldn't open, so she knocked away the loose glass and climbed out the window. The New York skyscrapers loomed above her, flakes of snow swirling through the air. There was no sign of Susan... no sign of anyone. Shit, was *this* what she had to look forward to? An eternity of solitude, doomed to walk the streets alone?

Charlie smiled.

After a decade of being abused by Susan, that didn't sound so bad. In fact, it sounded kinda great.

Then came a noise. A low growl, animalistic and feral.

"What the hell is that?" she whispered, searching for the

source. The streets were deserted, soundless, except for the vague suggestion of a quietly sung melody from far away.

Footsteps, to her left.

No, not footsteps.

Paws.

Another snarl.

The steps grew louder, faster. With no weapon and nowhere to hide, Charlie backed away. She crouched and snatched up a shard of glass. One corner pricked her thumb, an unfortunate moment to receive confirmation that even here, in the Great Beyond, she still felt pain.

The growl again. Closer, and from behind this time. Whatever it was, it was circling her.

Gripping the glass, Charlie turned, and there, right in front of her, was a squat English bulldog striding on muscular legs, a gold disc dangling from the pink collar around its thick neck. Its lips were drawn back, teeth bared.

"Oh my god," whispered Charlie.

The dog looked up at her, its eyes widening.

Charlie let the glass fall from her hand and dropped to a crouch. "Princess? Is that you?"

The dog tilted its head at the mention of the name. Then its mouth widened into a slobbering grin, and the dog bounded towards her. It leaped into Charlie's arms, knocking her onto her back, smothering her face with licks.

"Princess!" cried Charlie.

She wrapped her arms around the beast, hugging him, holding him tight. Tears flooded her eyes, and the dog paused licking long enough to bark excitedly, before resuming his sloppy greeting. Charlie held her beloved family pet and wept as she recalled the last time she had stroked his fur back in nineteen-seventy-four. She had been thirteen or fourteen when Princess — *Princess Elizabeth Cupcake,* to use her full title — had gone to the vet and never returned. Her mom said he had 'crossed the rainbow bridge' and was in a better place with all the other dogs, playing for eternity, and though Charlie had hoped he was happy, she missed him terribly. Her weeks of crying in the aftermath of his passing were why they had never gotten another pet.

She had begged Susan to let her get one, but the girl inevitably refused. Charlie thought she understood why. She had seen Susan around dogs, and they *loathed* her. It was as if they knew something was wrong with her mind. More importantly, Susan had no power over the animal kingdom. She couldn't control them the way she did humans.

And for Susan, control was *everything.*

Princess continued to smother her with doggy kisses. The sight of him made Charlie think of her parents. They were dead now, and had been for years. Susan hadn't allowed her to attend either funeral. In fact, she hadn't visited in the two years leading up to their deaths, and often tortured herself with the idea that her absence had contributed to their declining health.

Tired, Princess rested his chin on Charlie's chest.

"I've missed you so much," she said, her face wet from a mixture of tears and bulldog saliva. "What are you doing here?" The dog didn't reply. "Did you come to meet me?" asked Charlie. "Are you my guardian angel?" She smooshed his face and adopted a silly baby voice. "Are you my little gardy-wardy-en angel?"

It was the happiest Charlie had felt in a long time. The sensation felt unfamiliar to her, almost alien.

"Ding, dong, the witch is dead," she whispered, as she got to her feet. Princess stood with her, and together they gazed down the deserted streets. "Which way to go?" When the dog failed to make a decision, she started forwards. "How about this way?"

Princess padded alongside her. A minor tremor rippled beneath them, the ground shaking, and then it was gone.

"You feel that?"

Princess looked ahead and grumbled. Then, he farted.

Charlie raised her eyebrows. "Same old Princess," she said.

They wandered the streets, past empty stores and over-flowing trash cans, abandoned cars and quiet apartment blocks. After a while, Charlie noticed the curious melodic sound she had heard earlier. At first, she believed it was the whisper of the wind, but the further they walked, the more it sounded human. A distant song, hummed softly.

She followed it. Maybe someone else was around? If Princess was here, then perhaps her parents would be too? Or even—

No, she wouldn't get her hopes up. Banishing the thought, she kept walking, until she caught movement in her periphery. When she turned, there was nobody. It reminded her of the silent stress migraines she used to experience, when strange, transparent dots would float across her vision until she tried to focus on them.

Only when she stopped and examined her surroundings did Charlie understand. The movement did not belong to humans... it was the *buildings*. The change was gradual at first; vague swirling patterns on the walls that vanished when stared at. But soon the walls themselves were moving, the bricks reconfiguring themselves, changing the shape and structure of the surrounding blocks.

"You see that?" she asked Princess, and he snorted in response.

One apartment block had shrunk to half its size, the brickwork swallowing itself and shifting restlessly, as if the buildings themselves couldn't decide how they wanted to look, and kept trying on new styles.

Fascinated, Charlie watched for a while, then continued in what she thought was the direction of the music, which came and went in quiet waves. Ahead, she made out a strange, dazzlingly white building. It hadn't been there moments before, but the bricks from the surrounding edifices now flowed overhead in spirals towards the mysterious windowless structure, constructing it as she neared. By the time she was close enough to get a good look, it was taller than any building she had seen before, rising until it obscured the moon, casting the street in deep black shadows.

Charlie approached, looking to Princess for comfort. The dog was unconcerned, panting in his usual manner, tongue lolling out of his mouth like the village idiot. A glance back confirmed that the buildings she passed earlier had given their lives in the making of this giant, featureless brick behemoth. Where she had walked before was now a desolate wasteland. If she squinted, she could still see the crashed car, though it no longer rested against a wall.

Another light quake rumbled beneath their feet as Charlie stood in front of the ominous black doorway. What lay beyond? Heaven? Hell? Or nothing but a great void, an endless sleep?

"Well," Charlie mused out loud for the benefit of Princess, "If it *is* hell, it can't be any worse than the last fucking decade."

And with that, she and her faithful companion stepped inside.

A door — which seconds earlier hadn't existed — slammed shut behind them.

Charlie nodded to herself. "Okay," she said. "No backing out now."

And with that, she took her first bold step into the unknown.

4

———

THE DARKNESS EXPLODED INTO DAZZLING LIGHT, SO BRIGHT that Charlie shielded her eyes to protect her scorched retinas. She stood, eyelids clamped shut, and waited. The smell hit her first. A nostalgic scent of freshly mown lawn, and the sizzle of meat over an open fire. Faint voices and laughter resounded from nearby, and when she dared to look, she found herself...

...in a bedroom. She glanced around, taking in the view, and stumbled backwards onto the bed in shock. That the bed was behind her came as no surprise, for she knew the room well. She had grown up here, after all, spending a good portion of the first eight years of her life in her childhood bedroom.

It was unchanged.

The violet bedsheets, the dresser with the reading lamp. Goober, her beloved teddy bear, lay across the pillow to keep it warm, the way he always did. Princess snuffled around the room, giving every square inch a damn good sniff.

"Oh my god," breathed Charlie.

There was her little desk, a sheet of paper on top with a crudely scribbled drawing of her house in reds and greens and yellows. She flopped down on the bed, and Princess joined her, cuddling in close as she stared at the single crack on the ceiling. That crack, more than anything, proved she was home. It had always been there, comforting in its familiarity. She looked at the framed pictures on the wall, at—

"Huh," she said, sitting up and squinting.

Her Monkees photo — that her dad had brought her from a visit to LA — was upside down. It was the only one. The family portrait was correct, as was the photo of the horse they had met in a field. Only The Monkees, Davy and Mickey and Michael and Peter, hung the wrong way. Sun shone through the open window, and she left the bed, forgetting about the photo. Princess hopped down after her, and Charlie peered out the window, her heart hammering in her chest. There they were.

Her parents.

She watched them from afar, gripping the window frame. They looked so *young*, her dad cleanly shaven, her mom resplendent in golden curls and a red and white striped bathing suit. Charlie's nails dug into the wood. Could it be real? Was this a mirage? Was this...

No, she didn't believe in that place. Not the way it was spoken about in church, anyway. And yet—

"Oh," she said, her eyes brimming with tears as a young girl capered towards her parents in a blue bathing suit. She ran with the carefree attitude of the innocent, hair streaming behind her, gangly prepubescent legs pumping madly, as if the devil were on her tail. The girl threw her arms around her mom's waist, and Charlie swallowed hard.

It was *her*.

Young Charlie ran from her mom and jumped into a

paddling pool. Her feet slid out from under her and she landed on her butt with a splash, her parents chuckling at the casual misfortune.

Charlie turned from the window, heading for the door, almost tripping over Princess as she did so. She reached for the handle and hurtled down the stairs, Princess in hot pursuit. The smell of childhood summers filled the air, cloying and sweet, and when she burst through the back door she emerged in the backyard. Her parents stood by the grill, hamburger fat sizzling onto the coals and spitting sparks.

"Mom!" she called out. "Dad!"

They ignored her, lost in their idle small-talk. Her dad flipped a burger, and she walked closer on legs that trembled beneath her.

"Mom?"

They couldn't hear her. She tugged on her dad's sleeve, gingerly touched her fingers to her mom's arm.

"...I was thinking," her mom was saying, "that maybe we should move."

"I thought you liked this place?" her dad replied distractedly.

The woman looked over at Young Charlie playing in the pool. "I do. But it would be good for Charlotte. There're no other kids around here. It'd be nice for her to make some new friends."

"Or *any* friends."

Her mom sighed. "I know. She just seems so happy being by herself."

"*Mom!*" screamed Charlie. "Can't you see me?"

The ground shook beneath her. No one but her and Princess noticed. The dog growled, while overhead, a blanket of heavy thunder rumbled across the sky.

Charlie wept as her parents went about their business, clueless as to her presence. "Come on, mom," she cried, then looked at her father. "Dad? I'm right here!"

Her father turned towards her, and for a second, Charlie thought he had heard her. Then he peered beyond her, his face crumpling into confusion. "Jenny," he said. "What the fuck happened to our house?"

"Language, please. Charlotte's right over—"

Then she saw it too. Her jaw dropped a little, their comical expressions of surprise straight out of a Saturday morning cartoon. Charlie wiped the tears from her eyes and followed their gaze.

"Fuck," she said.

The house was not as she remembered. It was, however, *exactly* as it looked on the drawing on her desk upstairs. The sides of the building were wobbly red lines like a crayon scrawled onto thin air, while yellow scribbles filled in most of the blank space, the front yard and street visible through the many gaps. The back door and windows were colored green in crooked, childlike approximations of squares and rectangles.

"Has it always looked like that?" her father asked.

Her mom waited a moment before saying, "I guess it must have."

"Then maybe it *is* time to move."

A splotch of yellow appeared on the wall, as if a great invisible teardrop had landed on the page.

"Mama!"

Charlie recognized the voice as her own. She turned to the paddling pool, a pit opening in her stomach as she saw her younger self splashing in the shallow water, except it wasn't water, it was thick, viscous blood that coated her body, that plastered her hair to her face. In hung in sticky globs from her fingers, oozing down her shoulders and arms.

"Look, mama. The water's gone red!"

Charlie heard her parents scream, and as they raced towards the inflatable pool, their bodies collided with her and knocked her to the ground. She scrambled to her feet and ran for the bizarre, hand-drawn green door of her house.

It opened, and, instinctively, she closed her eyes, witnessing the flare of brilliant light behind her eyelids. This time, she smelled a different type of grass. Loud music assailed her ears, dozens of raised voices competing with the strange sounds. She opened her eyes and bit back a scream.

People, everywhere. The lights were low, and bodies swept past each other like an alcoholic ballet, women carrying drinks, men in absurdly baggy pants leaning on tables and smoking, no one paying her any attention. She was thankful for that small mercy, at least. It was a party, but she knew no one, recognized nothing. Princess howled at the noise, and she bent to pick him up. His stocky frame was heavy, but she cradled the frightened animal, enjoying the warmth of his hairy body.

An older woman with a terrible haircut staggered towards her holding a large glass of red wine, and bumped into her, releasing the contents of the wine glass over Princess and Charlie's dress. The dark stain looked like blood on the bulldog's smooth fur.

"Oh my god," said the woman, "I'm so sorry."

But Charlie was already backing away. She didn't like it here. In fact, she *hated* it.

"Please," the woman called after her, producing a handkerchief. "Let me clean that up for you!"

The room — and the people inside it — glitched like a

blast of television static, vibrating Charlie's insides. She screamed at the foul sensation, shoving through the crowd, ignoring the angry remarks hurled at her by disgruntled partygoers. Where was the exit?

Princess squirmed in her arms, and she brought him down to the ground. If anyone could find a way out, it was him.

"Go pee," she whispered sharply, two words that had always acted as a trigger for the dog to run towards the nearest door. Charlie worried too much time had passed, that he would have forgotten the command... but Princess was a good dog. He ran forwards, dodging drunken revellers, hunkering low and scrabbling between people's legs, stopping occasionally to ensure Charlie was close behind.

"I'm sorry," the woman with the wine shouted. God, was she following? Why wouldn't she leave her alone?

The dark stain spread across Charlie's dress like mould. All she could think of was herself as a child, sitting in the paddling pool, drenched in blood. The image made her nauseous. Panic and uncertainty jostled in her mind, and she placed a hand over her mouth, afraid she might vomit from the stress. For a moment, she lost Princess, and then the dog uttered three clear barks. She found him by a door, his little shoulders hunched like an angry parent. The crowd began to chant, starting at ten and working their way down.

As they reached two, Charlie exited through the door and slammed it shut behind her. She collapsed to her knees and threw up. The involuntary expulsion of her dinner hurt her stomach, and she cried as she stared into her own vomit. Princess crept closer, attempting to sniff the foul puddle.

"No," said Charlie, sniffing back a string of snot that dangled from her nose. "Don't eat my spew."

Princess grumbled, then flopped heavily onto his belly, gazing hungrily at Charlie's puke.

"You're disgusting." She patted the dog's head. "But that's why I love you." She smiled at the dog and her heart broke a little as she remembered how upset she had been when he had died. And now, here he was again, the faithful pooch by her side. It brought the reality home.

She was *dead*.

It explained the sight of her parents, she supposed. But what good was seeing them when she couldn't hold them, or tell them how much she loved and missed them? She glanced to her right, staring down a long, white corridor she had seen before, once, in what had felt like a dream. Lynette had helped her find it that day in the park, after Michelle... *exploded* in the dinner hall. They had sat together in blossoming friendship, Lynette explaining how to step into the unseen corridors of her own mind.

There are doors, Lynette had said. *So many doors, more than you can count. Can you see them?*

With Lynette to guide her, she had trod bravely into her own unconscious, unlocking a lifetime of memories. Never again had she managed to find that corridor. And for the first time since that day, she was here again, in the corridor of happy places. The doors stretched on forever, further than she could see. So what now? Try one? Try them all? Did she have time? Charlie leaned back against the wall, thinking. Would she age here? Could she die? Or was she destined to spend eternity walking the length of the infernal corridor, entering door after door and—

"Princess, no!" she shouted, as she noticed the dog edging closer to the puddle of vomit. He gazed up at her with wide, surprised eyes, then shuffled backwards. "Come on," she said, walking to the nearest door. She hesitated before it. What lay beyond the threshold?

Princess lumbered to her side, and with a troubled sigh, Charlie placed her hand on the cold metal and pushed it open.

"Okay, boy," she said. "Let's see what's behind door number one."

5
___

...That bitch that bitch that fucking bitch that cunt I'll kill her...

SUSAN LAY MOTIONLESS ATOP THE HOOD OF THE CAR, UNABLE to move. The bizarre tilt of her head enabled her to look down the length of her body. Razor-sharp pieces of glass pierced her skin. A bone erupted from her forearm. Worst of all, her dress was bunched up around her waist, exposing her bare ass to the small crowd of onlookers.

One of them, a reedy man with a mustache and thick glasses, stood by her, pressing his stubby fingers against her broken neck.

"She's still breathing," he called out to the others. "Where the hell is that ambulance?"

He wore an expression of concern, but as Susan delved into the shallows of his mind, she tasted his desire, felt the tingle in his pants as his eyes kept returning to her ass. He wanted to fuck her... to spread her cheeks wide and ram his cock into her tight asshole, right up to his balls, the way his wife never let him.

Susan wished she could kill him... but she had to conserve her strength.

Because despite her power, and despite the terrible, wonderful things she could do to people, Susan could not defeat death.

Over the ringing in her ears, she heard a siren as the ambulance arrived on the scene. *"Stay back,"* someone shouted. Fuck, she wished they would leave her alone. Sure, she was on borrowed time — hell, she could see a piece of her *brain* on the hood — but she wasn't finished yet. She had one final task to complete.

Revenge.

Susan knew the satisfying taste of revenge better than anyone. She meted out punishments to all who wronged her, and whether it was public sexual humiliation — her favorite, she had to admit — or violent death, the thrill of vengeance never waned. But no one was more deserving of the honor than Charlie. For what better reason for revenge than betrayal? Charlie had stabbed her in the back. After all Susan had done for her... disposing of their bullies, making it so they could spend their lives together, and all while wearing the revolting flesh suit of that cunt Lynette, the slut who had tried to come between them. Susan hated that body. She wanted to destroy it... and she would, in time.

But not until she punished Charlie. She would find her... and then, she would kill her. No, killing was too easy, too predictable. Instead, she would drive Charlie mad. She would annihilate her puny mind and turn her into a raving, brain-dead lunatic, a hollow shell walking the corridors of her own insanity until her feeble bones splintered and crumbled to ash.

Then, and only then, would Susan allow Charlie to die.

But first, she had to find her. She had to—

A thin wheeze escaped her lips. Though her eyes were shut, she saw everything around her down to the minutest detail. A paramedic in a white shirt and black tie loomed over her. "She should be *dead*," he whispered, inspecting her with disbelieving eyes. He tried to lift her head, but the cold weather had frozen her cheek to the hood. Susan felt the skin stretch and break, hot blood spilling onto the metal, steam rising.

...Clumsy fucking asshole, stupid motherfucking incompetent shit...

"I need some help over here," he shouted.

A female paramedic came to his side, leaning on the car so as not to slip on the icy road. "How is she?"

"Real fucking bad. I can't believe she's still alive. She's a fighter, that's for sure."

Susan knew what he was thinking. That she would be better off dead. That with her head the way it was, she would be irreparably brain damaged. That she would never walk, or talk, or even *think* again. A vegetable, something to be pitied for a while, and then forgotten about.

She hated him. She wanted to—

...save your strength save it save it for Charlie save it for revenge save it for her destruction think about it imagine it oh god oh god it'll be so good so good so good so...

"Anyone in the car?" asked the male medic.

"Kinda. They're missing their head."

"Shit," said the man.

Susan tip-toed through his mind. Norman was his name. Norman Conroy. He was married, but he harbored a crush on his co-worker, the woman standing opposite him. Jean... Jean Aldocini. They had shared drinks and a quick kiss the previous week at a Christmas party, and this thought was at the forefront of the man's mind, even as he stood in front of a dying woman with her *fucking ass exposed to the world.*

...fix my dress you putrid fucking slime fix it fix it fix it or I'll pull your guts out...

"You find the head?"

The woman gestured behind him, and Norman turned. Charlie's head had been brutally severed, her face frozen in a chilling grimace.

...that's nothing compared to what I'll do to you...

More paramedics arrived, accompanied by two firefighters. The medics hurried towards Norman and Jean with a stretcher, while the firefighters inspected the car door.

"Gonna need the Jaws of Life to get this open," one of them said. Susan didn't understand the reference, so she searched his mind, locating the image of a hydraulic cutting tool used to extricate crash victims from damaged vehicles. It looked like a giant steel claw, and her first thought was, *what damage would that do to the human body?*

A sizeable crowd had gathered around the vehicle, a bunch of ghouls gawping voyeuristically at the carnage and, so Susan thought, her ass.

"Would somebody get these people back?" shouted Norman, as the firefighters raced towards the car carrying their metal-cutting tool, a third man lugging the small generator that powered the implement.

The pair with the stretcher arrived and looked expectantly at Norman.

"She's stuck to the hood," he said, "but she doesn't have long. We don't have time to do this politely."

...don't you fucking dare...

Susan looked through his eyes, rifling through his darkest memories. Most people kept them hidden deep within the recesses of their psyches, but Norman's were easy to access. She saw a man on a couch with a gun in his limp hand, blood dribbling from his forehead, his pregnant wife behind him on the floor, the bullet having traveled through the man's head and into her belly. She saw charred, smoking corpses in the wreckage of a downed airplane. She saw the mangled arm of a woman who had tried to retrieve her wedding ring from the waste disposal unit in a restaurant.

Norman Conroy had seen death before. He knew better than most when someone didn't stand a chance, and right now, he was thinking that Susan had *minutes* to live.

That was okay. Susan didn't *need* much time. Because where she was going, time moved differently. It slowed, sometimes so much that it even traveled backwards. It was how she had found time to swap bodies with Lynette as she fell to her death from the school roof, pushed by Charlie...

...Charlie...

She should have known back then. Charlie didn't deserve her. No one did.

No one in this whole, miserable, stinking world.

The medics lifted her head, the hard skin of Susan's frozen cheek ripping from her face and remaining on the hood like meaty residue in a frying pan. Then they rolled her onto the stretcher with half her face missing like the fucking Phantom of the Opera. But that wasn't what mattered to Susan. She cared not that her face — the face of that bitch Lynette — had been disfigured, nor that the medics had all but given up on her chances of survival.

No, what really galled Susan was that they *still... hadn't... fixed her fucking dress*. From her outside vantage point, looking down on the macabre scene like a goddess, she saw she was naked from the waist down, her neatly trimmed pubic bush streaked white with frost.

She recalled that night, that happy night when she and Charlie had danced on the roof, and how moments later Greta and her goons had cornered her on the rooftop, tearing her dress, stripping her to her underwear, threatening to do more, to take it all, to leave her naked and exposed for the whole school to see... and now it was happening again.

It was happening *again*.

Susan knew she shouldn't react. There were more important matters to attend to. Finding Charlie, torturing Charlie, and watching Charlie die. Time was running out, and yet...

...fuck it...

There was *always* time for a murder spree.

A cold shiver ran through Norman Conroy's body as he laid the blanket across the dying woman on the stretcher. That alone was not enough to interest him. It was the middle of winter in New York City, after all, and shivering was to be expected. But there was something different about this palpitation. It reminded him of one of his mother's favorite sayings.

"Like someone just walked over my grave," he muttered, recalling the exact phrasing and intonation of his dear departed mom. Death came for all, he supposed. Young or old, it didn't matter to the reaper. When it's your time, it's your time, and there ain't a damn thing you can do about it.

He glanced down at the woman, still in awe of the way she clung to life, and silently prayed for her death. It would be best for everyone, especially her friends and family, who would have to devote their savings and the rest of their lives to looking after her. And as for her friend, well... she was in even worse shape. Norman looked over to where the severed head of the woman's companion had lain half-buried in the snow.

It was gone.

"Hey, has anyone moved the—"

He paused mid-sentence, the words deserting him as he noticed the two firefighters by the smoking wreck. One was pressed up against the vehicle, held in place by his colleague, who brandished the hydraulic cutting tool, the fearsome blades against the sides of the man's head. Blood fountained from his damaged cranium as the blades, designed for slicing through car doors, clamped shut. The top half of the firefighter's head ruptured in a fountain of gore like a burst balloon. His hands jerked wildly before his lifeless body slumped to the ground.

"What are you doing?" screamed Norman.

The man turned to him, but before he could so much as sneer, the front of his face exploded as a bullet slammed into one cheek and out the other. A second shot struck him in the throat, then a third, a fourth, a fifth, peppering his body, making it spasm.

Norman gazed, stunned, at the cop who had opened fire. The officer made eye contact, and for one horrifying moment, Norman saw the terror on the man's face. Then he placed the barrel of his firearm to his crotch and pulled the trigger. The scream tore through the night, high-pitched and ungodly, though it was as if no one had told the rest of his body. Calmly, the cop raised one leg and shook it until the tip of his severed penis dropped from his pant leg and splatted wetly onto the ground.

The other cops had begun firing on the crowd. Men and women shrieked and ran, the rain of bullets felling them like trees in a storm, the blood leaking from their punctured bodies and staining the snow.

Norman backed up. He turned to the medics who had arrived with the stretcher. One of them carried the decapitated head of the car crash victim by the hair. He swung it mightily, the head smacking hard into the nose of the other medic, who Norman knew only as Hulk, a nickname the man had gone by for many years due to his large stature. Hulk took the blow calmly, even as blood cascaded from his newly broken nose. He took a step towards the other man.

"Stop!" screamed Norman. "Have you all gone crazy?"

As all hell broke loose, he searched for Jean, praying she was alright. When he turned back to his colleagues, Hulk had the other man by his hair and slammed him down onto the hood, where moments before the girl had lain. He yanked the man's pants down, then his briefs.

"Hulk... listen to me," said Norman.

But Hulk was *not* listening.

The big man drew back a fist.

"Please God, no," said Norman.

But God was nowhere to be found, certainly not when Hulk rammed his fist into the screaming man's anus. Unable to look away, Norman trembled in shock as Hulk forced his limb inside. At first, it seemed it wouldn't fit. But as Hulk's brawny arms flexed, and he dug his heels in, the tender flesh tore with a stomach-churning squelch. Soon, he was up to his wrist in the ruptured orifice, a flood of murky shit and dark blood flooding from the man's ruined asshole and steaming on the snow.

Somehow, Hulk kept going. His elbow was no longer visible, the man dangling from his arm like a monstrous puppet.

"I don't want to do this!" roared Hulk, as he reached his other hand between the man's legs and grasped a flap of loose skin. He lowered his head towards the blood-drenched crevice. "This isn't me!"

As an EMT, Norman had heard fear before. The screams of the dying, the confusion of an accident victim... this was worse, because it was a man he knew and respected and trusted. Nothing made sense... *nothing*. Norman realized he was hyperventilating. His body was numb, and he was going into shock.

"Jean?" he barked, not recognizing his own hollow voice.

As Hulk inserted his head fully inside the man's torn and bleeding anus, muffling his nightmarish screams of horror, Norman felt something forced against his back. A machine fired up, and before he could do anything about it, the external defibrillator unit sent four-hundred joules of power coursing through his body, firing Norman against the car. He struck it hard, then fell backwards onto the ground, the bed of snow breaking his fall. Wearily, he looked up at Hulk, who was emerging from his victim's lower half with coils of stringy intestines clamped in his jaw, his head coated in excrement. The big man was crying, even as he bit down on the slippery tubes and crunched them between his teeth.

"I'm sorry, Norman," said Jean. The defibrillator paddles fell from her hands, and she stomped through the snow to where the car accident victim's severed head lay on its side. Jean frantically unbuckled her black pants, tugging them down her thighs. "I... I can't help it," she sobbed, as she squatted over the head and unleashed a torrent of piss all over it.

"Jean," croaked Norman. "Why?"

It was then he heard the laughter; cruel, mocking tones coming from the girl on the stretcher, the one he *knew* should be dead. She continued laughing, shrieking with delight, until blood spilled from her mouth and she started to choke. She was staring at the stream of urine splashing onto the head of the woman she had been traveling with.

"Fuck you, Charlie," she spluttered. "Fuck... you..."

Her eyes closed.

She's lost her mind, thought Norman, and as Jean finished peeing and ran at him, leaping onto his prone body and slashing him with her nails, gouging strips of flesh from his unprotected face and neck, he realized they had *all* lost their minds.

"May God have mercy on us all," he whispered, as the woman he secretly loved took his nose between her teeth and wrenched it clean off.

6

———

CHARLIE FELT THE SAND BETWEEN HER TOES AS WAVES whispered sweetly against the shore. Upon arriving at the beach, where she had spent a family holiday many years ago, Princess had gone nuts, running in wide circles. The ocean called to Charlie, and she answered by slipping out of her clothes at the water's edge and wading in, gasping at the chilly sensation.

She laughed at Princess, who tentatively dipped one paw into the cool liquid. Princess had always treated water with extreme caution, unless it was in his bowl, and he retreated, plonking himself down on the sand.

"I won't be long," she shouted, splashing into the water with a squeal of delight, the ocean rising to meet her, covering her waist, her chest, her shoulders.

If only she could have meditated like Lynette had tried to teach her. Maybe then the last ten years of her life, trapped in that cold tomb of an apartment, would have been... well, if not *enjoyable,* then at least bearable. She could have escaped the soul-crushing drudgery, and the constant abuse and demands made of her. She could have retreated from Susan's wild temper, even transported herself somewhere pleasant during their all-too-frequent fuck sessions. As time passed, Susan's emotions had amplified to frightening levels. When angered, she was a whirlwind of violent madness. When jealous, she would fly into rages and torture Charlie, telling her it was all her fault. And when she was horny? Well, that was worst of all. Her insatiable desire for new and twisted stimuli stunned and appalled Charlie. The things Susan made her do in her quest for depraved ecstasy were the darkest periods in Charlie's meagre existence. At night, she would dream of happier times, but after a while, even the dreams faded, leaving her with nothing.

It doesn't matter, she thought. *It's over now. It's all over.*

The nightmares... the atrocities... the threats, the violence, the fear... it was finished. Done.

Refreshed, Charlie swam back to shore, where Princess lay on his belly, his exercise having evidently tired him out. Charlie emerged from the sea and ran her hands through her wet hair, wringing it out. It felt weird to have long hair again, after years of the Princess Diana cut Susan preferred. She couldn't understand why she had ended up as an eighteen-year-old again, but absolutely nothing about this made sense, so she refused to dwell on it. She glared at the underwear Susan had chosen for her, and kicked sand over the torn, skimpy panties, burying them.

When she slipped into her dress, the soaked material clung uncomfortably to her body. What she needed, she reasoned, was a change of clothes, preferably of the stretchy, comfortable variety.

An idea formed, and she turned to Princess, smiling.

"Hey, boy. Wanna go shopping?"

The mall was, inevitably, full of people.

Charlie hesitated by the entrance. She hadn't been around a crowd of this magnitude for a long time, and the sight of so many bodies mingling and talking and living their quietly desperate lives filled her with a powerful sense of dread. "They can't see you," she said to herself, crouching to stroke Princess's fur.

She was surprised she had been able to find the mall straight away. After leaving the beach and finding herself back in the corridor, she had tried the nearest door and appeared precisely where she wanted to be; in the Monroeville Mall, Pennsylvania. Was that how it worked? Did she simply have to think of a specific memory, and whatever door she picked would automatically transport her there? Well, she supposed, she had all the time in the world to put the theory to the test.

On her single visit to the mall, during a family vacation, she recalled feeling stunned by the overwhelming amount of shops and diners. Of course, by the eighties, malls were literally *everywhere*... but none could replicate the awe-inspiring impression of that summer day in seventy-seven when she had first set foot in the Monroeville. The following year, George Romero had released his zombie epic *Dawn of the Dead*, a film shot on location in the mall, and that she had caught at the drive-in with Susan in nineteen-eighty, back when she was still successfully hiding in Lynette's skin.

God fucking damn it, why was every memory tainted by Susan? Every last fucking one.

"I gotta move on," she said, and Princess grumbled in agreement, or perhaps because he was hungry, Charlie couldn't tell. Steeling herself, she started through the busy shopping mall, leaving soggy footprints on the floor. An unlucky patron stepped on one and slipped, the teenager's friends laughing at him as he brushed himself off and tried to play it cool. "Sorry," said Charlie, though no one heard her.

She lifted Princess and carried him as they rode the escalator, then placed him back down as they headed for JCPenneys, enjoying the click-clack of his little claws on the floor. As she neared, another mild tremor shook the foundations, and a single tile fell from the roof.

"Don't remember any earthquakes," said Charlie, forgetting about it as she reached the ladies' clothing section. Compared to what she was wearing back in nineteen-eighty-nine, the garments were charmingly dated, but Charlie had always enjoyed the fashion of the seventies. She browsed the racks, seeking the perfect outfits to lounge around her memories in, dumping baggy tees and skirts into a cart and shouting, "Sorry, forgot my Amex," at the oblivious checkout girl. Then something caught her eye. She paused, staring at the blue peplum dress, the one she had bought here and worn to the dance, that fateful event that ended in disaster and bloodshed.

Charlie ran her hands over the soft material. God, she had looked so pretty. Tears welled in her eyes, and — in the middle of the aisle — she stripped naked and slipped into the blue dress. It was snug, the way it had been that night.

Tight in all the right places, Susan had giggled, before cheekily slapping Charlie's round ass. They had been so in love back then.

So in love.

She took the dress off and discarded it, enjoying the liberating feeling of being naked in a crowded shopping mall, dozens of shoppers unaware of her presence. With a final sigh, she walked to the underwear section and selected the biggest, comfiest underpants she could find, then dressed in sweatpants and a baggy tee.

Before she left, she found a pretty summer dress and stuffed it in her cart, alongside *one* matching set of lacy bra and panties.

"Hey," she said to Princess, as if the dog had rebuked her. "I might have to look my best sometime. In case... y'know..."

But she couldn't bring herself to say it out loud.

In case you meet Lynette?

It could happen. If this was heaven, or some weird approximation of it, wasn't there a chance — however small — that they could find each other again? That they could reunite and spend the rest of their days together?

Lost in her fantasies, she wandered aimlessly through the mall until she arrived at the indoor ice rink. There, she parked her cart and leaned on the barrier, watching the skaters glide across the ice, dodging and weaving like birds in flight. Amongst the laughing young people, she spotted her childhood self, all snug in a winter coat and scarf, unsteady on her rented skates, but smiling regardless.

A song played over the speakers, the same melody she had heard at the crash site. Only this time, there was no voice, just the gentle strum of an acoustic guitar.

Beside her, Princess grumbled. The dog turned around, his ears alert, paws firmly planted.

"What's wrong?" asked Charlie. "Princess, you okay?"

At the sound of his name, the dog glanced back at her, then stalked from the rink, his body low. Charlie abandoned her stolen shopping cart and followed, as the dog picked up speed. "Slow down," she called out, but Princess broke into a loping run, pulling away from her. Increasing her pace, Charlie jogged after him, occasionally colliding with shoppers who looked around, bemused, before going about their business. They passed the hardware store, the gun store, a vacant unit, a... wait, no, it couldn't be...

Skidding to a stop, Charlie gazed at the comic book store. *Kryptonite Komiks,* read the sign. "That wasn't here," she said, taking a step closer, the ground beneath her rumbling. *Kryptonite Komiks* was the store she had visited with Susan back in eighty or eighty-one, on a visit to Boston. It hadn't been in the Monroeville Mall. Had it?

She checked Princess hadn't run off — the dog sat waiting for her with an impatient side-eye — and walked to the door, reaching for the handle. She placed her hand around the metal and quickly withdrew it.

"Shit!"

The handle was scalding to the touch. She gazed at the red burn forming on her palm and moved backwards.

Inside, the lights went off.

A sharp bark from Princess caught Charlie's attention, and when she looked back at the store, it was gone. In its place was a nothingness, vast and black. She trembled before the void, a sense of deep insignificance penetrating every fiber of her being. A low, droning buzz emanated from the depths, and Charlie felt it beckon her.

Princess barked again, loud and clear. Charlie forced herself to turn from the emptiness and walk away. The buzzing receded as she did so, replaced by the murmuring voices of the shoppers. Funny... she hadn't even noticed their absence.

She found Princess pawing at a door, raking his claws down the wood and leaving shallow grooves.

"You need to pee?" asked Charlie as she opened the door and walked through, trying to forget about the disappearing comic book store and the strange, dark pit it had left behind.

The corridor looked different, somehow. Older. The

once gleaming white paint was yellow and peeling, and a meandering crack ran the length of the wall. Princess padded down the middle, avoiding a puddle into which murky water dripped steadily from the ceiling.

"How long was I gone?" muttered Charlie.

She drew level with Princess, who had stopped, and now sat on his hind legs, staring forwards. For the first time, Charlie saw what she assumed was the end of the corridor, a blaze of brilliant light so intense she had to close her eyes. It grew stronger and stronger, until she was forced to turn her back on it, shielding Princess with her body until the light fizzled out.

A dog howled.

It wasn't Princess, who was wrapped up in Charlie's protective arms.

Another howl.

Princess wriggled free and scampered down the corridor.

"Wait!" yelled Charlie, turning to stop the foolhardy beast. "We don't know what..."

She couldn't finish the sentence. Not when she realized what she was looking at.

It was a rainbow.

Close enough to touch, it stretched from the floor to high above them, the colors shifting and blending, forming *new* colors, ones Charlie didn't recognize. And there, at the bottom, stood a single golden retriever, its soft fur billowing in a non-existent breeze. The retriever bounded down from the rainbow and strode towards Princess, who leaped to his paws and met the dog halfway. Princess circled the retriever, sniffing its hindquarters, then looked back at Charlie.

She understood.

The rainbow bridge was *real*. Her parents had told her

about it when Princess passed, that magical bridge that all dogs must cross when their time with the humans was up.

When they've taught us all they can teach, her mom had said.

And now the rainbow bridge was here, in front of her... in front of Princess.

Sadness rose from within as the bulldog waddled back to her, the retriever waiting patiently. There was a wisdom in its eyes that suggested a lifetime of, well... *retrieving* other dogs.

With his stubby tail lowered, Princess brushed against Charlie's legs. She crouched and held him, ruffling his fur, kissing his head.

"It's okay," she said, tears welling in her eyes. "It's... it's where you belong." Princess snuffled close, and Charlie wept. There was so much she wanted to say to her small friend. She wanted to explain that every time they had bathed him, it had been for his own good, and how running her hands through his fur had been so soothing, and how she adored his loud snores, and how... and how...

There were too many things to say, so she settled on just one.

"You were the best friend I could ever hope for."

Princess looked up at her, his own eyes wet and glassy. He licked her face, sneezed, then hopped down and walked towards the bridge.

"I'll miss you, you silly dog," said Charlie.

Princess paused, and turned back one last time. Charlie raised her hand and waved goodbye. "I love you," she said, and then she buried her face in her hands as her last remaining friend climbed onto the rainbow bridge and began his ascent. When she managed to look up, Princess was barely visible. She heard a cacophony of barks and howls from above, as the residents welcomed their newest member to the fold.

The retriever remained at the bottom of the rainbow, its face impassive.

He waited for you, a voice said. *All these years, he waited. To see you one last time. To show you everything would be fine.*

The voice was in her head, yet she knew where it came from.

"Look after him," she said. "He's a good dog." Through the river of tears, she saw the retriever nod.

They all are, the dog said, and with that, the retriever turned and jumped gracefully onto the rainbow. The light grew brighter, blindingly bright, and Charlie clasped her hands over her eyes. She lay there for what felt like hours, and when she finally mustered up the courage to look, the rainbow bridge — and Princess — had vanished.

7
___

Charlie got to her feet.

The corridor had returned to normal, apart from the fissure along the wall, which had grown. Thoughts dashed through her head. Princess and the rainbow bridge... heaven... the mall, her childhood, her parents... had she gone mad? Was that it? Had she lost her mind, and, in reality, she was lying in her and Susan's apartment bashing her skull off the floor in the grip of insanity? And if not — if she was really dead, and really *here,* wherever this was — then what the hell was she supposed to do now? Walk the corridors forever, gazing in on memories but unable to interact? An endless, twenty-four-hour movie marathon, with no one to talk to, no one to hold her? Was *this* what had driven Susan mad during her time in the coma?

Alone, alone, always alone.

She wandered through the nearest door, emerging in the Monroeville Mall. This time, without Princess toddling along beside her, she felt lost and confused, a ghost in need of an exorcism. Despite the knowledge that she could visit her parents whenever she wished, she no longer wanted to.

It would be too hard, too torturous to watch them, like a grieving widow replaying home video recordings of her deceased partner.

She reached the ice rink and watched her younger self happily skate in circles, until the lights dimmed and a warning came over the speaker letting the patrons know the mall was closing. The skaters vacated the area, leaving Charlie alone with her thoughts.

What to do?

She knew what she *wanted* to do. Find Lynette. Be with her, see if she was okay. But it would be the same as her parents, wouldn't it? She could *watch* Lynette, peering in on her like a pervert hiding in a cupboard... but it didn't feel right.

"Might be different," she said out loud, for at that moment, she *needed* to hear a human voice.

A familiar tremor rattled the building. Charlie gripped the barrier to maintain her balance. When she looked at the ice, it had cracked, a long split running from end to end. Music drifted ethereally from below.

That song, the one she kept hearing.

It was such a pretty song. Only this time, as she listened, a lone voice sang along.

> *"Lonely night in winter, I was feeling blue.*
> *Life was slipping by me, don't know what to do."*

The voice was fragile, unsure of itself, delicately stretching for the high notes as if afraid to be heard. Charlie knew it well.

It belonged to Lynette.

> *"Til the day I met you, baby, and the clouds did clear,*

That's just how it happens when you're standing near."

Drawn by the siren song, Charlie clambered onto the ice.

"Lynette?"

Her foot slid out from under her, and she dropped, shivering, to her hands and knees.

The song continued.

Lynette sang louder, growing in confidence.

"I wish that I could tell you how you make feel,
How only when I'm with you do I think I'm real."

"Lynette!" screamed Charlie. Was it her? Was it really, truly her? On all fours, she slid over the slippery surface alongside the crack, following it to where it widened.

"But I wish I had the courage buried deep inside,
So when you are around I wouldn't have to hide."

Charlie kicked her way along, her heart racing. She was nearing the widest point of the opening. The verse had ended, but still the phantom player strummed, building towards a chorus. Charlie slowed herself, wrapping her freezing fingers around the edge of the crevasse and pulling herself the rest of the way. She gazed through the gap.

"Oh my god..."

There she was.

Lynette sat in her room on a wooden chair, wearing a loose white vest, the guitar resting on her lap.

"Lynette!" shouted Charlie. The girl was *right there*, twenty feet below her.

Lynette didn't look up. She strummed a bum chord and winced, her fingers sliding dejectedly down the fret.

"Lynette, it's me! It's Charlie!"

The girl sighed. A tear rolled down her cheek, and she tried the chord again, getting it right this time, and launched into the chorus.

"And you, can't see,
How the sun, shines on me,
When you're here,
My troubles go away."

"Lynette!" screamed Charlie. Could she fit through the gap? It was quite a drop. She couldn't guarantee she wouldn't break her leg, or her neck...

Lynette had stopped playing. She looked thoughtful, then tried the chorus again, altering the words.

"And you, can't see,
How the sun, shines on me,
When you're near,
My troubles melt away."

The ice numbed Charlie's body, chilling her through the insubstantial tee shirt and jogging pants, yet she hauled herself as far over the gap as she could manage and stared down at Lynette, so near, so close...

"Lynette! Lynette!"

The girl hit another wrong note, and stopped, laying the guitar to one side. Did she—

"Charlie?" she said. She stood, glancing around the room.

"Up here! I'm up here! Look up!"

Lynette ran both hands through her hair. She stalked to the window and stared out. Charlie slammed her fist against the ice. Dammit, Lynette couldn't hear her!

"Fuck it," she said, and slid around until she was parallel with the crack, one leg cautiously dangling over the edge. "Here goes nothing."

Something grabbed her other ankle. Charlie tried to turn, but she found herself yanked backwards, her chin smacking off the ice and forcing her teeth into her lower lip. Back she went, speeding across the abrasive rink. She dug her nails in as she slid away from the crack, away from Lynette, leaving a trail of smeared blood across the ice.

"Oof!" she grunted as she smashed into the barrier, and then the invisible hand lifted her, dragging her over. She crested the barrier and slammed onto the other side, the impact knocking the breath from her. Charlie choked and spluttered blood. She kicked out, but there was no one to strike. The steps loomed ahead of her, and she flipped onto her back, closed her eyes, and braced herself.

The first stair whacked painfully against her ass, as her invisible assailant hauled her up and onto the next one, each impact causing her to yell in pain. She thought of Lynette, and how close they had been to making contact, and then she hit the next step, and the next, her tee pulled up to her neck, her bare skin scraping along each sharp edge.

At the top of the stairs, she crashed through the glass door that led to the mall, shards of shimmering crystal raining down, slicing her belly and arms.

"Stop!" she cried, but the phantom hand pulled her faster through the empty mall towards the escalators. "No!" roared Charlie, anticipating the violent impact of the metal staircase, and the sharp edges tearing her skin to shreds.

Seconds before the collision, she veered left, her whole body swinging around and smacking against the wall.

Too late, she realized she was heading for the indoor fountain, a large circular bowl surrounded by bushes and shrubbery. The branches scraped at her skin as she bundled through them, hitting the stone fountain so hard that she bounced into the air and came—

—splashing into the ocean, saltwater filling her lungs, the hand tugging her down, deeper into the depths. She kicked with her free leg, momentarily breaking the surface and seeing the beach, full of vacationers lounging on recliners, their children building sandcastles and running, screaming, having a good time. She disappeared underwater again, pulled hard, and when she looked down, she could make out a shape, an outline as the water moved around the invisible figure dragging her to her death.

Then the world seemed to flip. Whoever had been dragging her let go, and Charlie pivoted, kicking until her head was out of the water. She gasped for breath, gripping onto the side of... a bathtub?

Hauling herself over, she landed with a thump on the bathmat. A quick glance at the clock with the garden birds on it and the obnoxious orange wallpaper revealed she was back in her childhood home. She scrambled away from the tub and hugged her knees to her chest, shivering in her sodden clothes. God, she was home. It was safe here.

It had to be.

She heard her parents talking downstairs, the house alive with activity, and right now, Charlie wanted to be around people, whether they were aware of her presence or not. She stood, not caring that her white top clung to her body like she was at a spring break wet tee-shirt competition, nor that her jogging pants sagged below her hips due to the weight of the water. Clutching the waistband with one hand, she reached for the door handle.

And *that* was when she heard it.

The bathwater shifting, slapping against the side of the tub in miniature waves and splashing to the floor. She didn't *want* to turn around. She wanted to leave, to see her family, to dry off by the fire and smell dinner, maybe even taste it.

But she had to look.

With a deep breath, Charlie turned. The water was red, and it rippled as if—

"No," said Charlie, as the bathwater parted, a head rising, followed by two hands, thin and angular, clamping onto the lip of the tub.

"Hello, lover," said Susan, her wet hair hanging over her face like a black cloak. "Did you miss me?"

8

———

Charlie tried to run.

Where Susan was concerned, there was no such thing as the fight-or-flight response... there was *only* flight. But before Charlie could move, a tight grip formed around her neck, lifting her off her feet, water dripping from the tips of her toes into a shallow pool beneath her. Unable to speak due to the pressure on her windpipe, she could only watch, helpless, as Susan emerged fully from the tub.

It was Susan as she remembered her, the way she had looked during the hospital visits, when Charlie would read her stories and tell her about school and brush her hair and weep by her side. The Susan she had loved, and who she had danced with on the roof. Only now, she looked different. Her features were askew, a funhouse distortion. One eye — ringed with dark shadows — was too high, the other a little too low, like a living, breathing Picasso.

She stood before Charlie, a spectacle of sadism, and glared at her.

"I can't... breathe..." gasped Charlie, her vision blurring.

Susan relaxed her psychic grip on Charlie's throat. "Better?" she said, and smiled, baring crooked teeth of wildly different sizes.

Still Charlie hung in the air. "Susan, please—"

"Don't fucking talk to me," she sneered. "You don't get to talk, not unless I say you can." She spoke the way a corpse that had washed ashore would, her voice gargling with filthy black water that spilled out the side of her mouth and through the gaps in her teeth. "You tried to kill me," she said, regarding her like a butcher sizing up a slab of meat.

"No, I just—"

"You wanted to break up with me. Is that it?"

"I..."

Susan limped closer. "You wanted to *kill* me?"

The unseen fingers tightened around Charlie's throat. Her temples throbbed as if doors were repeatedly slamming shut on her head, the pain so intense she wanted to scream.

But Susan wouldn't let her.

"I gave you everything. I gave you my *love*. But it wasn't enough, was it? Nothing is ever good enough for *Charlie,* is it? My obsession... my queen... I tried to please you. I never let any harm come to you. But I was never enough, was I? Because I wasn't *her.* That bitch, that cunt, that fuck. Out with the old, in with the new, am I right, *Charlie?*" She spat out the name with venomous sarcasm.

Charlie barely heard her, such was the overwhelming sensation of her skull compressing. Blood dripped from her nose, and her bladder released, sending warm liquid trickling down her legs.

"Susan..." she croaked, eyes half-closing. "You're... hurting me."

"No amount of pain could hurt you the way you hurt me. No amount of suffering could equal the way you've made me suffer. I tried so damn hard to trust you, Charlie. To put my faith in you, to believe you loved me back. And all this time, you were scheming. You whore, you bitch, you slut, you *fuck, you cunt! Fuck you! Fuck you! Fuck you!*" She was screaming now, and as she did so, the room rumbled, the violent tremors causing the bathroom cabinet to drop into the basin, the mirror smashing into hundreds of long shards.

Weapons, Charlie thought, but they may as well have been miles away, for Susan had control, and Charlie was a prisoner in her own treacherous body. Only one thought consoled her. That if Susan was here, then back in the real world, she was probably dead. And if she was dead, that meant she couldn't harm anyone anymore. She—

"No, I'm not dead yet," said Susan, smiling so wide that one eyeball bulged from its socket, ready to pop out. "What, you think I can't read your mind?" She lurched closer, until Charlie felt her noxious breath against her skin. "I told you before... I'm a fucking *god* now." She caressed Charlie's cheek with the back of her hand. "There's nowhere you can run that I won't find you."

With a simple tap on Charlie's nose, the powerful choke-hold vanished, and she crashed limply to the carpeted bathroom floor. There she lay, sobbing and gasping for air. Could she talk her way out of this, convince Susan to change her mind, to forgive her, to give her one more chance at redemption? She could try...

But she didn't want to.

Because death — true, utter death — was preferable to the life she had been living. Living! Ha, that was a joke. A lifetime of torture and punishment and humiliation, of being on the receiving end of furious tantrums and jealous rages, of being locked away and hidden from the rest of the world like a closely guarded and long-forgotten secret. No, if it came down to it... Charlie would rather die.

She looked up at Susan's twisted face, and said, "Would you just shut up and kill me already?"

Susan's smile oozed from her face. "Say that louder."

Charlie half-laughed, half-cried. "Kill me. Get it over with. I'm so sick... to *death*... of your bullshit."

Susan stared at her for so long that Charlie thought she had broken. Then, she simply said, "No."

"Do it. Do it, you bitch. *Do it!*"

"No," Susan repeated. "You're already dead. Where's the fun in dying twice?" She kneeled and placed a hand on Charlie's breast. "I have a much better idea." At once, Charlie's body stiffened, and she rose to her feet like Nosferatu, leaving the ground and hovering.

"You think I'm mad, don't you?" the girl ranted. "You think I'm crazy. Who knows, maybe I am? But you don't know the meaning of the word. I'll show *you* crazy."

"What are you talking about? What are you saying?" roared Charlie. "Kill me!"

Susan wasn't listening. "I'm gong to drive you out of your mind. I'm going to break you, Charlie, my love. And only then, once I've taken *everything* from you, will I leave you to wander the corridors of your own fractured sanity." She stopped, sniffed the air. "Is that turkey I smell? Is your mom preparing Thanksgiving dinner?"

The blood drained from Charlie's face. "Don't you dare..."

"Your mom always liked me," Susan continued. "More than my own. She was always so accepting of our love. It'll be a shame to kill her. Well, for you, I guess. Not for me."

"You wouldn't," sobbed Charlie.

Susan chuckled. "I slit my mom open from her cunt to

her tits and bathed in her blood, *Charlie*. So yeah, I don't think killing *your* parents will prove too challenging. Especially your dad. Seemed like a nice guy. If I'd been straight, I might've had a crush on him. I wonder what he looks like with his own dick in his mouth, hmm? You ever wonder that, Charlie? You ever stay up late at night and wonder that while fingering your fucking pussy?"

Unable to move her limbs, Charlie wept. "Please, leave them alone, and kill me instead."

"Already told you, lover. There's no fun in that. So stop whimpering like a little bitch, and let's go see your family. It's been a long time since I saw them." She grinned. "And now I wanna see them bleed."

9

WITH A SNAP OF SUSAN'S FINGERS, THEY WERE DOWNSTAIRS IN the dining room.

"No!" yelled Charlie, as she struggled against psychic bonds that clasped her arms and legs together tighter than any rope. She floated above the ground in the corner of the bustling room, as — oblivious to her presence — her family and friends busied themselves with the festivities. Her mom was in the kitchen with her best friend Gladys, the two gossiping as they wrestled the turkey out of the oven, the bird brown and glistening and heavy. Meanwhile, her dad was looking out the window and telling nobody in particular that it looked like snow, and that winter was going to be a tough one this year.

"Where's Charlotte?" someone asked, and Charlie turned her head far enough to see her beloved mawmaw lounging on the couch with a crocheted blanket over her legs. The old lady blew kisses at Gladys's infant son Rudy, who lay snugly in his stroller.

"Charlotte?" repeated her dad, still staring out the window as the sun set over the neighboring buildings. "Oh, she's upstairs. Or out with her friend." He shrugged "I don't actually know."

"Frank, would you help with this damn turkey?" her mom called from the kitchen. "Gladys has arms like a T-Rex."

"I do not!" shouted the woman in mock anger.

Charlie watched it all in sorrow and frustration. For a few seconds, she even forgot about Susan, so wrapped up was she in the small-scale drama of a typical Bonner Thanksgiving dinner. God, how she missed it. The people, the conversations, and the inebriated games, followed by snuggling up on the couch to watch a movie and taking bets on how long mawmaw would last before falling asleep and spilling her brandy over the carpet, which happened every year without fail. It was one of the great Bonner family traditions.

Her dad reluctantly left the window and helped the women struggle through with the bird balancing on the silver platter. They laid it in the middle of the table and stood back, admiring the noble beast that had given its life for their gluttonous enjoyment.

"Gets bigger every year," Charlie's dad said.

Her mom sighed. "And you say *that* every year."

"If something's worth saying, it's worth saying twice," her mawmaw interjected.

"Twice, sure," said her mom. "But not twenty times."

"Look at them," Susan whispered. "They have no idea what's coming."

"Don't," was all Charlie could say.

"Don't what?" asked Susan, adopting a guileless tone that didn't suit her.

Charlie glanced at her parents, at her mawmaw, at Gladys and her young son. "Don't hurt them."

"Oh Charlie," said Susan, wrapping her arms around Charlie's waist, seeking her flesh. "Your naiveté is charming." She slid her hands under Charlie's shirt, her breath hot and panting against her neck.

Charlie's dad sniffed the air. "Is something burning?" he asked.

"Can't be," replied her mom. "Turkey's out."

"I don't smell anything," said Gladys, as she set up the wooden high chair by the side of the table.

"No, something is definitely burning."

Gladys rolled her eyes. "Then go check."

"Why me? I'm already sitting down."

"I know," said Gladys. She crossed the room to retrieve Rudy from his stroller. "You've been sitting down all day while your wife and I prepared dinner."

"Well, I can't argue with that," he said, sliding his chair back and heading for the kitchen.

"Boobooboobooboo," Charlie's mawmaw babbled. She leaned over the stroller, waving her fingers at Rudy and smiling.

"Okay, little guy," said Gladys. "Time for your first Thanksgiving—"

She paused mid-sentence and stared into the stroller.

"Where's Rudy?"

Dark smoke plumed through the kitchen door.

"God, no," breathed Charlie.

"Uh oh," said Susan, kissing Charlie's ear as she clumsily kneaded the girl's breasts.

Her dad emerged from the kitchen with his oven mitts on, carrying a metal tray, upon which rested a steaming black lump of charred flesh. His face was deathly pale. "It's... I don't... how could..."

The tray fell from his gloved hands and crashed to the

floor, disgorging the crispy infant corpse onto the carpet. It broke apart on impact, tiny limbs crumbling from Rudy's lifeless body.

"Susan! Fucking stop!"

"This," the girl said, as she dug her nails into Charlie's breasts, "is just the fucking *beginning*."

The room erupted in chaos.

"Rudy!" screamed Gladys, frozen to the spot. She turned to Charlie's mawmaw. "You did this!"

The older woman looked up at her, uncomprehending, even when Gladys raced for the dining table and snatched up the meat fork. She ran for Charlie's grandmother and plunged the knife into her sternum with both hands. It cracked off bone, gashing open her skin and unleashing a flood of blood.

"You did this! You senile old bitch!"

She brought the fork down again. Charlie's mawmaw raised a protective hand, the twin blades stabbing through the thin flesh.

"I don't know what's happening?" the elderly woman cried, and then the fork plunged into her face, the prongs bridging her nose and piercing the tear ducts of both rheumy eyes.

Charlie screamed in horror. Why was no one stopping Gladys? She looked to her parents, and understood why.

Her mom sat at the table, clutching her belly. It was swollen, reminding Charlie of the photo above the mantel from when her mom was eight months pregnant. The buttons on her dress popped open like champagne corks as her belly inflated, stretching the skin to breaking point.

On the other side of the table, Charlie's father placed his hand flat on his empty plate and stared at it. Beneath the skin, something squirmed.

"What is that?" he said, as his flesh contorted. He choked, doubling over and gagging as a narrow, wriggling black worm slipped out of his mouth and slopped onto the table. It thrashed like a fish gasping for air.

"Look at that," said Susan. She toyed with Charlie's nipples, squeezing them between her serpentine fingers. "I don't even know what that is!"

"Make it stop!"

But Susan didn't. And she wouldn't, not ever. Charlie knew this all too well.

Her mom roared in agony. She had never heard her mother make a noise like that before, shrieking and hammering the table as tiny beads of blood formed across her distended abdomen. More blood trickled from her ears, her eyes filling with scarlet tears. As her stomach ballooned, fit to burst, her hands frantically sought something... anything...

Her fingers closed around the handle of the six-inch boning knife.

"No," said Charlie. "Mom..."

The woman thrust the knife into her gut with a deranged yell. If she expected her belly to deflate, she was wrong. The knife stuck out from her like a candle on a birthday cake. At first, nothing happened. A small amount of blood dribbled from the wound, running down the curve of her stomach. Her belly rumbled... and then the knife erupted from the skin, flying across the room and embedding itself in the wall. The blood followed, a ludicrous crimson geyser that shot out with machine-gun ferocity.

"It's not enough," Charlie's mom cried. *"It's not enough!"*

Horrified, Charlie returned her gaze to her mawmaw, and soon wished she hadn't. The woman's face resembled tenderized beef, the sagging skin hanging in chunky clods from her smashed and mutilated face. Unable to defend herself, she had let Gladys annihilate her with the meat fork. Charlie noticed one of the prongs was missing, and when her grandmother's head lolled back, the snapped shard of metal in the woman's eye socket caught the light of the fire and glowed softly.

As the carnage unfolded, Charlie watched with a dazed numbness. Though she wanted to look away, to close her eyes and shut the nightmare out, Susan wouldn't let her. She didn't even notice Susan slide her jogging pants down to her ankles.

"What the fuck are you wearing?" asked Susan, snapping the elastic waistband of the voluminous panties Charlie had selected in the mall. "Are these what you wear when I'm not around? Don't you *want* to look sexy for me?"

Charlie didn't answer. She heard nothing, her mind shattering as her family tore itself apart.

Her dad wielded the electric carving knife, running the whirring blade across the top of his hand, slicing veins and tendons, the metal grinding against his knuckles as he screamed. Dozens of the thin worms squirmed free from between his exposed muscles, but now his entire *arm* was a mass of slithering beasts.

"Get them out of me," he sobbed, blindly hacking at the limb with the electric knife, long, slippery creatures spilling from jagged slashes in his skin. They landed at his feet, and he stomped on them, crushing their slender bodies and sending gouts of bile-like greenish slime spurting across the carpet.

He didn't even notice his wife, or the five distinct streams of blood that spurted unceasingly from her bloated abdomen, redecorating the walls a Stygian scarlet.

Susan ripped Charlie's underpants off and pressed her

hand between her legs, rubbing her pussy. "Get wet," she snarled. "And hurry, or I'm putting my whole fist up there *dry,* bitch."

Gladys wandered past them in a stupor. She didn't notice the remains of her son on the floor, and trod through them, leaving ashen footprints on her way to the kitchen.

"Let's see where she's going," said Susan, casually inserting two fingers into Charlie's vagina and dragging her through the air. As they passed her mom, the woman burst, the explosion drenching the room in blood and entrails. Flaps of skin rained down like leaves on a fall morning, stringy intestines plopping onto the table.

Charlie reeled from the horror of it all. Her dad lay on his back, one hand clutching the carving knife, the other scooping out handfuls of squirming monsters from the cavity of his belly, gargling blood and howling in crazed agony. Her mother dripped from the ceiling, from the lampshade, down the wooden television cabinet. Susan positioned Charlie in the kitchen as Gladys kneeled by the open door of the oven. The heat blazed inside, a miniature hell.

"Think she can make it all the way in?" asked Susan.

It's not real, they're just figments of your imagination, Charlie tried telling herself. *They're dreams, memories... they're not real...*

Gladys placed her hands inside the oven. Steam rose from her palms as her soft flesh crackled and burned.

Susan spread Charlie's ass cheeks apart, her tongue flicking against her asshole. "Did she make it?" the girl asked, her voice muffled between the plump mounds.

By the time Gladys was halfway in, her skin had gone from red to a dark purple. The woman screamed, and screamed, and screamed some more, as she hauled herself into the cramped space. Her legs poked out, so she reached for her ankles and pulled, snapping her lower limbs at the knees. Bone burst through ruptured muscle and sinew, and she folded her legs fully in and slammed the oven door shut.

Susan ran her tongue up the crevice of Charlie's ass, following the trail of her spine. Then she whirled Charlie around to face her.

"How was it for you, lover?"

"They're not real," she whispered, the phrase becoming a mantra. *"They're not real."*

"Sure looked real to me."

"No. Not real. Nothing's real, not anymore."

Susan released her, and she slumped to the floor, naked and defeated, curling into a ball and weeping.

She tried to imagine the corridor, that magical space accessible only through meditation. Lynette had shown her how... so why couldn't she find it? Over the years, she had tried hundreds of times, always without success, and now, more than ever, she knew it was her only way out. She needed to relax, to clear her mind, but it buzzed with atrocities. How many times could she witness the destruction of her family before she went truly, irretrievably mad? One more time? Two?

Stop thinking about it! Meditate!

What was it Lynette had said...

It's all about breathing. Breathe in... and breathe out. Keep the rhythm.

She tried. Oh god, she tried. But every time the corridor appeared in her mind, the sanctuary bleached to white nothingness.

> *And you, can't see,*
> *How the sun, shines on me...*

Lynette's song shimmered into her head like a heat haze. Could she use that? What was the next line? Dammit, think! She couldn't remember.

> *And you, can't see,*
> *How the sun, shines on me...*

The corridor... she saw it. She was *in* it. The doors, the ornate brass lamps... she ran, reaching the nearest door, grasping the—

"*Charlie.*"

Susan's voice.

"*Are you there, Charlie?*"

The corridor jolted at a forty-five degree angle, sending Charlie slamming into the wall. No! She had to get to the door. She crawled along the wall to reach it.

"*Charlie, are you listening to me?*" barked Susan.

> *And you, can't see,*
> *How the sun, shines on me...*

So close... so near!

She gripped the handle, the corridor spinning, hurling Charlie around until the centrifugal force became so strong that she stuck to the wall like a fly to flypaper. Behind her, hairline fractures spread out in a wide oval, encircling her. She tried to raise a hand, to reach for the door handle, but gravity defeated her.

The room kept spinning.

From behind one of the doors, she heard Lynette's song. Charlie called her name, but her voice was ripped from her throat. Air rushed against her back as the cracks widened, bigger and bigger until—

They split, sucking her through the wall with the force of a freight train. She saw the wildly revolving corridor alter itself, bending and warping until it formed a perfect circle, and then...

...nothing.

10

———

WHEN CHARLIE OPENED HER EYES, SHE WAS LYING FACE DOWN in the grass. The sun was pleasing against her bare skin, and she pushed herself up and sat on an overgrown lawn in a residential street.

She peered both ways, searching for Susan and finding no trace. Instead, her gaze settled on a man standing by a purple Oldsmobile, two suitcases resting on the driveway. He glanced furtively from side to side, then produced a pack of Rothmans from his shirt pocket and lit a smoke while sheltering behind the open trunk of the vehicle.

Lynette's father.

Instinctively, she hid her nakedness, even though she was invisible to him. But something about the scene struck her as odd. She was sure Lynette's parents' Oldsmobile had been the color of cheap mustard, not purple.

The house was as she remembered, the only incongruous detail being a small white horse in the yard. It looked at her, then turned and ran down the street, its hair streaked with dried blood. It passed a little boy mowing his lawn, and then the mailman, who didn't appear to notice.

For a moment, everything felt normal again, as if the murder of her family had been nothing more than a bad dream. And the more she thought about it, the more she decided it was precisely that.

A dream.

Her parents couldn't die... they were already dead. What Susan had done to them had been a trick. A sleight of hand.

"It wasn't real," she told herself, the horrifying imagery replaying itself in her head. "It was just a movie. A sick movie." Still... seeing it, watching it happen before her eyes... it had almost driven her mad. She could never bear witness to that again.

Her heart — and her mind — would be unable to cope.

Carefully strummed acoustic notes wafted through the open window on the upper floor.

Lynette's song.

It played again, a lighthouse beacon on a tempestuous night.

With trepidation, she stood and walked barefoot through the grass, heading for Lynette's house. Would it be like before? Would Lynette come bounding down the stairs as she entered, pretty as a picture? That had been the moment Charlie had fallen in love with her. Though they hadn't known each other long, she couldn't argue with her heart. Love was a fickle mistress. It didn't always make sense, and nor did it have to.

Love just... *was.*

"Come on," she said, standing in the doorway. "Go in."

But she wasn't sure if she should. To see Lynette again — the real Lynette, not Susan's grotesque charade — and to not be able to talk to her... after all that had happened, that would be the final straw. There were only so many heartbreaks her poor, damaged organ could take.

If anyone can see you, it's Lynette, her mind argued.

"And what if it's another trick?" she replied. She looked down at her naked body. Her breasts bore pink scratch marks from Susan's nails, and she shuddered. Susan killing her family may not have been real — *it wasn't, it wasn't, it wasn't* — but the way she had raped Charlie was undeniable.

"Not for the first time," she said, a bitter tear rolling down her cheek.

From down the street came a colossal crash. Charlie snapped her head in the direction. A car lay on its roof on the sidewalk. The mailman dropped his bag and jogged towards the vehicle, and as it exploded in a ball of flame, it sent him flying through the air, his shirt and shorts blazing with fire. He landed on the road in front of a pickup, the wheels thudding over him.

She glanced over in a panic at the little boy with the lawnmower, his legs poking out from beneath the hulking green machine that spat out blood and hair and chopped clumps of flesh.

"God, no..."

She was here.

Susan had found her again.

With a final look back at Lynette's father — the trunk was closed, his headless body prone on the driveway — Charlie sprinted through the door and up the stairs, Lynette's song getting louder, louder. She reached the top and flung herself through the bedroom door, landing in a naked heap on the floor, and there, *there,* was Lynette, cross-legged on the bed with her guitar, and beside her...

"*You can't get away,*" said Susan. She stroked her hand through Lynette's hair, the girl unaware of the violation. Susan looked worse, somehow, her face seemingly in the process of reconfiguring itself, the features drooping like a wax candle. Her arms were no longer at her shoulders. One protruded vilely from her waist, the other from above her right breast.

She looks like Mr. Potato-head, Charlie thought madly.

"Did you think she could protect you?" sneered Susan, her voice different, a mutant growl. What the hell was happening to her?

A force of immense power gripped Charlie in boiling hands. She screamed as Susan unleashed wave after wave of violent energy coursing through her.

"Why could you never love me like this?" asked Susan. "What did she have that I didn't?"

Charlie dug her nails into the carpet as the pain passed. "I did love you," she grunted, tasting blood in her mouth. She spat it out. "You know I did."

"And you, can't see," Lynette sang obliviously, *"How the sun, shines on me."*

"What the fuck is this?" asked Susan mockingly. "Did she write you a fucking *song?*" She laughed so hard that several teeth pierced her runny, yolk-like lips, while a festering sore on what was once her forehead popped, oozing green pus down the bizarre assemblage of features that constituted Susan's face.

"You thought this maudlin bitch would be your savior? This melancholy *cunt?* She couldn't even save herself. You should see how pathetic her life has been." Susan fixed Charlie with a dazed stare. "Here. Let me show you."

Charlie's vision exploded in white light, revealing a young Lynette, aged maybe fifteen or sixteen. She hobbled through some kind of suburban wasteland with a group of kids in pursuit. They quickly caught up to her.

Susan stood by Charlie's side. "Watch this."

One of the kids — a girl — grabbed Lynette's shoulder and spun her around.

"Please," said Lynette, "I won't—"

A vicious right-hook stung her cheek. Lynette fell backwards, landing in a thick puddle of mud. When she tried to rise, another girl booted her thigh and shoved her. They crowded around, rolling her over and forcing her face into the mud. Lynette struggled against the bullies, but she was powerless against such odds. While four of them held her down, the others rifled through her schoolbag, stealing her money and emptying the rest of the contents into the dirt. They ran off, laughing, leaving Lynette face down in filth and scum.

"Please stop," said Charlie.

"It gets better," said Susan. "Your girlfriend is a real fuck-up."

Now Lynette was in a movie theater, a bucket of popcorn balanced on her lap. Charlie and Susan stood in front of the screen, as a young boy slunk his way down the aisle. A couple of other kids watched from the balcony, giggling as the boy raced along the row behind Lynette with his hand raised, palm open. Before she knew what was happening, he clapped his hand mightily against her ear. Lynette screamed and dropped from her seat, spilling her popcorn across the floor. When she stood with her hand over her ear, blood leaked between her fingers.

"They popped her eardrum that time. Made her half-deaf. A cripple."

"Don't show me any more," sobbed Charlie.

"We're just getting started. This pathetic bitch has led the sorriest little life I've ever seen. I want you to understand the mistake you made when you chose her over me."

Charlie felt sick. She projectile vomited over the front

row of theater patrons, her bile soaking into the viewer's hotdogs. One man took a bite, blissfully unaware of the spectral retchings that coated it.

"This next one might be my favorite," said Susan.

The theater gave way to an alley. Charlie wanted to fall to her knees and scream, to look away, to give up and just... fucking... *die*. She knew this place. She had seen it before, in dreams. Sometimes, in bed, Susan's feverish night terrors leaked into Charlie's brain, infecting her sleep. She shared her captor's wild visions, her impossible ecstasies, her dreadful fantasies. Lynette's brutal rape had been one of Susan's most frequently recurring dreams. Charlie had never known if it was real — a by-product of Susan taking over Lynette's mind — or a morbid flight of fancy.

Now she knew it was true.

"Lynette," she whimpered, as Susan accompanied her down the alleyway. A large group of teenagers blocked Lynette from their view, screeching with delight and egging the boys on.

"Let's take a closer look," said Susan, following the trail of scattered rocks that the teens had pelted at Lynette, forcing her into the dead-end. Drops of blood formed another part of the grisly trail, giving way to ripped and shredded clothing.

"Stop!" cried Charlie. If Susan was attempting to break her spirit, it was working. "Please! I'm begging you, I don't want to see! Do you hear me? I don't want to fucking see it again!"

They stepped over the torn panties of the girl Charlie loved, moving through the crowd of whooping onlookers, now only a wall of boys between them and the horrifying assault.

"*Do it!*" yelped one boy, his voice breaking mid-sentence.

"*Turn her straight!*" shouted another.

It became a chant.

"*Turn her straight! Turn her straight! Turn her straight!*"

"*No!*" screamed Charlie. "*No!*"

Susan laughed. "Look at her! Look at your savior now!"

They approached the boys, drawing closer, drawing *level*, passing them. One boy remained. He was on the ground with his back to them, his pants and underwear bunched up around his knees, his sweaty ass thrusting, pounding.

But something was wrong.

The boy with the crewcut, his discarded switchblade resting near his hand, howled with each violent jerk of his hips. And as Susan and Charlie walked around him, they both saw what was missing.

Lynette.

The girl was nowhere to be seen. Instead, her rapist stabbed his chubby erection against the ground, the tip scraping the rough concrete, tiny fragments of gravel embedded in the fat, purple head.

"It hurts!" he cried, as the sharp stones grated his penis, leaving a red smear on the concrete. "It hurts!"

"Where the fuck is she?" asked Susan. They both turned to the gathered throng. The crowd was cheering on a boy tearing his cock to shreds by fucking the sidewalk... yet no one had noticed the missing victim.

The alleyway melted, becoming an unfamiliar high school locker room. Here, a group of girls in gym clothes and underwear took turns slamming their bloody fists into a dented locker, presumably aiming at Lynette... who wasn't there.

Susan gripped Charlie by the hand so hard she thought it might break. "Where is she? Where has she gone?"

They spun around, no longer in the locker room but in a

pink bedroom adorned with posters of Elvis Presley and Angie Dickinson in *Police Woman*. A repugnant man in his fifties, wearing sagging gray underpants and nothing else, brought a leather belt down against an empty bed with staggering ferocity.

"You been a bad girl, Lynny," the man slurred drunkenly. "And bad girls get a *whippin'* from their uncles." He beat the bed mercilessly, and Charlie shuddered at the thought of Lynette being on the receiving end of the harsh strikes. "Now quit your bellyachin' and mebbe I'll let you taste a cigarette after."

"Where is she?" yelled Susan, her scream so violent it caused the room to shake. The wardrobe toppled and crashed to the floor, the lamp swaying so hard on its cord that the bulb hit the ceiling and shattered. Even the foul man in the underpants stopped whipping the bed and looked around, puzzled.

"Hell's goin' on?" he muttered, the makeshift lash dangling from his hand like a used condom as Susan searched for Lynette. With each stomping step, her left arm dropped lower and lower on her body, until her knuckles dragged across the carpet.

"Where is that cunt? I'll kill her!"

"Who are you?" asked the man, gazing at Susan in bewilderment, and she chopped her hand repeatedly through the air, razor-sharp red lines appearing across the man's gut, his arms, his legs, his head. The pieces slipped away from each other, large chunks of meat thudding to the floor as his body crumbled.

Susan turned and stared at Charlie. Her eyes were upside down, and when she blinked, the lids rose like she was a lizard. "You did this," she spat, drool spilling down her elongated chin as she clomped towards Charlie, grabbing her wrist and tossing her onto the bed. She stooped and picked up the leather belt, which was still clutched in the firm grip of the disgusting man's severed hand.

"You did this!" shrieked Susan in a lunatic pitch, as she brought the belt whistling down on Charlie's lower back. Pain flared as the hard leather split her skin.

"Where is she?" demanded Susan, as the belt came down with a savage crack across Charlie's spine. "I can do this for a long, long time," she said, the belt smacking dryly across Charlie's exposed thighs. "I can do this forever!" Harder and harder Susan attacked her, viciously whipping her. Charlie felt an unseeable force flip her onto her back, and she stared up into Susan's deranged face, before the belt whacked excruciatingly across her breasts.

"Stop! I'm begging you, stop!"

Susan didn't. Manic glee shaped her expression into something resembling human, but the eyes betrayed her. Her mind was no more. Charlie's legs spread apart, wide and waiting, as Susan eyed her with the blood streaked belt in her hand.

"Last chance," she said, smacking the leather against Charlie's inner thigh, bringing it perilously close to her vagina. Red welts formed across Charlie's bare flesh. "Where is she hiding?"

Charlie gagged from the pain. She swam in and out of consciousness as Susan let the belt dangle over her crotch, the wet leather brushing her labia.

She closed her eyes.

"Just kill me," she whispered, and waited.

There was a long silence, before Susan said, "So be it." She kneeled on legs that bent the wrong way and put her head between Charlie's things, tenderly kissing her. "Goodbye, Charlie," she said, rising to her hunched form and raising the belt. "Goodbye, Charlie's cunt!"

She leaned back, then swung, the belt screeching through the—

Her arm froze in midair as a hand shot out of nowhere and caught her wrist. Susan turned towards the interruptor, the desecrator of her holy sacrifice, ready to destroy them.

"*You,*" she said with a ghastly sneer.

Lynette held her wrist in an iron grip, her face set, eyes narrowed. She glanced once at Charlie, then smiled at Susan.

"Get the fuck away from my girlfriend," she said.

11

———

Lynette.

Charlie saw her. She *heard* her. Despite all she had seen, all she had done, she struggled to believe it. She scrambled backwards over the bed as blood surged from Susan's eyes. Floods of it, like someone had stuck a firehose up her ass. The blast displaced one of her eyeballs, knocking it loose. The orb dangled from the optic nerve, and Susan tried to shove it back in.

Lynette tilted her head, raising Susan up, her feet leaving the carpet.

"What's happening?" roared Susan as she rocketed towards — no, *through* — the wall, leaving a gaping hole in the brickwork.

"Come on," Lynette said, turning to Charlie. "We don't have much time."

Without a word, Charlie took Lynette's hand. Her legs wobbled as she stood, but there was no chance to reacclimatise. Lynette hauled her away, and they were off, racing through the front door. As they passed the hole in the wall left by Susan, Charlie saw the insane girl charging towards them.

"This way," said Lynette, as they departed the collapsing bedroom and reappeared in the familiar corridor.

An ear-piercing shriek boomed after them.

Charlie glanced over her shoulder. Susan was on their tail, closing the distance fast. A brick wall rose in front of her, and she smashed through it with ease.

"Shit," said Lynette. "She's too strong."

"But where are we going?"

"Elevator. Almost there."

More bricks blasted apart behind them, Susan's footsteps echoing after them. Ahead, the floor started to split, the corridor cleaving in two.

"Get ready to jump," said Lynette, the crevice widening before Charlie's eyes.

"I can't make that!"

"You can do it. I've got you. Ready? Jump!"

Lynette leaped first, gripping Charlie's hand, the pair soaring through the air. Lynette landed gracefully on the opposite side, but Charlie realized she wasn't going to make it. Panicking, she held her arm out, searching for—

Lynette grabbed her trailing arm and yanked her up, the great fissure yawning behind them. Where was this elevator Lynette had mentioned? And *why* was there a fucking elevator? Where did it go?

She looked back in time to see Susan reach the broken floor. Rather than jump the gap, she scaled the side wall and scurried across like a spider.

"Here it is!" shouted Lynette.

The elevator was one of those old-fashioned ones Charlie knew from the movies, a metal cage with doors that opened manually. Lynette hauled the bars aside, sparks shooting from the grinding metal. She stepped in, pulling Charlie in with her, and slammed the bars shut. Two buttons were set into the brass panel, one marked C and one marked L. Lynette jabbed the L button, and the elevator jolted as Susan caught up. She smashed into the bars, shoving her arms between them. The gaps were narrow, and as she forced her forearms in, the sharp edges tore thin strips of skin and muscle from the grasping limbs. Lynette and Charlie pressed against the back of the elevator as Susan groped for them.

"You bitch," she snarled. "You fucking *bitch*. How are you doing this?"

"What do you think I've been doing for the last ten years?" yelled Lynette, and then the elevator began its descent. Susan tried to pull back through, but she was too slow. Her arms caught on the rising floor and were torn off, the elevator jerking as it sliced through muscle and bone. The two limbs hit the floor, fingers still twitching even as the appendages dissolved into steaming piles of bilious goo.

The giant metal contraption juddered to a halt. Lynette opened the bars and dragged Charlie into the corridor, shouting, "Quick, this way!"

They bolted towards a door, appearing in the same bedroom they had left only moments before, except this one was unmarred by destruction. Heading straight for the wardrobe, Lynette opened it and stepped inside. Charlie hesitated before the ominous black void, before a voice called from the darkness.

"Hurry!"

She entered, finding Lynette in the vast hall of an art gallery. They crossed the room towards a fire exit. Lynette kicked it open, revealing an abandoned warehouse. "We have to go deep. Somewhere she'll never find us."

From room to room they traveled, building to building, city to city, each door narrower than the last, until they were climbing down manholes and crawling through air vents. Before claustrophobia had a chance to dig its claws in, they exited the dusty metal tunnel. Cold air blasted Charlie's face as she emerged onto a platform hundreds of feet high.

A dam. They were standing atop a dam. All around was the most beautiful natural vista Charlie had ever seen, a sprawling series of mountains and rivers and forests and lakes, as far as the eye could see. Lynette stepped to the edge of the platform, while Charlie hung back. Ever since Susan's accident at the dance, she had feared heights.

"Come here," said Lynette.

Charlie looked down through the metal bars between her feet, her stomach curdling. "It's too high."

"Do you trust me?"

Charlie looked at her. "Of... of course I do."

"Then come here." Lynette smiled. "Please."

Closing her eyes, Charlie took three quick steps. She stumbled and Lynette caught her, pulling her into an embrace.

"Kiss me," she said. "And don't let go."

Charlie did. She kissed Lynette, their lips locking together, the taste exquisite.

"Remember," Lynette said between hungry kisses. "Don't let go."

They toppled sideways, the air rushing by as the two girls, in each other's arms, fell from the platform. Charlie was frightened. The fall should kill them. And yet... if she was to die now, together with Lynette after all this time...

then it would be okay. Everything would be worth it for this one...

...last...

...perfect...

...kiss.

12

CHARLIE AWOKE BENEATH FRESHLY LAUNDERED SHEETS, HER head resting on a spongy pillow. The lights were dim, and she tried to sit.

"Careful," said Lynette.

Charlie turned in her direction. There, by the side of the bed, sat Lynette in a black satin nightie. In the faint light, she handed Charlie a glass of water. There were so many questions... and there would be time for them. For now, only one question truly mattered.

"Lynette... is it really you?"

The girl nodded almost imperceptibly. "Yeah. It's me."

Charlie's body relaxed. Tears sprang to her eyes, and she pulled Lynette onto the bed, shuffling over to make room. There, they held each other, crying together, their foreheads touching.

"I never thought I'd see you again," said Charlie. "The *real* you, I mean. Not..."

"I know."

"I've dreamed about this moment. I never wanted to give up hope, or stop believing, but after a while... she broke me.

And I *did* give up. I wanted to die, and then I *did,* and things only got worse."

"Don't think about it," said Lynette, kissing Charlie's nose, her cheek, her lips. "You're here now. With me."

"But where *are* we?"

"My house."

"That's not what I mean," said Charlie quietly. "Are we... are we in heaven?"

"I don't know. I don't think so. If it is, then it's pretty messed up."

"Tell me about it," smiled Charlie, before a grim idea took hold. "Can she find us? Are we safe here?"

"We're deep in my subconscious. Only I — and now you — know the way."

"But she might have followed us. She could be outside, ready to—"

"Baby, she would have been here by now. You've been out for a month."

"A month?"

"Time's funny here," said Lynette, without elaborating. "How you feeling?"

"Okay." She ran her hands down her body. Lynette had dressed her in silk pajamas, the material welcomingly cool against her skin. "What about you? Have you been... *here*... all this time?"

"Yeah," the girl whispered sadly. Then she brightened. "Come on, let's go for a walk. It's a beautiful day out there."

"Out where?"

Lynette smiled. "You'll see." She hopped out of bed and padded to the thick drapes that obscured the window, pulling them apart. The light of a blisteringly sunny morning flooded into the room, blinding Charlie. She slid out from under the covers, squinting through the brightness, and walked towards the window.

She gasped at what she saw.

"No fucking way..."

The first thing she noticed was the Eiffel Tower. But before she asked if they were in Paris, she realized the monument was set against a backdrop of the Canadian Rockies, the snow-covered peaks shimmering in the sun. To the left was the open sea, a golden strip of sandy beach separating it from a series of stunning architectural triumphs. Charlie didn't recognize most, but she did spot the Taj Mahal amongst them. Directly below was a massive courtyard with a glass pyramid in the center. People walked to and fro, adults talking, children playing, everyone going about their lives without a care.

"They can't see us," said Lynette. "But it's nice to have people around. It can get lonely sometimes."

"I don't understand," said Charlie. She gestured out the window. "Where are we?"

"My little kingdom."

"Did you..."

"Build this? Yeah. I learned how. You can too. I can show you."

Charlie chuckled doubtfully. "I'm not good at that sort of thing. Remember when you taught me how to meditate?"

Lynette placed her hand on Charlie's arm. "That was your first time."

"I never got any better at it."

"*Never?*"

Charlie shook her head, enjoying the way her long hair brushed across her face. She had forgotten what it felt like. "If anything, I got worse."

"Well, you've got all the time in the world, now," said Lynette. "And you've got..." — she half-shrugged — "...me."

"That sounds good," said Charlie, and they embraced, holding each other close. Charlie nuzzled into Lynette's neck, breathing in her scent. A miserable, awful part of her brain fought back against her happiness.

It's not her, a voice said, dripping with pessimism. *It's Susan. She's fooling you again.*

She tried to ignore it, but what if the voice was correct? It wouldn't be the first time she had fallen for it...

No. The way Lynette held her, the shy way she spoke, like she didn't want to be a bother... it was different to Susan. Or, at least, what Susan had become. This was sweeter, more tender.

"You wanna go to the beach?" Lynette whispered.

"Not yet," replied Charlie. She reached for the hem of Lynette's nightie, letting her fingertips brush the cool, supple flesh of her thighs, then raised the flimsy covering, sliding it over Lynette's body, revealing matching black satin panties. She looked to Lynette for confirmation. The girl nodded, lifting her arms above her head to allow Charlie to continue disrobing her. She wore no bra, and Charlie — who had ached for Lynette's touch for over a decade — couldn't help herself. She kissed the girl's breasts, her limbs trembling with nerves and excitement.

Lynette unbuttoned Charlie's pajama top. They faced each other with the awkwardness of new lovers, and then Lynette giggled.

"Sorry," she said, embarrassed. "I just... I can't quite believe it."

Charlie laughed too. It was so far from her prior sexual experiences, which had been fraught with violence and degeneracy and nightmarish tension. To stand with someone, near-naked, and laugh — god, to actually laugh in pleasure and delight — was an alien concept to her.

Until now.

She put her arms around Lynette, their bodies becoming one, and kissed. Charlie felt Lynette's hands on her pajamas, tugging them over her ass. She stepped out of them and stood naked, the marks from Susan's whipping visible, but fading.

Lynette looked up, and licked her dry, nervous lips.

"Make love to me," she breathed.

Charlie smiled, a tear forming in the corner of her eye. "I thought you'd never ask," she said.

After, they lay in bed together, enjoying the easy post-coital silence. Charlie lay on her belly, her eyes closed, while Lynette sat on the backs of Charlie's legs.

"It's funny," the girl said. "I live among humankind's greatest artistic achievements. From my window, I can see the Eiffel Tower, the Hagia Sophia, the Colosseum, the Guggenheim. Every day, I walk past buildings by Gaudi, Le Corbusier, and Frank Lloyd Wright, all in the space of two blocks. Heck, I live *in* the Louvre, above works of art powerful to make people cry, to change lives." She smacked Charlie's ass. "But nothing — and I mean *none* of it — compares to the natural beauty of your ass, Charlie Bonner."

Charlie chuckled and squirmed with delight as Lynette kissed her butt cheeks.

"This ass saved my life one time, you know that?" said Lynette, between warm kisses on Charlie's posterior.

"What do you... *mmmmh, that's nice...* what do you mean?"

"When I was trapped in my own mind... by *her*... I couldn't find my way out. I was lost, and people were chasing me. People who wanted to hurt me, Charlie. But then I found you, in the memory. Remember that time in school I told you about? How I followed you, staring at your ass until I was late for class?"

"Yeah."

"It was that memory that brought me out. I followed your ass all the way out of her prison, and escaped. You saved my life." She playfully smacked Charlie's rump again.

"And now you've saved mine," said Charlie. "Guess that makes us even."

"Guess so."

Charlie swallowed, and said, "You can smack it harder, if you like."

Lynette waited a moment, then spanked Charlie. "Like that?"

"Yeah. Like that. It's nice."

"Are you sure? I don't want to hurt you."

"I don't mind if you do," said Charlie, grinning. "Anyway, you can always kiss it better."

Later — their desires sated, albeit temporarily — the pair got out of bed. They showered, then Lynette introduced Charlie to her walk-in closet, which turned out to be a normal wooden wardrobe that somehow led to a Sears department store. They wandered the aisles, picking out clothes and goofing off, the way they had never been able to during their all-too-brief time together.

Dressed in flimsy summer dresses, they ran hand-in-hand through the streets, Charlie marveling at the ceaseless parade of incredible buildings.

"It's so beautiful here," she beamed, dizzy from the sensory overload. "How did you do it?"

"Took a lot of practice, but once you know how, it's easy. And, I can change it any time I want."

"No way."

"Sure. Watch!" Lynette placed her hands on Charlie's shoulders and pushed her. Surprised, Charlie stumbled backwards, falling, landing—

—in the warm ocean, the water breaking her fall.

She laughed, pulling Lynette under with her, the pair swimming in the sea, surrounded by unnatural fish and plant-life that glowed a lurid, pulsing neon. When they left the water, laughing, Charlie walked ahead of Lynette to show off her ass through the wet — and nearly transparent — dress. She loved the way Lynette looked at her. With love, and with respect, and — *yes* — with lust.

"So you can do anything you want?" asked Charlie as they lay on sun loungers wearing bikinis they had picked up in Sears. All around them, people went about their business, ignoring the two girls. Families and groups of friends and couples and everyone in between, all enjoying a gorgeous day at the beach.

"Not anything," answered Lynette, her eyes hidden behind dark sunglasses. "But a lot. Within reason."

"Show me."

Lynette looked thoughtful. "It's quite loud here, don't you think?"

"Guess so," shrugged Charlie.

The volume of the people ebbed away like the tide, getting quieter and quieter until... they were silent, and all

Charlie heard was the sound of the waves crashing against the shore and the occasional squawk of a gull.

"That better?" asked Lynette.

"Shit. No wonder you beat her."

The volume roared back, louder than it had been before, making Charlie scream. Lynette concentrated, controlling it, bringing it down again.

"Sorry," she said. She looked troubled. "I didn't beat her, Charlie. I took her by surprise, that's all. She didn't expect me to challenge her, and that's how we escaped. But I couldn't kill her, no way. If she ever found us here..."

"I thought you said we were safe?"

Lynette removed her sunglasses. "And I hope I'm right," she said, gazing out to sea, where a yellow dinghy bobbed across the surface. "For our sake, I *pray* I'm fucking right."

13

Susan was dying.

She had known for a while, ever since the car crash. Back there, in the *real* world, she didn't have long to live. That was fine, she reasoned. In here, she had days, even *weeks* left, time she had planned on spending torturing Charlie until she was nothing but a broken mind in a useless body.

And then Lynette showed up and ruined *everything*. That bitch... that fucking wretched cunting *slut*.

"I'll kill her," she slurred. "I'll kill them both. Kill them, kill them, kill them."

She would turn this whole damn place upside down if she had to. She was familiar with Lynette's mind, after having spent months raiding it for information, for backstory to her character. And it had worked, for a while. Charlie had really believed she was Lynette. What galled Susan the most was how *happy* Charlie had seemed. Why? Why was she happy Susan was dead? They were supposed to be in love.

"I'll never leave you," she remembered Charlie saying. *"I'll*

love you forever, I promise."

Yeah, sure. Until some new pussy came along.

She looked forward to killing Lynette. That bitch took everything from her, and yet circumstances had forced Susan to inhabit her foul, wretched body for *ten years*. She hated seeing Lynette's stupid face in the mirror, hated the weight of her heavy breasts. But most of all, she hated the way Charlie had looked at her in those early days, her eyes full of adoration and longing.

"Both going to die," Susan sang, her voice that of a someone who had recently crawled from the grave. "Both going to die, both going to die."

Lynette had hurt her. She wondered if the bitch knew how badly. Back in reality, her life was slipping away. Worst of all, the closer she got to death, the more her body deteriorated. In front of the cracked full-length mirror in Lynette's bedroom, she saw herself.

She was a monster.

It was as if she was made of rubber and elastic, and a particularly imaginative child had tried to bend her into the most revolting position possible. Her torso twisted to the side, her arms bursting from the middle of her chest and her lower back. Her legs were like a goat's, her feet strange, flat puddles. But it was her face that bothered her the most. Her face, once so beautiful, was a torrid nightmare. Nothing was in the right place, or the right way up. Every time she moved, the different parts jostled around like a shaken snow globe, coming to rest wherever they wanted. Her skin, too, had abandoned her. It shuffled down her face in layers of peeling strips, the top of her skull visible through the remaining clumps of hair. Boils peppered her flesh, the pustules popping with alarming regularity, sending foul-smelling thick pus down her abhorrent abomination of a face, where it dripped from loose skin that sagged from her chin.

Charlie would *never* want to fuck her *now*.

And it was all thanks to Lynette. That bitch bitch bitch bitch bitch.

She had to find the pair of escapees, and find them fast. Every step Susan took left a sticky, blood-flecked residue on the floor. Her body was failing, her powers weakening. If she didn't locate them soon, she may not have the strength to kill them both. She had to do something, had to get help. Help with finding them, help with subduing them... and help with destroying them.

She left the bedroom and entered the dark corridors of Charlie's mind, as the ground shook beneath her, and thunder rumbled overhead. She had a plan. It was simply a case of putting it into action. Did she have time? Yes, if she conserved her energy. The lights around her dimmed in response, and Susan lurched off towards the next door, leaving a trail of fleshy, liquid footprints.

She would get the help she needed. Then, she would storm Lynette's mind, and tear the entire place apart until she found the truant lovers. If there was enough time, she would torture them first, or maybe make them torture each other, until they grew to loathe the sight of each other's stupid face. Yes, that would be poetic. She would enjoy that.

She would enjoy watching them suffer.

And as they cried for mercy, begged for the reaper himself to envelop them in his icy cloak... she would kill them.

Then — and *only* then — would Susan allow herself to die.

14

———

THEY STROLLED FOR HOURS, HAND-IN-HAND, AFRAID TO LET the other go for fear they would lose each other again.

Charlie spoke of what her life had been like, omitting the most graphic, upsetting details, and finishing with the car crash and her experiences in the afterlife. Lynette listened, occasionally interjecting and then apologizing for doing so.

"I'm used to saying what I want, when I want," she admitted. "Living on your own for so long erodes your social skills, I think. And mine weren't great to begin with."

"I don't mind," said Charlie, as she gazed in awe at an unfinished church Lynette had referred to as La Sagrada Familia. "It's nice to hear your voice again. The way it's *meant* to sound." She thought for a moment. "I'm glad she stopped trying to get the intonations right. After a while, she just sounded like Susan, only higher pitched. So when she shouted at me, or said horrible things, it didn't sound like *you* were saying it."

"It must have been awful."

Charlie didn't know what to say to that. It *had* been

awful. An unending nightmare of violence and sexual torture. She had long thought she would never enjoy sex — or any form of intimacy — again. But in Lynette's arms, she felt safe. Safe, and loved. What else mattered?

"How about you?" Charlie asked, changing the subject. "What have you been up to since you died?"

"There's a sentence you don't hear every day," smiled Lynette. The smile faded. "It took a while for things to be okay. I was trapped, locked in my worst memories. Forced to relive them, over and over."

Charlie nodded. Susan had shown her some of them, though she didn't mention that. If Lynette wanted to talk about those, then she would, in her own time.

"Eventually, I learned how to change things. How to control the memories. See, you *can* change them, with enough effort. You just gotta learn how."

"How long did it take you?"

Words deserted Lynette. Her lip quivered, a teardrop rolling down her cheek. "A long time," she said quietly, and turned away.

"I'm sorry," said Charlie.

"It's okay. It's over now."

A sudden tremor rattled the windows in the surrounding buildings. Charlie stumbled as a sizeable chunk of rubble crashed to the ground nearby.

"Quakes are getting worse," said Lynette grimly.

"When did they start?" Charlie asked, although she knew the answer before Lynette said it.

"Around the time you arrived."

Charlie looked at the broken masonry. It was bright blue, which was odd, as it didn't match any of the buildings. She left Lynette, curiously drawn to the rock. It was several feet wide, and as blue as the—

"Oh," she said, as she kneeled by the unusual rock. She reached towards it, *into* it, feeling the cold air blast her hand.

"What's wrong?" asked Lynette.

Charlie didn't answer. Instead, she gazed up at the sinister black hole high above them, from where the chunk of sky had fallen.

"Well, that's probably not good," she said.

Susan took the first door in Charlie's memory, emerging in a shopping mall.

Snorting out a stream of blood and mucus, she staggered the length of the mall on strange, twisted limbs, passing hundreds of people. As she did so, the people halted and dropped whatever they were carrying. Mostly it was shopping bags, but sometimes it was a cigarette or even, on one occasion that made Susan laugh, a child. One-by-one, ignoring their discarded belongings, the people turned and followed her like a procession of lemmings, their faces betraying not a hint of emotion.

By the time she arrived at the ice rink, the line snaked back through the mall further than she could see. They were deathly silent, arms dangling by their sides, eyes focused unquestioningly on their new master.

Susan was tired. The mental strain of controlling hundreds, possibly thousands of people, took a toll on her already fragile mind. But not knowing the full extent of Lynette's powers, she couldn't take any chances.

The people left the rink and headed towards the exits, hobbling clumsily on their skates. With a sigh, she made them remove the footwear, though a lone figure continued skimming across the ice, oblivious to her inaudible siren call. Susan watched the teenage girl, rage boiling her blood, her gnarled fingers closing into an attempted fist that resembled a stack of trimmed tree branches.

"Charlie," she said, spitting out the name like a hex.

Blissfully unaware, the young Charlie skated unsteadily, a determined look plastered to her face.

"We could have been so happy together," said Susan. She glanced at her army. It wasn't enough. Not yet, anyway.

But that didn't matter.

Her final act of destruction was only beginning.

15

"So, he's right out on this... this bridge, or something," said Charlie breathlessly. "If he falls, he's gonna die, for sure. There's nowhere else for him to go... he's *trapped.*"

Lynette leaned in close. "So what happens?"

Charlie sat back in her beach recliner, and smiled. "Then Darth Vader says... '*Luke... I am your father.*'"

Lynette was stunned. She couldn't believe it. "No... that's impossible."

"That's what Luke said."

"But... but *Vader* killed Luke's dad. Ben Kenobi said so."

"He was lying. Well, sort of. Anyway, Luke can't take it, and he jumps off the bridge."

"He dies?" gasped Lynette. She was so near the edge of her recliner she was in danger of falling off.

Charlie shook her head. "He lands on the Falcon, and they escape."

"Thank god," breathed Lynette. She shuffled backwards as her recliner started to tip. "They can't kill Luke. He still has to get together with Leia."

Charlie pulled a face. "Yeah, about that..."

"What? They *kissed*, remember? In the first film."

"Oh, that's the other thing. It's not the first film anymore. It's the fourth."

Lynette stared at her, brow furrowed, her dark sunglasses masking the bafflement in her eyes.

"*Star Wars*," said Charlie, "is now called *Star Wars Episode Four: A New Hope*. They've not made the first three yet."

"What the fuck are you talking about?"

"It's hard to explain. Anyway, Darth Vader is Luke's father, and I'll let you stew on that for a while. Later, I'll tell you all about *Return of the Jedi*. Or Episode Six, if you prefer."

"I do *not* prefer, thank you very much." Lynette shook her head. "Oh my god. Vader is his *dad*."

"The whole theater went nutsoid. The line around the block was so long, I had to wait in it for hours."

"I bet it was worth it."

"It was," Charlie agreed. "Hey, could we watch my memory of it? Then you could see it with me! I could show you all the horror films you missed."

"Any good ones?"

Charlie laughed out loud. "Oh, like, soooo many. I lived in New York, so I didn't go to the drive-in anymore. Instead, there were all these horrible, grimy theaters, where people took drugs and jerked each other off, and the films were the kind you'd *never* see back home. There was one called *Maniac*, where this guy stalks women and scalps them. It was so gross." It was funny, she thought. Being with Lynette, she felt herself reverting to her teenage language. "So what do you say? Could we go into my memories and watch them? I'd fuckin' *love* to show you *Dr. Butcher M.D.*"

"Dr. Butcher?"

"Yeah. *He makes house calls*," giggled Charlie, mimicking the film's trailer.

Lynette smiled sadly. "That would be amazing, but I don't think we can risk it. She knows your mind too well. Probably spent a lot of time in there. She might find us."

"Yeah, I guess you're right," said Charlie, and took a sip of her piña colada.

The two girls were on the beach again, wearing matching striped bikinis, ice-cold cocktails resting on the small plastic table between them. Since the last quake, no more sky had fallen, though the black hole was still observable above them.

Charlie looked out to sea. "What's out there?"

"Nothing," said Lynette. "The world just stops."

"So weird."

"You get used to it. The only problem is, there's never anything new. No new films, no new songs... it's the oldies station, twenty-four-seven."

"Music's changed a lot in ten years," said Charlie. "Rap is really popular right now."

"Rap?"

"Yeah, it's songs, but instead of singing, someone talks quickly over the music."

"That sounds awful," said Lynette.

"No, it's good! It's not just talking, it's very, y'know, rhythmic."

"Sing me a rap, then."

Charlie rolled her eyes. "You don't sing a rap. You *rap* it."

"Fine. Rap me a rap."

Charlie sat up, placing her feet in the sand. Overhead, the gulls circled, cawing relentlessly. "Okay. Uhh..." She imagined a Run-D.M.C. style beat in her head, and rapped, *"My name is Charlie and I eat a lot of Barley."*

Lynette screwed up her face in horror.

"Wait, wait," said Charlie. "Let me try again." She heard the beat again. *"Your name is Lynette, and, I, ummm, I... I take you to the vet."*

"Uh-huh. And people listen to this?"

"It's better than it sounds. It's hard to do, okay?"

"Sure," said Lynette, clearly unimpressed.

"Don't be a meanie when you're wearing a bikini," rapped Charlie.

Lynette turned to her. *"You keep giving me sass, and I'll spank you on the ass."*

Charlie felt her face go red. She looked at her drink. "That doesn't sound so bad," she grinned.

"Well," said Lynette, rolling over to get the sun on her back. "The jury's still out on rap music."

"It's good, I swear," said Charlie, as her gaze traveled up Lynette's tanned legs and over the gentle curve of her butt. Lynette caught her looking, and smiled. God, she was so beautiful.

"I love you, you know," Charlie blurted out.

"I love you too," said Lynette. "I remember when I first told you that. It just came out. I was worried you'd think I was a psycho."

"Why would I?"

"We'd only known each other a few days."

"Sometimes, that's all you need to know for sure."

They looked at each other, then dissolved into giggles. "You're such a loser," said Lynette.

Charlie launched into a feeble impersonation of Ben Kenobi. "Who's the biggest loser? The loser, or the loser who loves her?"

Lynette kicked sand at her, and Charlie squealed. "No! I've just put lotion on!"

"So what?" laughed Lynette, putting her hands on Charlie's recliner.

"Don't you da—"

She tipped it. Charlie rolled off and onto the sand, the coarse grains sticking to her lotion-smeared body. "You bitch!" she laughed, getting to her feet and chasing Lynette, who zig-zagged through the crowded beach, laughing all the way. Charlie caught up with her, grabbing her striped bikini bottoms and yanking them down. She tackled Lynette, the two girls rolling over one another, laughing and play fighting until they came to a stop, Lynette on her back, Charlie on top.

"Kiss me," said Lynette.

Charlie wanted to — she wanted to do a lot more than kiss, for that matter — but first she had something she needed to ask.

"Hey, about that song," she began.

"What song? Another one of your raps? Here's one for you. *Take off all my clothes, or I'll punch you on the nose.*"

"Lynette, I'm serious," said Charlie, though confronted by such a poor rap, she struggled to keep a straight face. "You know what song I mean. The one you were playing. It was how I found you. I kept hearing it, everywhere I went."

"Oh... *that* song." Lynette squirmed in embarrassment and tried to wriggle out from under Charlie, who put her weight on Lynette's hips to prevent her from leaving.

"No way," said Charlie. "I got you right where I want you. Now c'mon... tell me about that song. I loved it."

Lynette looked anywhere but at Charlie. "I wrote it for you," she said. "Ages ago. I had this stupid idea that if I played it every day, for long enough, that one day you'd hear and come find me. That a dumb song would somehow bring us together."

Charlie let the tears fall, surprised she hadn't exhausted her supply yet. "Looks like it worked."

Lynette half-smiled. "Well, it took you long enough."

Charlie chuckled, and rolled off Lynette. "Sing it for me."

"No."

"Why not?"

Lynette only shrugged.

"Come on, don't be shy. You owe me one."

"How?"

"Because I'm covered in sand."

Lynette chuckled. "That's not *my* fault."

"Oh no? And who tipped me *onto* the sand? And, come to think of it, who *insisted* on applying handfuls of lotion to my butt?"

"Okay, that's fair," said Lynette, failing to hide her grin as Charlie stood, brushing sand from her ample cheeks.

"See? I'll be finding grains of sand up there for weeks."

"Okay, okay, I'll do it," she grumbled with a smile. "Jeez, you're harder work than I remember."

"Get used to it." Charlie crossed her arms. *"Well?"*

"What, you want me to sing *now?* Without my guitar?"

"You're telling me you can move the Eiffel Tower from Paris, but not conjure up a guitar? Quit stalling."

Lynette sighed, and lifted a guitar that a second earlier hadn't been there. She took a deep breath, placed her fingers on the strings, and—

"It's not finished, you know," she said. "I'm still work-shopping the lyrics."

"Play it for me."

Lynette nodded. She took a deep breath, placed her fingers on the strings, and—

"You promise not to laugh?"

Charlie promised.

"Okay," said Lynette. She took a deep breath, placed her fingers on the strings, and—

"It's just—"

"Oh, play the damn song already!" laughed Charlie.

"Fine." Lynette strummed the opening chord. "Just saying, it's not done yet." She took a breath, strummed the chord again, and launched into the song.

> *"Lonely night in winter, I was feeling blue.*
> *Life was slipping by me, don't know—"*

At once, the heavens opened, torrential rain pouring from non-existent clouds and battering the hollow wood of the instrument. Charlie grinned wryly.

"You did this!" she said.

"I didn't, I promise! I—"

A bird fell from the sky. It was a gull, an enormous one with a wing span of several feet, that landed between them, thudding to the newly wet sand with its neck broken. Both girls looked at the sky in surprise.

"What the hell?" murmured Charlie, before another bird hit the beach. Then another, and another, more and more of the dead creatures raining from above, their heavy bodies slamming into the sand and creating deep impressions.

Lynette's face was pale and frightened. "I'm not doing this."

One falling bird struck Lynette on the shoulder. She leaped to her feet, her expression sending a chill down Charlie's spine. They hunched over, covering their heads from the rain and the avian downpour, and ran from the beach. The street fared little better, the birds hammering onto the empty road and deserted sidewalks with enough force to rupture their bodies, plumes of feathers exploding with each solid impact, accompanied by fresh, spurting blood.

"The Louvre," shouted Lynette, and she *had* to shout, for the noise approached apocalyptic levels. Some birds died on contact, others squawked and flapped useless wings as they lay dying. It was a maddening, hideous sight, thought Charlie, as she tried in vain to avoid stepping on the carcasses as she ran.

They arrived at the gallery, leaving the fluttering insanity outside.

As their bare feet slapped off the marble floor, they slowed, turning to face the entrance, gazing in stunned silence at the carnage.

"That ever happen before?" panted Charlie. She looked down at her feet. They were soaked in blood.

"No," said Lynette. The shrieks of the dying birds grew louder, reaching a cacophonous fever pitch. "Let's not stay here." She took Charlie's hand, leading her from the entrance towards—

"Oh fuck," she said.

"What's wrong?" asked Charlie, and then she saw it too.

And when she did, she couldn't help but scream.

16

BODIES.

Bodies *everywhere,* ravaged, torn to shreds and strewn across the floor. Blood poured down the gleaming marble of Antonio Canova's sculptural masterpiece, *Psyche Revived by Cupid's Kiss,* while Lisa del Giocondo screamed from within the oak frame of the *Mona Lisa,* her serene face contorted into a ghoulish grimace.

A hand groped at Charlie's leg, and she backed away from a dying woman, whose flayed skin was draped over the *Venus De Milo,* giving the famously damaged statue the illusion of arms.

"It's not possible," said Lynette. "She couldn't... she can't..."

"Is it her?" urged Charlie. "Lynette, is it her? *Has she found us?*"

"It's not possible," Lynette repeated. A door thumped open behind them, and the girls turned towards it. Black smoke belched from the doorway, a small river of blood pouring through. Faint footsteps reverberated inside, before a fire alarm screeched through the hall.

A figure appeared, torn and bleeding. It was a woman, her hair burned off, skin sizzling. She stumbled in their direction, both eyes reduced to white and yellow liquid that ran down her face like fried eggs.

It was Charlie who first noticed she was carrying the severed head of an elderly man, gripping it by his thinning white curls. She turned towards the pair, holding the decapitated head aloft.

"It's you she wants!" bellowed the disembodied head.

The woman raised her arm and pointed at them.

"Both of you!" the head shouted. "See what she did to us? *See what she did?*"

At once, the bodies that lay on the ground twitched, forcing themselves to stand, rising as one grisly mass of slaughtered, decaying flesh. Those that couldn't stand, crawled, their open mouths emitting ghastly utterances.

Charlie ran from the hallway, pulling Lynette by her hand, the girls breaking into a faltering run as their feet slid beneath them on the blood-slicked marble. They exited the gallery and staggered through the mass of dead gulls, heading back to the beach as, behind them, The Louvre burned, huge flames stretching to the broken sky.

"*My home,*" Lynette muttered. "*She destroyed my home. I built it, and she destroyed it.*"

"What are we going to do?" said Charlie. "Does she know we're here?" She looked around for a trace of Susan, for a sign she was here. Perhaps she had passed through, killed the denizens of the gallery, and then carried on?

"I don't know," said Lynette, rubbing her trembling hands together. "I don't..."

She trailed off, as the sound of creaking metal assaulted their ears, booming across the landscape. The iron legs of the Eiffel Tower buckled, groaning under the weight of the structure.

"It's gonna fall," whispered Charlie, sizing up the distance between the monument and themselves. Her quick calculations resulted in her screaming, *"It's gonna fucking fall!"*

They glanced around at the narrow street. There was nowhere to turn, the buildings crammed together. And so they ran, heads down, desperate not to trip on the mounds of gull carcasses. The beach was ahead of them, not far... not too far...

Charlie dared to look back. The tower was indeed crumbling, and heading straight for them, with no escape route in sight.

"Magic us out of here!" roared Charlie, but Lynette's face was ashen with fear. Were they out of reach? A cursory glance suggested no, not yet. The tower was falling in slow motion as the metal struts strained to keep it upright. Then it hit the ground, directly behind them, in a tangle of twisted iron that sent shockwaves along the street, powerful enough to knock them both off their feet.

Charlie's heart tried to hammer its way out of her chest. The girls looked at each other, then ahead at the beach.

The water was boiling.

Bubbles shot to the surface, thousands of them, the ocean red with blood.

It was Susan who appeared first. Or what *used* to be Susan, but was now a disfigured, misshapen atrocity. A man followed her, rising from the water. Another dredged himself from the depths, then a woman, *another*, a vast legion of faceless drones emerging. It was only then that Charlie realized the sea itself was draining away, the tide dropping like bathwater. The sky, too, splintered, great shards of broken blue glass raining from above.

"What do we do?" asked Charlie.

Lynette surveyed the throbbing mass of bodies that stretched to the horizon as the sand absorbed the last droplets of ocean. "Too many," she said. "She's built a fucking *army*."

"We have to do *something!*"

Lynette shook her head. "We're fucked," she whispered.

The army, led by the ghoulish approximation of Susan, stamped their way across the beach, heading towards them, the fallen tower blocking their only way out.

~

...found you...

~

The voice was in Charlie's head. She looked at Lynette and knew she'd heard it too.

"We have to run!" said Charlie.

"Nowhere to run *to*." There was defeat in Lynette's voice. "She'll always find us."

"Then we fight!"

The army approached, a disparate gathering of normal, everyday people in sweaters and shirts and dresses and hats, some of whom she vaguely recognized but couldn't place. Charlie stooped and picked up a rock that had been hurled her way by the collapsing tower. She held it, squeezed it.

"What are you doing?" asked Lynette.

"I'm not going down without a fucking fight," she growled. "She's not gonna take me alive." She gazed at the people, and as they neared, she began to pick out faces. There was Bella Cruikshank, her childhood babysitter. And Martin Popol, who had been in the year above her. Relics of her past, coming back to haunt her, to kill her. She spotted Mohammad from her local deli, who used to sell her candy and ask how her day was going, and — what the fuck, it couldn't be — *Sylvester* fucking *Stallone,* who she had once bumped into in the street.

"They're from my memories," she said. "She's built an army out of my motherfucking *memories.*"

Time was slipping through their fingers. Or perhaps more accurately, time had caught up with them.

Lynette turned to her, eyes wild. "You go. I'll hold them off."

"No. It took me this long to find you. I'm not gonna leave you now. We're in this together, you and me. Forever."

"There'll be *nothing left,*" said Lynette. Tears rolled down her cheeks. "She's destroying everything I've built, everything I've worked for. My home, my life. I can't have her destroy you, too." She looked Charlie dead in the eyes. "I can send you away. I can do it. Maybe I can even kill her, if I'm lucky." She tried and failed to choke back a sob. "But not with you here."

The mob was nearing. Lynette turned and fixed them with a steely gaze. Immediately, the front line of Susan's soldiers fell to their knees, clutching their heads.

"I hate this," said Lynette softly, averting her gaze as the heads burst, one after the other, in crimson explosions resembling a gruesome firework display. Charlie hurled her rock, striking one woman in the face. She went down hard... but so what? So fucking what? There were thousands more, advancing unhurriedly, safe in the knowledge that the two girls posed no threat.

Charlie didn't care. She would rather die than become Susan's plaything again. At least she had tasted happiness, if only fleetingly, on this final, glorious day with Lynette. If it had to end here? Then so be it.

Lynette battled on. Her skin grew paler, veins bulging on her forehead and neck. The two girls backed away as the army marched onwards, Susan no longer visible behind the horde. Charlie's heel kicked an iron bar, a piece of shrapnel from the fallen French monument, and she picked it up. It was weighty, but there was enough adrenaline pumping through her system to enable her to swing it like a woman possessed.

The people were slow and clumsy. She brought the bar down on a woman's head and split her skull. When Charlie placed her foot on the woman's stomach and wrenched it free, blood fountained from the wound. She swung again, this time wielding the weapon like a baseball bat and striking someone's jaw, horrified to realize it was her third-grade teacher, Mr. Lamont. The metal bar shattered his mandible, catching on his chin and tearing the skin away, leaving little below his bushy mustache but a drooping tongue.

"Sorry," she said, taking a swing at the next person without pausing for breath. She glanced at Lynette. The girl had dropped to one knee. A vein on her temple had burst, blood pouring down her skin, dozens of the zombies bearing down on her. Charlie abandoned her post and hurried to her girlfriend as another of the mindless drones grabbed Lynette from behind.

"Put her down!" yelled Charlie, slamming the bar against the man's spine. He shrugged the blow off and hurled Lynette at her. They collided, falling to the ground. Charlie got to her feet, but Lynette was weak. She remained prone, staring at the man until the skin dissolved from his face, forming a thick paste of blood and melted flesh that dribbled down his torso, revealing a shrieking skull, exposed and severed carotid arteries spurting frenziedly in all directions.

"Too many," wheezed Lynette, before turning onto her hands and knees and ejecting a mouthful of bloody vomit onto the carnage-strewn street.

Charlie dragged her away from the oncoming onslaught... but the downed tower blocked the way. The army advanced, crushing the bodies of their fallen comrades beneath their feet.

"Stay there," said Charlie, laying Lynette down and gripping her iron bar. She looked at the fragile girl, and an awful thought rippled through her mind.

Kill her.

It would be merciful. They were both going to die today. Or worse, be captured and tortured for all eternity by Susan. Death was the only way out.

Above, most of the sky had crumbled to pieces, leaving bitch black nothingness in its wake. Only a thin sliver of blue remained. Soon, it would all be gone.

A hand grasped Charlie's bare leg.

Lynette.

Resignation was written all over her face.

"It's over," she said, and looked at Charlie with wet, pleading eyes. "Hold me one last time."

Charlie hesitated. A man in slacks and a blazer approached, and she smacked him with the bar, then gripped it in two hands and plunged it into his chest. He staggered away, the bar jutting from his chest and back, his still beating heart impaled on the end. Then he fell, swallowed by the horde, vanishing into the murk of braindead drones.

Charlie went to Lynette, dropped to her knees, and wrapped her arms around her. They held each other and wept, as hands groped over their bodies, scratching and clawing, blocking out the last vestiges of daylight.

"I love you," said Lynette, placing her hand on Charlie's chest, between her breasts. "I loved you all this time, and I'll love you forever." She looked into Charlie's eyes. "I'm sorry."

Energy flooded through Charlie's body, pulsing in brutal waves from Lynette's palm.

"No," she said, then Lynette jerked in a violent spasm, sending Charlie spinning away, her body a ragdoll hurtling through space at a crazed velocity. She shot into the air in time to see the horde descend on Lynette, and then the world was rushing by her like shooting stars, a meteor shower of forgotten, ineffectual memories. She tried to scream but couldn't, couldn't even *breathe*, the wind sucked right out of her as she gained speed, faster and faster, until her body and mind conceded defeat.

As her eyes closed and she blacked out, her last thought was—

17

"Lynette?"

At first, Charlie was amazed she was still alive, until she remembered she was actually *dead*. She was back in the corridor of her mind, with its muted color palette and wall sconces and endless, endless doors. Her chest stung from Lynette's touch, a faint pink handprint between her breasts the only rapidly vanishing evidence of her lightning speed journey.

She placed her hand on her chest, experiencing a charge of static as her fingers aligned with the fading pink mark.

Lynette had saved her life.

"Goddammit!" shouted Charlie, pounding her fist off the floor. "I told you not to! I told you we'd stay together..." She broke down. How could Lynette have done this? It was... it was *selfish*.

For what good was being here without Lynette? What fucking good? Was she supposed to live out the rest of her days in this rotten fantasia of empty memories?

She needed to get out of here, out of this corridor. Somewhere quiet, where she could reflect. As she walked, she noticed the doors were in a state of disrepair; some boarded up, others hanging on loose hinges, broken handles rolling across the floor. She thought about Princess. Doggy heaven had to be better than whatever the fuck *this* dumb bullshit was. Oh, what she'd give for a hug from him right now!

"Princess?" she called, out of desperation more than hope. She wondered if he missed her, and figured he did.

He always was a good dog.

She pushed open a door, visualizing her local library, and entered.

A place of solitude for Charlie during her childhood, the library was even quieter than usual today. No cheery librarian's greeting, no surreptitious coughing, no whispering voices. She wandered past the desk, through Crime Fiction, via Biography & Autobiography, then up the stairs to the second floor. There, beyond the Music and Film & TV sections, sat three comfortable chairs next to a window that overlooked the local park. She used to sit here for hours, devouring books by Richard Matheson and Ray Bradbury and Robert Bloch and Shirley Jackson, pausing between chapters to gaze out the window at the kids playing baseball and the strolling lovers and the golden oldies feeding the ducks.

Now, there was no one outside. The park was empty, and Charlie was all alone.

She couldn't go on like this. Lynette — in her well-meaning way — had cursed her. She could sit here and read every book in the damn library, and then what? Do it all over again?

Perhaps Lynette was still alive? And if so, could she rescue her? Ah, that was a fucking joke. What would she do, take the elevator down to Susan and try to reason with her? Try to *kill* her?

Maybe.

The Mall. There was a gun shop in the Monroeville Mall. If she armed herself to the teeth, picked up some ice hockey gear for protection, and...

No, that was stupid. She was an idiot for thinking that. Susan's army outnumbered her a thousand to one. They would kill her in a heartbeat.

But she couldn't leave Lynette alone down there. A failed rescue attempt was preferable to sitting here waiting to die. After all, Susan had found them before. How long until her minions roamed through Charlie's memories, searching for her? At least this way, she could get the drop on them. Surprise them. Susan would never expect Charlie to have the balls to come for her. Or would she?

"Fuck!" she shouted, her mind in turmoil. "Fuck, fuck, *fuck!*"

The window cracked, an icy cobweb spreading across the pane until it reached the edges. Then it shattered.

Charlie stared uneasily at the broken pane, a curious tingle emanating from her chest. Avoiding the glass beneath her bare feet, she walked towards it.

"Did I do that?" she wondered aloud.

A sound, coming from behind.

She spun, staring down the labyrinthian rows of shelved books. Was someone else here?

Footsteps.

She was definitely not alone. The intruder shuffled quietly, but she heard the creak of their leather shoes, the air rushing through their nostrils. Charlie picked up a long shard of broken glass. Should she confront them? Or hide?

"Who's there?" she asked in a tremulous voice.

The noises stopped.

"Is that you, Lynette?"

Of course it's not. She would have replied the first time.

She took a step forwards, and the nearest shelving unit toppled, crashing to the ground in front of her and disgorging books all over the floor. A man stood behind it, a man in an expensive fur coat that failed to hide his bulky, muscular frame. He stared at her, meaty hands clenched into fists, his dark hair tumbling over his shoulders. She recognized him instantly.

Anyone would.

"Oh, no fucking way," said Charlie, as Sylvester Stallone stepped onto the downed bookcase and lumbered towards her. "Stop," she said, trying to project an air of confidence. "I'm warning you. Don't, uh, come any closer."

"Pardon me, sweetheart," he said in his distinctive mumble, the exact three words he had spoken to her in the early nineteen-eighties, when they had accidentally collided on Franklin Avenue. She remembered the thrill and excitement of touching a Hollywood star, of having him speak to her.

Now, she brandished a puny piece of glass as he closed the gap between them. "Stay back!" she commanded, as the realization set in. She had to kill him.

She had to kill motherfucking *Rambo*.

He didn't stop. "Pardon me, sweetheart."

She waved the glass threateningly. "This is your last chance, Mr. Stallone."

"Pardon me, sweetheart."

He reached for her, and she brought the makeshift weapon sharply up, gouging flesh from his forearm. He muttered in discomfort, gazing at the blood bubbling from his torn skin.

"Pardon me, sweetheart," he said, and lunged for her. She stabbed him in the gut, twisting the glass, and he threw her backwards into a bookcase. It toppled, the colossal crash shaking the library's foundations. Winded, Charlie rolled from the shelving unit onto her knees, catching her breath as the cinematic strongman ambled towards her. He took her by the arm and threw her across the room. She smacked into another bookcase. This one wobbled, then overbalanced, striking its neighbor, which in turn, hit another, the shelving units dropping one after the other like a domino rally.

Ignoring the chaos, Charlie crawled for the window. Stallone caught her, lifting her by the hair and tossing her onto the pile of broken glass. Hundreds of sharp points pierced her bikini-clad body, slicing her open. She rifled through the pieces, selecting a good-sized one, but before she could use it, Stallone booted her in the stomach. Glass crunched beneath her as she scurried backwards, leaving a sparkling trail of blood.

She lifted a handful of tiny shards and threw them at Stallone. They bounced harmlessly off his face and sternum as he leaned over and picked her up by the throat. Charlie had enough time to grab another handful of glass, and as Stallone raised her high, she shoved the shards into his face, rubbing them there.

"Pardon *me*, sweetheart!" he said, a slight change in intonation the only clue that she had hurt him. She lashed out with a flurry of kicks to his stomach and crotch, and he tossed her away again. This time, she landed on her shoulder, bouncing off the hard floor.

Stallone strode purposefully towards her.

Everyone knows they're going to die someday, she thought. *But nobody thinks they're going to be murdered by Sylvester Stallone.*

She laughed a freakish, high-pitched giggle, her grip on

sanity ebbing away, and leaped at Stallone, surprising him, gripping the glass in his stomach and wrenching it free. She plunged it into his chest, then back out again, hacking at the dense muscle of his powerful torso. Blood fountained from myriad wounds, drenching her, splattering her face, her mouth, her breasts, as he wrapped his fingers around her throat and lifted her, carrying her frenzied body towards the broken window.

"No!" she screamed, as she stabbed the glass into Stallone's eye, rupturing the orb. Nothing stopped him. He paused at the window, Charlie's feet dangling thirty feet above the concrete sidewalk.

"Pardon me, sweetheart," Stallone said, then hurled her through.

Charlie's whole body was alive with electricity as she flew backwards. She felt nothing, not even the wind rushing against her bare skin, her eyes clamped shut. Shit, she was about to die for the second time this week. She waited, ready for the impact that would steal the life from her...

...and waited some more.

When she cautiously opened her eyes, she was staring into the mangled, savaged face of Sylvester Stallone, framed by the broken window. She looked at the ground far below, and realized she was levitating. She didn't know *how* the fuck she was doing it, but it felt natural, like walking or talking. And when she imagined Stallone's head exploding...

...*boom!*...

...it did, his skin splitting as his skull enlarged to absurd proportions, blood spraying from his nostrils as the pressure built, before erupting in a wild detonation of brain, skin, and bone. He stood there a moment, his spinal column protruding from the stump of his neck, then plummeted through the window to the sidewalk.

Charlie remained suspended in midair. Her head ached with the worst migraine of her life. She needed to... she needed to...

She floated to the ground, landing awkwardly next to the gloopy mess that had once been an Oscar-winning film star, and said the only thing appropriate for the situation.

"What... the... *fuck*..."

18

SUSAN GAZED UPON LYNETTE'S LIMP, HANGING BODY, AND tried to smile. Her jaw contorted, immense pain shooting through her face as her few remaining teeth ground together.

Snap!

She winced as another tooth cracked. Rolling it around on her tongue, she licked it clean, then swallowed the shard of bone. If her body was going to fall apart on her, then at least she could keep the pieces somewhere safe. So far, her insides hadn't rebelled as badly as her limbs and facial features, though the bizarre slits — almost vaginal in appearance — that had formed on her arms and neck had caused her some concern.

Currently, her failing body was of secondary importance to the bitch in front of her, the one strung up by her wrists and swaying back and forth from the ceiling. Her followers — as she had christened them — had overpowered Charlie and Lynette... or so Susan had believed. But when the smoke had cleared, and the followers had backed off as instructed, only one remained.

"Hello," she said, as Lynette's eyes flickered open.

The girl looked at her in confusion, which quickly turned to horror as she discovered her predicament. She tried to move, to wriggle free, the binding digging into her wrists and drawing blood as her feet kicked uselessly.

"I never knew what Charlie saw in you," Susan slurred from her chair, which consisted of six of her new female followers bent over and balancing atop each other to form a twisted throne, their nude bodies entwined, arms broken and tied together like shoelaces to prevent them from moving. The women wept as Susan rested on them, and the sound of their sniveling was perfection to her ears.

It was difficult for Susan to walk, so gnarled and distorted had her body become. She figured that back in reality, she was minutes away from death. Seconds, possibly, though she no longer had the strength to leave this place and check. Controlling the minds of thousands of followers, while simultaneously blocking Lynette from using her *own* powers, was an extraordinary exertion.

"I spent a lot of time in your body," said Susan. "I know it intimately. Better than Charlie ever could. Better than you, even."

Lynette said nothing, dangling before Susan in her torn bikini, the scratches and bites across her skin surrounded by dark, dried blood.

"I know everything about you. Your hopes and fears, your darkest desires. What makes you happy, what makes you sad, what makes you come. There's *nothing* I don't know about you. And still, armed with that knowledge, I couldn't understand what she saw in you. Every morning I'd wake up and have to look at your face in the mirror. I hated it before, of course, but I grew to *despise* it. Not just because you're ugly, which you are. But because *she* couldn't see it." A stream of blood dribbled down her chin. "When I fucked her, it was *your* name she screamed."

Susan pushed up from her squirming throne and dropped onto all fours. It was the only way she could move. She writhed clumsily towards Lynette and gripped her tightly, pulling her mangled body up into a standing position. Her face was level with Lynette's breasts, and she gazed at them with one large bloodshot eye. She had to keep the other one closed, as it had turned one-eighty and now stared into her own skull.

"I have a question for you," said Susan. "One simple question."

Lynette said nothing.

"Look at my body... look at my face... and ask yourself... do you think Charlie could love me now?"

Lynette's face was blank. Susan knew she was deciding which answer would cause her the least amount of pain.

"I said... do you think Charlie could love me now?"

"I... I don't know," said Lynette. Her head hung, and she sobbed.

"Do you think... *anyone*... could love me now?" She dug her nails into Lynette's soft belly and raked them down, carving open layers of skin. Lynette screamed.

"Answer me!" demanded Susan.

"Maybe?" sobbed Lynette.

"Look at this!" said Susan, pointing to a puncture on her bald head. "You see that? That's my *asshole*. It's on my head, you stupid cunt. My asshole is on my head, and you're telling me someone could still love me? You're saying that *Charlie* could still love me, with my asshole on my fucking head?" She clenched her sphincter muscles to prove her point, and Lynette gagged.

"I don't know. Maybe? Yes?"

"Shall we find out?"

"Please," begged Lynette. "Let me down."

"I said, shall we find out?"

Lynette shook, but she was tied tight. "What are you talking about? *What the fuck are you talking about?*"

Susan's hands fumbled for Lynette's tits, squeezing them. Lynette shrieked, and when Susan let go, she left wet flaps of her own shedding skin stuck to each breast.

"All that time hating your body," said Susan, "and now, here I am, *jealous* of it." She stooped low, yanking the striped bikini bottoms down and letting them dangle around Lynette's ankles. "I remember the smell of your cunt. It was your best feature." Susan shifted her body, pressing the nose on her shoulder between Lynette's legs and taking a long sniff. "Still good. I always wondered if it tasted as sweet as it smelled. Maybe *that* was why Charlie liked you."

"Just kill me, you fucking psycho!"

"Kill you?" Susan laughed, displacing another tooth. This one disappeared beneath her tongue, and she felt it break through her sagging skin. "No, I'm not going to kill you. I *need* you, because Charlie will come for you. I know she will. You see, Lynette... I'm tired... and I'm *dying,* and I can't go chasing after her anymore. But she'll come here to try to rescue you. Because for you, she'd do *anything.*"

One of the slits on Susan's arm bulged, momentarily distracting her.

"What's this now?" asked a bemused Susan, as a glistening pink tongue wriggled its way through the gap. "Well, that's new," she said, the voice coming in stereo from both her mouth and the orifice on her arm. "Let's see what this does." With difficulty, she half crouched, holding her arm between Lynette's legs. The foul tongue probed the girl's pussy, slurping wetly.

Lynette threw up, the vomit spilling from between her lips and splattering Susan's head. Susan withdrew her arm, her single eye narrowing with malicious intent, malodorous gunk leaking from the tear ducts.

"You're lucky I plan on keeping you alive," she said, holding her arm to her head and letting her new tongue lick the chunks from her bald cranium. "Until Charlie arrives, at least. But I don't know how long she'll be, and a girl's gotta have her fun, y'know?"

Her lipless mouth clamped down on Lynette's left breast. Though her front teeth were mostly gone, she retained her molars, and used them to bite the girl's nipple, sinking into the juicy flesh. She wrestled with the breast, pulling roughly, feeling the skin stretch. Hearing Lynette's frantic cries only made her bite harder. She wrenched the nipple free, blood filling her mouth as she savored not only the taste and consistency of the bitch's flesh, but her helplessness and humiliation.

She chewed for a while, the soft bud surprisingly crunchy, then swallowed. Lynette bucked and thrashed against her bindings. "Please!" screamed Lynette. "Please, I can't take it anymore!"

"Oh, you can, bitch. You can, and you will." Susan smiled. "We're just getting started. Until Charlie gets here... you're all mine."

19

IN THE MONROEVILLE MALL, CHARLIE STARED AT HERSELF IN the mirror of the JCPenney womenswear section. She wore fresh clothes, though already the blood from her wounds seeped through them.

"Okay," she said, gazing at her reflection. "You can do this." She concentrated hard, staring at the glass, willing it to shatter. Her body tensed. "Break," she whispered. *"Break."* Was it her imagination, or did the glass buckle? No, it *was* her imagination. The mirrored surface was resolutely untarnished. Trying a different tactic, she relaxed her eyes, hoping to feel some kind of magical energy flowing through her.

The mirror remained unblemished.

"Shit."

She was Luke Skywalker without an Obi Wan Kenobi to guide her in the ways of The Force.

Still, she felt stronger than before thanks to a peculiar power lurking within her. If only she could learn how to harness it on command! In the library, she had blown up Sylvester Stallone's head, and now she couldn't even warp some glass. Of course, she had been stressed before, the fear of imminent death coursing through her veins. Had *that* been what unlocked her power?

Whatever the reason, she needed to figure out how to use it. But every second spent trying to make glass explode, or move something telepathically, was a second wasted. Lynette was out there, a captive in the depths of Susan's mind. And she needed help.

Charlie's first stop had been the Monroeville Mall, because she sure as shit wasn't going into battle wearing a bikini. Not a single human remained in the decimated building, save for some scattered corpses that looked to have been trampled to death during a mass exodus. Large parts of the mall were missing; sections of the floor no longer existed, giving way to deep voids that beckoned to her with silent promises of sweet, empty oblivion.

"And you, can't see, how the sun, shines on me," she had sung quietly as she browsed the department store racks, picking up comfortable underwear, stretchy pants, a tee shirt, and a pair of running sneakers.

She tried not to think of how terrified she was.

Her next port of call was the sporting goods section. Time was of the essence, she knew, but she also couldn't rush into things unprepared. This would be her only chance. If she failed, she would die, and so would Lynette.

"Don't even think that," she said, fastening an ice-hockey goalie mask to her face. She peered out from behind the vintage nineteen-seventies mask, unable to shake the image of her favorite slasher movie killer, Jason Voorhees. By the time she had died, in eighty-nine, eight of the films existed. She wondered how many she would never get to see.

Her final port of call was Gunner's Den, the firearms store. There, Charlie picked out a pump-action shotgun.

Only once she caught a glimpse of herself in the window did she realize how ridiculous she looked. Who was she kidding? One shotgun, a hockey mask, and some half-baked powers she wasn't sure she could use, let alone control?

It was certain death. She may as well walk into a lion's den with a hot dog up her ass. Laying the shotgun on the counter, she leaned against the nearest wall, her body trembling as reality hammered at the door.

Rescue Lynette? What a moron. Susan had been murdering innocent people for years, and Charlie had never been able to save a single one. Shit, she hadn't been able to save herself. Really, when she thought about it, she struggled to come up with one single good thing she had *ever* done in her wasted life.

"One hundred percent rate of failure," she smiled, then started to cry.

Look at yourself. You're pathetic. A nobody, a pawn in someone else's game. Give up.

The words didn't shock her. She had told herself the same many times before, and believed them unquestioningly. Nothing had ever gone right for her. Even her brief tastes of happiness were stolen from her. She almost wished she hadn't found Lynette again, because otherwise she would have placed the shotgun barrel in her mouth and pulled the trigger without debate.

But she *had* found Lynette, and their brief reunion was the happiest Charlie had felt in a long time. Maybe the happiest she had *ever* felt. A lifetime spent with Lynette sounded like perfection.

Charlie wiped her eyes. This was no time for tears. Ever since she had arrived here, she had done nothing but cry.

Cry, cry, cry.

"Well, I'm through crying," she mumbled, then raised

her head. "You hear me? I'm through running." She lifted the shotgun, and slung a backpack full of shells over her shoulder. "And I'm through *fucking crying!*"

Lynette was out there.

And if there was a chance — no matter how slim — that the two of them could be together, then Charlie had to take it.

If necessary, she would storm *hell* to find her.

20

CHINTZY MUZAK TINKLED FROM THE ELEVATOR, PLAYING A panpipe rendition of Lynette's song. It was all Charlie needed to hear. She stepped inside, the bulky shotgun cradled in her sweaty hands. The elevator interior was as before, with one key difference.

There was a third button alongside the ones marked C and L. With grim inevitability, this one bore the letter S, with a handwritten note next to it that read,

ENTRY FOR OFFERISED PERSONAL ONLY

Charlie recognized the sign from the spelling mistakes. At the school dance, it had been taped to the door that led to the roof.

"Susan," she said, her finger hovering over the button.

Was this a bad idea?

Probably.

Was Lynette already dead?

Maybe.

Would she make it out alive?

Unlikely.

Did she have any other choice?

"Absolutely fucking not," said Charlie, and pressed the S button. The elevator began its final descent.

Now, there was no turning back.

The bell dinged to signify Charlie's arrival at the lower level.

Susan's *mind*.

She didn't know what to expect, but knew it wasn't gonna be pretty. So when she pulled back the bars and stepped into raw sewage, she wasn't wholly surprised. The murky liquid rose to her knees, with a uniquely revolting stench akin to a corpse found floating in a septic tank.

Candles lit the corridor, melting from ancient, rusted candelabras. As she waded down, something bumped against her ankle.

"Jesus," she whispered, unable to tell if the rotten body belonged to a man or a woman. Two rats scurried on its chest, nibbling the flesh and screeching excitedly as the macabre vessel sailed by.

More bodies floated in the shallow river. Was she walking in corpse juice? Bile rose in her throat. There were no doors in Susan's corridor. Rather, steel bars sealed the doorways, enabling Charlie to gaze through without entering.

What she saw was a series of abominations.

In one room, a man crouched on all fours on a stained mattress, a ball-gag in his mouth, while Susan — in Lynette's body — affixed a strap-on to her hips. It was no ordinary sex toy. In place of the phallus was a rusted saw blade. She rammed it into the man's anus, his eyes widening in surprise and agony as she thrust in and out of him, blood gushing in waves over Lynette's thighs.

Transfixed by the wanton violence, Charlie was unable to look away. Lynette — no, it was Susan, dammit, *Susan* — angled her body so that the blade hacked downwards, opening the man up. His insides flooded the mattress, entrails slopping out and—

Charlie threw up into the revolting river. She turned her back on the sickening vision, staring through the opposite barred entryway. Inside, a nude woman levitated in a forest, screaming, her arms and legs spread out wide in a X shape, her legs continuing to rise until she was performing the splits... and then she *did* split, her legs going vertical, cleaving her vagina open, the rip traveling to her belly button, unleashing torrents of dark blood on the woodland floor as Susan snapped her in two like a wishbone.

"No," moaned Charlie, turning away and walking onwards, keeping her eyes dead center, listening to the cries and whimpers and guttural sobs of Susan's many victims as she passed by. Several times she heard what sounded like her own voice, crying out for mercy, begging and sobbing, but she refused to look. She was already teetering on the precipice of madness, and it wouldn't take much to send her careening over the brink.

More bodies floated by, more limbs, heads, guts, an endless tide of human detritus.

"Is it too much? I feel like it's too much."

Charlie paused. She recognized Susan's voice from the old days, from *before*. Placing a hand on the bars, Charlie peered into Susan's high school bedroom, where the pair of them stood, Susan fussing over her dress in front of the mirror.

"Would you stop worrying? You look terrific," said memory

Charlie, and on the other side of the bars, the real Charlie watched, her eyes filling with tears as Susan pulled the fabric up over her bust.

"Just a little higher," she said. *"My nipples are practically on show."*

It was the night of the Clinton High Summer Ball, and they had been so happy. Nervous, of course. Terrified, even. But happy. Their first proper outing as a couple, and though they had invited dates — Decoy Boys, Susan called them — they would be together, in public, in their prettiest dresses, smiling at each other from across the dance floor. If they had known then the trouble that Susan's red dress was going to get them into, they would have stayed home. If only she had changed, or decided not to go, or...

Or what? What, precisely, was she wishing for? If Susan had never been pushed through that skylight, would they still be together? Would she have never met Lynette? And would that have been *better?*

The thought appalled her. She loved Lynette, and would do anything for her... but she had also loved Susan. The way they looked at each other in the memory, their touches, their kisses. Things could have been so different.

"Stop it," she said. There was no point considering it. Not now, anyway. She had spent too long dreaming about how differently her life could have turned out, and all for nothing. There was no changing history, no going back. Her life was an unmitigated disaster, and always had been. Like an inverse-Midas, everything she touched turned to liquid shit. She had no friends, no achievements, no life.

Just Lynette. Sweet Lynette, who had waited ten years for her return, singing her sad song and never giving up hope. Now she needed help, help that only Charlie could provide. For the first time in her life, Charlie was *needed* by someone.

And she would not let Lynette down.

She watched herself kiss Susan through the bars, then shook her head as she remembered what Susan had done to her.

"I'll kill you, bitch," she said, the shotgun trembling in her hands.

This was it. The end. There would be no more fucking around.

One of them had to die tonight.

One of them simply *had* to die.

21

THE SONG PLAYED FAINTLY, AND CHARLIE SANG ALONG AS SHE traversed the disgusting corridor. Lynette was calling to her, and though the damn room never seemed to end, at least she knew her girlfriend was still alive.

The melody grew louder with each step, the water level dropping, until a wall of stacked corpses formed a dam that blocked her passage. Charlie shoved the bodies from the top of the pile to clear the way, then clambered over soft, dead flesh that disintegrated at her touch.

There, she found a door, built from what looked like solid gold.

It sparkled in the candlelight, an impossible mirage in a tarnished hell. With her shotgun raised, Charlie approached, nudging the unlocked barrier open with her foot.

The song faded away.

"Okay," she whispered. "Let's do this."

She opened the door fully and entered, unprepared for the lush, decedent interior. It was a *mansion,* a garish palace fit for royalty, from the plush pink carpet to the intricately carved rail on the wooden staircase on the far side of the room. Every piece of metal was a gleaming golden monument to tackiness. An opulent chandelier hung from the ceiling on a thick chain, and paintings and photos adorned every square inch of wall.

"Oh, fuck me," breathed Charlie.

Every image in the vast room — every painting, every framed photograph — was of her.

The photos were snapshots of Charlie's life. There she was as a mewling newborn, cradled in her mother's arms, and her first day of kindergarten, of school, her birthdays. The girl in the photos laughed, cried, smiled, shouted, *lived.* There she was with Susan; the first time they held hands, their first kiss, that night they bathed together, Susan crying with laughter as Charlie constructed a foam beard and mustache and pretended to be a fancy gentleman.

The paintings, however, appeared to be stylized ideations of make-believe summers spent abroad with Susan, the pair of them capering on the beach in their underwear, then laughing in front of the Egyptian pyramids in their underwear, then — most inexplicably of all — surrounded by penguins, chasing each other through snow... in their underwear, naturally.

It was absurd, a catalog of demented fantasies... and it didn't end there. A marble statue had been carved into a likeness of the pair of them embracing, Charlie cupping Susan's breast, huge, angel-like wings spreading behind her. Another sculpture was of Charlie in repose, her eyes closed, head resting on a pillow, a thin blanket pulled down far enough to reveal her unclothed buttocks. A sign above it read:

BY ORDER OF MANAGEMENT —
DO NOT TOUCH, KISS, OR FUCK THE EXHIBITS

"Jesus," said Charlie with a shake of her head. She traversed the room towards the golden staircase, avoiding the steely gazes of a hundred Charlies staring at her from within their wooden frames.

It was a ghoulish museum in her honor.

"Why?" she asked softly as she climbed the stairs. "I'm just *me.*"

At the top, she stood before a stained glass window depicting herself in field, wearing a white robe and smiling benevolently as celestial light shone in a halo from behind her head.

There were two doors. One promised:

THE TEMPLE OF ASS

while the other apparently led to:

THE PANTY ROOM
GIFT SHOP
EXIT

"I'm not going to the fucking *temple of ass,"* she grumbled, taking the door on the right and leaving the weird room of paintings behind. A dark hallway stretched before her, lined by hundreds of carefully framed and mounted pairs of panties. "Fucking maniac," said Charlie, as she wandered past a lifetime's worth of her underwear. Cotton and lace and satin, plain and striped and polka-dotted, they were all here, with brass plaques beneath them. She stopped to read one of the inscriptions.

"Red Nylon and Black Lace Low Rise Panties
1979-1981"

Charlie shook her head in disbelief.

At the end of the long room stood a full-size glass display case. Inside was a nightmarish wax effigy of her, clad in what appeared to be — judging from the unwashed bloodstains — the original dress she had worn to the Summer Ball. Laid out along the bottom of the case were more of her belongings; her handbag, a half-drunk bottle of vodka, her shoes, panties, stockings, and earrings.

The display brought dark memories of that night flooding back. How helpless she had felt as she crouched by Susan's limp body, screaming for someone to call an ambulance. The guilt, the feeling she was responsible, that she shouldn't have left Susan alone, that she could have somehow saved her.

"I'm sorry, Susan," she said. "I'm sorry you didn't fucking *die* that night."

She followed the signs for the exit, emerging in a well-lit lobby with an unmanned reception desk and a small open-plan gift shop that offered tee shirts bearing images of Charlie's face, tears streaming from her eyes, the slogan "SEE YOU LATER CHARLIE-GATOR" printed above in a bold font.

"Bet those really fly off the racks," she said, perusing a stand of ten cent souvenir postcards, each one with a different shot of her butt. "Should pick one of these up for

Lynette," she muttered darkly, fighting against the overwhelming — and ever-increasing — insanity of the situation.

Ahead, artificial light streamed through glass doors. She left the gift shop and crossed the lobby, stepping out of the building and into what appeared to be a football stadium. The stands at either side were cloaked in darkness, the beams of the huge spotlights directed on the fifty yard line, where one small figure lay.

Charlie started forwards, the wet grass squelching beneath her feet, rain battering her face.

"Lynette?"

The figure didn't move. As Charlie approached, she saw they were lying face down, naked and covered in blood.

It had to be her.

She ran, the rain falling in sheets around her.

"Lynette, it's me! It's Charlie," she said, as she put her hands on the girl's back, trying to avoid the hideous scars that criss-crossed the wet flesh. Carefully, she rolled Lynette over, and when she saw what Susan had done, she let out a hitched sob. Lynette had been viciously beaten. Her face was puffy and swollen, her nose broken. Several teeth were missing, and the bruises and lesions spread down her torso and arms like a disease. One nipple was gone, ragged flesh framing the bloody laceration, while teeth-marks dotted what skin remained to be seen beneath the blood.

One eye fluttered open. "Ch... Charlie?"

"It's me. Don't worry, I'll get you out of here."

"It's a trap," groaned Lynette.

Charlie helped her up. "I know. But it's okay. Together we can—"

The stadium lights burst into life, every stand suddenly

bathed in glowing golden light, revealing a sold-out crowd of *thousands* of people.

Susan's army.

The drones sat in silence, all eyes focused on the two young women in the center of the pitch. Then, as one, the horde got to their feet.

"Shit," said Charlie, reaching for her shotgun. She looked at the weapon. What good would it do?

"Go," said Lynette, her voice pitifully small. "Please. While you still can."

"I told you before, I'm not leaving you."

The people in the stands shuffled along the rows, moving towards the pitch in unhurried fashion.

Lynette wheezed a ragged sigh. "We can't beat them. We can't beat *her.*"

"*She's right,*" said Susan, the low voice booming over the speaker at such a volume that Charlie winced.

"*Go,*" urged Lynette, and she was sobbing now, her face a cracked image of desperation.

Charlie only shook her head. "It's okay," she said. "I got this."

The army flooded the pitch, ambling towards the two girls, but there was no sign of Susan. Charlie stood, taking the shotgun with her.

"Where are you, bitch?" she shouted. "Come out and face me!"

"What are you *doing?*" asked Lynette.

"I told, I *got* this."

Susan's mad laugh echoed throughout the stadium, so loud that one speaker exploded in a whine of feedback. "*Oh, Charlie,*" said Susan. "*You sweet, stupid cunt.*"

"Come out and say that to my face!" bellowed Charlie, turning as the army slowly surrounded her, maintaining a distance. She raised the shotgun and blasted one of them in the stomach, leaving a gaping, sanguinary hole. The man swayed a moment, then fell away, replaced by another of the mindless drones.

"I'm not sure you have enough bullets, Charlie," said Susan. Her voice was odd; muffled and wet, like it was coming from a radio at the bottom of a pool.

"I don't need them. I got something else to show you." She recalled the way she had levitated, and concentrated, trying to do it again. *"Come on, come on,"* she whispered. It didn't work. Trying a different tack, she stared at the heads of the drones nearest her.

Explode, explode, come on, explode already!

She tried just *one* of them, but that, too, was useless. If it was indeed stress that fed her power, then she had plenty to go around right now. So why wasn't it working? It had before, for fuck's sake!

"...oh Charlie, quit making a fool of yourself..."

Susan's voice came from within her mind. "Get out!" she shouted, smacking her head with her palm. *"Get out!"* She glanced down at Lynette. The girl's tear-streaked face stared back at her.

"She's in your head," the girl said sadly. "She's been there the whole time."

Charlie reloaded the shotgun, ejecting the empty shell, and fired again at the throng that crowded around them. One girl — who she thought might have been in the grade above her at school — dropped to the ground in a welter of spurting gore.

They were closing in on them. Charlie took aim... and

froze. Her finger hovered over the trigger, but she couldn't pull it.

"*Charlie,*" said Susan, and this time the voice was close, a few feet behind her. Charlie wanted to turn her head, but she was a statue, another tasteless sculpture in Susan's ghoulish museum. A hand clasped her shoulder. "What did you think? That you could beat me? That you had gained powers in a matter of seconds that took me years to master?" She laughed. "You fucking fool. You pathetic, fucking stupid, spineless little cunt."

Charlie concentrated hard.

Come on, you can do it! You can—

"Are you still trying?" laughed Susan. "Here, let me help you."

Charlie rose off the ground, her arms dropping limply to her sides, the gun sliding through her fingers and hitting the turf.

"It was *me*, Charlie. Your little fight with Stallone, your levitation… *I* did that. I gave you hope, so you'd come and find me."

"That's not true!"

"Ah, but it *is* true." Susan sighed. "I'm tired, Charlie. I'm very, very tired. I didn't have the strength to come for you myself, so I sent someone. I could easily have had him bring you here, but to give you hope, to make you think you stood a chance… it was funnier that way, don't you think?"

"You're lying!"

"Fine," said Susan. "Let me demonstrate."

A cry from behind. "*Stop!*" Lynette shouted. "*What are you doing?*

Charlie tried to turn her head to see the girl, but from the neck down, she was a functionless, broken marionette. It didn't matter, because then Lynette staggered before her, the torrential rain washing the mud and blood from her naked, brutalized body.

She placed her hands on Charlie's shirt and tore it open.

"This isn't me," said Lynette. "I'm not doing this!"

"I know," said Charlie, tears streaming down her cheeks as Lynette tugged her pants and underwear down. "Susan?" she shouted at her unseen adversary. "You're sick in the head, you bitch."

"Sticks and stones," said Susan. She was closer now, her voice bleeding into Charlie's ear.

Lynette finished stripping Charlie, leaving her naked below the waist except for her socks and one sneaker. All the while, she sobbed apologies.

Charlie tried not to think of what Susan had planned. Sexual humiliation and violence were her stock-in-trade, but what vile acts were left for Susan to perpetrate upon her? She had spent the last decade being used by Susan in cruel, sadistic sex games that left her feeling hollow and dead inside. What else could she—

"Oh god," breathed Charlie, as Lynette picked up the shotgun, supporting it in her pale hands. "Susan, whatever you're doing, *stop*. Please. Think about this, please, *just think about what you're doing!*"

"I never wanted to hurt you, Charlie. Never. And if sometimes I got carried away? Well, that was because I loved you too much. Is that a crime? Loving someone too much?"

Lynette — puppeteered by Susan — angled the shotgun towards Charlie's crotch.

"Susan! Susan!" yelled Charlie. "Don't! Please, dear god, don't do it!"

The shotgun barrel nudged her labia, and she screamed as Lynette thrust the cold metal inside her.

"How does it feel?" cooed Susan. "How does death feel inside your cunt?"

It felt repulsive.

Grotesque.

Lynette's grip shifted, her finger wrapping around the trigger. "Don't make me do it!" she cried. "Please... don't make do it..."

"Right up the snatch," laughed Susan. "What a way to go, huh?"

"For god's sake," sobbed Charlie. "Don't do it!"

"Too late," said Susan. "You're not my girlfriend anymore."

She laughed at that... and then Lynette pulled the trigger.

22

———————

CLICK.

Nothing happened.

Click, click.

The gun was empty. Charlie stared at the ineffectual weapon as Lynette continued to squeeze the trigger.

"A bit of fun," said Susan. "You didn't really think I'd *shoot* you, did you? Charlie... where's your imagination?"

Charlie had no words. She was exhausted, she wanted to throw up, and most of all, she wanted to kill Susan. Not hurt her, nor maim her, but *murder* her. The entire rescue attempt had been a ruse. Susan had known her every move, making her think she stood a chance, only to rob her of hope at the last second. And now the last second had arrived. There would be no escaping this time.

"No," Susan continued. "I wouldn't do that. I always liked your cunt."

A single spotlight exploded, dipping one section of the stadium into inky darkness.

"We could still be together, you know," Susan whispered

from behind, remaining out of sight. "It doesn't have to end like this."

"What?"

"I'm talking about *us,*" Susan said patronizingly. "We could start again, start afresh. Time is all kinds of fucked-up here. Forwards, backwards... if you leave at the right time, who knows where you'll end up?"

"What do you mean, *leave?* Is there a way out of here?"

"Individually, yes. But for us to leave together... that's more difficult. But I have an idea. If you're willing to try, then maybe we'd be together again. Like the old days. You remember the old days, Charlie? When we were young? I'd even be myself again, not stuck in that fucking meatbag over there." She leaned in closer, and Charlie gagged on the stench. "So what do you say?" she asked conspiratorially. "Wanna try?"

Charlie looked at Lynette. Her body was frozen, the shotgun still in her hands.

"Only if you save Lynette too," she said.

"No, she's not part of the deal."

"That's the only deal you're getting, Susan. Spare her life, and I'll do it. I'll come back with you."

Susan mulled the proposition over. "You know you'll never see her again, right?"

Lynette looked up at her with melancholy eyes. "Charlie, don't. I'd rather die."

"And you know you'll never see her again?" asked Susan, more insistently.

Charlie swallowed hard. "Never." She looked at Lynette, saw the hurt and confusion on her face. "You deserve to live."

I love you, she mouthed at the girl, afraid that Susan would fly into a rage if she heard the words aloud.

"So," said Charlie, "do we have a deal?"

"On one condition. I need you to prove yourself. You've let me down before, lover. Like the time you tried to *kill* me. I need to know you'll never do that again." Bony fingers caressed her spine. "I need to know you still love me."

"I do," she lied. "I love you, Susan."

Something slimy brushed against her skin and dripped down her bare legs.

"Then I ask only one thing," said Susan, as she finally stepped out from behind Charlie. "Prove you're still mine."

Charlie couldn't help it. She screamed at the sight.

"Make love to me," said the hideous, misshapen monster that once was Susan. *"Make love to me."*

23

———

Charlie stared in mounting horror at the freakish deformity. Not one part of the shambling lump resembled Susan. The girl appeared to be *inside out*.

Spongy pink mass coated her form, exposed veins threading through distorted limbs that jutted like stumpy tree branches. Bulging eyes glared at her, six of them, no, *seven*, bloodshot and crusted. Strings of intestines hung from the soft flesh, looping around before disappearing back inside, reminding Charlie of the slides at a water park. There was no face, nothing resembling one, while dripping purple tongues slobbered from narrow slits in all the wrong places.

"Come to me," the mouths sang in ghastly harmony. "Make love to me."

When Charlie realized she had full control of her body, her first instinct was to run. But where, and how? Even if she somehow cleared the thousands of people that stood sentinel around her, where would she go? There was nowhere to run *to,* and she couldn't leave Lynette behind. No, she had to do it.

She had to take one for the team.

If she proved herself to Susan, then they would all be okay. After all, Susan had said so.

And you believe her, right?

Of course not. But what choice did she have?

"Take your clothes off," said Susan. "Let me see you, let me touch your skin..."

Charlie did as asked. She removed her torn tee shirt and took a step closer to the putrid creature, fighting back the urge to vomit.

"You could still love me?" asked Susan. It sounded like a challenge.

"Yes," replied Charlie. She stood inches from the pustulating fiend, the powerful odor overwhelming in its rank fetidness.

"Then take me, *here,* with everybody watching."

Charlie wasn't sure where to start. She gingerly placed her hands on Susan, trying not to grimace at the soft, sticky touch. Her palms came away wet with blood. Something grabbed her ankle, and she looked down to see a hand extending from Susan's lower half. It gripped her, and then more hands found her waist, her shoulder, pulling her close. Their bodies pressed together. Squirming entrails brushed Charlie's stomach, tongues lapping at her legs, her breasts sinking into the skinless torso as two enormous, toothless mouths sucked on them.

"No," moaned Charlie, the sensation too foul, too obscene. "I can't!"

But it was too late.

The hands pulled her closer.

A shapeless thing that had once been a head quivered, vibrating so hard that little chunks of muscle dropped off. It split in two, long strands of gossamer-fine mucus straining to hold it together. The halves closed over her head, forcing her lips against a delicate, pulsing sac-like organ.

The sac burst, reedy tentacles reaching into her mouth and latching onto her tongue. She tried to scream at the abhorrent invasion, but couldn't. At least three hands, maybe more, grasped at her buttocks, kneading and squeezing them, scratching and slapping.

Charlie fought with every last ounce of her strength, but she was powerless against Susan. The tentacles spread down her throat, choking her, and she became aware of something slithering up her left leg, winding its way past her knee and around her thigh.

She knew where it was going.

The hands gripped her ass cheeks, spreading them apart, the slimy member wriggling its way inside her.

Charlie wept in darkness, the repulsive split head acting as a protective cocoon, depriving her of most of her senses. She heard nothing, saw nothing, heightening the appalling sensation of the organs that probed unceasingly inside her. There was nothing she could do but wait. Wait and think and... meditate.

Meditate.

The word flashed in her mind like a neon sign outside a strip joint. But what was the point? It had never worked before. Well, only that one time in the park, when Lynette had been there to guide her.

But wasn't Lynette there now, just a few feet away?

Picture yourself in a corridor.

That's what Lynette had said. Well, that was easy. She had been there recently.

Charlie envisaged the corridor with herself standing in it, the image emerging with spotless clarity.

I'm doing it, I'm really doing it, she thought, the room shaking as some new abomination guzzled at her vulva.

No!

She focused her attention, steadying the corridor, even as lamps exploded around her. She wouldn't let Susan kick her out this time. Cracks split along the walls, the paint peeling like diseased skin.

It's all about breathing, she recalled Lynette saying. *Breathe in... and breathe out. Keep the rhythm.*

She tried. Standing in the corridor, she leaned one hand against the wall and breathed... in... out... in... out...

A nearby section of roof caved in. She had to move, had to find help.

Help? Ha! Who the fuck was left to help her? They were gone, all gone. Everyone she had ever met — hell, everyone she had ever *encountered* — was standing in a circle watching in silence as a sentient blob raped her in a football field.

There was no one left.

Unless...

"Shit," said Charlie, as the idea struck her. Would it work? Was it even possible? She didn't know, but goddammit, she had to try. It was her — and Lynette's — only chance.

As the corridor shook violently, and fire erupted around her, Charlie took off running.

Only one person could save them now.

24

———

L YNETTE WATCHED HELPLESSLY AS S USAN SUBSUMED C HARLIE, their bodies merging with painstaking slowness. The longer it went on, the more their surroundings seemed to crumble, almost as if Susan was the only one holding everything together, and the less she concentrated, the more the fragile illusion deteriorated.

One of the spotlight stands toppled, crushing some of the waiting army, while a low tremor rumbled endlessly. A sinkhole opened up, swallowing several men and women, who tumbled soundlessly through the widening gap.

The world — this world, this hellscape they currently inhabited — was ending.

She doubted Charlie believed Susan's lies about saving them and bringing them back to reality. They were dead, and there was no coming back from *that*. If there *was* a way out, Lynette would have found it. Heaven, Hell... whatever this place was, it was strictly one-way.

The painted clouds on the sky above them split open, a deluge of water pouring in as the artifice continued to reveal itself like a film set collapsing atop the actors.

Lynette noticed the pain in her mauled breast had returned. That was good. It meant Susan, so wrapped up in absorbing Charlie, was losing control. Her infantry, too, were recovering what little sense they possessed, glancing around at each other in confusion, none of them quite sure why they were crowded into a football stadium, or what to make of the grotesque spectacle they witnessed.

Lynette flexed her fingers, focusing all her energy on regaining mastery of her limbs. The shotgun remained in her hands, the open backpack full of shells within reach... if only she could move her damn arms.

Charlie's body melted into Susan's, their grim union almost complete.

Lynette's arms tingled, and she managed to close her eyes, drawing on reserves of strength she wasn't sure she possessed. Limbs that had previously been immobile began to itch, and when the excruciating pain hit, Lynette knew she was on the right path.

Susan's eyes — all of them — were shut, and with agonizing ponderousness, Lynette made her move, staggering sloth-like towards the bag of shells, each step helping to vanquish the forced lethargy.

In her periphery, she noticed some of the drones snap to attention. They turned to her, eyes locked on their target... yet, for now, they remained stationary.

Shit, shit, shit.

She took another step, pitting her own mental fortitude against Susan's, fighting back against the cognitive brick wall the psychopath had erected around her mind.

Almost there...

Lynette glanced at Susan. Only Charlie's back was visible, scrawny veins burrowing into her spine and taking root.

The tips of Lynette's fingers brushed a shotgun shell, the

tactile nature sending waves of freedom up her arm. The further she got from Susan, the easier her movements became. She slid the shell into position, turning to face—

Susan's eyes opened. They opened, and looked directly at her.

Lynette had to act fast, but she couldn't risk hitting Charlie. As the clumsy hands of the army grasped at her shoulders, she aimed low... and pulled the trigger.

This time, the gun fired.

Susan's foot detonated, blood and tissue splattering in a wide radius. Her mouths screamed as she toppled like a felled redwood, her juicy, slick form hitting the ground with a vile splat.

Charlie's limp body rolled out of her, the coiled, blood-soaked tentacles retreating from her various orifices at high speed.

At once, everything went to hell.

Susan's army, so regimented before, lost their discipline. They stared at their hands, they screamed, they tried to run, knocking each other to the ground and clambering over the fallen bodies, crushing them to a pulp, while overhead the heavens cracked like a spiderweb, disgorging vast quantities of blood that flooded over the horrified mob. Lynette shielded her face and stared into the fractured sky. A single gigantic eyeball gazed back at her, its iris a blue pool of thrashing, mutilated bodies.

"Oh god," said Lynette. She hoped it wasn't.

As huge chasms wrenched the pitch apart, she ran for Charlie, dragging her slack body away from Susan.

"Charlie! Charlie, wake up!" The girl did not stir. Lynette slapped her face, hating to do so. "Charlie, please!"

Susan's twisted form undulated, the flesh bubbling like a pool of primordial ooze. Lynette lifted Charlie, ignoring her own pain, and hefted the girl onto her shoulder as a single human hand burst through the dissolving slime that had once been Susan.

"No, no," muttered Lynette as she staggered through the flock of wailing civilians, who scratched and lacerated their own faces, raking nails down their skin. A colossal crash rang out as one of the stands disintegrated, the pieces washed away by a river of blood that flowed alongside the pitch.

"Wake up!" screamed Lynette, fighting through the havoc, barging aside anyone who got in her way, only to find...

"Fuck!" she shouted, as the crowd parted to reveal Susan's remains, two arms protruding from within like something was trying to claw its way out. She turned and ran the opposite direction, ensuring she remained in a straight line, using the one remaining floodlight tower as a guiding star.

She stumbled and fell, releasing Charlie and watching as her girlfriend, who had risked everything to save her, tumbled gracelessly onto the grass, her limbs loose and flaccid, eyes closed.

And there, right in front of them, was Susan, emerging from her old form like pus from a cyst, a sheen of pink film breaking across her face, blood raining down from the sky, the watchful blue eye of madness peering down from high above.

Susan clawed at the layer of stretched flesh, bursting it open, her rebirth complete. She shambled to her feet, looking as she had before, once upon a time, before derangement had infected her every pore.

Lynette shook Charlie. "Wake up! Please, you have to wake up!"

"You stupid fucking cunt," growled Susan. She glared at Lynette, the fires that burned around the stadium casting macabre shadows across her face. "You took her from me. She was *mine,* and you took her." She hobbled forwards. "Twice! You took her from me twice!" Her naked body trembled in fury. *"She was mine, and you took her from me!"*

Suddenly Susan composed herself. "Your death," she said slowly, deliberately, "will be beyond belief."

Lynette shook her head, gripping Charlie's slack hand in her own. She gazed into the girl's face — so tragic, so beautiful — and cried. A single tear landed on Charlie's cheek, and she leaned forwards, taking her in her arms and kissing her reverently, the way those lips deserved to be kissed.

"When you're near," she whispered, *"my troubles melt away."*

"I love you," said Charlie, so softly Lynette thought she was imagining it.

"What?"

Charlie's eyes half-opened. "You heard me," she said, and then — against all odds, despite everything — she *smiled.*

"I got us some help," she said.

25

———

GOLDEN LIGHT BATHED THE STADIUM IN A HEAVENLY GLOW.

"The fuck is this shit?" muttered Susan, staring at the flaring radiance, the heads of her minions tilting, following her gaze.

A shimmering, phosphorescent half-rainbow appeared in the sky, seeming to end somewhere within the mass of bodies. It glistened a moment in quiet majesty, and then a single, small figure ambled forwards.

"Is that... a dog?" asked Lynette, squinting through the dazzling light.

"No," answered Charlie. "That's Princess Elizabeth Cupcake."

The dog barked once, the sharp report echoing across the stadium.

"I'm sorry, is *this* your cavalry?" cackled Susan. She shook her head. "I'll tear that dog to—"

Another canine howled in response. Then another, more and more until the noise was deafening. Princess bounded down the rainbow bridge, leading the charge as hundreds — no, *thousands* — of dogs appeared, following him. They kept coming, paws thundering against the rainbow, an unending tidal wave of wagging tails, wet noses... and sharp teeth.

"Kill them all!" shouted Susan, as her horde turned on command to face the determined pooches.

The first dog to leave the bridge and leap into action was a Labrador named Bertie, a Good Dog who enjoyed rolling in the grass and chewing socks. Bertie leaped at the closest assailant, clamping his powerful jaws against the man's throat and ripping it out, blood gushing over Bertie's fluffy yellow coat. Scampi, an Irish Setter and a Good Dog who disliked the rain but loved having her belly tickled, threw herself at a snarling woman, using her paws to shove the woman onto her back.

Princess, who was of a more diminutive stature, went straight for one man's groin, his teeth breaking through the thin shorts and sinking into his penis. Princess shook his head back and forth, tearing the ragged member loose. His new chew toy tasted bad, and he spat it out and ran for the next man.

"What the fuck!" screamed Susan. "Kill those fucking dogs!"

Charlie watched in stunned awe as Susan's army — the faceless humans that lived only in her memory — fell one by one, more dogs pounding down the bridge and vaulting into action.

She laughed. The whole thing was fucking ridiculous, she knew, and yet here they were, every dog that Princess could rally doing their damnedest to help them. And why? Well, she supposed it was like the old retriever had said... because they were *all* Good Dogs.

Three chihuahuas nipped at a woman's ankles, biting at her Achilles tendon, savaging it until she fell, the dogs scurrying out from under her falling body. One was too slow, and a Newfoundland — who was a *Very* Good Dog, because he had saved his family from a fire by barking loud enough to wake them — snapped the small dog up in his jaws in time, depositing her, unharmed, amongst her friends in another concerted attack on some poor bastard's ankles.

The army toppled as the dogs cut through them, still more entering the fray, long ears rippling behind them. The sound of human screaming mixed with howls and barks. Charlie saw one Rottweiler racing past with a hand in his mouth, while other dogs bit and tore at the belly of a guy she recognized from a party a long time ago who had repeatedly pinched her ass.

"Rip his guts out!" she cried, and the dogs — for they were indeed Good Dogs — did as asked. One small black Pomeranian scampered by, dragging the pervert's entrails behind her like a string of sausages stolen from a butcher.

Susan stood amongst the carnage, bellowing profanities. "Fucking kill them, you bastards! You fucking useless cunts!" She turned to Charlie, fixed her with a murderous stare. "You *know* I hate dogs," she said, and raised both arms.

Charlie's throat constricted, her feet leaving the ground as Susan choked her from afar. Lynette, too, rose up, her legs feverishly kicking.

"You cunts deserve each other," said Susan, bringing her hands together, the motion causing the girls to fly towards each other, their foreheads striking with a dull thud. It hurt like hell, and when Susan slammed them against each other for a second time, Charlie's nose smacked into Lynette's cheek, breaking it.

Susan was squeezing too hard. Charlie's neck tightened, the pressure on her windpipe impairing her ability to breathe. She crashed into Lynette again, with enough force to dislocate her shoulder.

"Go on," laughed Susan. "Kiss her! *Kiss her!*"

If she had been crazy before, then now she had lost even the vaguest semblance of sanity. She thrust the couple together, their skulls cracking against each other, blood pouring from Charlie's nose, her eyes watering. She didn't know if she would be dead before she lost consciousness.

The dogs were making their way through the army, their progress impeded by the sheer volume of bodies as the mindless drones formed an impenetrable wall around Susan.

"I could have saved you!" the girl shrieked. "I could have saved you, but you fucked it up like you fuck *everything* up!"

She spread her hands into a Christ pose, gearing up for one final killing blow. As Charlie's vision faded, she caught a glimpse of Princess. The dog leaped onto the back of another bulldog, then hopped onto a Great Dane, using them as a stepladder, bounding from the tall dog onto the head of one of the men, using *him* as a springboard, jumping from shoulder to shoulder, too fast for anyone to stop the crazed hound.

Susan noticed him too, and she turned, letting Charlie and Lynette drop to the grass. In her whirlwind of madness, she held both hands out to the dog, trying to control him... forgetting that she couldn't.

Princess hurtled through the air, teeth bared, jowls flapping the way they did when he used to put his head out the car window on a long drive.

"Fuck!" yelled Susan, as Princess slammed into her, his teeth penetrating her cheek. Susan pounded her fists against the dog's sinewy torso, but he refused to let go, not until he tore the skin from her face like a wet, fleshy rag.

They burst through, *all* of the dogs, as Susan's army dissolved in bewilderment, their glorious leader lying on her back as hundreds of feral teeth mangled and lacerated her skin, tearing her fingers from her hands, biting huge chunks of muscle from her legs. A bloodhound excitedly chewed at the exposed bone, pulling it with such ferocity that it came away from the leg. More dogs grappled playfully for the prized treat, three of them clamping their jaws over it in a savage tug-of-war.

"Stop!"

The voice belonged to Charlie. The dogs halted at her command, and she got groggily to her feet as a tremendous tremor vibrated the ground. She looked across the field, at the unbridled carnage, at the mounds of ravaged corpses and severed limbs.

"Sit," she called.

The dogs sat.

She helped Lynette up, and the two embraced, before stumbling arm-in-arm towards Susan... or what was left of her.

Lying in a pool of blood, she was missing a leg, and one arm had been gnawed to the bone, teeth marks dotting the skeletal limb. Half of her face was gone, one eye punctured, the other dribbling from the mouth of a corgi.

Still her chest rose and fell, her breathing slow and labored.

She wasn't dead yet.

Charlie kneeled by Princess and ruffled his fur. He responded by licking her hand, and a wave of sadness hit her.

"My best friend," she said, as the tears fell. Princess offered a paw, and she shook it. Lynette crouched beside them, and she too shook Princess's paw.

"It's an honor," she said, her voice hoarse.

With great effort, Charlie stood and surveyed the scene, dogs as far as she could see, each sitting still. "You're all Good Dogs," she said, and at the sound of her words, a million tails started to wag. "Thank you," she sobbed, holding onto Lynette. "Every one of you."

Princess barked in response, and the dogs — those Good, Good Dogs — filed back onto the rainbow bridge.

They watched them go, a parade of loving obedience, Princess the last to leave. He gazed upon Charlie, then Lynette, and turned away, bumbling past the retriever, who waited at the bottom of the bridge, corralling his flock.

He's lucky, said the wise old retriever. *Most Dogs have one best friend. But now Princess has two.* The retriever smiled. *His heart is filled with joy.*

He looked past them and uttered a sharp *woof.* Charlie turned to see a little black pug next to Susan, one leg raised as he peed on her shoulder. Then he scampered towards the bridge.

Farewell, said the retriever, as the rainbow bridge faded from view, leaving a field of broken, bloodied bodies in its wake.

Using each other for balance, Charlie and Lynette gazed down at Susan.

"What now?" asked Charlie, as lightning forked across the sky in a garish outburst.

"Is she dead?"

"Not yet."

"Then I guess we have to finish her off." Lynette looked at Charlie. "Do you want me to do it?"

Charlie shook her head. "It's okay. It should be me."

She wasn't sure she had the strength. After everything she had been through — the pain, the torment, the madness, the torture — it would all be over soon. She collapsed to her knees by Susan's side, and stroked her hand through the girl's matted, bloody hair.

"I'm sorry it had to end like this," she said. "But sometimes you can be a real cunt, you know?"

Susan laughed, which turned into a coughing fit as she spat up lungfuls of dark, black blood.

"Something funny?" asked Charlie, as Lynette loaded the shotgun and handed it to her.

"Actually," croaked Susan, "yeah." She smiled a horrible smile. "What... do you think... is going to happen... when you kill me?"

It was Charlie's turn to smile. "I don't know. But Lynette and I... we're going to be together. And we'll be happy."

Susan laughed again, spitting out more blood. "You stupid bitch. You think you're in heaven? In the afterlife?" She managed to move one arm to her head, and tapped at her temple with a bloody, fingerless stump. "You're in *here*. You're in my head."

"No," said Charlie, glancing at Lynette for confirmation.

Lynette looked worried.

"Before you died," said Susan. "I brought you inside. I protected you. She," — she gestured feebly at Lynette — "was already here. All this time."

"She's lying, Charlie. Kill her."

Charlie pumped the shotgun, loading the first shell. But she didn't pull the trigger. "What if she's right?"

Susan let out a ragged, wheezing sigh. "Look around you. It's already falling apart, isn't it?"

Charlie turned as a wind whipped through the stadium, the corpses crumbling to ash and whirling through the air like snow. The grass, the remaining stands, even the edifice of the museum fragmented into tiny mosaic pieces, caught in the wind and blown sky high.

"You'll be free, soon," said Susan. "Back to reality... at some point in time. I don't know when. It was... too much for me to control. Too much pressure... even for me." Her expression turned serious. "But when I go... I'll take your memories with me. I'll take your *minds*. You'll be nothing. Empty shells, lost and alone. You'll *never* find each other again."

"I don't believe you," lied Charlie, gazing beyond Susan at a world turning to dust before her eyes.

Susan's malevolent laughter rang in her ears. "Too late," she said, her breathing slowing, slowing... stopping. *"See you later... Charlie-gator..."*

More lightning split the night, literally tearing the sky in two. The great eyeball above them closed, shutting out the desperate screams of the tortured souls that swam in its cruel iris.

The wind howled, the very air around them fragmenting.

Charlie took Lynette's hand.

"It's happening," she said. "Oh god, she was telling the truth."

Lynette stared at her, her jaw set. "Then let's get the fuck out of here," she said.

26

———

T**HEY** **RAN** **FROM** **A** **WORLD** **THAT** **DISINTEGRATED** **AROUND** them, their broken and battered bodies begging for mercy, for relief from the physical pain and mental anguish they had faced their whole lives.

But how could they outrun death itself, the very destruction of their world, of their minds? If it was true that Susan had stored their memories, their *lives,* inside her own head, then what did that mean? What would happen when she no longer existed?

Charlie glanced over her shoulder at the tornado of swirling debris, the field crumbling behind them, the ground giving way. She wiped blood from her eyes. Lynette was lagging, Charlie practically dragging her along. "Jump!" yelled Charlie, as the pitch split in front of them, and they vaulted the gap, leaping over a hellish, flaming abyss.

"Stop," said Lynette.

"What? We can't!" Charlie grabbed the girl's arm and hauled her forward.

"I said, stop!"

She looked at the girl, the world coming down around them. "What is it? It's catching up!"

Lynette closed her eyes, concentrating. Blood spurted from both nostrils, and she pointed behind Charlie. "Get in!"

"Huh?" She turned to see Lynette's 1955 Ford Thunderbird. It was the same one they had shared their first kiss in, with its broken rear window and dented side panels and rusted paintwork.

They ran for the vehicle, Lynette piling into the driver's seat. She flipped the sun visor down and the key fell into her lap.

"You okay to drive?" asked Charlie.

"No," said Lynette, squinting through her swollen, bruised eyes. "Did you ever learn?"

"No."

Lynette jammed the key into the ignition. "Decision made," she said, and the engine roared into life. The battered old vehicle lurched and stalled. "Useless fucking thing," said Lynette, trying again, this time getting the car in motion. She slammed the pedal down, accelerating past a few wretched stragglers from Susan's army.

One of them was on fire. In fact, fire seemed to be raining down from the broken sky, balls of churning flame striking the pitch and embedding themselves there.

"Brace yourself," said Lynette, as they careened towards a barrier, smashing through it, finding themselves on a desert highway, the sun high and bright.

"Are we—"

"Not yet," said Lynette. "Look behind you."

Charlie glanced in the rearview. Unable to believe her eyes, she loosened her seat belt and pivoted around, staring out the back windshield. The stadium, and its pitch black night sky, were in pieces, forming a giant tidal wave that thundered high above them. The desert floor was breaking apart, shards of sky and sand and cacti and even remnants of a gas station swirling through the air like smoke. Other cars had stopped by the side of the road, the drivers getting out to stop and stare at the calamitous destruction, unaware of their impending deaths.

"They're not real," Charlie reminded herself. "This is all just in Susan's head."

"Left or right?" asked Lynette as they approached a fork in the road, the speedometer nudging eighty. Charlie wondered how fast the old wreck could go. "Left or right!" screamed Lynette.

"Left," she said decisively. "No, right!"

Lynette spun the steering wheel so hard the vehicle almost tipped. Two tires left the road, and for one hideous second, they thought they were gonna roll. Then the Thunderbird righted itself, and they took off down the highway, except now it wasn't the desert, it was the Las Vegas strip, and the street was jam-packed with cars.

"Fuck!" shouted Lynette, veering onto the sidewalk. She tried to avoid the pedestrians, but they stood slack-jawed in their colorful shirts and sunglasses, many pausing to snap photos of the impending collapse of their small world.

Thud!

The first person hit the hood, smashing the windshield and tumbling over the soft roof.

"Lynette!"

"It's okay," the girl said through gritted teeth. "It's like you just said," — *smack!* Another tourist bounced off the car — "They're not real!"

Charlie tried to recall a time that Susan had visited Vegas. Back in the early eighties, she used to disappear for days, which were the happiest times of Charlie's life with the maniac. She supposed Susan could have — *crunch!* A pedestrian fell in front of the vehicle and they bounded over her — gone for the weekend without telling her.

"It's still coming," said Charlie, looking back. Behind them was nothing but a monstrous black void that hungrily devoured all in its mighty path. "We can't outrun it!"

"You don't know that," said Lynette, though she was crying, steering wildly to avoid the people. A huge sign that said FRONTIER in Old West writing hung at an angle, crashing down atop several cars, crushing the occupants. Lynette spun the wheel to avoid it, briefly driving along the road and scraping against oncoming cars, sending up showers of blazing sparks.

"Oh god," said Charlie, pointing through the windshield.

Lynette could say nothing. She, too, saw the passenger jet falling from the sky, speeding towards them in the middle of the strip. The wings were aflame, the back half of the jet missing and spewing out black smoke.

"Hold on," Lynette grimaced, turning the vehicle and crashing through the glass doors of a hotel as the airplane hit the road behind them in a ball of blinding light, the impact shattering windows for miles around and sending the already precarious world tilting. The Thunderbird entered the lobby and annihilated the reception desk and the clerk, before coming to a violent, screeching halt.

Steam belched from the engine. Charlie tried her seat belt and found it was stuck, so she slid out under it and looked at Lynette.

The girl was unmoving, her forehead resting on the steering wheel.

Charlie limped around the car, noticing the lobby was

tilting at a slight angle, potted plants and computer chairs rolling towards her. She wrenched open the driver's side door. "We have to go," she cried, unbuckling Lynette's seat belt and swinging the girl's legs out of the car.

Her eyes remained closed. "I don't... know if I... can."

"You have to! You hear me? You fucking have to!"

Charlie reached into the vehicle and dragged Lynette out, forcing her to stand, though the rapidly tilting floor played havoc with their balance. Outside, the Vegas strip was in chaos. People ran screaming past the hotel lobby, hundreds of car horns blaring, the passenger jet burning up in the street.

"Wait here," said Charlie, leaving Lynette to lean against the Thunderbird. She jogged as best she could towards the shattered doors, avoiding the glass, and looked out. The void was getting closer, swallowing everything. Whole buildings crunched and distorted, bricks and mortar spiraling through the air as the world continued to tilt on its axis.

Running now, despite the pain, she made it back to Lynette.

"Come with me," she said, putting her arm around her girlfriend's waist and helping her through the lobby. It was like walking uphill, the building approaching a forty-five degree angle.

"Where are we going?" asked Lynette softly. Charlie wondered if she had a concussion.

"The elevator," she replied. It was the only place she could think to go. She hammered the button and waited, planting her feet in the entrance and gripping onto Lynette for dear life as the room continued to slowly turn.

The elevator dinged, and they rolled inside, lying across the mirrored walls. Charlie hit the button for the top floor, watching the madness unfold as the doors slid shut. There had to be a way out. Maybe a helipad on the roof with a waiting copter and pilot? Or a glider, or... or... or fucking *something,* dammit! It couldn't end like this. Not after all they'd been through.

They slid down the mirrored surface as the elevator spun, landing on the ceiling next to the maintenance hatch. Charlie crawled towards it and peered through. They were approaching the top floor.

"Almost there," she said to Lynette, cradling the girl's head on her lap. She was in bad shape. They both were. Without the benefit of adrenaline, she wondered if either of them could move.

The doors opened noiselessly.

She placed her hands under Lynette's shoulders and hauled her out. Where the hell were they? It was a small, dark room, with a rickety metal staircase leading down and...

"Of course," she said, as the realization dawned. She saw the misspelled sign — ENTRY FOR OFFERISED PERSONAL ONLY — attached to the door, and knew precisely where they were. "All roads lead back to Susan," muttered Charlie, as she half-pulled, half-carried Lynette through the metal door and emerged on the roof of Clinton High School.

The skylight pulsated with colorful disco lights, the house band's rendition of The Jackson Five's *ABC* seeping into the night, as Charlie laid Lynette down on the cold concrete. She stood, gazing out over the town.

Like everything else, it was caught in a whirling maelstrom. The hospital was already gone, along with the Town Hall and the library. She tried a different direction. The park was missing, replaced by emptiness and desolation. She spun again, searching for one direction in which they could run, but it was all-encompassing.

There was nowhere left to go.

Panic set in. Sheer, blind panic. She hyperventilated, tears streaming down her face, turning in circles at the encroaching end.

"There's... we can't... I..."

A limp hand grazed her leg, and Charlie looked into Lynette's eyes. The girl shook her head and said, "Sit with me a minute, Charlie."

"There's no time. We have to... we have to..."

"We don't have to do anything. Except be with each other."

"But—"

"Charlie, please." Lynette swallowed painfully. "Sit with me. Be with me when the end comes."

The void reached the car park, the cars splintering into tiny slivers of white light, before being sucked into the awesome power of the black hole. Charlie took one last look across the town she had called home for many years, and sat next to her girlfriend.

They clasped hands.

"It's not fair," said Charlie.

Lynette nodded sadly. "I know." As the apocalypse approached with calculated slowness, she laid her head on Charlie's shoulder. "I love you," she said. "From the moment I saw you, I just knew it in my heart."

"I love you too. I wish we'd got to spend more time together."

"We did, though," wheezed Lynette. "And that day together was the greatest of my life. I used to imagine you somehow finding me, and worried that maybe I'd misremembered you, that you were no longer the girl I fell in love with, that you'd changed. But I was wrong to think that." She turned her head towards Charlie. "You're everything to me."

Charlie didn't know what to say to that. Instead, she kissed Lynette, a kiss of long-repressed passion and desire. It was a great kiss. Despite the taste of coppery blood and salty tears, it was a fucking *terrific* kiss.

Screams rang out through the skylight as the darkness consumed the dancers in the school hall, the music cutting out as the band members dissolved, leaving nothing but silence. No wind, no birdsong, no crickets, no cars... they were all gone. Nothing remained except Charlie, Lynette, and the school rooftop.

"Sing for me," said Charlie. "Sing your song."

Lynette shivered. "I can't," she whispered. "I'm so... tired."

"You *have* to. For me. Listen, we don't know what's coming, right? We don't know what's going to happen. Susan said she'd destroy our memories, sure, but so what? We found each other before, didn't we? I found you here, thanks to *your* song. So sing it for me, one last time, and I swear, whatever happens next, I *will* find you again. Wherever you are, wherever I am. We'll find each other."

Lynette's lip quivered. She was growing pale, the red blood on her face a shocking contrast to her fragile, porcelain skin.

"Okay," she rasped. "I'll try."

She gazed out over the approaching abyss, tears running down her cheeks.

> *"Lonely night in winter, I was feeling blue,*
> *Life was slipping by me, don't know what to do,*
> *Til the day I met you, baby, and the clouds did clear,*

That's just how it happens when you're..."

She coughed up blood. It spilled down her chin.

"...when you're standing... near."

The last word was almost inaudible. Lynette's eyes closed, and Charlie held her tightly.

"I wish that I could tell you how you make feel,"

sang Charlie. God, she hated her voice. It wasn't melodic and pretty like Lynette's. But Lynette couldn't sing right now, so it was up to Charlie to do it for her. It was okay. There was no one else around to hear.

"How only when I'm with you do I think I'm real.
But I wish I had the courage buried deep inside,
So when you are around I wouldn't have to hide."

Her voice cracked, and powerful sobs tormented her broken body. She gazed longingly at Lynette, kissed her forehead, and sang, as the void devoured the rooftop, a circle closing in on her like the spotlight on a theater stage.

"And you, can't see,
How the sun, shines on me..."

She couldn't do it, couldn't finish. The darkness reached her feet, the skin peeling away, revealing raw musculature, beads of blood rising into the air like leaves caught in a fall breeze. There was no pain, the sensation akin to the numbness of placing cold feet into a hot bath. She watched the layers of her flesh unravel, her bones rotting to dust, as the circle grew smaller.

"Hey," said Lynette in a small, small voice. Charlie gazed into her eyes. "You didn't finish…"

Charlie clenched her jaw. "Finish it with me, 'kay?"

Lynette nodded.

"And you, can't see," they sang together.
"How the sun, shines on me,
When you're near,
My troubles melt—"

And then there was nothing.

27

"*Charlie?*"

The voice roused her.

"*Wake up, you're gonna be late for school.*"

With a yawn and a stretch, she slid her legs out of bed and rubbed groggily at her eyes. What time was it? A digital alarm clock on a bedside table told her it was seven forty-five.

Forcing herself to stand, she unpicked her underwear from the crack of her butt and tugged her nightdress down.

The room was unfamiliar. There was a bed, and a writing desk and chair, and a table lamp, and a wardrobe, and posters, and Christmas lights, and... there, on the mirror...

Photographs.

They covered the glass from top to bottom, and she peeled one off. Two young girls looked back at her, grinning foolishly, but she didn't recognize their faces. She removed another photo, this one a faded Polaroid of a child sitting in a sandbox and waving a green plastic spade over their head. Again, nothing. She tore more photos from the mirror, staring at them before discarding them. A family posing with mountains in the background, a girl ice skating, two girls in swimsuits eating ice cream, a dog asleep on its back, a tall building, *another* girl eating ice cream, a man and a woman holding a baby, more girls, more ice cream, more and more until not a single photograph remained on the mirror.

And for the first time, she looked at her reflection.

It was *her*.

The girl from the photos, the one smiling and laughing and eating ice cream, so much ice cream.

She was that girl.

And she had no idea who she was.

PART III

AFTERDEATH

28

―――――

December 31st 1999

The party was lame.

It was fast approaching midnight, the start of a new decade, and all anyone wanted to talk about was The Millennium Bug, which apparently meant that all the computers were gonna reset at the toll of the bell and planes were gonna fall from the sky and hospital life support systems would switch off, or some bullshit. And to make matters worse, there was a never-ending soundtrack of fucking *swing* music. Big Bad Voodoo Daddy, The Brian Setzer Orchestra, Cherry Poppin' Daddies... it was awful.

Charlotte stared out the penthouse window at the New York skyline and toyed with a cigarette carton. She didn't want to be here — she had just broken up with another in a long string of meaningless girlfriends — but Jerry from work had *insisted*.

"You can't bring in the new year on your own," Jerry had said.

But Jerry was wrong. She absolutely *could* do that. In fact, she had done it before, many times, and thoroughly enjoyed her own company. Jerry, however, was the kind of guy who could bludgeon even *Charlotte* into submission with his relentless good nature, and so she had acquiesced.

God, she regretted it.

She often wondered if she should leave New York and head back to Clinton. The band hadn't worked out, the label dropping them unceremoniously after one failed album. They had split after that, and it was too late to find another group of willing musicians. She was approaching her forties, and the music business was a young person's game. It hardly seemed worth staying here when all she was doing was working in a comic book store and scraping by. All she had to show for her six years in The Big Apple was a crummy rented apartment, no close friends, and a litany of disastrous relationships.

Still, it was easier to meet women here. She doubted many — *any?* — lesbian bars had sprung up in Clinton during her absence. That place was backwards. How had she managed growing up there as a teenage lesbian? She would never know. She remembered *nothing* before the age of sixteen. The doctors said it was shock from the death of her girlfriend, Susan, who had passed away in her sleep. They also said that, in time, she would recover her memories.

She never did.

Susan... the name meant nothing to her.

Now, Charlotte Bonner looked out over the Hudson and prayed that, sooner or later, the DJ would run out of swing records to play.

"Fuck it," she muttered, and lit up a cigarette.

"Hey, you can't do that in here," some twenty-something dickwad in a blazer and slacks said to her.

"Bite me, loser," snarled Charlotte, and blew a puff of smoke at him.

The guy coughed overdramatically, shook his head, and walked away.

"Fucking preppy asshole," she said, then decided she'd had enough. She wanted to head back to her apartment and ring in the new year the correct way — by rocking out to AC/DC's *Hell's Bells*.

"Sorry, Jerry," she whispered. "This party blows."

Trying to remember where she had left her jacket, she pushed away from the window, too fast to avoid the woman.

"Shit!" said Charlotte, as they bumped into each other, the glass of red wine in the woman's hand spilling down the front of Charlotte's white Metallica tour shirt.

"Oh my god," said the woman. "I'm so sorry!" She rummaged in her handbag for a handkerchief. "May I?" she asked, holding the cloth an inch from the reddening stain on Charlotte's chest.

"Sure," she sighed, her escape momentarily halted.

"I'll soak as much up as I can," said the woman, carefully dabbing at Charlotte's breasts. "Then, it's best we get salt on it to draw out the stain."

"Salt?"

"Yeah, it works. We'll lay it out flat and cover it with—"

"We lay it flat? So, I'm supposed to just sit here with my tits out? I didn't know it was *that* kind of party."

"Oh," said the woman. "Sorry, I wasn't thinking. Whenever I spill wine, I'm usually at home."

"You spill wine a lot?" asked Charlotte, unable to hide the sarcasm in her voice.

The woman didn't pick up on it. "Uh, yeah. Sometimes."

She shrugged, and half-smiled. "I guess I don't have a lot going on these days."

Here we go, thought Charlotte. *Another bored housewife with a sob story.* At least she was nice to look at. Despite the frumpy dress and bad haircut, the woman's radiant beauty shone through. Was she looking to get laid? Charlotte had fucked her fair share of bored housewives looking for an injection of excitement in their humdrum lives, and they were some of the best lays of her life.

The woman continued dabbing her handkerchief at Charlotte's breasts. "I don't get out much," she was saying. "The last of the kids left home this year, so my husband said I should learn how to socialize again. Though honestly, I was never any good at it."

"Same," said Charlotte. "I didn't even want to come here tonight. I was happy at home, alone."

"That sounds perfect," smiled the woman. A tear formed in the corner of her eye, and a strange sensation overcame Charlotte.

"You ever get déjà vu?" she asked.

The woman looked up at her. "Sometimes, yeah."

"I've got it right now. Isn't that funny? I'm pretty sure I've never met you before."

"I'd remember," the woman said, blushing. "I don't think I'd forget you." She looked away, as if the words caused her physical pain, and turned to leave.

Charlotte stopped her. "Hey," she said. "Where are you going?"

"Sorry. I think I'm drunk. I just... you ever look back on your life and think about what a disappointment it's been?" Before Charlotte could answer, the woman continued. "I do. Constantly. And I shouldn't, because I'm married to a man who loves me, and we have two great kids, and I know I'm supposed to be happy, but... I'm not. I thought there was more to life than this." Her face was beet red. "Sorry, I don't know why I'm telling you this. I don't even know your name."

"I'm Charlie," replied Charlotte, surprised at herself. She never went by the name Charlie. Only her parents used it, and they were long dead.

"Charlie," said the woman. "That's pretty."

"So are you."

Charlotte gently stroked the woman's hands, then leaned forwards and kissed her on the cheek. The woman turned her head, their mouths finding each other... and then they parted.

"I'm sorry," said the woman. "I... I don't know what came over me. My husband is upstairs."

"It's alright. You're not the first bored housewife I've kissed. I get it, you're curious, that's—"

"It's *more* than that," the woman said. "I feel like I've missed out on everything. *Literally.* Half of my life is missing, I don't remember it at all, and somehow I ended up married to the man who got me pregnant, and I think I *forced* myself to fall in love with him, which isn't fair, because I know he loves me, and I try to be a good wife, but then I also know that... that the woman he loves isn't the real me." She shook her head, tears rolling down her cheeks. "The kids are grown up now, and I don't know what I'm going to do other than drink myself into oblivion. Because I'm not happy, Charlie. I pretend I am for the benefit of his friends and family, but it's not true. I'm living a lie."

Well, this escalated quickly, thought Charlotte. What started as a cheeky New Year kiss had now become a heart-to-heart. Normally, she wouldn't be in the mood, but there was something about this woman...

"Look, if you're not happy, then leave. Find what makes *you* happy. You only get one chance at life."

"Not true," the woman said. "I had *two*. I woke up one day with no memory, and had to start again. And I blew it."

"Wait. You lost your mem—" Charlotte started to say, and then the woman kissed her again. It was a great kiss, fueled by desire. A *perfect* kiss.

"Lynette? Where are you?"

The woman pulled back sharply. "Oh god," she said, her eyes darting around.

Charlotte licked her lips, butterflies dancing in her stomach. "What?"

"That's my—"

"There you are, baby," said the well-dressed man with graying hair, as he wrapped his arm around the woman's — Lynette, he had called her — waist. "Come on, it's almost midnight." He glanced at Charlie, then back to his wife. "Who's your friend? Ah, I'm sorry, it'll have to wait. We gotta go!"

Lynette smiled sadly at her, failing to mask her true feelings. "Sorry. Duty calls. It was nice to meet you, Charlie." She hugged her, whispered, "I'll never forget you," and dutifully trotted after her husband.

"I thought I'd lost you," he was saying. *"It's almost midnight, and I need someone to kiss!"*

"Me too," said Charlotte as she watched them go, mingling with the crowd until she could no longer see them. She exhaled deeply, relishing the tingling in her limbs. That kiss... it was like none she had ever experienced, and Charlotte had kissed a *lot* of women. She wanted to chase after the woman and tell her.

Maybe she should?

She stood by the window, hesitating. Why *not* tell her? What did she have to lose? Lynette had awoken something long-dormant within her. Charlotte wasn't sure quite *what* she had awoken, but it bore further investigation.

"Fuck it," she said, making her mind up. She had let every opportunity at happiness slip through her fingers all her life, and she wasn't going to let it happen again. "I'm gonna tell her."

"Ten!" chanted the partygoers.

The countdown had begun. A new century beckoned. And what better way to greet it than with a kiss from a beautiful woman, one who made Charlotte feel as giddy as a schoolgirl?

"Nine!"

She shoved through the crowd, grinning. This was so unlike her! If she paused for even a second, she knew she would give up on the idea.

"Eight!"

A couple were making out in a doorway, the guy's hand up the chick's shirt, copping a feel.

"Excuse me," said Charlotte, barging past them.

"Seven!"

She entered the main room, gazing at the mass of people gathered around the huge forty-inch TV screen.

"Six!"

There were so many people. She ran from couple to couple, fighting her way amongst them.

"Five!"

Panicking, Charlotte spun, searching for Lynette.

"You looking for someone to kiss?" asked a bearded man in a *Clerks* tee shirt. "I'm available."

Charlotte ignored him.

"Four!"

She wasn't here. God-fucking-dammit, where was she?

"Three!"

Had she left? Had she gone home?

"Two!"

Wait, what about—

Charlotte elbowed desperately through the partygoers, spilling drinks and not caring, until she broke free and raced across the room to the glass door that led to the balcony.

"One!"

And there they were.

"Happy New Year!" the crowd cheered.

Lynette and her husband kissed on the balcony, the wind ruffling Lynette's hair. Her eyes were closed, her husband's lips locked around hers.

Charlotte waited in the doorway.

Go, go, go! Tell her how you feel!

But she couldn't. She was being an idiot again. What did she think, that the woman was going to leave her husband and abandon her life because they had shared a drunken kiss at a party?

It was a stupid idea, and she was a fool for considering it. A useless, pathetic fool. No one had ever loved her, and no one ever would.

One day, she would have to accept that.

Charlotte turned away, grabbed her jacket from the bulging coat rack in the hallway, and headed for the door.

"You sure you're okay?" asked Gabe, as fireworks erupted across the night sky. He put his arm around Lynette. "You look like you've been crying."

"I'm fine," she said, glancing towards the party, half-expecting — *hoping,* even — to find Charlie there, waiting to kiss her, to take her away from this bland life she had never wanted.

But she wasn't.

Lynette turned back to Gabe and tried to smile. "Can we go home now?"

❦

Charlotte pulled her jacket tightly around her. It was freezing out, and she wouldn't be surprised if it snowed.

High above, luminous fireworks exploded in colorful bursts. She waited for a plane to fall from the sky as a result of The Millennium Bug, but none did. She shook her head. Planes didn't just fall from the sky. Some people will believe anything.

Licking her cold lips, she tasted Lynette's lipstick as she wandered the deserted streets. It was weird; she felt like she *knew* the woman intimately, like they had met before, many times.

"Maybe we were lovers in a past life?" she mused.

Who was she kidding? She was nothing but a failed rockstar who lived in Queens, and if she didn't want to freeze to death on the streets, she had better hurry up and get her ass home to bed.

The nearest subway station was a few blocks away, so she shoved her hands in her pockets and walked, kicking an empty can along the sidewalk. As she did, a song popped into her head, the way songs often do. Funny thing was, she couldn't place this one. Not the title, nor who sang it. But stuck in her head it was, and so, with the streets quiet apart from a distant siren, she sang.

"And you, can't see—"

~

"What's that song?" asked Lynette, as Gabe — forever the designated driver, especially as his wife always drank like she wished to forget — navigated the Plymouth Breeze through New York's streets at a sensible speed. He had never seen the city so quiet, he thought, as they drove past a lone woman with her hands in the pockets of a black leather jacket.

"What song?" he replied, glad Lynette was talking again. She had been quiet all the way from the apartment to the car, and he was worried.

"Oh, you know the one." She hummed the melody for him.

"I give up," said Gabe. "But I never was a big music fan."

"No, no, you *must* know it," she insisted. "It's famous. It's like... shit, I can't remember the words. You know it. It goes, uh...

"How the sun, shines on me,
When you're near..."

Gabe chuckled, and said, "It's the sorta meaningless crap I'd expect to hear from Madonna. Are you sure it wasn't her?" He nodded to himself. "Yeah, I think that's who it is. Madonna."

"You're probably right," said Lynette, the melody slipping through her grasp, the words lost in time. "It must have been Madonna."

~

A car cruised past Charlotte, idling at a stoplight, its windows frosted.

God, it was cold.

She walked briskly, keeping her head down, as snow fluttered from the sky like swirling ash, landing in her hair and on the tip of her nose.

"My troubles melt away," she said, smiling to herself as the last line of the chorus, the *one* line she couldn't remember, popped miraculously into her head. "That's it."

The power of song always amazed her. How a few words arranged in a certain order, coupled with the right melody, could truly lift the soul, even in its darkest hours.

> *"And you, can't see,*
> *How the sun, shines on me,*
> *When you're near,*
> *My troubles melt away."*

Yet as the stoplights turned green and the Plymouth Breeze took off down the street, the words seemed to evaporate from her mind. She tried to remember them, to sing them again, but the strange, sad song was gone forever, out of her mind and out of her life.

And as the snow blanketed the ground, and the deafening cacophony of the fireworks died away, the newly christened Charlie Bonner started to cry.

She was, once more, alone.

CARL'S AFTERWORD

I can't say for certain, folks, but I think *Psychic Teenage Bloodbath II* might be the first extreme horror novel ever adapted from a Christian musical.

It all started back in the eighties, when I was out of work and heavily in debt to the sort of people you *never* want to be in debt to. In the interests of keeping my fingers and toes and other, more *sensitive* extremities intact, I took a job as a caretaker at a local church.

One night I got talking with the priest, who had heard I was a writer and asked if it was true. I told him it was, neglecting to mention the fact I was also a washed-up alcoholic bum, and he told me he had always dreamed of putting on a show — a religious musical, to be precise — and asked if I had any interest in writing it. I said no. Then the crazy fucker offered to *pay* me for it, and I changed my tune.

He asked if I believed in God, and I said yeah, because of *course* I believed in Eddie Van Halen. Then he enquired if I had any experience writing religious material, to which I replied that yes, I had, thinking about a porno picture I had written in the seventies in which a muscular oaf in red body paint and tacky horns used his, uh, *pitchfork* on several golden haired angels in a very unconventional manner.

With that out of the way, I set to work on the dramatically titled *Heaven and Hell: A Religious Odyssey,* a sort of rock-opera for losers.

In the original story, a young couple — a man and a woman, of course — die in a car crash, and while the dude goes to heaven, his chick goes to hell because she's a sinner, a plot point the priest insisted upon, due to his belief that "All women are sinners, Carl. Some just sin less than others."

Now personally, I always had a preference for women who sinned *more* than others, but I went along with it. He put me in touch with a musician, and together we hammered out the songs, including such gems as *Touched by Jesus* and *Somewhere Over the Rainbow (Bridge),* a song for which we would have been sued to hell and back had anyone outside of the church ever heard it.

Obviously, the book you just read — and I sure hope you enjoyed it — has some pretty substantial changes from the original stage production, but the gist of it remains the same, with lovers searching for each other across some sort of afterlife. One part that is totally unchanged is the reason the show was canceled on its third evening.

The rainbow bridge scene.

Yeah, for some reason — drugs probably, alcohol *definitely* — I thought it would be a great idea to stage a scene where hundreds of dogs come to the rescue of our heroes, attacking the devil's minions and saving the day. Equally inexplicably, no motherfucker talked me out of it. Guess *they* were all drunk on communion wine or something.

Anyway, the first night went okay, all things considered.

There were eight people in the audience watching a cast of six, two of whom could actually sing, while the band consisted of myself on guitar and my co-writer on piano and synth. It wasn't a disaster, but when the rainbow bridge scene happened and only one sorry-looking mutt shuffled onstage and proceeded to urinate over the front row, two patrons got up and demanded their money back. This was especially galling, as we hadn't even *charged* for the opening night performance.

The next night wasn't much better. The priest — who was also the director — said the climax was falling flat due to a lack of dogs. I thought the problem was a lack of tits and ass, and tactfully suggested adding some nudity to distract people, but he said he had a better idea.

I should've known not to trust a priest.

And that was why, one week later, during the third and final performance of *Heaven and Hell: A Religious Odyssey,* our mad director unleashed a horde of twelve feral hounds on the audience. Yeah, you read that right.

You see, the priest had rounded up every stray neighborhood dog he could find and kept them in a cage until showtime on Saturday evening, at which point he released them during the opening bars of *Very Good Dogs.* Two parishioners were treated for bites, one for a twisted ankle, but most importantly, no dogs were harmed in the ensuing chaos, the mutts escaping out the front door.

The show closed for good after that, and I was canned from the job as if the whole thing was my fault for writing the scene. Or maybe it was because I just stood there laughing while the dogs ran riot?

Anyway, until next time,

Your friend,

Uncle Carl

EXTRA SPECIAL THANKS TO MY PATRONS

Abbey Lund
Adam Soll
Alexander Buschmann
Allie Vanderlaan
Amber Cassady
Amy Richardson
Anna Crossland
Anna the Cheddar Goblin
Audie Schultz
Barry Stentiford
Brendan & Honey Bunny
Brendan Fitz
Brian Forberger
Britain Gilgour
Brittany Ross
Brock and Alicja Reichstein
Cameron Roubique
Camille Sara
Carsyn
Cody Phillips
Cole Basaraba
Courtney Pearson
Danielle Chiarappa Perkowitz
Dawn Pearson
Destinie
Edward Helton
Elli Wade
Enda Doran
Eric Rumsey
Grayson Yoder
Gregory Martin
Hana Lewis
Hannah Castillo
Hannah Orr
James Hill
Jarrod Linehan
Jeb Caffee
Joctan Hernandez
Joe Brewer
Jonathan Whitely
Josh Heaps
Joshua Carter
Kaila R
Kate H

Kate H
KD Davies
Kevin Kelly
Kim DeCillo
Kirstin
Kyle Weseman
Landyn Tedrick
Lindsay Robertson
L.J. Dougherty
Luke Martin
Matt McCleland
Matthew House
Mel Kaye
Meredith Jensen
Michael Sjögren
Michelle S
Mike McDougal
Miss Boozy Baker
Neil Sheppard
Newton Webb
Nicola Swordy
Nicole Stephens
Noah Andruss
Patricia Palacios
Phoebe Thompson
Phillipillar
Phil Otter
Rebecca Vale
Rob Jeromson
Robert L
Roberto Hull
Rochelle Hennings
Ryan Orgel
Sam Munster
Sam Verner
Sarah Brown
Sebastian Ersson
Sonja Reich
Steve Stred
Susanne Bouwmeister
Tomáš Urbánek
Tyler Geis
Vickie Allan
Vivian

ABOUT THE AUTHOR

David Sodergren lives in Scotland with his wife Heather and his best friend, Boris the Pug.

Growing up, he was the kind of kid who collected rubber skeletons and lived for horror movies. Not much has changed since then.

His best known books include the gory and romantic fairy tale The Haar, the blood-drenched folk-horror Maggie's Grave, and the analog-horror fever dream Rotten Tommy. David also writes under the pseudonym Carl John Lee, publishing splatterpunk novels such as Psychic Teenage Bloodbath and Cannibal Vengeance.

ALSO BY DAVID SODERGREN

The Forgotten Island

Night Shoot

Dead Girl Blues

Maggie's Grave

The Navajo Nightmare (with Steve Stred)

The Perfect Victim

Satan's Burnouts Must Die!

The Haar

And By God's Hand You Shall Die

Rotten Tommy

Summer of the Monsters

Death Spell

Hard Luck Jenny

CONTENT WARNINGS

PART ONE

Suicide and suicidal ideation
Violence and gore
Sex and sexual assault
Homophobic bullying
Cannibalism
Necrophilia
Infanticide

PART TWO

Violence and torture
Rape and sexual assault
Infanticide
Homophobic bullying and abuse
Domestic abuse
No harm comes to any dogs, but there are references to dead
family pets
Suicidal ideation

www.ingramcontent.com/pod-product-compliance
Lightning Source LLC
Chambersburg PA
CBHW031738180726
48283CB00005B/1562